# TO SAVE MY DAUGHTERS

LOUISE GUY

Boldwood

First published in Great Britain in 2025 by Boldwood Books Ltd.

Copyright © Louise Guy, 2025

Cover Design by JD Design Ltd.

Cover Images: Shutterstock

A CIP catalogue record for this book is available from the British Library.

Paperback ISBN 978-1-83533-157-6

Large Print ISBN 978-1-83533-156-9

Hardback ISBN 978-1-83533-158-3

Ebook ISBN 978-1-83533-155-2

Kindle ISBN 978-1-83533-154-5

Audio CD ISBN 978-1-83533-163-7

MP3 CD ISBN 978-1-83533-162-0

Digital audio download ISBN 978-1-83533-159-0

This book is printed on certified sustainable paper. Boldwood Books is dedicated to putting sustainability at the heart of our business. For more information please visit https://www.boldwoodbooks.com/about-us/sustainability/

Boldwood Books Ltd, 23 Bowerdean Street, London, SW6 3TN

www.boldwoodbooks.com

# AUTHOR'S NOTE

This story revolves around the lasting impacts of domestic abuse, which occurred in the characters' pasts. While the abuse itself is not depicted in graphic detail, it is central to the theme that shaped their lives and relationships. Please be aware that the content may be triggering for some readers.

*For those still fighting – remember, you don't have to do it alone.*

# 1

As *Southern Insight*'s closing music rang through the TV studio, Tori Blackwood removed her earpiece and stood, relieved that the broadcast for the network's current affairs show was over. The familiar buzz of activity surrounded her as crew members bustled about, dismantling equipment and tidying up the set.

'Great job, Tori,' the technical director called as she walked away from the anchor desk in search of a water bottle. She nodded in acknowledgement, a small smile tugging on her lips.

'It was,' Penny, Tori's close friend and the show's producer, agreed, her power heels click-clacking on the polished concrete floor as she fell in step beside her. 'Are you sure we can't convince you to stay as anchor?'

Tori laughed and shook her head. 'Firstly, I don't think Marion would be too happy to return from maternity leave to find herself sidelined, and secondly, I love reporting – you know that. This has been fun, but I can't wait until Friday. Only a few more days until I can get my teeth into something interesting. Speaking of which, what have you got for me?'

'A few potential stories,' Penny said, handing Tori a bottle of water as they reached the refreshment area. 'First is the ancestry one I mentioned a while back.'

Tori tucked a strand of her wavy blonde hair behind her ear. 'I thought you said you couldn't get that one green-lit. That the overall feeling was that the human interest side wasn't hard-hitting enough.'

'Seems the production team have changed their minds,' Penny said. 'Viewers will love it. Especially when something unexpected is revealed. Let me get back to you on that one though. I still have a couple of issues to work through.'

'Sounds good,' Tori said. 'You said there were a few ideas?'

'There are. How do you feel about murder in a domestic violence situation?'

Tori unscrewed the water bottle cap and took a swig. 'As in, the victim was murdered?'

Penny shook her head. 'No, the victim was the murderer. It's a crime that happened almost thirty years ago that we've been given a lead on. The victim was sentenced to life for killing her abuser, despite claiming it was self-defence.'

Tori frowned. 'Why did she get life if it was self-defence and a known domestic violence situation?'

'It's complicated. But it's also a great story. And so you know, this one's come down from Gav. He wants you on it.'

'Really? He doesn't usually get involved with story allocation.' Gavin Barnett was the chief executive of *Southern Insight* and generally left the running of the show to Penny and the other producers. He'd joined the *Southern Insight* team a year after Tori had, which she was grateful for, as he was a childhood friend of her father's. She would hate for people to think he'd helped her get the job there. It had, in fact, been quite the opposite, with Tori making him aware the role was available.

'I think with ratings sliding, he's taking more of an interest.

This isn't the only story he's directing us to cover,' Penny said. 'And with this one, when you read the court information, it's crazy to think she was convicted, but I guess they wanted to make an example of her. Convey to the public that you can't just kill people, even though it appears to be self-defence. The problem is she did a terrible job in court. Pleaded guilty. Said she was defending herself and her daughters but didn't add much more than that. She was probably in shock. Her daughters were quite little, ten and six, and neither one confirmed their mother's story that their father was violent.'

'But you believe her?'

Penny nodded. 'From what I've read, yes. Gut instinct. That said, she's guilty. That's not what we're highlighting. It's whether her sentencing was fair.'

Tori shook her head. 'Imagine protecting your kids from a monster and then losing the right to watch them grow up. Are the daughters close to the mother? And what about other family and friends? Did she appeal the sentence?'

Penny laughed. 'I take it from the questions you're interested in the story?'

Tori joined Penny's laughter. 'I get carried away when I feel passionate about something. And yes, of course, I'm interested. Can I get whatever files and information you have on her? It'll give me the chance to get a head start before officially moving back into my old job next week. It'd be useful to find out visiting hours and the protocol we need to follow with the prison, too. Which one's she at?'

'Winchester.'

Tori frowned. 'But that's minimum security.'

'She was moved there a few days, maybe a week, ago. I'm assuming she might be up for early release, and they're transitioning her. She's been made aware of the story we're doing and in principle has agreed to be involved. There are a few conversations still to be had with the prison and her lawyer.' Penny glanced at her watch. 'I've got a stack of calls and need to get moving. Her file's on my desk with a sticky note with your name on it. Grab it or ask my assistant to get it if she doesn't let you in. She's rather protective.'

Tori smiled. 'That's one way to describe her. What's the woman's name? The one we're doing the story on?'

'Marlow. June Marlow.'

* * *

June smiled as the closing music and credits of *Southern Insight* filled the screen. She liked that one of the reporters, Tori Blackwood, had been filling in as the show's anchor and hoped the usual one would extend her maternity leave or, better still, not return. Tori brought something different to the show, something June couldn't quite put her finger on, but she knew without a doubt that she respected and liked her.

'That'll be you soon,' Doreen, a particularly friendly older woman who'd welcomed June the previous week to Winchester Correctional Centre, the city's new minimum-security prison for women, said. She pointed at the screen. 'Getting all famous and stuff.'

June chuckled. 'Famous for all the wrong reasons. I think they'll be blurring my face, so I won't be all that famous.'

'It's a good thing you're doing,' Doreen said. 'It's not easy – we all know that – having to revisit our pasts.'

The faraway look in Doreen's eyes told June that she, like many of the women June had met over the past twenty-eight years, had a story to tell.

Doreen snapped back to attention. 'Now, how are you settling in?'

June knew her smile was unusually wide for someone being asked how they liked a prison, but it was for good reason. 'Honestly, compared to Trendall, this is like one of those holiday resorts you hear about. Trees and bushland, and our own rooms. The library and this lounge area are cosy and nice, and we even cook our own food. It's incredible.'

Doreen's eyes widened. 'Maximum security was that bad?'

June swallowed. She'd survived the past twenty-eight years by keeping to herself, doing what she was told, and not getting involved in any altercations or arguments that seemed to arise daily between the other women or the women and the guards. July 22, 1995, had been the start of a nightmare that June felt she was perhaps beginning to wake up from. Although, if she was honest, the nightmare had begun well before 1995. Her husband, Alan Marlow, had a lot to answer for. The fact he was dead and unable to was nothing more than a relief.

Doreen was still waiting for an answer.

'Let's say I'd recommend you make this your last prison stay. You don't want to end up anywhere worse than here.'

Doreen shuddered. 'I think I'd curl up and die. Now, tell me, do you have any visitors arriving on the weekend?'

'Yes, I believe my youngest daughter will be visiting. I hope so, at least.'

\* \* \*

Luella Marlow sat at a corner table in the bustling Future Blend café, her sketchbook open and pencil in hand, her brow furrowed in concentration. With a frustrated sigh, she erased a few errant lines and started again, her pencil moving with deliberate strokes. The café buzzed with conversation and the clinking of cups and dishes, but Lu remained oblivious, completely absorbed in her work.

'Another coffee?'

Lu jumped at the sound of the café owner's voice. She looked up to find the short, dark-haired woman grinning at her.

'Sorry, didn't mean to startle you.'

A subtle flutter in Lu's chest prompted her to give a nervous smile. There was something about Ali that intrigued her. She was older than Lu by a few years, with gorgeous green eyes and a slim build, and she carried herself with a confidence Lu admired. 'I was in a different place altogether.' She glanced down at the page she'd been sketching on and folded the sketchbook cover over it. She'd been preoccupied with thoughts of her mother lately, and this was a drawing she didn't want to have to explain.

She looked around, realising the tables were full. Other than a few people waiting for takeaway coffee, it had been empty when she'd arrived earlier that morning. She glanced at her watch. She'd been here for two and a half hours. Her cheeks heated, as she realised she'd taken up a table that could have been used for people who'd order food rather than only a coffee.

She started to collect her belongings. 'Hey, I'm sorry. I had no idea I'd been here so long. I'll get going so you can use the table.'

Ali put a hand on Lu's shoulder. 'Stay. I love that you work from here; you know that. I always wanted this to be a creative space.' She nodded towards a guy sitting in the corner, head-phones on, laptop in front of him. 'Bryce's written his last three books at that table. Arrives at eight and leaves at four.'

'Yes, but he probably buys more than a coffee.' Lu could only imagine the shade of red her cheeks had now turned. So much for impressing Ali, but she didn't want to admit that her funds didn't stretch beyond the one drink. Her artwork wasn't selling in the quantities she'd like. In fact, it wasn't selling at all. She sighed. She needed to master online sales or become better at selling herself to galleries.

'You okay?'

Lu nodded and forced a smile. 'Need to get my big-girl pants on and sort myself out. I never expected to be in my thirties and still be a struggling artist. I should probably get a real job.'

Ali sat down on the chair across from her. 'You're still doing the dog walking?'

'Yeah. It covers the essentials, but that's about it.' She smiled. 'Anyway, it's not your problem, but thanks for the chat. And I will be a bit more conscious about how much time I spend taking up the tables. You're great about it, but if it was my business, I'd want people to buy more than one coffee if they're sitting here for hours.'

Ali looked thoughtful for a moment. 'How about you earn your keep?'

Lu frowned. While dog walking wasn't exactly glamorous, she wasn't sure about working in the café. When she walked through the door of Future Blend, something inspired her. If she associated it with waiting tables, she'd be concerned she'd lose that.

'Don't worry. I'm not asking you to clean tables or serve customers or anything like that. I have another idea.' Ali nodded towards Lu's sketchbook. 'How about you work on a few pieces for the café? I've been thinking about doing a bit of a refresh of the art we currently have, but I don't have the budget. I can, however, pay in coffee and food.'

Lu experienced a rush of affection towards the woman across from her. She had a reputation for her generosity and could see it being extended to Lu now. 'You've never even seen my work. How do you know you'd like my style?'

Ali locked eyes with her. 'I like your style, Lu. I liked your style from the first day you walked into the café.'

Nervous energy fluttered in the pit of Lu's stomach. Was Ali hitting on her?

Ali's lips curled into a smile. 'And I've been following you on Insta since you first mentioned your art. So, I do have a feel for your work, and I love your drawings.'

Lu let out a breath, slightly disappointed that Ali wasn't hitting on her. 'As much as I appreciate the offer, you don't need to do that. If you like my style, I'd be happy to make some pieces for you. I've spent enough time in the café as it is. I probably owe you ten pieces by now.'

Ali smiled. 'You don't owe me anything, and I'd only be happy if this was a business transaction.' She pushed back her chair and stood. 'Give it some thought, and if you're interested, let me know, and we can sit down and talk about themes and what I'm looking for. And I'm going to get you another coffee now and a delicious pastry to encourage you to say yes. This would work for both of us. You'd be doing me a bigger favour than I'd be doing you. It'd take a lot of coffee and pastries to pay for one of your pieces.'

A tremor of excitement ran through Lu. This was a genuine offer. An offer that would enable her to spend more time at the café. More time around Ali.

'And,' Ali continued, 'we can put something up on the wall to say that you're the artist. Who knows, it might lead to some more work for you.' She hesitated before pointing to the sketchbook. 'I probably shouldn't say anything because I have the feeling that drawing might have been private, but that's exactly what I'm looking for. Something that's powerful, raw with emotion and makes people think.'

Lu became uncharacteristically emotional at these words.

She waited until Ali returned to the counter before re-opening the sketchbook. The drawing showed a woman standing looking through a barred window at a garden where flowers were blooming under a vibrant blue sky. Lu had tried to capture a look of hope on her face but knew it needed more work. A young girl stood in the garden beyond the bars, reaching out towards the woman. Lu closed her eyes, longing and despair overcoming her.

There should be two girls reaching for their mother, not one. Both in the drawing and in real life.

# 2

As Cole Langrell blended the foundation over her skin, taking additional care to cover the scar that curled around the top of her brow, she did her best to ignore the incessant ringing of her phone. She knew without even glancing at the screen that it would be Lu. Why couldn't her younger sister text like a normal person? Well, if she was honest, she knew exactly why it was a call, not a text. As part of the process of avoiding her sister, Cole barely responded to her texts. She had no interest in discussing their mother. She hadn't since she was ten, so why did Lu think now was going to be any different?

She sighed, doing her best to push all thoughts of her family from her mind, and with swift, practised movements, applied a coat of mascara to her lashes and finished with a swipe of shiny lip gloss.

A knock on her front door had her drop her make-up back into her bag and hurry through the apartment. She hesitated as she neared the door. It was unusual for anyone to visit without messaging first, especially at seven o'clock in the morning. She spied through the peephole and was greeted by a large eye peering back at her.

'Jesus!' She jumped backwards. She couldn't help but smile at the peal of laughter that erupted on the other side of the door.

'Let me in, sis.'

Cole reluctantly pulled the door open. 'What do you want?'

'What sort of greeting's that?' Lu pushed past her in the direction of the kitchen. 'Coffee?'

Cole shut the door and made her way to the kitchen. Her sister was already sitting up on one of the counter stools, helping herself to a banana from the fruit bowl.

'Is your café closed today?'

Lu frowned. 'My café?'

'I thought you spent every morning at that café near you. That it was part of your routine that *"affected your creative energy if you varied from it"*?'

Cole was surprised to see red splotches appear on Lu's cheeks as she replayed the exact words her sister had used only recently when getting out of helping with some fundraising Cole was doing.

'I don't go there every day.' Her lips turned up in a smile. 'Today's proof of that.'

Cole sighed. 'As much as I love you, what do you want, Lu? I need to leave in twenty minutes.'

Lu peeled back the banana skin and took a bite, her eyes fixed on Cole. She swallowed her mouthful before speaking. 'I only need a coffee and ten minutes. So, you'll be early. You're already ready. Hair perfectly straightened – love the copper high-lights, by the way – flawless make-up, suit straight from the dry cleaners.' She nodded towards a navy backpack sitting on the kitchen counter. 'Let me guess. Lunch made last night is ready to take, and you need to fill your water bottle.'

Cole managed a wry smile, knowing that, at this point, it was easier to go along with Lu rather than object any further. She turned and popped a pod into the coffee machine, placed one of her favourite mugs beneath the spout and pressed the button. Thirty seconds later, she was pushing the mug across to Lu and starting the process again for herself.

'So,' Lu said. 'As you might have noticed, I've been trying to get in touch with you.' She cocked her head to one side. 'The six calls and twelve texts might have given that away?'

'And me not responding should have made it clear that I don't want to talk about that woman,' Cole said. 'I don't see why that's so hard to understand.'

'*That woman* is our mum,' Lu said. 'I know what she did is hard to accept, but for my sake and for Gran's too, it'd be good if you could try and get over it.'

Cole stared at her sister. '*Get over it*?'

Lu sipped her coffee. 'Mm, this is good. And yes, get over it. She's been punished enough. She was a *victim*.'

Cole closed her eyes, anger bubbling up inside her. There was no evidence to suggest her mother had been a victim of domestic abuse. Their father had been a kind and loving man. If he'd been abusive, surely she or Lu would have memories of it? Or her mother would have confided in someone? All they had to go by were her mother's words. Her father could hardly defend himself now. She opened her eyes. 'If she was being abused, she had options. She could have asked for help, but she didn't. She told no one. It doesn't ring true. Gran didn't even know what was going on. Can you honestly imagine not being able to confide in Gran?'

Lu shook her head. 'No, but I've never been put in a position like Mum was either. She was embarrassed and worried for her life and for ours.'

Cole took her mug from the machine. 'Let's agree to disagree, and *get over it*. Not likely.'

'Jeez. At least speak to her. Give her a chance to tell you the situation for herself. You might change your mind.'

'I'm not interested in changing my mind, and I'm not interested in talking to her. Her sentencing was clear. She was convicted of murder with an unbelievable and weak case of possible self-defence.' She held up her hands before Lu could object. 'I know how harsh that sounds, but they're the facts, Lu. Of course I'd like to believe the situation was different, but I can't. As far as I'm concerned she made a decision that left us without parents. I'll never forgive her for that, and I can't imagine there's any story she could spin that would change my mind.'

Lu shook her head. 'How did you get a job as a trauma counsellor when you won't look at your own situation?'

'Look at it? I've spent years in therapy because of my—' she raised her fingers in air quotes '—"own situation". I've gone over all of this a million times with numerous counsellors and nothing's changed. I can't remember the night, and I assume that's probably a good thing. Seeing your father murdered in front of you is something no one wants to relive. And no matter what you believe as far as murder or self-defence, the result that night was the same. Our father was killed by our mother.'

The pain that flashed in Lu's eyes immediately had Cole regretting her words. She closed her eyes and took a deep breath. She needed to calm herself and then she'd apologise. Getting angry with Lu wasn't helping anyone.

'Channel Six has approached her,' Lu said, and Cole's eyes flew open.

'That news show, *Southern Insight*, wants to tell her story.'

'What? Why? Surely the prison wouldn't allow that?'

'The prison has given permission so that she can help other

women who end up in situations like she did. While at the time she didn't feel like she had options, the story is to try and make it clear to women that there are alternatives and help is available. They don't want to see other women end up in prison for murder because they feel they have nowhere else to turn. But Mum wanted to check that we're okay with her telling the story before she goes ahead. She's worried it might bring everything back up for us, and she doesn't want to upset us.'

Cole shook her head. 'This is upsetting me. Having to talk about her. And she's right. I don't want her story spread all over the news again. It was bad enough when it happened. I certainly don't need her creating issues for me at work now.'

'How would it create issues at work? To start with, everyone knows you as Cole Langrell since you changed your name. If Mum talks about her daughter, Nicole, it's unlikely anyone's going to connect it to you.'

'I didn't change my name. I go by a nickname.'

Lu rolled her eyes. 'You were Nic to everyone growing up. Cole's hardly a normal abbreviation. And you changed your surname to Gran's, so it's unlikely anyone would put two and two together. And anyway, if someone did connect you and Mum, it could help one of your clients.'

Cole narrowed her eyes. 'Are you serious?'

'Deadly.' Lu's cheeks flushed scarlet. 'Sorry, bad choice of words. But yes, I am serious. People hearing your story could relate to you more. Know that your own life experience was what made you choose the profession that you did. It's not going to hurt.'

Cole snorted. 'I've spent close to three decades trying to hide the fact that she's my mother. I can't stop her from doing a news story, but she's not to mention me by name or make any reference to what I do or where I work. Make that clear to her, please.'

'Why don't you tell her yourself? I'm going to visit on Saturday. Come with me.'

Cole picked up her water bottle and filled it with filtered water from the tap. 'I have to get to work.'

Lu slipped off the stool. 'Come on. It's time you forgave her and moved forward. It would mean a lot to Gran and me. And Mum, of course. Don't make the next time you see her be because of a television story.'

A dull thud started in Cole's temple. This wasn't the first time Lu had asked her to visit their mother or talk to her. She picked up her bag and started walking toward the front door.

'Cole?'

She turned and faced her sister. 'I'm not going to forgive a woman whose actions killed our family. She…' She stopped and drew in a deep breath. 'I'm not having this conversation. I've spent enough years in therapy to know that going over this again now isn't going to achieve anything.'

'What about when she gets out? Are you going to avoid her then, too?'

'Yes. But she's a murderer, Lu. A murderer who's serving life. She isn't getting out anytime soon. You might not remember Dad, but I do. And there's nothing *Southern Insight*, or anyone else, can say that will convince me that killing our father was something he deserved or that it was in some way beneficial to us.' She glanced at her watch, turning back towards the front door. 'Now, let's go. I'm running late.'

# 3

Tori leaned back in her chair, waves of emotion overcoming her. She stood, shaking herself. One of the attributes that made her such a good reporter was the empathy she was able to show her subjects. However, the impact this had on her at times was hard to handle. She'd spent the morning trawling through old news articles on June Marlow and several other victims of domestic violence who were now behind bars for attacking their abusers. She found herself, as she did with most stories, imagining herself in the shoes of her subjects. Feeling the fear June no doubt felt for herself and her daughters. The utter despair the woman must have experienced when she was convicted and the grief she would have experienced for losing the life she had known.

'Hey,' Penny said, entering her office. 'You look rattled. What's going on?'

'Research,' Tori said.

Penny shot her a sympathetic look. 'Being an empath is what makes you so successful, you know, but you need to take care of yourself too. We don't want you to burn out.'

Tori nodded. She'd recognised her empath traits when she

started out as a journalist. She'd thought her reactions were normal until she saw others being able to distance themselves from their work and not becoming emotionally involved.

'Which story are you researching?'

'Domestic violence. The victims-behind-bars one,' Tori said.

'*Victims Behind Bars*,' Penny said. 'Great title for the segment.'

'I'm seeing if I can find other women in the same situation as June Marlow. Adding stats and numbers will make this story even more powerful.'

Penny nodded. 'See how you go. If you're going to reference other cases, make sure they show an injustice in the sentencing, like June's story suggests. I'm guessing you might come across some women who were more calculated in the attacks on their husbands. They aren't the ones we want to showcase. Now, I wanted to give you a heads-up that our friend, Alex Wilson, is going to contact you about collaborating on a story.' She fluttered her eyelids dramatically.

Tori frowned. 'Why are you so hung up on Alex? He's just another reporter here. We've worked together plenty of times in the past.'

Penny shrugged, her smile still intact. 'I don't know. I wanted to see your reaction. You two would be good together.'

'Nope. Not interested. He's a nice guy, but I'm not attracted to him. What's the story?'

'It's about trauma and how experiencing something traumatic can affect and shape later parts of your life. I bumped into him at the gym last night. This is another of the stories Gav has directed the network to do. Apparently, he'd already mentioned to Alex that this would be a complementary piece to the June Marlow story, and he'd like you to work together. If you can get interviews with the daughters and the mother, you could delve a bit deeper into the impact their mother's incarceration has had on them and potentially weave it into Alex's story. It would have had a massive impact on them.'

A shiver ran down Tori's spine as she placed herself in the shoes of the Marlow daughters. She couldn't imagine how they'd recovered from losing both parents at such a young age. To Penny, she nodded. 'Gav's right. The stories will complement each other. I'll reach out to Alex in the next couple of days.'

'*Gav's right.* That's what I like to hear.' Gav's deep voice was accompanied by his laughter as he passed Penny on her way out of Tori's office.

Tori smiled. 'Don't let it go to your head. I'm sure it's a first.'

Gav laughed again. 'Probably.' His smile was quickly replaced with a more serious expression. 'Now, I wanted to check in. How's your dad going? Any news?'

Tori shook her head. 'No, he's got some follow-up tests next week, but from everything he and Mum have said, they're routine. It sounds positive.'

'They got the cancer?'

'That's what they're telling me.' She frowned. 'Dad hasn't told you something different, has he? I wouldn't put it past them to protect me.'

Gav hesitated, causing alarm to flare in Tori.

'What?'

'Nothing. I was thinking that, yes, I think they would do anything to protect you, but that's not relevant to why I asked. I haven't seen or spoken to Dion in a few weeks. Which I must rectify. If you're speaking with him or your mum, tell him I asked about him, and I'll be in touch. I might leave it until after his next lot of tests, to be sure. See if I can get him out on the boat for the day. Do a spot of fishing, take a few beers and celebrate if he's had the all-clear.'

'I'll pass the message on,' Tori said, although she had a vague recollection that her father hadn't enjoyed the last outing on Gav's boat.

'Great,' Gav said. 'Now, I'll leave you to it. I'm looking forward to seeing what you come up with on the Marlow story. We desperately need some ratings boosters, and I'm counting on you to make sure that's one of them. See if you can get the daughters involved, too. The impact the situation has had on them will be incredibly powerful.'

\* \* \*

Cole had done her best to push away all thoughts of Lu and their mother and focus on her clients and workday. She'd worked at the government-funded Hawthorn Community Wellness Centre for twelve years as a qualified psychologist and trauma counsellor and loved her job. Now, as the afternoon sunshine streamed in through the windows of the Wellness Centre, she watched as five of the six group participants scribbled notes in their notebooks. It was impossible to miss the oldest participant in the room, sixty-seven-year-old Roberto Runci, with his exaggerated sighs and throwing his hands in the air in exasperation one minute and shaking his head the next. She'd seen it all before in her therapy sessions and quite often would wait for the participant to vocalise their issue, but today, she could see it was distracting the rest of the group.

'What's going on, Roberto?'

Roberto took his seat, shoved his hands deep into his pockets and stared at her.

Cole stared back. She wasn't going to force it out of him.

'Yeah, Roberto,' Tom Hargreaves said, 'you've obviously got something up your arse. Spill.'

Roberto shook his head before turning his attention and

pointing a finger directly at Tom. 'You, Thomas. You're what's *up my arse*. The fact that they let you in here is a joke. Watching you scribble down your notes for a trauma plan and coping strategies when nothing's even happened to you is basically insulting. Wake up and smell the *caffè*. Do you think jotting down a few notes makes you some kind of expert? Stai scherzando!'

Cole was aware that the four others in the group had stopped writing and were watching with interest.

'It's not our place to decide what impacts someone else, Roberto,' she said. 'Trauma comes in all different shapes and sizes, and regardless of where it originated from, coping strategies such as the ones we've discussed and will be planning for are relevant to everyone.'

Roberto continued to shake his head. 'Every person in this room, other than Weak Guts here, has suffered a terrible loss. We've got Joss, whose husband was murdered. *Mi dispiace,*' he added as Joss flinched. Cole didn't need to speak Italian to know Roberto was saying he was sorry. He used it so often in their sessions she was finding herself slipping into Italian on occasion.

Joss nodded, accepting the apology, before dropping her head into her hands. She'd been attending Cole's group and private counselling for two years since the stabbing took place, but it was still as raw as the day it happened.

Roberto continued. 'Shane lost his wife and daughter in a horrific accident. Lisa found her father, who'd hanged himself, when she was thirteen, and then this tosser—' he pointed at Tom '—thinks because he saw a dog get run over, he should be here. *È assurdo.*' He threw his arms in the air to amplify how absurd he found the situation.

'It was my dog.' Tom's face flushed with anger. 'And she was murdered. She wasn't run over. You have no right to tell me what I can or can't feel any more than I have the right to judge you.'

'But you do, you little *idiota*. Don't you?'

Tom shrugged. 'Hard not to if you're putting it out there. Big tough cop. Doing your best to intimidate all of us and make out you're so special. Do you think your late wife would think you're special, or a prick?'

'Okay, enough,' Cole said, placing one hand on Roberto's shoulder, half expecting him to leap from his chair and rip Tom's head off. 'This is a support group. You don't get to judge people's trauma or reactions or—' her gaze settled on Tom '—make deliberately insensitive comments.'

'Roberto, maybe you should spend more time working through your own issues,' Joss added, having raised her head from her hands. 'What you went through must have been tough, and focusing on Tom is a good way to avoid doing any work on yourself or facing what happened to you and your beautiful Maria.'

If it had been appropriate, Cole would have liked to have done a fist pump. Joss's words were heartfelt and meant a lot more coming from a fellow victim than they would coming from her.

'I…' Roberto's words tapered off, and he sagged beneath her touch.

'So,' Cole said, keen to change the subject, 'that's it for today's group. Spend some time finalising the coping strategies you feel are best for you and your situation, and we'll discuss them further during our one-on-ones. Next week, we'll be exploring triggers and trigger management. And, of course, reach out to me at any time. If you're struggling, don't wait until our one-on-one. You've got my number.'

The class collected their belongings and made their way out of the meeting room. Roberto was last to leave and turned briefly to Cole and gave her his trademark wink. '*Grazie, Capo.* See you next Wednesday. I'll see if I can perfect Maria's raspberry bomboloni. She would have wanted you to try one.'

Cole smiled. Roberto kept himself busy trying to perfect his late wife's favourite recipes. She patted her soft belly. 'I'll need to buy bigger pants if you keep spoiling me. But, if the bomboloni are as good as the cannoli you brought in last week, the new pants will be worth it.'

Roberto's booming laugh followed him out of the room as Ethan, another of the Wellness Centre's trauma counsellors, stepped inside.

'Nicely handled.'

Cole laughed. 'What, not objecting to more pastries or cakes or whatever bomboloni are?'

'No, the near punch-up earlier. I was passing when it started, so I stopped to listen. I think Joss nailed it when she suggested Roberto not deflect his own pain and anger onto Tom.'

Cole's laugh faded. 'I'm wondering if I should move Tom to another group. We've always mixed the clients regardless of the level of trauma, but I'm beginning to feel that the group sessions should all be level-one trauma or level two.'

'It's probably a good idea. Look, I'd better get back to work, but I wondered if you have time later for a quick chat. Perhaps over a coffee, or if much later, head out for a drink?'

'Is everything okay?'

He smiled, his dimples deepening. 'Of course. But I'm hoping to twist your arm and ask you for a favour.'

'Sounds intriguing.' Cole glanced at her watch. 'How about a drink at Pulse around six? I've got a couple of sessions still this afternoon and some reports to finalise.'

'Perfect, I'll swing by your office and pick you up. Oh, and Mike asked me to let you know that he's going to drop in to talk to you. He's also after a favour, I think.'

Cole raised an eyebrow. 'A day of favours! Any idea what it's about?'

Ethan shook his head. 'He mentioned his neighbours having problems, but that's all I know. He'll fill you in.'

Lu hadn't admitted to Cole earlier that morning that the visit to her sister, instead of her regular routine of coffee and time spent at the café, had been partly because she'd had two disobedient dogs to walk at nine o'clock and because she'd arranged to meet with Ali when the café closed at three to discuss artwork ideas.

She'd originally planned to drop in on Cole at work, but with her own day being moved about, the early visit had made more sense. She was disappointed but not surprised at Cole's reaction. She'd done her best to try and understand her older sister's feelings towards her mother's situation but could never put herself in Cole's shoes. There was only one difference between what the two girls had experienced the day their father had been killed, and that was that Cole had witnessed it, whereas Lu, who'd already been in bed and asleep at the time, had been spared that.

She'd had enough counselling to understand that Cole had experienced severe trauma and never recovered from it, but even knowing that didn't make it any easier that her sister wouldn't entertain the idea that their mother was a victim in what had happened. Even after years of counselling it was like talking to a brick wall when her mother was the topic of conversation.

Lu wondered how it would all play out. It was likely that June would be released, and it should be an incredible celebration and homecoming, but with Cole's attitude, this seemed unlikely. She squeezed her eyes shut. Sometimes, she was hit by emotions she found hard to contain when she thought about her mother, the death of her father and what was, in effect, the death of their family. Today was not the day to go there. She had a meeting at three and needed to be ready for it.

She opened her eyes and took one final look in the mirror, hoping that with the minimal make-up she wore, she'd achieved a natural look. She ran her fingers through her short blonde hair, wondering briefly what it would be like to feel Ali do the same. She gave herself a shake. This was a business meeting, and she needed to get her butt out the door if she was going to be on time.

She grabbed the portfolio she'd put together the previous night and pulled the door shut on the tiny studio apartment she rented in Elwood.

Ten minutes later, she sat at the one table that didn't have chairs stacked on it.

'You weren't in this morning,' Ali said as she placed two chai lattes on the table and sat down across from Lu. 'I was worried I'd scared you off.'

Lu smiled. 'No, re-arranged my day a little. I had to see my sister, so I did that first thing before wrangling a couple of dogs for an unenjoyable walk.'

Ali laughed. 'I assume you have a house full of them?'

'No, I'm pet-free at home. I do love dogs, but I'm happy for them to be my day job. I'll occasionally dog-sit, but it must be at the owner's home. My place is tiny. There's not even enough room for a goldfish. What about you, any pets?'

Ali shook her head. 'No, which is surprising as, when I was growing up, Mum used to bring every stray she found home.' She smiled. 'That's probably why I don't have pets. As ridiculous as this will sound, I think I was jealous of them.'

'Jealous?'

'Let's just say my mum was better at showering love on the strays than her kids.'

'I'm sorry.' Lu sighed. 'Families aren't easy, are they?'

'Sounds like we might have something in common in that area. Issues from childhood we'd rather not revisit.'

Lu cleared her throat, unsure how to respond, deciding it was probably best that she didn't. 'So, what were you thinking about for an artwork theme? Or were you thinking stand-alone pieces?'

Ali raised an eyebrow. 'That's a subject change if ever I saw one.' Her voice was gentle. 'Anything you want to talk about?'

Lu's eyes filled with tears, causing alarm to cross Ali's features. She reached out and laid a hand on Lu's arm. 'Hey, ignore me. I didn't mean to upset you. I sometimes need to learn to mind my own business.'

Lu wiped roughly at her eyes, annoyed with herself. She'd done her best to suppress her feelings earlier, and now, they were again rearing their ugly heads. 'Not your fault,' Lu said. 'I've got a lot going on. The visit to my sister unleashed a few emotions.' She took a deep breath. 'My mum went to prison when I was six for killing my dad.' She ignored the sharp intake of air that escaped Ali's lips. 'It looks like she might be getting out soon, and my sister, who has refused to have anything to do with her for the past twenty-eight years, isn't planning to make any changes to that.'

'And that's why you visited her this morning?'

Lu nodded.

'And she upset you?'

'She didn't say anything new or anything nasty, just made it clear that her position hasn't changed. She wants nothing to do with Mum, and that upsets me. I'd hoped we might be a family again one day, but Cole's going to stop that from happening.'

Ali hadn't removed her hand from Lu's arm and gave it a

gentle squeeze. 'I'm sorry you went through that. Your poor mum, too. In prison all that time. I can't begin to imagine what you've been through.'

Lu felt a rush of affection for the woman sitting across from her. 'You know,' she said, 'I think you're the first person I've ever told that story to who hasn't straightaway asked why my mum killed my dad. Most people are quick to assume she's some kind of monster.'

'Since owning this place—' Ali gestured around the café '—I've heard so many stories of difficult situations people have gone through or are going through. You start to learn quickly that things aren't usually cut and dried. I'm guessing that your mum probably had a good reason to kill him.'

'She did.' Lu started talking, telling Ali the whole story, from the abuse her mother had silently suffered, to the murder, and then to how it impacted her own life. She glanced out of the café window at one stage and noticed with a start that the sun was much lower in the sky. It was already nearly five, and they hadn't even started talking about the artwork.

Ali appeared as surprised as Lu that so much time had passed. 'I'm enjoying getting to know you. Do you have to be anywhere tonight?'

Lu shook her head.

'Great.' Ali stood. 'Let me grab a bottle of wine from out the back, and I'll put together a platter of food, then we can keep chatting.' She smiled. 'And maybe even get to talking about the artwork at some stage.'

# 4

With Ethan having given her the heads-up, Cole wasn't surprised when Mike popped his head around her office door towards the end of the day.

'Got a minute?'

'Sure,' Cole said, indicating to the seat on the other side of her desk. In her opinion, Mike was the perfect person to head up the Wellness Centre. In his early fifties, he was always well presented, his dark hair neatly styled and his clothing impeccably tailored, but most importantly, he had a calm but commanding presence and was respected by staff and clients. 'Ethan mentioned you wanted to ask me for a favour?'

Mike nodded. 'I know you've recently completed the advanced certification in...' he hesitated '...I'll probably get this wrong, but from memory dialectical behaviour therapy aimed at teens?'

Cole nodded.

'I thought it might be a way to get through to my eleven-year-old neighbour. She's not a teen in years, but definitely in attitude.

I think you might have heard about my neighbours. The two kids were placed in foster care recently?'

Cole nodded. 'I've heard about the domestic violence situation. The mother chose to stay with the husband rather than go with the kids.'

Mike nodded. 'I still can't get my head around it. It's hard to comprehend. But yes, there are two girls. Piper's eleven and she and her younger sister, Katie, have been placed together with a family, so that's good, at least. Katie seems to be doing okay, but Piper's having trouble sleeping and not doing well at school. She was previously an excellent student. It's not hard to imagine why she's struggling.'

Cole frowned. 'I'm a little confused as to why you're asking me to work with her as a favour. She sounds like a perfect fit for dialectical behaviour therapy, and we can certainly book her in for a session.'

'That's where the favour comes in,' Mike said. 'The tricky bit is Piper's refusing counselling. Hates the idea of coming somewhere like this and having to talk to someone.'

Cole nodded, unable to hide a smile. 'I can relate to Piper on that one. When it comes to my own counselling sessions, I'm never that keen either. Working with clients is not an issue, of course. I'm assuming the favour is a visit to the foster home? Made to look like a friendly drop-in as far as Piper's concerned.'

Mike nodded. 'We're working with social services on this one and she's already registered as a client but yes, the initial meeting needs to be away from the centre. Talk to her in her own environment or perhaps at the community garden. She's interested in gardening, which is why I thought you'd be perfect to try and connect with her. You've been incorporating working at the community garden with our clients for some time now and that might be the perfect venue to get her to open up. I'll need to get all the correct approvals in place, of course, before you visit her or suggest she might like to help out at the garden, but it could be the environment to get through to her.'

Four years earlier, Cole had successfully orchestrated approval from the board of the Wellness Centre to establish a horticultural therapy project. Her research had provided documented studies that this approach could help trauma survivors, including teenagers, to process emotions, reduce stress, and foster a sense of accomplishment and healing.

Cole had worked with a small team to turn an area of local parkland into a community garden. The garden was used by the Wellness Centre for individual and group therapy but also had a strong community member base who had transformed the area into a thriving vegetable garden.

'Perhaps tell her that I mentioned her, and you thought she'd be interested in seeing it, maybe even working in it.' He stood. 'Sorry, I've got to take a call in a few minutes. The day's disappearing as usual. I'll forward you the foster family's details and leave it to you to get in touch,' Mike said. 'And Cole, thanks. I'll owe you one.'

Shortly after leaving her office, Mike sent through Piper's foster carer's details and Cole called the number Mike provided. She spoke with Anne Gleeson, the foster mother, and organised a drop-in visit on Saturday morning. She'd have to give some thought to how she approached the situation, as eleven wasn't a little kid. Piper would probably see right through her if she tried to hide behind turning up to show her around the community garden. Why would a stranger do that, even if they were friends of a neighbour?

A few minutes before six, Cole slid her laptop computer into the backpack she used for work and added her water bottle to the side pocket.

'Ready?' Ethan appeared in the doorway of her office, a smile playing on his lips.

Cole couldn't help but notice how nice he looked, with his cobalt blue shirt enhancing the striking blue of his eyes. 'Sure am.' She slipped the backpack over her shoulder.

They made their way to the now empty reception area. The digital screen mounted on the wall to the side of the reception desk had been left on. Usually, it played company information and news on a loop, but tonight, it had been switched to Channel Six.

Anger surged through Cole as the opening credits for *Southern Insight*'s nightly current affairs show began to play. She stepped toward the screen and switched it off more forcefully than she'd intended.

'Wow,' Ethan said. 'Are you angry that reception left the screen on, or are you making it clear that you're not a fan of the show?'

Cole forced a smile. 'Not a fan of the show.'

Ethan raised an eyebrow. 'Sounds like there's a story in that.'

'Not one worth giving any energy to.' Cole walked through the automatic doors and out onto the footpath that ran along Glenferrie Road. She sighed as the sun's rays warmed her arms. 'I can't believe we've been cooped up in the office all day when the weather's so magnificent. Six o'clock, and it's still beautiful. I'm going to miss daylight saving next month when it ends.'

Ethan laughed. 'Nice change of subject, but I agree about daylight saving But, on *Southern Insight*, you might want to have a chat with Mike if you're against them. There's talk of a TV show doing a story on the centre and the long-term effects of trauma. I have a feeling it was them. Now, let's see if we can get a table at Pulse.' His hand gently touched her back as he guided her into the road. They waited for a tram to pass before continuing to the footpath on the other side.

Pulse looked busy, as it usually was midweek, but they found an outside table on the back terrace, which overlooked a lushly planted courtyard with a large fishpond and fountain.

'So,' Cole said once they'd placed their drinks order, and chatted briefly about their days. 'What's the favour?'

Ethan grinned and leaned back in his chair as one of the waitstaff appeared at their table with a tray containing their drinks.

'Gin and tonic?' she said, holding the tall glass up.

'That's me, thank you,' Cole said, accepting the drink as the beer on the tray was passed to Ethan.

'Cheers,' Ethan said, lifting his glass as they were once again on their own.

Cole clinked hers against Ethan's and took a sip. 'Okay, so back to you. I'm intrigued, but of course happy to help if I can.' Ethan was one of her favourite people, and she knew he'd do anything for her.

His eyes twinkled. 'Without even knowing the details? You're sure?'

Heat rushed to Cole's cheeks. She assumed his suggestive tone was a joke, but it left her a little rattled.

He reached out and put his hand over hers. 'Don't worry, I'm messing with you. Teasing you is quite a lot of fun.'

Cole slipped her hand out from under his and took another sip of her drink.

'So,' Ethan said. 'My sister's getting married, and my mum's been at me constantly about bringing a date. I was hoping you might come with me. It'd mean a weekend in Sydney, and I'd pay for everything. But, I should warn you that it's in a few weeks, so there's not a lot of notice.'

'Sure,' Cole said without hesitation. 'I could do that. I quite like weddings. All the hope and joy they bring. The start of something new and wonderful.'

Ethan raised an eyebrow. 'Are you taking the piss?'

Cole laughed. 'Why, because the likelihood of it lasting more than ten years is slim?'

'Twelve and a bit years the last time I checked, but yes, that's exactly why.'

'Nope. I like the optimism people have at the outset. If they could bottle that feeling and that love they had for the other person, imagine what an amazing world we'd live in. Of course, we see enough in our line of work to know that there's a much darker side to life and relationships. But I like the fairy-tale kind of feeling a wedding offers. It's like we all get to step out of normal life for a day or a night, depending on when it is, and get caught up in something quite pure and lovely.'

'I can tell Mum I'm bringing someone then?'

'Sure, why not.' Cole frowned. 'Although, are we lying and saying we're in a relationship?'

Ethan shook his head. 'No, I'll tell her exactly who you are. We're friends and we work together. I'm not expecting you to have to lie or anything.'

'Easy then,' Cole said. 'Let me know the details, dress code and all of that, and I'll make sure I'm available.'

'Will do. Now, your turn.'

'My turn?'

'Yes, that was a strong reaction to *Southern Insight*. I know you said it wasn't worth giving any energy to, but I'd still love to hear that story.'

Cole gulped her drink and made a point of looking at her

watch. 'You know, I promised Lu I'd drop in and see her tonight. I probably should go.'

Ethan opened his mouth as if to say something but closed it again. He took a large swig of his beer. 'I wasn't trying to pry, but if you ever want to talk about it, I'm always here.'

Cole sighed. 'I know, and I appreciate it.' She hesitated then continued. '*Southern Insight* wants to interview my mother for a news story, but I'm not supportive of the idea.'

Ethan frowned. 'Your mum? I don't think you've ever mentioned her before.'

Cole pushed her chair back and stood. 'For good reason, and to be honest, she's not someone I want to talk about now, or probably ever. When you said earlier that a news show was looking to talk to the centre, were you sure it was *Southern Insight*?' A tinge of unease rippled through Cole. Surely, they hadn't already worked out her relationship with her mother?

'Not completely sure, but I think it was. Mike knows some guy there: Alex something. He wants him to shine a light on the Wellness Centre and is hoping we can then leverage the exposure for fundraising. I assume, as we deal in trauma counselling, the story would be about that, or the centre in general.'

Cole allowed herself to relax a little. The two stories didn't sound like they were related, and as Lu had said, there was no reason anyone would make the connection between her and her mother. And even if they did, she would seek legal advice if necessary to ensure she wasn't mentioned by the program.

She'd been so deep in thought that Ethan was staring at her.

'You might end up in two stories on *Southern Insight*,' Ethan said.

'Nope. I'm having nothing to do with my mother. The one thing I can tell you is your opinion of me would change dramatically if you knew the truth about her and where I come from.'

Ethan snorted. 'That I doubt. Many of us working in this field do it because of how our pasts have shaped us. I wouldn't judge you. You should know that.'

Cole smiled, choosing to keep the words that sat on the tip of her tongue to herself. *It's not something I'm willing to risk.*

It was already seven thirty by the time Tori pushed open the door of her double-fronted Victorian cottage, her thoughts still occupied with the 'Victims Behind Bars' story. Usually, she did her best to leave her stories and the emotions that accompanied them at the office, but for some reason, she was finding it difficult with this one. Her own childhood could be described as nothing less than idyllic, so it was hard to comprehend the environments that others had endured growing up.

She was greeted with the aroma of sweet orange and peppermint oil as she stepped into the cottage. It was one of her favourite combinations for setting a positive and inviting tone in her home. *Her home.* It still blew her away that her parents had surprised her with the most amazing twenty-first birthday present almost seven years earlier when they'd handed her the keys to what was then a run-down property.

'We realise it needs a lot of work,' her father, Dion, had said, 'but owning it outright gives you lots of options. I can help with most of the work, and we'll get cheap rates on some supplies with my trade discounts.'

Tori had started crying, giving her parents the wrong message. She'd tried to pull herself together as her mother spoke worriedly to her father. 'Perhaps we should have told her earlier, given her the chance to decide if it's what she wants.'

Tori had wiped her eyes and put her arms around both of her

parents. 'I'm crying because I'm overwhelmed that you'd do something this huge for me, not because I'm upset. A property in St Kilda is my dream; you know that.'

Her father's chest was puffed out, and his smile was wide when they'd eventually pulled apart. 'I told you, didn't I, love, that St Kilda was the place to buy all those years ago?'

'Your father purchased the property as an investment in 1992,' her mother explained. 'St Kilda was an up-and-coming suburb then. It had some bad areas and some rather questionable people living in it, but with it so close to the city and the fore-shore, your father predicted it would be cleaned up and become highly desirable over the next ten years. He was right, of course, and buying here now would be impossible.'

'Tenants have paid the mortgage off,' Dion said. 'We gave the last one notice six months ago, and they moved out a few weeks back. The property's been cleaned, but like I said, it needs a lot of work. We wanted you to be part of the decision-making process regarding the renovations. And you still need to be careful, of course. The area, like anywhere, still has questionable people in it.'

Now, seven years later, Tori still walked through the front door every day loving that this was her home.

'Sunny!' Tori dropped her bag as her four-year-old ginger cat rubbed around her legs. She scooped him up. He nuzzled his face into her neck, his purr vibrating against her. She carried him down the hall to the central living and dining area and flopped down on the couch. He snuggled against her, loving his cuddles as always.

Tori sighed as her phone rang, interrupting their relaxing afternoon ritual. 'Sorry, Sun,' she said, moving him as she hurried to the hallway where she'd dropped her bag. She retrieved her phone.

'Hey, Mum,' she said, quickly retracing her steps to the couch where Sunny was now stretched out. She sat back down and continued stroking the cat's back.

'Hi, love, just a quick check-in.'

Tori smiled. Her mother started, what at times were daily phone calls, with the same words.

'Now, I'm confirming you're still coming to us on Sunday night to celebrate your birthday.'

'Of course.'

'And what about on Friday? Anything planned for your actual birthday?'

'Penny from work's organised a dinner for me on Friday,' Tori said. 'Just me, Jaime and Sam. The usual crew.'

'It's lovely that Penny's fitted in so well with those girls,' Sylvie said and gave a little laugh. 'From everything you've said about her I feel like I know her. It'd be nice to meet her one day.'

'Definitely,' Tori said. 'She's a bit full on compared to Jaime and Sam, but she's lovely.'

'Speaking of Jaime,' Sylvie said, 'Mary was over this morning for a coffee. She was quite upset.'

'Really?' Mary was Jaime's mother and best friends with Sylvie. The families had grown up next door to each other and both Tori and Jaime's parents were still neighbours.

'Yes, she's talking about doing some kind of DNA test that will tell her about her ancestors.'

'Like Ancestry or Heritage Link?'

'Yes, the second one. Heritage Link,' Sylvie said. 'She wants to find out more about her immediate relatives. I don't know if you remember, but Mary's adopted and has been adamant for years that she doesn't want to know anything about her biological parents or family. Jaime speaking of doing this test is really upsetting her. Do you think you could talk her out of it?'

Tori was silent for a moment. She remembered years ago when they were in the early years of high school doing a school assignment on family trees. Jaime was upset at the time that her mother wasn't interested in finding out about her biological family, but she hadn't realised it was something Jaime was still interested in.

'I can speak to her,' Tori said. 'I'm not sure if I'll be able to talk her out of it, but I'll try. I wonder if she's been talking to Penny?'

'Does Penny know about the tests?'

'She's considering doing a story on it for the show,' Tori said. 'It's a directive from Gav, I think. He's getting more involved with story allocation. There are some good hard-hitting stories being researched and then a few that are lighter, more human interest like the ancestry one. Anyway, I'm seeing both Jaime and Penny on Friday night, so I'll find out more then.'

'Thanks, love, I know Mary would appreciate anything you can do to stop her. If you're researching this one perhaps dig up some information on how it can ruin families and relationships and share that with Jaime.'

Tori laughed. 'I think the spin the show will be taking is the positive side. I'm sure there are plenty of happy stories about family reunions and that sort of thing.' She stopped laughing as a thought occurred to her. 'Do you think Mary's hiding something that she doesn't want Jaime to know?'

Silence greeted her.

'Mum?'

Sylvie cleared her throat. 'Based on how upset she is, I'd say that's very possible, and if that's the case, it should be her choice as to whether her secrets are revealed.'

Ten minutes after they'd ended the call, Tori gave thought to her mother's words, that it should be Mary's choice to reveal her secrets. A part of Tori agreed, but the reporter in her knew that the best story and ratings would come from the shock value of secrets being revealed when the keeper of the secrets didn't want them to be. If *Southern Insight* did do a segment on ancestry, this was the angle that would rate.

\* \* \*

It was close to nine by the time Lu and Ali had agreed on a direction the artwork for the café would take. It had been one image that Ali had seen on Lu's Instagram page that had influenced the way she wanted to go.

'What I love about it,' she'd said as they looked at the image of the lone daffodil shooting up through the crack in the pavement, 'is the hope it presents. That in amongst the ugly concrete jungle, this one flower has the strength to bloom. It's so powerful, Lu. I looked at it, and I thought that it could be me. That no matter how tough times get, I can still be the best I can be. I can succeed, and I will.'

Lu's cheeks had flushed with heat as Ali talked with such passion about her work. She used symbolism in all her artwork but wasn't always sure if people understood what she was trying to achieve. She loved that Ali not only understood but was also applying it to her own life.

'I think I'd like a series that combines nature and hope,' Ali continued. 'Perhaps a rainbow after a storm, a flower turning towards the sun. Happy for you to come up with the ideas, of course, following that theme of hope.' She hesitated. 'I don't know if you'd let me display it, but that piece you were working on yesterday was so powerful. I now understand that it was your mum, so realise it might be a personal piece and too private to share.'

Lu considered her response. 'I'm not sure to be honest. With her possibly being released, she's been playing on my mind. I don't usually draw her directly like that, but I was finding it hard to focus this week.'

'Why this week?'

Lu cleared her throat, willing the tears that were pricking the backs of her eyes to stay away. 'My mum was recently moved from a maximum-security prison to a low-security one. That's all part of the early release process. Anyway, on Saturday, I'll get to hug my mum for the first time since I was six. My gran will, too. I know it doesn't sound like a big deal, but it is. It's more than a hug. It's symbolic of the journey we've been on, which has taken a massive change in direction. One that hopefully will see her home in a matter of weeks.'

Ali's eyes were raw with emotion at this. She reached for Lu's hand. 'It sounds like a big deal to me.'

# 5

June's heart swelled as her mother and Lu walked towards her in the outdoor visiting area. It was the first time since her incarceration that she'd been allowed to have an outdoor visit, with the previous process being much stricter at the maximum-security prison. She'd even been informed that she would be allowed to hug her visitors at the beginning and end of the visit. There would still be prison staff nearby supervising, but it was a much more relaxed environment than she was used to.

Her eyes filled with tears as her mother's worried face came closer. Her poor mum. How had she survived her sentence? Losing her daughter to the prison system, trying to hold her head high amongst family and friends who believed June to be a cold-blooded killer, and then raising her two daughters on top of all of that.

It was too much to have asked anyone, but if she'd had to have anyone on her side, Elena Langrell was the woman she would want there. She'd taken the whole situation in her stride as if this was normal and expected. June was racked with guilt whenever she thought of her mother. She'd been widowed herself only three years before June was incarcerated, and in many ways, June's situation had robbed her of an opportunity to start again or to retire at an age where she could enjoy it. Her mother was always quick to dismiss such thoughts: *'Don't be ridiculous, Juney, you'd do the same for your girls. You know you would.'*

Now, she stepped forward as the two women reached her and opened her arms. Tears ran down her cheeks, mirroring her mother's as they hugged. They held on tight, their bodies convulsing together as the enormity of the situation hit them.

'Marlow,' the prison warden closest to them called, a mild warning in her tone.

June gave her mother a quick squeeze before pulling away. She turned to Lu, whose cheeks were as wet as her own and pulled her close. She caught the sweet citrus scent of Lu's hair and felt the soft curves of her grown daughter's body. She didn't wait for the prison officer this time but reluctantly released her daughter, smiling at her through her tears. 'I don't want to lose privileges to do that again before you leave. Now, come and sit down.' She indicated to the table and chairs that were positioned in the sun, overlooking a neatly manicured section of lawn. Other tables were positioned in the visiting area far enough away from each other to provide some privacy.

'This is amazing,' Lu said, looking around. 'What a shame they didn't have you here for your entire sentence.'

June nodded. 'I know. In many ways, I feel like I've already been released. It's a good transition, I guess, as it would be daunting going from maximum security back into the real world. I think the adjustment, even from here, will be tricky enough.'

'Speaking of that,' Elena said, 'is there more news about an early release?'

'I'm meeting with Mackenzie, my lawyer, on Monday,' June

said. 'She seems to think I could be released as early as a month or six weeks.'

Elena clasped her hands together. 'A month or six weeks would be wonderful.'

'It's not guaranteed, but it is possible. I want to make sure that speaking with this television show won't cause any problems. I'd hate to be trying to help others and end up ruining my chances of early parole.'

'Have they given you further information about the interview?' Lu asked.

'No more than I shared when you last visited. They basically want to hear what happened before...' she hesitated and cleared her throat '...before your father's death and my sentencing. They want women to know that there are centres that will offer help and places to reach out to anonymously so that what happened to me hopefully doesn't happen to anyone else.'

'What about the fact that it was self-defence?' Lu asked. 'The legal system seemed to ignore that, but will *Southern Insight*?'

'That's why I need to get some clear guidelines from Mackenzie,' June said. 'Everything that happened leading up to that day is fine to talk about, and I won't be saying anything that I haven't already disclosed, but the fact that the legal system didn't believe me, when I said it was self-defence, is possibly an issue. Anyway, I'll get some advice around that. Mackenzie has said she'll attend the interview with me and stop them if they ask anything that could cause problems. She's also having it written into the agreement that she gets to review all footage prior to it going to air. So does the prison administration, so I hope that everyone vetting what I say will therefore make it okay to use.'

'It's a good thing you're doing, Mum,' Lu said. 'We won't want another family to have to go through this.'

'I think the main concern from Mackenzie is if they ask me the question of what – knowing what I know now – I'd do if I could turn back the clock. The support they're talking about wasn't promoted or talked about like it is today. I now know that it existed in the form of shelters and Lifeline, but I didn't have the courage to reach out to them. I was embarrassed. Alan was a highly respected member of the community, the church and his workplace. My real answer is that I'd do exactly what I did again. I can't say that, though. That's not showing remorse or ticking any of the boxes required to get released.' She forced a smile. 'Let's change the subject. I'll tell you more about that once I have the details. It's likely they'll want to interview you both and Nicole, but I'll leave that for all of you to decide yourselves.'

'I'm trying to talk Cole around,' Lu said. 'I don't think she's going to budge, though. Hopefully, she'll come around when you're released.'

June wasn't sure she'd ever get used to Nicole being called Cole. Beyond photos that her mother had shown her, she'd had no contact with Nicole since the night of Alan's death. Other than during the first few months of incarceration when, in trying to come to terms with what had happened, she'd refused all visitors, she'd seen Lu at least once a month for the duration of her time. She'd been reluctant to allow a child to visit, but her mother had been adamant. *You did nothing wrong, Juney. You were protecting yourself and your family, and your girls need to grow up knowing that. They need to know that they can't rely on the legal process either, and seeing you enduring your situation will help them grow into strong, capable women.*

Nicole, however, had refused from day one. June had initially understood why her daughter chose not to visit, but as the weeks, then months and years passed, she'd be lying if she said she wasn't hurt that Nicole hadn't changed her mind and wanted to see her. She thought of her eldest daughter every day and wondered what they would say to each other if they were to speak. From everything Lu and her mother had told her about Nicole, she knew that she blamed June for the situation her imprisonment left their family in. She blamed her for killing her father, who she'd loved fiercely. It did, however, surprise her that Nicole had gone into a field of work that had her working with trauma victims daily. Had, at no point, she questioned her mother's situation and believed that she was, in fact, a victim?

'Your room's ready,' Elena said, breaking into June's thoughts.

'My room?'

Elena smiled. 'Yes, remember the second family room? The girls used it as a playroom and then a teenagers' retreat. I've had that turned into a lovely room with a bed and sitting area. You'll have your own space if you want it. That room leads into the main bathroom too, which you'll have mostly to yourself.'

'It looks amazing,' Lu added. 'There's one thing missing from it... you.'

June smiled. 'Thanks, Mum. I'm not sure how long it will take me to get a job and get out of your hair. I don't think prospective employers will be beating down my door to sign me up.'

'You can stay as long as you like. Forever hopefully,' Elena said. 'I'll enjoy the company.'

'It's all rather surreal right now,' June said. 'I can't imagine being able to wake up when I want to and not have to follow a schedule set by others. Mind you, it's much more flexible here. There are all sorts of activities and training available. Now, let's talk about the two of you. Lu, what's been happening? What are you drawing or painting now?'

Ninety minutes after they arrived, Lu and Elena were once again hugging June. There were fewer tears this time, but the tight squeeze Elena gave June conveyed how much she'd missed her and how excited she was that this terrible ordeal had an end in sight.

It was later that evening, as *Southern Insight* came onto the television, that June questioned her decision to agree to be part of the show. While there was a part of her that was nervous about going back into society, she couldn't wait to leave the prison system either. She wanted what was left of her life back and in no way wanted it jeopardised by an interview.

* * *

Cole ignored the ding of her phone, another text from Lu. She knew her sister and grandmother had visited the prison that morning, but she didn't want to hear about it.

She pulled up outside the Gleesons' plain brick house, wondering what kind of reception she was going to get from eleven-year-old Piper.

Anne Gleeson was in the driveway cutting back a hedge that ran along the fence line when Cole stepped out of the car and walked in her direction. Anne smiled at her with a warmth that instantly confirmed why the Gleesons were foster carers. Cole's gut told her that these two girls were lucky to be placed here.

'You must be Cole,' she said as Cole reached her. 'Mike told me that he thought you'd be perfect for chatting with Piper. We appreciate you doing this – and on a Saturday, too.'

'It's no problem,' Cole said. 'We work flexible hours to allow for after-hours and weekend appointments, but I'm rather wondering what kind of a reception I'm going to get. I tend to deal with adults more than kids, and they come to us asking for help. This is a different situation.'

'It is,' Anne agreed, 'and certainly not one we expect you to be able to wave a magic wand and fix. Piper needs an adult she can trust and confide in. But she's had the two most important adults in her life let her down, so there's no guarantee she'll ever trust a grown-up again. Come in and meet her and Katie.'

Cole knew how that felt, although she recognised that she had been lucky to have her gran when she was Piper's age. 'Do the girls have other family?' she asked Anne as they walked towards the house.

'They do,' Anne said. 'The maternal grandparents are alive but unfortunately haven't shown any interest in the girls since they were born. I think we're all hoping their mother's going to step up.'

Anne smiled as the sound of squeals came from within the house as they stepped inside. Cole's eyes went to the photo frames that lined the walls of the passageway, and she followed Anne along. 'Are these all of the kids you've fostered?'

Anne nodded. 'Yes. Anywhere from a few days to a few years. We've had eighty-six kids placed with us since we started fostering twenty-five years ago. We're looking forward to adding Piper and Katie to the wall,' she said as they entered a family room where the two girls were playing with a small fluffy white dog. It had a pink ribbon tied to its collar and something that looked suspiciously like a tutu around its tummy. 'Aren't we, girls?'

'Yes!' the younger of the two said. 'I want Bruiser to be in the photo too.'

'This is Cole,' Anne added. 'Piper and Katie,' she said, pointing to each girl as she stated their names. 'Cole's a friend of mine who's dropped in to say hi.'

Cole smiled at the girls. 'Please don't tell me that dog's named Bruiser.'

Katie giggled. 'He is. I think he should be called Princess, even though he's a boy. What do you think, Cole?'

Cole grinned. 'I think that would be more suitable, looking at what he's currently wearing. Maybe you could call him Princess B.'

Anne groaned. 'Don't let Zane hear you call him that. He wanted a big dog and was going to call it Bruiser, but when we got to the rescue centre, this one needed a home the most. He was filthy and malnourished. You'd never believe it now, but we couldn't not take him home. Zane insisted he'd grow into his name, so we kept it as Bruiser. Looking at his tutu, I'm not sure it's working out as Zane had quite imagined.'

'Why are you here?' Piper asked, eyeing Cole suspiciously. 'Are you going to make us talk about our parents and what happened?'

Cole did her best to pretend to look surprised. 'Um, no, that wasn't the plan. I heard that one of you was a keen gardener, and I run a community garden a few blocks away. I wondered if you'd both like to come and give me a hand. There's quite a bit of planning and planting to be done this weekend. Are either of you interested?' She looked from Katie to Piper.

Katie turned up her nose. 'I don't like to get dirty. Piper's better at gardening than me. I'm good at watering, though. Maybe once everything's planted, I could come and do some watering to help?'

Cole smiled at her. 'That would be great, Katie. How about you, Piper? Do you have any plans for the next few hours? I could use some help, but there's no pressure. Only if you feel like it.' It was easy to see Piper struggling with her decision. It was clear that she was keen but also suspicious of Cole. She was going to have to play this casually to gain Piper's trust. 'No need to decide now. Anne's got my number, and if you change your mind and would like to come along, she can give me a ring. I usually spend a few hours over the weekend in the garden and often a night or two after work. Daylight saving makes it easier to do that. During winter, it's only on weekends.'

'That'd be great,' Anne said. 'The girls are still finding their feet here, so I'm sure they'll be looking for activities to do in the coming weeks.'

'Great. Lovely to meet you both,' Cole said, 'and Princess B, of course. Hopefully, I'll see you in the garden one day.' She smiled once again at the girls and followed Anne back down the hallway.

'Sorry,' she said as they reached the front door. 'That didn't go well. You could see the hostility radiating off her from a mile away.'

Anne sighed. 'It'll take time before she trusts anyone. I'd hoped the lure of the gardening might be enough, but she's tougher than I imagined.'

'Cole,' a tentative voice called up the hallway. 'Could I come with you today?'

Anne raised an eyebrow and mouthed, 'Unexpected.'

'That'd be great,' Cole called back. 'Have you got some older clothes that you don't mind getting dirty?'

'How about those jeans with the tear in the knee,' Anne said. 'Pop those on and one of your older shirts, and then you can go with Cole. I'll get a drink bottle for you from the kitchen.'

'Success,' Cole whispered, and grinned as Piper ran off to get changed.

* * *

Tori sipped her peppermint tea as her eyes flicked across the screen, reading as much information as she could find online about June Marlow. As the crime had been committed in 1995, it was limited, but the old news archives still had some feature stories about her.

It was hard to comprehend that June Marlow had spent more than Tori's lifetime behind bars.

Tori couldn't imagine what June must have gone through prior to the night she killed her husband. It was incredible to think that she'd ended up in prison for what looked, from everything she'd read so far, like a clear case of defending herself and her children. However, one statement she'd found in the archives said that on that night, Alan Marlow hadn't been given the chance to physically hurt June or either of the children. The abuse had escalated from verbal to him threatening her with a knife. June had produced a knife of her own and killed him before he had a chance to hurt her.

Tori sighed as she continued to read. It appeared June hadn't told anyone of the abuse. Not her mother, friends or the police. No one, other than June herself, could confirm it happened at all. Even her two girls, both quite young at the time, were unable to confirm that their father had been aggressive or physically violent. The oldest daughter, Nicole, had even stated: '*My daddy was the best daddy in the world. He would never have hurt us.*'

Tori wondered what the relationship between June and the oldest daughter was like now. Had she forgiven her mother as she grew older and understood what had transpired?

Tori started making notes as she continued to read, a flutter of nerves unexpectedly rippling through her. She stopped for a moment. Why was reading about this woman and thinking about interviewing her making her nervous? She knew the answer without giving it too much thought. She had the chance to give June Marlow a voice. A voice she hadn't had prior to the night she killed her husband.

She was interrupted by a text. Alex Wilson. He'd beaten her to making contact.

Free to chat?

Tori didn't bother to text a reply. Instead, she called Alex straight back.

'That was quick,' Alex said. 'Thanks for calling back on a Saturday. Did Penny give you a heads-up?'

'Some brief info,' Tori said. 'You're doing a piece on trauma and how it's affected people long term.'

'Yes, particularly looking at adults who experienced trauma as kids or in their teens and seeing where they are today. I've suggested we also interview some teens too who are going through trauma now and catch up with them again in five or ten years to do this again but have the footage of them as they're going through their issues. That would be powerful.'

'It would,' Tori agreed. 'Although they might not be up for it if they're experiencing trauma at the moment.'

'Can we catch up?' Alex asked. 'Penny mentioned you're working on another story that might feed into this one.'

'I am,' Tori said. 'It's about victims of domestic violence who are behind bars, for fighting back against their abusers. As you can imagine, it's a topic that's trauma-filled. I'm sure there will be some crossovers.'

'I'd say there will be,' Alex said. 'I'm hardly in the office, which is why I haven't dropped in to see you. Every story I'm working on has had me travelling around. I'll be back on Monday, though. How about we meet for a drink after work, say six? I've got quite a lot to chat with you about, so we could even grab a bite to eat at the same time if that suits you.'

Tori hesitated. As much as Penny thought she and Alex were

compatible, she wasn't interested in him like that. She was happy to meet him but would make it clear that it was a work meeting only if she needed to. 'Let's aim for the drink and go from there. I'll have an hour or so, but I'm a bit swamped for anything longer.'

'Perfect. Let's meet at Drakes at six.'

# 6

Lu hugged her grandmother, declining the invitation to come in for a cup of tea as she dropped her home following the visit to the prison.

'Or a glass of wine, if you prefer,' Elena said.

Lu laughed. 'It's a bit early for wine. No, I've got a client to meet at two and then some other work to do.'

Elena laughed. 'A client. And what's this client's name? Fido or perhaps Bear or Daisy?'

'Fred Astaire. One of the snooty, well-paying clients that I can't be late for.'

Elena raised an eyebrow. 'People are so ridiculous when it comes to their pets. It was good to see your mum today, wasn't it? She's looking much happier than any time I think we've visited.'

'The combination of finally being able to hug us and the thought of getting out, I guess,' Lu said. 'It'll be strange to have her home, won't it?'

Elena nodded. 'But lovely.' Her smile quickly faded to a frown. 'Except for Cole. I'm not sure what we're going to do about her.'

'I'm trying to wear her down,' Lu said. 'I'm hoping if I bug her enough about speaking to Mum that she'll end up giving in and agreeing to at some stage. I even called her work last week and asked for the name of the therapist she's seeing. I wanted to check that they knew what was happening.'

'And did they?'

Lu shook her head. 'No, it's all confidential and they wouldn't provide the counsellor's details. But I honestly think if we can get them in the same room and Cole gives her a chance to explain, she'll be able to see Mum's side of the story. To believe her that it was self-defence.'

'Cole's such a closed book,' Elena said. 'You know, one of the psychologists she saw after it happened said to me that Cole's refusal to believe June was acting in self-defence may have been a result of the fact she did see what happened. And if she had witnessed a calculated murder, which I can assure you that I don't believe for one minute was what happened, it would explain the fact she'd repressed the memory and won't give June the time of day.'

'Mum didn't plan to kill him,' Lu said. 'But maybe it seemed like that to Cole.' She sighed. 'As she won't talk about that night, won't talk to Mum, and does her best to run a mile whenever it's mentioned, we might never know. Although, I will keep trying to wear her down.' She glanced at her watch. 'I'd better run. Fred Astaire's waiting.'

As she manoeuvred the white Jeep from her gran's house in Malvern to the streets of South Yarra, she directed her in-car system to call her sister. She doubted Cole would pick up, but as Lu had said to Gran, she'd wear her sister down eventually. As expected, the phone clicked through to voice mail. She didn't bother to leave a message. She'd text her when she was walking Fred.

As she had the thought, a text pinged her phone, indicating a voice message had been left while she was calling Cole. She grinned. Maybe her sister was going to communicate after all. She instructed the car to play the message, her stomach flip-flopping when a husky voice played through her speakers.

'Hey, it's Ali. Just wondering how today went and if that hug was everything you dreamed it would be. I hope it was.' There was a beat before Ali spoke again, her voice sounding uncharacteristically nervous. 'And I'm home tonight if you feel like some company. I know today would have been huge, and if you feel like debriefing with someone, I'd love it to be me. Drop by. It's the apartment behind the café. Otherwise, I'll see you Monday for a coffee and some art chat.'

Lu had held her breath the entire time Ali was talking. Everything in her voice suggested this invite was more than someone reaching out as a friend. Or was Lu reading too much into it? She groaned. She was useless at dating. What played out in her head was never what played out in real life. She wasn't sure why she was so bad at it. Cole said it wasn't her. It was both of them. They hadn't had parents setting an example of how to interact in a relationship, so they had no idea. On this one, she'd have to agree with her sister.

Nerves rattled through her. She would play this cool. Turn up at Ali's with a bottle of wine and expectations that Ali was reaching out as a friend. That way, she wouldn't be disappointed.

She nodded to herself as she pulled to a stop outside Fred's South Yarra mansion. She could play it cool. Couldn't she?

* * *

Cole had been pleased to see Piper's face light up when they reached the community garden. There were plenty of garden beds to dig over and replant, but a large section of the garden was also thriving with summer produce.

'Hey, Cole,' John, one of the regulars, had called as they arrived. There were plenty of people working the beds, and most of them called out hello or gave a friendly wave.

'People are nice here,' Piper said as Cole handed her some gloves.

'I guess they've all got a similar interest,' Cole said. 'It's always lovely when you can chat to people about something you're interested in and not have to talk about normal life. I'd much rather talk about tomatoes or herbs than what's going on in the world or even what's happening at work.'

Piper nodded. 'Me too. I'd rather talk about dirt than my life right now. It's a much cleaner subject.'

Cole glanced at the little girl, relieved to see the corners of her lips turned up in a smile and a glint in her eye. She handed Piper a garden fork. 'How about we dig over these two beds,' she said, pointing at two empty beds that lined part of the herb garden. 'We've got some zucchini seedlings ready to plant once the beds have been prepared.'

Cole was impressed as she watched Piper turning the soil. She was about to ask who'd taught her to do this but stopped herself. The most likely answer was one of her parents, neither of whom Cole wanted to bring up yet.

They had worked in silence for over half an hour when Cole left Piper to finish the digging while she retrieved the seedlings from the greenhouse.

She returned carrying a large seedling tray. Her phone pinged with a text as she placed the tray beside one of the garden beds. She took the phone from her pocket and glanced at the screen. Lu *again*. Would she never get the hint that she didn't want to hear about Lu's visit to the prison? Regardless of that, this was supposed to be about Piper right now.

'You look kind of annoyed,' Piper said as Cole shoved the phone back into her pocket. 'Was that someone you didn't want to talk to?'

'It was my sister,' Cole said.

'Don't you like her?'

'I like her a lot,' Cole said. 'But she wants me to do something I don't want to do. Something I don't even want to talk about, if I'm honest.'

Piper nodded, and Cole could see that the little girl understood exactly where she was coming from.

'Let's plant these, shall we?' Cole nodded at the seedlings.

'Three rulers apart,' Piper said, causing Cole to smile.

'Rulers?'

Piper nodded. 'My dad said to think in rulers. Some seedlings need one ruler, some two and others, like zucchini, are better if you place them three rulers apart. Our school rulers are thirty centimetres, so it's easy to estimate.'

'Clever,' Cole said. 'I'll start thinking in rulers moving forward.'

'Dad had some great ideas,' Piper said as she expertly took a seedling from the tray and used a trowel to dig a hole for it. 'He was a good gardener.'

'And teacher from the looks and sounds of it.' Cole nodded towards the seedling Piper had planted.

Piper nodded and continued planting the seedlings. Cole decided not to push the conversation any further. She had a feeling that Piper would open up when she was ready.

As the young girl planted the final seedling, Cole glanced at her watch. 'You know, we've probably done enough for today.

How about I treat us to a milkshake, and then I'll drop you back at the Gleesons'? They do great ones at Carlson's, which is on the way.'

Piper's eyes widened. 'Yes, please. Anne and Zane took me and Katie there when we first came to live with them. It was the best milkshake I've ever had.'

'Let's go and wash up our tools and ourselves, and then we'll head off. I'll send Anne a message to let her know our plans. Does that sound good?'

Piper nodded.

Fifteen minutes later, they sat across from each other in the American-style café. 'I thought you'd get a coffee or something an adult would drink,' Piper said, her surprise obvious that Cole had ordered a strawberry milkshake. 'Anne had coffee, and Zane had a beer when they brought us here.'

'God no,' Cole said. 'As you said, these are the best milkshakes ever, and I love milkshakes. I'm not missing out. How's your vanilla one?'

Piper smiled. 'Delicious.'

Cole's phone pinged with another text. She glanced at it and then switched the phone off. Was Lu ever going to let up?

'Was that your sister again?' Piper asked.

Cole nodded. 'How did you guess?'

'Because your face went dark like you were annoyed. Sisters can be so annoying.'

'They can,' Cole agreed. 'Mike, your neighbour, is someone I work with. He said you and Katie were pretty close.'

'We are,' Piper said. 'Someone needs to look out for her.'

Cole nodded. 'Definitely a big-sister responsibility. Mike mentioned you've had a pretty hard time at home lately. Katie's lucky to have you there to protect her.'

Piper sipped her drink, her eyes fixed on Cole as if she was weighing her up. Eventually she released the straw from her lips. 'I need to protect Katie. To prove to her that even though Mum didn't protect her, I will.'

'That's hard that you feel like your mum wasn't looking out for you and Katie.'

'It's not just what I feel, it's what happened,' Piper said, her teeth gritted.

Cole held up her hands. 'Hey, I wasn't suggesting it didn't. I just know that it's hard when adults let you down, that's all I meant. And especially when it's your mum.' Cole swallowed. She knew what it was like to be let down by your mother.

'Do you hear of other stories like us?' Piper asked. 'Where the dad hits the family, and the mum lets him get away with it.'

Cole nodded. 'Unfortunately, quite a lot.'

'Why wouldn't our mum protect us?'

'I can't speak for her as I don't know her, but what we often see is women who've not only suffered abuse – whether it be physical, verbal, emotional or all three – but their partner has made them believe that they deserve the treatment they're getting. They're so pushed down that they don't have the belief that they deserve any better and even if they do, they don't have the strength to do anything about it.'

Piper nodded, a faraway look in her eyes. 'That kind of makes sense. My dad hit Mum a lot. He even kicked her and told her she was useless. He hit me and Katie too. I wish I'd been stronger. Maybe I could have stopped him. Hurt him. Maybe even killed him.' Her face flushed red with these words. 'I didn't mean that. It just came out.'

'You don't need to apologise,' Cole said, doing her best to push all thoughts of her own situation from her mind. 'If he was hitting your mum and you guys, then yes, he should be made to pay for it. Killing him would be extreme and would probably ruin your life as you'd spend most of it in some kind of prison, but calling the police and getting help would be a starting place.'

'You probably think I'm awful.'

Cole shook her head. 'Not at all. A lot of us have struggled growing up.'

'You struggled?'

Cole nodded.

'Did your dad yell at you, or hit you?'

Cole's gut started to churn. She couldn't talk too much about her own life with a client, especially an eleven-year-old. She'd have to tread very carefully.

'I actually don't remember a lot of what happened when I was a kid, but my parents weren't in the picture from when I was about ten, and my sister and I were raised by my gran.'

Piper frowned. 'Weren't in the picture. What does that mean?'

'Just that something happened, and my dad died, and my mum went away. It's complicated.'

Piper nodded and Cole hoped she'd leave it there.

The little girl remained deep in thought, before looking up at Cole. 'Can I ask you something?'

'Of course,' Cole said, hoping it was going to be about Piper and her situation rather than Cole's.

'You said you were raised by your gran. Did you still see your mum?'

Cole shook her head.

'Do you hate her? Because I feel bad that I hate mine. You're supposed to love your mum, aren't you?'

Cole swallowed. Why had she agreed to this? As much as she wanted to help Piper, it was crossing too much into her own situation. She did her best to push thoughts of her life away and remain professional. 'I don't know that I'd say I hate her. I do know that I haven't forgiven her for not being there for me and my sister. It's tricky and every situation is different. The thing about hating your mum is what it does to you on the inside. It can eat away at you and make you feel miserable.'

'How do I stop hating her?'

'Talking about it helps,' Cole said. 'That's what I see a lot of in my job. That by talking through these kinds of situations people begin to understand a little bit more about why someone acts in a way that they do. It can help.'

Piper nodded, her face relaxing. 'Talking to you has helped a bit. But I feel better that you didn't say I shouldn't hate her 'cause that would be like saying what she's done is okay. Katie says that Mum loves us and is coming back for us, but I don't think that's true. I heard Anne talking to Zane, and she was saying that Mum was choosing to stay with Dad even though he beats her.' Tears filled the little girl's eyes. 'Why would she choose him over me and Katie?'

Cole wanted to scoop the little girl into her arms and comfort her.

'I don't know,' she said. 'It's hard to understand. Like I said earlier, I don't know your mum, so it's hard for me to even guess why she'd do that, but all I can say to you is that it's horrible. It's horrible for both you and Katie, and I'm so sorry you're in this situation. I hope that your mum can explain to you one day why she's making this choice, but even if she does, it doesn't make it any easier, does it?'

Piper shook her head, wiping tears from her eyes. 'I don't think she's allowed to see us, not that I want to see her anyway.'

Piper's words were at complete odds with the pained look on her face. It was obvious to Cole that she very much wanted to see her mother and to be comforted by her. To be told that, of course, she loved Piper and Katie and would put them first.

'I understand that,' Cole said. 'The not wanting to see her. I wouldn't want to see my mum if she suddenly appeared.'

Piper slurped her milkshake, causing a high-pitched bubbly sound to fill the air. She grinned at the unexpected noise.

Cole laughed, relieved at the mood lightening and an opportunity to change the subject. 'We should get you back to Anne and Zane's. Katie's probably spray-painted the dog pink by now.'

'Hopefully,' Piper said, pushing her empty milkshake to the side. 'Bruiser's a stupid name for it, but we can't say that to Zane. We wouldn't want to upset him. He's nice. Did you know that they've had over eighty foster kids?'

'Anne did mention it,' Cole said as they walked out of the café and back out onto the street.

'That makes me feel a bit better,' Piper said. 'That we aren't the only ones who've got bad families.'

'It's hard, isn't it,' Cole said, 'when all your friends have normal families, and you're the one who got something different? I used to get teased that my mum was so old 'cause people thought Gran was my mum.'

'There's a boy at school who told me that my mum hates me,' Piper said. 'And that's why she let Katie and me go into foster care. I kind of hate him.' She sighed. 'Except he's probably right.'

Cole put an arm around Piper's shoulders, conscious that the little girl tensed at her touch but then, after a few steps, relaxed. 'I think there are some horrible people in the world, Piper, and the key is to surround yourself with the nice ones. Like Anne and Zane.'

'And you,' Piper said. 'Do you think I could come to the gardens with you again?'

'I'd love you to,' Cole said. 'I usually drop in Wednesday

afternoon if you want to join me. We can check with Anne, and I'll pick you up on my way through.'

'I'd like that.'

* * *

June looked up from the journal she'd been writing in as Doreen came into her room.

'How was your visit yesterday? Your daughter looks a lot like you!'

She closed the notebook and smiled at the woman she already considered a friend. While she'd only been at Winchester for a short time, Doreen was the one woman who'd made an effort to make her feel welcome and help her settle in, a strangely bizarre concept for a prison.

'Honestly, being able to hug Lu and my mum was like Christmas. You don't realise how much you miss human touch until it's taken from you. It's like this piece has been missing, which may be something I can get back now. How about you? I saw you had a visitor.'

Doreen nodded. 'My son. He comes to tell me how angry he is and how he can't forgive me.'

'What?' June was shocked. 'Why would he do that? And why do you let him visit?'

'Because I deserve it. I let him down, and he needs me to hear that.'

'But he visits every week. Does he say the same thing each time?'

Doreen nodded.

'And what do you say?'

'I ask his forgiveness generally, and he says no, and then he leaves. I'm counting on the fact that he keeps coming back and wants to accept it but can't. Hopefully that will change.'

June thought of Nicole as Doreen spoke about her son. She'd always assumed that if she could get her in the same room and have a conversation, she'd be able to convince her that she'd done nothing wrong. Listening to Doreen made her realise that perhaps she'd been naive in this outlook.

'Your mum looks like a lovely lady,' Doreen said.

June's eyes instantly filled with tears. The love her mum's hug had conveyed was still wrapped around her. As bad as she felt for her two girls, she felt even worse for what her mum had been through. Not only dealing with her own pain and grief at June's situation but having to deal with the two little girls as well. It was more than anyone should ever be asked to handle.

'Sorry,' Doreen added, noticing June's distress.

'She's amazing,' June said, wiping her eyes. 'I feel awful for what she's been put through.'

'Why?' Doreen asked. 'All she's done is support you, knowing that what put you in prison was the right thing to do. You need to remind yourself of that. While the system might have let you down, you did nothing wrong. That's the message you need to get across in the television interview, too. Otherwise, what's the point?'

June stared at Doreen. 'What do you mean?'

'I mean, what's the point of telling your story if you don't make it clear that you were fighting for your life and that of your girls? That your mum has borne the brunt of it with raising the girls as a result, and that the system is – for want of a better description – fucked.'

June's eyes widened. While she was a convicted criminal, Doreen was well-spoken and articulate. She'd held her cards close to her chest in the brief time June had got to know her, but as she was in for insider trading, June assumed she was from a professional, well-educated background. Hearing the woman swear was a shock.

Doreen laughed. 'You've come out of maximum security, yet me swearing shocks you. You're an interesting character, June Marlow. Just remember, you've got a chance to tell your story and to help others. Make sure you do, okay?'

June nodded, knowing without any doubt that Doreen was right.

## 7

Cole hadn't been able to get thoughts of Piper out of her mind on Sunday and found herself looking through the file that Mike had registered at the Wellness Centre on the two girls when she arrived at work on Monday morning. There was nothing in it that she hadn't already learned, but she still felt compelled to read all the documents associated with it.

'Thank you.'

Cole looked up as Mike walked into her office, his tailored suit and polished black shoes suggesting he had some important meetings that day.

'Anne called me after you left on Saturday. Said it was the first time since Piper and Katie had been placed with them that Piper seemed to relax a little. That she'd obviously had a good time with you.'

'She's a great kid,' Cole said and then shook her head. 'No child should have to go through what she has. She thinks her mother hates her, because of her choice to stay with her husband.'

'I think most people would draw a similar conclusion,' Mike

said. 'Not that she hates them necessarily, but that she loves an abusive alcoholic more than she loves them. I'm sure we'll find there's a lot more to it than that. From what I've seen of her, her self-confidence and self-worth have been stripped away by her husband. It's hard to pick yourself straight up after that happens.'

'I'd like to speak with the mother. Do you think social services would approve a visit?'

'They should. We work directly with them on several cases and this one is no different. Speak with them and, assuming it's approved, we'll document everything and lodge all the right requests before you visit. Not that I need to tell you, but everything needs to be done by the book. Now, have you seen Ethan?'

Cole shook her head. 'I don't think he's in yet.'

'If you see him, can you let him know I'm looking for him? He might have mentioned that there's a current affairs program looking to do a story on the centre. I'm going to ask him to work with them.'

Cole's stomach churned. '*Southern Insight*?'

Mike nodded. 'It should be good exposure for the clinic. We'll have to be careful who we include and ensure all the sign-offs are in place. You're welcome to be involved if you're interested?'

Cole forced a smile. 'Definitely not interested, thanks. I'll chat to Ethan and let him know that I'm happy to approach any of my clients he feels would be good to put up for it, but I personally don't want to be involved.'

'Camera-shy?'

Cole laughed, hoping it sounded natural. 'Exactly. And Ethan's going to look much better on camera than any of us. No offence.'

Mike laughed. 'None taken, and I agree. On the male side, anyway. His looks will probably bring in more business alone.

While I think of it, Ethan mentioned you want to split up your Wednesday trauma group. To categorise them by trauma levels?'

'Yes, there's some extreme variances in what people have been through, and it's causing some issues.'

'Leave it for now, okay? I know who you're talking about, but there's a lot more to Tom Hargreaves's case than he's so far shared.'

'There's more to seeing his dog being killed?'

Mike nodded. 'I heard that Roberto had a problem with Tom being in the group, but it's where he needs to be. Turns out one of my mates on the force was there the night Tom's world fell apart. His dog's death is only part of his problems.'

Mike went on to tell Cole Tom's story.

Her stomach churned as he finished speaking.

'See if you can get Roberto to deal with his own issues because if Tom ever admits the truth, Roberto's going to feel awful.'

Cole nodded. Learning what she'd just heard from Mike, Roberto feeling awful was an understatement. Part of her wanted to contact Tom immediately and offer him a private session to talk through what had happened, but the sensible side of her knew for best results they needed to try and draw the story out of him. Have him initiate it.

She turned her attention back to the documents on Piper as Mike left her office, grateful for the distraction from Tom's case. Assuming social services approved a visit, she'd need to give some thought to what she said to Piper's mother before she made contact. She was conscious that she had her own demons sitting in the background and needed to be careful not to bring any of them into this situation.

\* \* \*

Lu hummed to herself as she pulled the Jeep into traffic, heading away from Elwood towards Malvern. Her thoughts shifted back to Saturday night. It had been magical. She'd arrived at Ali's with a bottle of wine, expecting to be talking about the visit to her mum. However, Ali opened the door and didn't hesitate. She'd pulled Lu into a tight embrace, only letting go so she could smile and laugh.

'Your heart's beating a million miles an hour.'

'I wasn't expecting that, that's all,' Lu said.

'You've had a big day,' Ali said. 'An exceptional day, I'm guessing. Getting to hug your mum for the first time in so long.'

Lu nodded. It had been huge. Wonderful, but huge.

'So, I wanted today to be a day of other firsts.' She pulled Lu to her and kissed her. 'I've wanted to do this since I first met you.'

'Really? But you were seeing someone then?'

'Which is why I didn't,' Ali said. 'But since that ended, it's been on my mind... a lot. I wasn't sure until recently as to how you felt. But the last few days have given me a bit more of an idea about that.' She pulled Lu towards her and kissed her again.

Now, on Monday afternoon, Lu understood it was something special. It wasn't one night or a bit of a flirtation. It was in the early days, but her feelings for Ali were reciprocated.

Lu had spent most of Sunday and part of Monday morning at the café, working on the first of the five pieces Ali had commissioned. She wasn't sure whether to feel awkward or elated when Ali had dropped a kiss on top of her head while serving customers. Did they want this to be public knowledge already? She quickly lost herself in her design, a smug feeling suggesting that, yes, she was happy for anyone to know what was going on.

'You free tonight?' Ali had asked, raising her eyebrows suggestively as she placed a latte in front of Lu.

Lu grinned, about to say yes, when she remembered she had

dinner plans at her gran's. Could she invite Ali along? No, it was far too early, and it wouldn't hurt to play a little hard to get. 'No, sorry, having dinner at my gran's. Another attempt to get my sister to come around.'

Ali nodded. 'Tomorrow night then? We could go out for dinner. Take a picnic down to the beach and go for a walk?'

'Sounds perfect,' Lu said. 'Although I do have a client at six. I can meet you after unless you'd like to come along?'

'As in a four-legged client?'

Lu nodded.

Ali agreed to meet Lu to walk the dog before having dinner and *whatever else the night brings.*

Now, as Lu got ready to tackle the afternoon traffic she was looking forward to seeing Gran and Cole. However, the reality was that it would probably end with Cole storming out like she usually did. But Lu liked to think her glass was always half full, and tonight, that meant she'd be able to talk Cole around.

\* \* \*

As Tori approached Drakes, the popular inner city wine bar, the warm February evening air was filled with the clanging of tram bells and the hum of conversation from passers-by. Wafts of garlic came from a wood-fired pizza oven, adding a mouthwatering aroma to the vibrant atmosphere. She spotted Alex at a prime outside table, which overlooked the Yarra River. He raised a hand when he saw her, and she made her way to the table.

'Nice spot,' she said, placing her bag on a spare seat before sliding into the chair across from him.

He smiled, the golden flecks in his brown eyes catching the light. 'I love nights like this in Melbourne. I know we complain year-round about the crappy weather, but a night like tonight is a great reminder of why we love this city.'

Tori laughed. 'You should do a tourism ad for Melbourne. You sell it well.'

Alex joined her laughter. 'Not sure they'd want me referring to the *crappy* weather. Now, what would you like to drink? I've started with a cider, but happy to move to wine if you'd like to share a bottle?'

'Cider's fine,' Tori said as one of the waitstaff approached and took her order. She didn't want to give him the impression that she was settling in for anything more than a quick chat. She waited for the waiter to retreat to the bar before moving straight to the purpose of their catch-up.

'Penny gave me a bit of detail about your story but didn't go into too much depth about how we could work together or potentially leverage the details from one story for the other. What were your thoughts?'

'Honestly, I'm guessing that your story might be of more use to me than mine to you,' Alex said. 'If you're talking to women who are in prison because of trauma, then that's full on. While I don't expect to use any of their stories, some of the trauma their extended families would have gone through would be interesting to explore.'

Tori thought of June Marlow's story. She wasn't sure if the daughters would necessarily want their information shared across another story.

'I guess the question is, why would they share it with you?' Tori said. 'With my story, the benefit to them is that it shines a light on unjust sentencing. We're calling it *Victims Behind Bars* for a reason. We believe these women were victims. How could sharing their trauma for your story be of benefit to them?'

Alex sipped his cider as he considered his answer. 'It won't necessarily benefit them directly. The point will be to share their stories so that other people realise that if they suffer trauma or any of their family or friends do, you don't dismiss it and assume people will grow out of it. You need to check in on them, get them help and make sure it's dealt with. Otherwise, it has the potential to mess people right up.'

'Have you confirmed some people for your story?'

'A couple, but I'm also meeting with a community centre in Hawthorn during the week. They run programs and groups specifically for trauma counselling. It'll most likely be Thursday morning. You should come along.'

Tori nodded. It would be interesting to see what the centre did. It might be a resource that was promoted during the *Victims Behind Bars* story. They wanted to ensure they provided plenty of options for help to the audiences watching. More than putting a phone number on the screen.

'I'd like that,' Tori said. 'Send me the address and a time, and I'll meet you there.'

'Will do. Now, I know you said you only had time for a drink, but those pizzas are smelling good. Can I tempt you?'

Tori's stomach rumbled, answering the question for her.

Cole pulled to a stop in her gran's driveway and switched off the car. She took out her phone, knowing she'd missed at least two text messages on the drive over. Both were from Ethan asking her to call him. She sent him a quick text explaining she was out for dinner and would give him a ring after. A thumb-up came back.

Now, shortly after being greeted by her gran and Lu, Cole stood staring at the old playroom that had been her and Lu's teenage retreat for years. When they'd finally left home, their gran had removed the posters that plastered the walls but hadn't changed the room all that much, as she didn't use it often. When it was Gran on her own, she tended to use the living room at the front of the house, which had a television and her comfortable armchair. It was the room she'd retreated to throughout Cole and Lu's teenage years, no doubt to give herself a break from them and to muffle the loud music they liked to play.

Now, the room had been transformed. The old couch, which had once been pushed up against a wall for optimal television viewing, had been re-covered in a cool blue fabric and been repositioned close to the large bay window that overlooked the back garden. A coffee table sat between it and the window, creating an inviting space to sit and relax. A double bed had replaced the couch's previous position with new bedding and some bright yellow cushions placed on it. The walls had been freshly painted, and when she looked down, Cole saw the carpet had been removed, and the boards beneath them had been polished. Nausea churned in the pit of her stomach. It was real. Her mother was coming home.

'Looks good, doesn't it,' Lu said, joining her in the doorway. 'Gran's spent ages doing all of this.'

'She did it herself? The painting and everything?'

Lu shook her head. 'No, I painted the walls, and we got someone to do the floors. But Gran chose all the colours, and she re-covered the couch and made the cushions. Mum's favourite colour is yellow. Upholstery and sewing were always Gran's specialties.'

'She's coming home?'

'Most likely,' Lu said. 'She doesn't have a date yet, but it could be as early as a few weeks.'

Cole thought she might be sick. From the age of ten, when her mother was incarcerated, she'd done her best to block out anything to do with her. She'd spent multiple hours as a kid in counselling but had spent a lot of that tuned out, refusing to engage. As an adult, she continued to go through the process of regular counselling but without being able to recall what she'd seen that night, the process seemed redundant. She could hypothesise until the cows came home but until she remembered exactly what happened, she had to stick with her gut and what she believed to be true.

But now, if her mother was to be released and would be living at her grandmother's house, the house she considered her childhood home, where would that leave her?

'You're going to have to see her at some stage. You do realise that, don't you?' Lu said. 'Especially if she's living here.'

'This is *our* home.'

'It was her home as a kid, long before it was ever our home. And anyway, the house in Mount Waverley is technically our childhood home.'

'Not to me, it isn't. This is, but it won't feel like that once she's here.'

'Once your mother's here?' Their grandmother came up behind them.

'Sorry, Gran,' Cole said. 'I'm struggling to get my head around her coming back, that's all.'

'Love, you need to have a conversation with her. You work every day with people who've been through traumatic experiences, and while we know you can't remember what happened, you need to give her a chance to explain the exact circumstances. Life isn't always black and white. Your mother had good reasons for doing what she did.' She held up a hand before Cole could respond.

'Come back to the kitchen. Dinner's ready, and I don't want anyone storming out because of this conversation. We'll all agree to change the topic and not talk about your mother again until after we've finished dessert. At that time, if you want to leave, I won't stop you.'

Cole smiled. Her gran knew her well enough to know that storming out was exactly what she was on the verge of doing.

Over dinner, Lu shared with them that she'd been asked to do some drawings for Future Blend, and she hoped it might lead to some more paid commissions.

'Is that why you're looking so happy tonight?' Elena asked.

The dark red splotches that appeared on Lu's cheeks suggested it was something or someone else that had caused that.

'Who is she?' Cole asked, unable to help herself.

'Who said there's anyone?'

Cole shared a look with Elena, and they both laughed.

'Your face is a dead giveaway,' Elena said. 'You don't have to tell us anything if it's early days, but it's nice to know that there's someone making you feel like that.'

Lu took a sip of wine. 'There is someone. But yes, it's new, and I'm not sure if it's anything more than a business arrangement.'

Elena's mouth dropped open. 'A business arrangement. You mean you're paying someone?'

Cole started to laugh. She was sure that wasn't what Lu was suggesting, but her grandmother's interpretation of the comment and the horrified look on her face was priceless.

'What? Of course not,' Lu said. 'I meant it's one of my clients who might turn into more than a client, that's all.'

'You're dating the dogs now?' Cole said, trying to keep a straight face.

Lu rolled her eyes. 'One of my *art* clients.'

Relief flashed across their grandmother's face. 'Thank goodness. It's bad enough we've got one family member in prison. I don't want another involved in some form of pros-titution.'

Cole laughed again, and this time, both Lu and their grand-mother joined in. Lu had an incredibly infectious laugh, and by the time they stopped laughing, Cole was wiping tears from her eyes. 'Thank you,' she said to her grandmother. 'I didn't realise how much I needed that.'

Elena reached across and squeezed her hands. 'Pleasure, hon. We all need less worry and more laughter. Now, I hope you've left room for dessert.'

Once they'd finished eating, Cole packed the last dish into the dishwasher and turned it on as her grandmother poured boiling water into the teapot and placed it with three mugs on the table.

'You okay?' Lu asked, breaking into Cole's thoughts. Her mind had wandered back to thinking about her mother and what she'd say to her if she had to see her.

'Yes, fine, thinking about work,' she lied.

Lu raised an eyebrow. 'That I doubt. Why can't you admit that you're thinking about Mum and you're not sure what to do? That way, we could all discuss it at least and try and help you.'

'Try and push me into doing something I'm not ready to do, you mean.'

'What, speak to her?'

Cole nodded. 'And forgive her. I know you think I've blocked it out and given it no thought at all, but of course I think about it. And more than think about it, it's a regular item for discussion with my own therapist, but the conclusion I come back to every time is that I can never forgive her. She took our father from us and then lied about what he'd done. You were old enough, Lu. When was he ever abusive towards Mum?'

'Are you really a psychologist? Do you even work in a trauma centre?' Lu asked, her voice rising with anger. 'If you answer yes to either of those questions I can't believe you'd ever disbelieve a woman who said she'd been abused without speaking to her or hearing her story? While she's in prison, you have all the power. You can choose to accept a call from her or visit her. She has no choice, and all she wants to do is talk to you. Ask you to hear her side of the story. But no, you're exerting power, which I get, because you feel the need to protect yourself, but it's totally unfair to Mum. I can't imagine you ever agreeing with one of your clients that this is the right way to handle the situation.'

Cole stared at her sister. Lu was right. She'd never thought of it in those terms before, but she was holding the power. Although it had been pointed out in more than one counselling session that she had the option to visit her mother, but her mother didn't have that option. She guessed it was a somewhat similar conclusion. She gave herself a shake. Whether she was holding the power or not was irrelevant.

'This is different,' she said. 'I was there. We were there. We know he was a good man.' She closed her eyes momentarily before opening them and taking a deep breath. 'I can't believe I'm engaging in this again.' She turned to her grandmother. 'Did you ever see signs of abuse?'

Gran shook her head. 'No, but that's because he was careful with what he did, never bruised her face and never hit you kids. She has scars on her body, Cole. Burns from his cigarette butts.' Tears filled her grandmother's eyes as she tried to speak. 'And they're just the physical scars. He traumatised her, and then she's endured nearly three decades in the prison system because he threatened you kids.'

'She says he did,' Cole said. 'But he wouldn't have hurt me or Lu. We were everything to him. He told us that all the time. Don't you remember?' She turned to Lu. '"*My darlings, my good girls.*

*You are my everything and always will be.*" He used to sing it to us like it was a song. I remember him singing me to sleep when I was little. Surely you remember that?'

'I remember some things about him,' Lu said, 'but I also believe Mum that he threatened us. Why would she kill her husband if something extreme hadn't happened?'

Cole opened her mouth and closed it again. When she had allowed herself to think about her mother and the situation, she'd never been able to come up with any reason for what her mother did. 'I don't know,' she said in the end. 'I was there that night. Yes, I blocked it out, but the therapy I've had tells me it's because I witnessed a premeditated murder play out. Mum thought I was in bed like you were, and she killed him. She didn't realise I was watching.'

'You remember that, or parts of it?' Lu asked.

'No, and that's the problem. That is the most likely scenario as to why I blocked it out.'

Lu shook her head. 'Don't you think it's possible you blocked out a struggle and him threatening her first?'

Cole sighed. 'I don't know exactly what happened. I do know that she decided to kill him, and she did. I'm not deliberately blocking the memory. There's part of me that's curious to know exactly what happened that night, but then my gut tells me not to push it. Maybe I don't want to know what happened? And that's what I need to listen to, as that will be the part of me that knows best, if what I'd find out would be so horrific, it'd be impossible to recover from.'

Lu reached across and squeezed her arm. 'I hope that you'll be able to move beyond it and remember how amazing Mum was to both of us before that night. She's still that same person, Cole.'

'She's right, love. The outside looks older, but what's on the inside is still the mum who loves you with every fibre in her body. She'd give anything to be able to tell you that.'

Cole pushed the chair back and stood. 'I'll give it some thought, okay?'

It was impossible not to see the look of disbelief that shot between Lu and Elena.

'Really, I will.'

'You're not saying that to shut us up?' Lu asked.

'Not this time.' Cole sighed. 'I can see she's coming home, and I'm going to have to face it at some stage. Let me process that, and I'll come back to you. Right now, it's getting late, and I've still got some work to do tonight.'

'I'm proud of you,' Elena said. 'And thank you. I know what it's taking for you to do this.'

Cole's gut twisted with guilt as she saw the pain flash in her gran's eyes. Lu had been right; she was trying to get them off her back, but her gran deserved more.

\* \* \*

June stared in the mirror of the communal bathroom. In a few weeks, it was likely she'd be back out in the world. A world that had continued without her, not even noticing her absence. She'd been thirty-six when she'd been convicted. Her skin had been flawless, and her blonde hair was long and shiny. Now, she was sixty-four, but honestly, she imagined people would misjudge her as being at least seventy. Her hair was more grey than blonde. It was limp and certainly not shiny, which she assumed could be attributed to the prison-issued shampoo and conditioner, but it also seemed thin and lifeless. Perhaps this would change once she was released, although she was sure it was also due to stress.

But it wasn't only her physical changes that June saw when she looked in the mirror. It had been nearly three decades since that night, and the woman she was back then was a distant memory. She used to believe him, every word, every insult – every blow was something she thought she deserved. She never told anyone. Why would she? He had convinced her she was worthless, and for too long, she believed him. She was scared, small and silent. Now, though? Prison had stripped her of illusions. The fear was gone, replaced by something harder. Anger, yes, but not just at him. Anger at herself for ever believing him, for letting it go on for so long. And sadness – grief for the life she'd lost, for the years she could never get back.

If her stress levels had been graphed from when she'd arrived at the maximum-security prison right through to today, she knew that the lines would fluctuate greatly and always show some level of distress. The first few years had, of course, been awful. With the initial arrest, then waiting to be sentenced, the pain of losing her girls, her mum and her freedom. That she'd married a monster; the grief had been enormous. There was never a morning that she hadn't woken worrying about the girls. As the years passed, her worry turned more to sadness about what she was missing out on.

An extra level of sadness existed whenever she thought of Nicole. She understood why her daughter wanted to pretend she no longer existed, but she had thought that would change as Nicole reached adulthood. That it hadn't, had been a shock to June and even more distressing. For years, she imagined that one day Nicole would appear as a visitor, having remembered what happened that night, knowing that June hadn't carried out a premediated murder as she believed, and wanting to talk about it. To understand more and hopefully rebuild their relationship.

But, as Nicole reached her mid-twenties and then thirties, June had understood that it was unlikely to ever happen.

Both Lu and Elena said that Nicole had no recollection of what happened that night, yet she still refused to talk to her mother. It was a response June never understood. Wouldn't part of her want to believe that her mother hadn't done anything wrong? That she was defending herself? And surely, if nothing more, she would want to have a conversation about it?

'You look deep in thought,' one of the younger inmates said as they washed their hands in the basin.

'Not a lot else to do around here than think.'

'You've got that right. There's still half an hour before lights out. Doreen and a couple of others are about to play poker. Feel like joining in?'

June nodded. The one thing she had learned during her time in prison was that anything that acted as a distraction and passed the time was a good thing.

# 8

Despair settled over Cole after she'd hugged her sister and gran goodnight and driven away in the direction of home. She'd done a good job of hiding away from her mother and having nothing to do with her and no association with her, but whether she liked it or not, that was all about to change. Rather than burying her head in the sand it would be better to be prepared.

The thought of more therapy sessions focused on her mother made her shudder. She'd been speaking the truth when she said her mother's situation often came up in her weekly counselling sessions, but they weren't the focus as they had been for many years after her father's death. What she needed was the equivalent of herself, a trauma counsellor who would ask the right questions. She wiped away a tear as an ironic through filled her mind. She could make a list of all the right questions to ask herself; she knew that already, but she also knew that up until this point, she was unable to answer any of them.

Would she be willing to take the risk and go down that path? An image of Ethan filled her mind. She'd promised to text him after she left dinner. She trusted him, and he was excellent at what he did. She dismissed the thought as quickly as she had it. It would be crossing a professional boundary and she wanted to keep her personal life and story out of the Wellness Centre.

Her phone rang as she turned from Malvern onto Glenferrie Road. Ethan's name appeared on her display. She must have been channelling him.

'Hey, I was about to text you. I've just left my gran's.'

'Hey, you, I wasn't sure that you'd pick up. Sorry for the late call.'

Cole laughed. 'It's eight thirty.'

'I know you said you'd call me, but you know what I'm like... impatient! It's about the wedding. I've booked the flights. It's an eight o'clock flight on the Friday night with a return flight on Sunday afternoon. I figured we could relax Sunday morning and go out for brunch before returning to the airport. Does that work for you?'

'Sounds great. Is there a dress code or anything else I need to know?'

'Black cocktail dress. They're going for a black-and-white theme, but I think the only female allowed to wear white is the bride. It'll look like something out of Antarctica, like we're a bunch of penguins.'

Cole laughed, already picturing her black Ted Baker cocktail dress she'd only worn once a year ago. It would be perfect.

'And I'm happy to go shopping with you if you don't already have something and pay for it. I don't expect this to cost you anything. You're doing me a huge favour.'

'I've got a dress already. The one I wore to the awards night last year. Hopefully, you don't remember it, and you'll think it's new.'

Ethan gave a low whistle, causing Cole to blush. 'The black one with the slit up the leg? I remember it. You looked stunning and will do again at the wedding. Thanks again. You're saving me from a fate worse than death.'

'I don't know. You might meet someone nice at the wedding.' She smiled. 'Your mum could have set you up if she's that keen for you to settle down.'

'Luckily, I'm not going to find out. Now, speaking of mums, how's it going with yours? I'm assuming it was a topic that came up at your dinner tonight.'

Cole paused.

'You don't have to discuss it with me. But I'm available if you ever want to chat.'

'No, you're right. They're pressuring me about my mum and being open to talking to her. It's been twenty-eight years, for clarification.'

'Twenty-eight years since you spoke to her?'

'Yes.'

Ethan let out a low whistle. 'You would have only been a little kid. You must miss her.'

Tears filled Cole's eyes. Rather than tell her it was a long time to hold a grudge or ask directly what had happened, he'd hit on the most important aspect of all of it. She did miss her, and that was why she was so angry with her. She'd done something that had taken both parents away from her.

'I do,' Cole admitted. 'But it's a long story and a difficult one.'

'Where are you now?' Ethan asked.

'Leaving Malvern. About ten minutes from home. I don't suppose you're nearby. I really don't feel like being alone right now.'

'Text me your address and I'll be waiting for you,' Ethan said. 'I'll bring a bottle of wine, and we can either open that, or I'll make us some tea. You don't have to tell me anything about the situation with your mother if you don't want to, but I'll be there if you do. In the worst-case scenario, we can watch *Love Island*. There's a new season on.'

Cole laughed. 'I didn't pick you as a fan.'

'Reality TV is my thing,' he said, and Cole could hear the smile in his voice.

'So, what do you say?'

'See you soon.'

\* \* \*

After insisting they split the bill, Tori discovered her phone and keys missing from her bag and remembered she'd left them on her office desk. She and Alex parted, agreeing that he would confirm the time on Thursday for the visit to the community centre.

She walked back to the office, reflecting again on what a nice evening it was. The sun was only just sinking below the horizon. She'd enjoyed her dinner with Alex; he was easy company, but there was no attraction, which was probably a good thing as he'd been telling her about the recent trip he and his new girlfriend had taken. She couldn't wait to share that nugget with Penny.

She used her alarm code to let herself back into her office. She was in the process of retrieving her phone and keys when Penny appeared in her office doorway. She moved into the office and flopped into the visitor's chair. 'I'm knackered.'

'I'm not surprised,' Tori said, moving around her desk and sitting down. 'I came in at eight, and it looked like you were on your second or third coffee. What time did you get here?'

'Six,' Penny said. 'Ratings are down, and I need to get something happening. As much as I don't want to worry you, it's a bit stressful right now. We need some hard-hitting stories. I've got a couple more for you. I'll send through full details tomorrow.'

'I met with Alex,' Tori said. 'I'll be going to the community centre with him on Thursday to research the trauma story. So that might help with ratings. It's one that Gav directed, isn't it?'

Penny nodded, her lips twitching. 'Dinner with Alex?'

'A drink and a woodfired pizza, so yes, you could say dinner.' Tori folded her arms. 'He was telling me all about Hawaii, where he just holidayed with his *girlfriend*.'

Tori couldn't help but laugh at Penny's disappointed face.

'Girlfriend?'

'Yep. So, you can get off my back now, okay?'

'No, I'll have to find you someone else. And Friday would be the perfect day to do that, don't you think?'

'Definitely not. That's the last thing I want for my birthday, thank you very much.'

Penny stood. 'I should get on with some work. But are you still good for Friday night? Sam's booked Luna Noir.'

Tori smiled. 'Definitely. It'll be great to get us all together. Mind you, I could do without getting any older.'

Penny laughed. 'There are many of us who would kill to be your age. Let's catch up before Friday, and you can fill me in on how the Marlow story's going.'

\* \* \*

Cole pulled into the underground parking of her apartment block and sat in her car for a moment, gathering her thoughts. She took a deep breath, willing herself to keep it together. Was she ready to tell Ethan her story? She sighed. She wasn't sure why she continued to hide it. Maybe she should tell everyone, then she wouldn't have the concern that people would find out. They'd already know.

She stepped out of the car, the night air cool against her skin, and walked towards the lifts, pressing the button for the third floor. As she reached her floor and the lift doors opened, Ethan, holding a bottle of red wine, was standing in the lift lobby waiting for her.

'You were quick,' she said.

'It's only a five-minute walk from my place,' he said. 'How are you holding up?'

Cole managed a faint smile. 'I'm okay. Come on in, and we'll open the wine.'

They made their way down the corridor to Cole's apartment, the familiar scent of sandalwood essential oils greeting them as she let them in. It was a comforting aroma, one that usually helped Cole relax. She hoped it would have the same effect tonight.

Ethan set the wine on the kitchen counter and turned to Cole. 'Wine or tea?'

'Definitely wine. This conversation might need something stronger, but we'll see how we go.'

Ethan nodded and busied himself opening the wine. Cole took two wine glasses from the cupboard before indicating the living room to Ethan. She sank into the plush armchair, the weight of the evening pressing down on her.

A few minutes later, Ethan joined her, handing her a glass of merlot. He settled onto the couch across from her, his expression open and attentive. 'So,' he began gently, 'do you want to talk about it?'

Cole took a sip of her wine, the warmth soothing her throat. She set the glass down and took a deep breath. 'My mum murdered my dad when I was ten.'

Ethan's eyes widened slightly, but he remained silent, and she continued. She spoke uninterrupted for five minutes, laying the full story out for him. 'So now you can probably understand why

I haven't spoken to her recently.' She couldn't help but smile as the words came out. 'Lu would jump all over the *recent* comment and ensure you knew exactly how many years, months, days and minutes it's been.'

Ethan leaned forward, his face full of concern. 'I'm so sorry. That must have been incredibly traumatic for you.'

'It was,' Cole admitted, her eyes filling with tears. 'And now, she's getting out. I don't know how to cope with that. I don't know if I can face her or if I even want to.'

Ethan reached out, placing a comforting hand on hers. 'You know, we've both dealt with a lot of similar cases in our line of work. It's different when it's personal, but we know the tools and methods to navigate this kind of trauma.'

Cole nodded. She'd had similar thoughts after spending time with Piper on the weekend. The cases were different, but in many ways, the approach would still be the same. But for Cole, being so personal, she wasn't ready to deal with it. 'It's... it feels so overwhelming,' she finally said. 'I figure I'm going to have to see her at some stage. I can try and avoid her forever, but if I want to have a relationship with Lu and with my gran, that's not going to work. I kind of hate her even more for putting me in this position.'

'Start with what feels right for you,' Ethan suggested. 'Take it one step at a time. Perhaps decide, to begin with, when you're willing to see her. Though it might be easier to see her while she's still in prison.'

'Why?' The last thing Cole wanted was to visit her mother in prison.

'Because you're safe while she's still locked up,' Ethan said. 'Not to say you won't be when she's out. It's just that if you visit her there, you'll have control over the situation. You can walk away knowing she can't come after you.'

Cole nodded. 'You're right, but there's part of me that would prefer to wait until she's released.' She managed a wry smile. 'Partly because that might never happen, and then I won't have to deal with anything.'

Ethan laughed. 'You've certainly got your avoidance tactics sorted. Go with the flow, I'd say. And hey, if you need a distraction, I'm always up for watching whatever reality show's on. There's nothing like appreciating your own life when you watch the *stars* of those shows and how messed up most of them are.'

Cole laughed softly, the tension easing. 'Alright, I'm not sure *Love Island* will be my thing, but happy to give it a go.'

## 9

When Tori woke on Tuesday morning, her mind was preoccupied with thoughts of June Marlow. She'd arranged a visit to June at Winchester Correctional Centre, but with the approvals required, it was looking like that would take at least a week, if not more, to confirm. In the meantime, she decided to reach out to June's family.

It had been easy enough to track down Luella Marlow, June's youngest daughter, and her mother, Elena Langrell, but she wasn't able to find anything about Nicole, the eldest daughter. Hopefully Luella or Elena would be able to give her Nicole's details. For now, she needed to contact them and check if they'd be happy to participate in the story.

Her first call was to Luella, who picked up on the first ring.

'Luella, this is Tori Blackwood from *Southern Insight*. You might be aware that we're in the pre-production stages of a story focusing on victims behind bars.'

'God! Don't call me that. No one does. It's Lu. And yes, I heard that you want to interview Mum.'

'That's currently being arranged, but we'd also like to interview all immediate members of the family, including yourself, your older sister and your grandmother. And, of course, anyone else who was affected by your mother's incarceration.'

'I'm happy to be involved,' Lu said, 'but my sister's already said she won't. She's not spoken to my mother since the night my dad died, which will give you a good indication as to how she feels about it all. And you won't find her easily either. She changed her name the minute she turned eighteen and will kill anyone who provides it to you.'

Tori heard the smile in Lu's voice and knew that she was going to like this woman. It also explained why Tori had been unable to track Nicole down.

'Would you be available to catch up for coffee?' Tori asked.

'Of course,' Lu said. 'I spend most mornings at Future Blend in Elwood. Do you know the café?'

'It's around the corner from me,' Tori said. 'I live in St Kilda. Would you have any time this week?'

'I tend to work from the café, so whatever suits you,' Lu said. 'I'll be the one with the sketchbook tucked away in one of the corners. Ali, the owner, knows who I am, so ask her to point you in my direction.' She laughed. 'I'll definitely recognise you, but I can't guarantee I'll be paying attention to anyone coming in or out.'

Tori smiled. 'Sounds good. I'll drop in tomorrow morning and see if you're there.'

She ended the call looking forward to meeting with Lu Marlow. She could only imagine what the woman must have gone through. The other sister, however, was going to be more difficult. If she hadn't spoken to her mother for the entirety of her incarceration she was hardly going to speak to a journalist.

Tori's phone rang as she gave thought to how she might be able to approach Nicole Marlow, or whatever her current name was, assuming she was able to track her down to begin with. She checked the caller ID and smiled.

'Hey, Mum, what's happening?'

'Hi, love, checking in. It's been ages since we've seen you.'

Tori laughed. 'If you call a week ages, then I guess it has been. We did speak a few days ago too! But I'll see you on Sunday.'

'That's why I was ringing. I was going to cook a birthday dinner for you, but Dad thought you might prefer to go out. He said to tell you that nowhere is off limits if you want to choose somewhere.'

Tori frowned. That was unlike her money-conscious father.

'Tori?'

'Is there bad news? Has the cancer spread?'

'What?' The worry in her mother's voice was evident. 'How do you jump to that conclusion from a dinner invite?'

'Because Dad's never one to spend big at a restaurant. It's not his thing.'

Her mother gave a soft chuckle. 'I think he expects you know that and would choose somewhere affordable if we did go out. It's not that he doesn't like to treat us. He finds it hard to justify when we can cook such nice meals ourselves. But, in answer to your other question, Dad's got some follow-up tests on Friday, but from everything the doctors have indicated, we're not expecting any bad news.'

'Good news only!' she heard her father call from somewhere near her mother.

'Tell Dad I said hi,' Tori said. 'And if you're happy to cook on Sunday, that would be lovely.' And it would. Her mother was an excellent cook. She could have made a career in it but had always said it would ruin her passion if she did. So, she'd followed her own mother's footsteps and had become a dental nurse. Now, in her early sixties, she chose to work part-time at a local practice.

'Wonderful,' her mother said. 'Now, tell me what stories you're working on.'

'Before I do, Gav was asking how Dad is. Said to tell him he'd get in touch in the next week or so. I think he's going to offer to take Dad out on the boat again.'

Silence greeted her.

'Mum?'

'Yes, I'm still here. The thing is, Dad didn't enjoy that last outing. It's nice of Gav to check in, but I think Dad's happy to stay away from him. I'm not exactly sure what happened the last time they caught up, but Dad came back quite agitated and said something along the lines of Gav was getting too big for his boots.'

'Really? That's strange. They've been friends for so many years.'

'They have. Don't let it worry you. You have to work with Gav, and no doubt your dad will come around and want to see him again. Now, tell me about work.'

It was forty minutes later that Tori ended the call and stared at the phone. Her mother had asked a lot of questions, which she often did, about Tori's work, but tonight she seemed to find problems with the stories Tori was talking about.

'It's not that people aren't interested in trauma and domestic violence,' she'd said at one point, 'it's that we want to hear something positive and uplifting.'

'Unfortunately, that's not the type of news that rates well,' Tori said. 'Sure, we'll put in a good news story here and there, so it isn't all doom and gloom, but the whole objective of a show like *Southern Insight* is to instigate change. To get people talking about issues that need to be addressed. The domestic violence story is a good example. Have you got any idea of how many women are rotting away in jail for defending themselves? It's hardly fair, is it.'

Tori continued when her mother didn't respond.

'And the long-lasting impact of trauma, too. People don't always realise how much an event can affect someone in the long term, or even come back when they're older and mess with them then.'

'But what about the families and friends?' her mother said. 'Maybe they don't want these stories dragged up again.'

'So, they should forget about the victim and move on?'

'Of course not. That's not what I'm saying.' Sylvie sighed. 'I don't know what I'm saying other than, after Covid and then your father's health scare, I just want some good news.'

Tori's heart went out to her mother. 'Of course you do. The best advice I can give you is not to watch the show or any other news program. Then you won't have to give it any thought.'

'I wish it were that easy, Tori.' She gave a wry laugh. 'I'd have to stop going to work, the book club, playing tennis and volunteering if I want to get away from the stories on *Southern Insight*. Everyone always wants to tell me how they watched you on the show and then asks my opinion on the story. I'm a celebrity by association.'

'I'm sorry.'

'Don't be silly. You've got nothing to be sorry about. You know how proud I am. I love the attention most of the time.' She sighed. 'I don't know what's wrong with me tonight. I'm probably a bit on edge about Friday, and I shouldn't be, as the doctors have assured us the tests are routine.'

Tori could understand her mother's concerns. Cancer wasn't something that generally came with good news, so it was normal to be expecting the worst. She hoped with all her heart that they were at the end of her father's cancer journey.

They ended their call and she picked up her laptop, deciding to see what she could find on Luella Marlow before their meeting in the morning. Hopefully, her parents would get good news on Friday, and her mum would be her usual cheerful self again on Sunday.

* * *

Tori pushed open the door of the rustic café, and the scent of freshly brewed coffee and baked goods greeted her. It was one she quite often dropped into on the weekend, as she enjoyed the hippy vibe, and the cosy feel the mismatched furniture and colourful cushions gave off. Shelves lined with organic products and potted plants enhanced the comfortable, earthy feel.

Scanning the room, Tori spotted a woman waving at her from a corner table. Her expression was a mix of curiosity and apprehension. Tori took a deep breath, feeling the weight of the conversation they were about to have settle over her.

She slid into the chair opposite Lu. 'Thanks again for meeting me,' Tori said, trying to keep her tone light. 'Sorry to interrupt your work,' she added, nodding towards the large sketch pad Lu had closed and pushed to one side.

Lu nodded, a smile playing on her lips. 'It's no problem. I'm doing a few pieces for the café, so there's no better place to start the initial sketches. It's also my regular coffee place, and the pastries are to die for.'

Tori glanced around, taking in the peaceful ambience. 'It's perfect,' she said as a waitress approached their table.

'Hey,' she said with a smile that appeared to only be for Lu.

Tori couldn't help but notice the faint flush of pink that tinged Lu's cheeks.

'What would you like?' she asked and then laughed and

turned to Tori. 'Or should I say, in addition to Lu's chai latte and Danish, what can I get you?'

'I'll have a flat white and whatever Danish Lu's having,' Tori said, handing over her menu. 'I have a feeling she has good taste.'

The waitress hesitated a moment, picking up on the questioning innuendo in Tori's tone. She glanced at Lu. 'She does.'

Tori raised an eyebrow after the waitress left. 'Girlfriend?'

'Was it that obvious? And no, nothing official. The start of something.'

'Nice,' Tori said, genuinely meaning it. 'And it's Valentine's Day, so you could have a fun day ahead.'

'God no,' Lu said. 'Sorry,' she added, seeing Tori's surprise. 'It's one of those days that reinforces traditional gender roles. I'm not a fan. Ali isn't either, as you can probably tell by the lack of anything Valentine's in the café today. Other than that.' She gave a slight nod to a couple sitting by one of the windows, their fingers entwined as they spoke lovingly to each other and a dozen long-stemmed roses lying on the table next to them. 'Which is lovely, of course. Don't get me wrong, I just don't want that on a day that's so commercialised and forced.' She grinned. 'But you enjoy whatever you've got planned and ignore my rant.'

Tori returned her grin. 'I'll keep all of that in mind if I get the sudden urge to purchase rose petals or heart-shaped chocolates. Now, as you know, it's your mum that we're including as part of our *Victims Behind Bars* feature, which means that we want to find out as much as we can about her family and the impact the situation has had on you. Nothing you say to me today will be used without your permission, and ideally, if you agree to it, we'll want to interview you and use that footage to support the story.'

The smile Lu had been sporting moments earlier was replaced with seriousness as she nodded. 'I'm happy to be involved if the focus is to show Mum as the victim that she is.

She shouldn't have spent any time in prison. Instead, a large percentage of her life has been wasted.'

'It's an awful situation,' Tori agreed. 'Which fundamentally is the reason for us doing this story. There have been plenty of stories about domestic violence in the last few years, trying to shine a spotlight on it and ensure people know where to get help, but this is a different angle that we're taking. There are too many women in prison, and no one, other than their families, knows why. We want to focus on the victims and make people aware that this can happen, so, where possible, you need to ask for help rather than take the law into your own hands.'

'I've followed quite a lot of stories over more recent years,' Lu said, 'and many of them did get ruled as self-defence. Mum's was a bit unusual in that no one knew that anything was going on, and she couldn't prove it. But from what Mum told me, that's not what you're focusing on for the story, is it?'

Tori shook her head. 'No. As much as I'd like to say we're here to fight for her and have her conviction overturned, that's not the story, and with her pleading guilty was never likely anyway. It's more about showing the fallout from the conviction. How it impacted your mum, of course, but also how it impacted your family.'

Lu nodded. 'It had a massive impact on us.' She went on to tell Tori about what she could remember from that night, which wasn't a lot other than how scared she'd been when the police had arrived, and then Gran had taken her to her house. They'd never gone back to the house, but instead, all their belongings had been packed up and brought over to Gran's. How for the first few months, Lu would rush home from school every day, expecting the police to realise a mistake had been made, and her mum would be waiting for her with her favourite lemon drop cookies that she loved to bake. She continued with a brief outline of how her own teenage years had been shaped by losing her parents.

'It sounds like your gran did a lot for you,' Tori said as Lu finished talking and took a bite of the pastry the waitress had delivered along with their drinks.

'We were incredibly lucky to have someone like her,' Lu said. 'I know Mum feels terrible that she got left to do everything for us, but Gran never made us feel like we were a burden. She loved us so much and made sure we knew it. She also made sure that we knew how much Mum loved us.' Her eyes darkened. 'Cole wouldn't believe that, though.'

'Cole, as in Nicole?'

Lu nodded. 'She was always Nic before Mum went to prison, but then changed her name to Cole and took on my gran's maiden name as her surname.' She clasped a hand over her mouth. 'I wasn't supposed to share that with you.'

Tori smiled. 'If it's any consolation, I would have found her without your help. I had planned to ask you and your gran, but if neither of you had provided that information, I can source it easily enough.' She didn't let on that her regular checks had turned up nothing so far. However, she could always pull a few strings with the police and others if necessary. 'I'll reach out to Cole, but don't worry, I'll also respect her right to tell me to go away. Now, tell me what it means for your mum to be released after all these years.'

Lu took another sip of her latte and then began to speak. 'I don't know how to answer that. It'll be amazing, of course.'

'But?'

'But I'm concerned as to how she'll fit back in. She has Gran and me, but that's about it. She and my dad had some friends, mostly work colleagues of my dad's, who all disowned her when she was convicted.'

'What about friends of her own?'

'According to Gran, her closest friend was one of the neighbours. But they moved away after it happened. The shock was too great for them, and they decided they couldn't live next to the house where their friend murdered her husband. Other than them, Gran's never mentioned anyone. You could ask her when you speak to her.' Lu took a deep breath, her eyes fixed on the latte glass. 'The main thing I want from this story is for the world to understand that my mum's crime wasn't a crime. It was an act of survival. She was an abused woman. My father...' she paused, her voice faltering '...I've now learned was a monster behind closed doors. She was too scared to tell anyone what was happening. The night he died was self-defence. She was fighting for her life. She would be dead if he wasn't, maybe me and Cole too.'

Tori listened intently, feeling the gravity of Lu's words. The café around them seemed to fade away as the story unfolded.

'I need people to see her side, to understand that she wasn't some kind of cold-blooded killer. She was a victim who fought back when she was forced to. It's about telling her truth,' Lu continued, her voice gaining strength. 'I hope that if the story gets out, it will help others in similar situations. That it will show them that they're not alone and that they need to speak up and make people aware of what's going on.'

Tori nodded, waiting as the waitress hovered by their table.

Her smile was replaced with concern as she looked at Lu. 'Everything okay here?'

Lu forced a smile. 'All good, thanks.'

Ali looked at Tori. 'You're not upsetting my customers, are you?'

'Of course she's not,' Lu said.

Ali shrugged. 'Just checking. Now, how about more coffee?'

'Maybe some water,' Tori said, doing her best to hide her amusement at the woman's protectiveness of Lu.

'Sorry about that,' Lu said when Ali left them. 'I'm not sure if I should be happy she's looking out for me, or concerned that she's going to smother me.'

'Early days, as you said,' Tori reminded her. 'I thought it was cute. Getting back to what you said earlier about your sister refusing to have anything to do with your mum or this story, do you think the story could help her?'

Lu nodded. 'I hope that if she sees the news story and hears what Mum went through, it might help her come around. She needs to have a conversation with her. I'm sure she's painted her into being some kind of monster in her mind, rather than the amazing mother she was when we were little.'

'We'll tell your mum's story, Lu. We'll make sure people understand the truth.'

Lu nodded, a tear escaping down her cheek. 'That means more than you know.'

The two women sat in silence for a moment.

'You're right about these pastries,' Tori said, licking the sugar from her lips and doing her best to lighten the sombre mood. 'They are to die for. Does Ali make them? Does she run this place?'

'It's her place, but I think she gets the pastries supplied by a local baker,' Lu said.

Tori raised an eyebrow. 'You'll have to watch your waistline if you two get together. These are dangerous. The two of you look like you'd be good together though. Just my gut feeling, nothing more.'

Lu blushed. 'I think I can honestly now say you are my favourite television personality.'

Tori laughed. 'How many was I competing with?'

'That I can't share.' Lu smiled and popped the remaining piece of the pastry into her mouth.

'I'll get the bill on my way out,' Tori said, standing. 'I'll be in touch with you again in the next few days to discuss the filming schedule. I'm hoping to meet with your mum and grandmother over the next week so I can put some more concrete plans in place. And...' she nodded towards the counter where Ali was serving someone '...good luck.'

The blush on Lu's cheeks deepened as Tori grinned and went to pay.

# 10

After Mike shared that Tom Hargreaves had larger problems than he'd led the group to believe, Cole hadn't made any changes to the participants of her Wednesday trauma group. She was hoping that Roberto would arrive early so she could have a word with him. Ask him to lay off Tom until they learned his real story.

Fifteen minutes before the session, she was arranging chairs for the group when Roberto entered the room with a broad smile on his face.

Cole laughed when she saw him. 'You know you're at a trauma counselling session, don't you? You're not supposed to look so happy.'

'But I'm happy to see you, *mia bella*. How could I not be happy when I see you on San Valentino?' He presented a heart-shaped box from behind his back and held it out to her. 'For you.'

Cole was touched. Roberto had brought her many gifts over the time he'd been in the trauma group, but to make a deal out of Valentine's Day was lovely. She smiled as she accepted the box. 'Can I open it?'

'Can you open it? *Devi aprirlo*! My Maria would be mad if you didn't.'

Cole laughed and lifted the lid from the box to find heart-shaped biscuits sandwiched together with a layer of chocolate between them and dusted with a fine sugar coating.

Roberto beamed proudly at her. 'Baci di dama. I made these for Maria on San Valentino every year. She loved them.'

'They look delicious, Roberto. Thank you. This means a lot to me. I'm sure that you're missing Maria today.'

'Today's no different. I miss my heart every day. But she would be happy for you to try these. She knows you are helping me, as do I.'

Cole put the box down, put her arms around Roberto and hugged him. 'Happy Valentine's to you too, Roberto.'

Roberto blushed.

'Now, before the group arrives, I wanted to talk to you about Tom.'

Roberto threw his arms in the air, a look of distaste crossing his face, and sat down on one of the chairs that Cole had put out.

'Before you say anything, I want to share something with you that's confidential. Can I have your word it goes no further than you?'

Roberto looked up at Cole, a flicker of interest in his eyes. 'Of course, *mia cara*. I am a man of honour.'

'Okay, so Tom has shared with us that his dog was killed, and he witnessed it.' Cole ignored Roberto's eye-roll. 'I've since learned that there is more to Tom's story than he has shared, and his trauma is much greater than what he's let us believe.'

Roberto edged forward on his chair. 'What happened?'

'I can't share the details at this stage,' Cole said. 'The chief executive of the centre advised me of this and said he would prefer the group to find out when Tom is ready to share his real circumstances. But, in the meantime, I wanted to ask you to lay off him. To be aware there is more to his story and wait until it is revealed. I know you'll be upset with yourself if you continue to dismiss Tom and then find out what he's dealing with.'

Roberto's eye-roll was quickly replaced with concern. 'Oh my, I hope he will be okay. I shall talk to him.'

'You promised not to tell him that I've shared this with you.'

'And I will not. I was a detective. I will find out the truth, and I will be subtle.' He laughed as her face gave away her thoughts about Roberto being subtle. 'Which I imagine you cannot believe.'

Cole smiled. 'I believe you were excellent at your job, and—' she held the heart-shaped box up '—I know how much you care about people. So, if you can combine that to show Tom some kindness, it would be appreciated.'

Roberto nodded, and Cole moved away. Joss and Shane entered the room, followed by Tom.

Roberto got to his feet. 'Thomas,' he said, clapping the other man on the back. 'It is good to see you, my friend.'

Cole inwardly cringed. This was hardly subtle.

'I wanted to apologise for last week. I was unkind, and I hope you will accept my apology. My Maria would have been upset with me, so I come today to make amends.'

Tom looked to Cole, who shrugged. Roberto hadn't wasted any time in acting on his plan to get Tom on his side. 'Um, thanks, I guess,' he said and took a seat next to Joss, who looked equally surprised.

'Okay,' Cole said as Lisa slipped into the room and sat down. 'Let's begin with a quick recap of the coping strategies we discussed last week before we move on to triggers.'

The hour passed quickly with a much more constructive discussion than the previous week. Roberto, true to his word, had not goaded Tom or made any unhelpful comments. He asked him a couple of pointed questions, which only Cole would have seen as him digging for information.

As they were winding up the session, Ethan and Mike appeared in the doorway.

'Can we have a word with your group?' Mike asked.

'Of course.' Cole looked to Ethan, who mouthed 'news story'.

Mike turned to the group and smiled. 'We've been approached by one of the media channels who are doing a story on trauma and how experiencing something traumatic can affect and impact your life. They're going to be talking to some of our clients who were impacted as children by events to learn how those events shaped the rest of their childhoods and them as adults. I realise for some of you that even opening up in a group like this is challenging, but if any of you feel that you'd like to find out more and potentially be involved in the interviews and story, let Cole, Ethan or me know. We're hoping the Wellness Centre will be represented by quite a few of our clients.'

Cole looked around the group, not expecting any of them to want to be involved.

'Which news show is it for?' Lisa asked.

'*Southern Insight*,' Ethan answered. 'We were approached by Alex Wilson, one of the reporting journalists.'

'I'll do it,' Lisa said without hesitation.

Cole was surprised.

'Really?' Joss said. 'You'd want your story to be public?'

Lisa blushed. 'Maybe. I don't know. But I'd like to meet Alex Wilson. He's hot.'

'Okay,' Mike said, unable to hide his grin. 'I'll add Lisa to the list, and if anyone else is interested, let one of us know. Ethan will be working with the show to get the interviews organised and to provide further information.' He turned to Cole. 'You might want to give him a hand and be involved?'

Cole shook her head. 'No thanks. I'll leave this one to Ethan.' She'd be giving Ethan a heads-up about not mentioning her to Alex or anything about her relationship with June Marlow. She knew it was a female reporter doing the story on her mother, but that didn't mean they didn't share information, and the last thing she needed was for them to put the dots together and work out who she was. She couldn't believe her bad luck that this story had coincided with the one on her mother.

* * *

Lu pushed all thoughts of Tori and her mother's story from her mind and continued working on the sketch for the café. She spent a lot of time on the details of the broken chain she was drawing. She'd move on to the butterfly emerging from a broken link next. She loved the idea of the chain representing adversity and the butterfly symbolising hope and transformation.

She was jolted from her thoughts as Ali sat down across from her, with a plate loaded with a couscous salad sitting on a bed of leafy greens. 'Lunch,' Ali said, pushing it closer to Lu without touching any of her sketching materials.

'I don't expect lunch as well as coffee and pastries,' Lu said, although she had to admit, the salad looked delicious.

'All meals will be supplied to the artist while in residence, as per the contract,' Ali said. 'And you are in residence, so lunch is supplied.'

Lu laughed. 'What contract is that?'

'The one I make up as we go along,' Ali said. 'And thanks for last night. I had a great time with you and Mr C.'

'Good,' Lu said. ''Cause Chips loved you.' And he had. The

little white Pomeranian she walked every Tuesday night for his elderly owner had taken an instant liking to Ali, running all around her legs excitedly barking and then rolling straight onto his back so she could rub his belly.

The two women had ended up deciding on a relaxed dinner of burgers from Gregory's, an up-market burger place that had recently opened and offered a takeaway window on St Kilda's foreshore. They sat on the beach as the sun set and chatted while Chips ran to and fro, collecting the ball they threw for him. It had been a lovely and relaxing way to spend time together away from the café.

Ali glanced at the sketchbook, which Lu had closed. 'Am I allowed to see, or do you prefer to get to a certain stage or finish a design first? I know our author over there—' she nodded towards Bryce '—won't let anyone read a word until he's almost ready to publish.'

'I'm a bit like that too,' Lu said. 'I like to get something exactly as I like it before I have other people's input. Hope that's okay?'

'Of course, it is,' Ali said, entwining her fingers with Lu's. 'I love that you know your own mind and your own value. I wanted to check that you were okay after the reporter left. It looked like she upset you.'

'She didn't. It's the situation that's upsetting. I can't wait to be a few months down the track, and we're in our new normal with Mum home. Whatever that might look like. Hopefully, with Cole on board and everyone living happily ever after.' She gave a wry smile. 'The rose-coloured glasses might get shattered along the way, and knowing Cole, it'll be by her. But who knows, there might be some miracle that changes her outlook on everything.'

\* \* \*

Cole hadn't expected Mike speaking to the group about participating in the *Southern Insight* story to throw her mind into turmoil like it had that afternoon.

Once her session with the Wednesday group had finished, she'd gone for a walk to try and clear her head. Ethan had intercepted her as she'd come back into the centre an hour later.

'You okay?'

Cole shook her head. 'The TV story's thrown me. I don't want to be involved.'

Ethan led her down to one of the meeting rooms where they could shut the door and have some privacy.

'Because of your mum?'

She nodded. 'It's the same show that's telling the story of victims behind bars that my mum's part of. I don't want them to know who I am or make any links to this story. Can you promise me you won't mention me or my relationship with June Marlow to them or to anyone?'

'Of course,' Ethan said.

Cole sighed. 'When's that wedding again? I'd like to get away. Maybe we could stretch it out to cover a couple of weeks while reporters are roaming around.'

Ethan smiled. 'It's still a couple of weeks away, but don't worry about reporters. They have no reason to deal with you. I'll make it clear that due to the nature of our work and the confidentiality, they need to deal with me on everything, and I'll set up the interviews with those who have agreed to be involved. They're coming in tomorrow morning to discuss requirements and have a look around the centre, so you might want to make yourself scarce.'

Cole could feel her heartbeat quickening at the thought. She took a deep breath. She needed to pull herself together.

'Now, to change the subject, Mike mentioned you'd had a successful meeting with Piper Dixson on the weekend.'

'Piper!' Cole glanced at her watch, relieved to see it was only four thirty. 'I've been so caught up feeling sorry for myself that I'd completely forgotten. She's helping down at the community garden. I'd better get organised. I said I'd collect her at five today.' She narrowed her eyes. 'Why did Mike mention her? Nothing's happened has it?'

'No, he mentioned that he thought you'd be good for her, that's all, and that she might be good for you too.' He gave a little laugh. 'I think you could say that about most of our clients, though, that they're good for us. We learn something from all of them.' He raised an eyebrow, 'Even if it's how good Italian biscuits are. Roberto knows how to spoil you.'

Cole smiled. 'He does, and I love him for it. The box of biscuits is on my desk. Help yourself. Now, I'd better get over to the Gleesons' to pick up Piper. Let me know if you want to catch up later in the week or early next week about the wedding plans. You can give me the rundown on everything I need to know.'

# 11

June looked around the decorated rec room, unable to hide her surprise at the effort some of the women had gone to. 'I would have thought most of them would want to forget about Valentine's Day altogether,' she said quietly to Doreen. 'Isn't it a reminder of what you're missing out on?'

Doreen shrugged. 'Honestly, I think any excuse to do anything around here is jumped upon. If Bill was still alive, I'd be more worried about *who* he was spending Valentine's with than missing him. I'm guessing there are quite a few husbands and partners of this lot still enjoying themselves tonight.'

'It'd be hard,' June said, 'to get out and find your partner had moved on with someone else.'

'Not a problem you're going to face,' Doreen said. 'Sorry,' she added, taking in June's horrified expression. 'That came out wrong.'

June forced a smile. 'It's fine. You're right, of course. It was just a bit hard to hear.'

'Do you miss him?' Doreen asked. 'Your husband?'

'I miss the person I first met,' June said, 'but he disappeared many years before he died. I can thank Mr Jack Daniel for that. His greatest love, as it turns out. He was a different man before he started drinking heavily.'

'You might meet someone else when you get out,' Doreen said. 'A fresh start, a new man.'

'I don't think any man will look twice at me. And to be honest, as I killed the last one, they're probably better off staying away.' She laughed as she said this, quickly clapping her hand over her mouth. 'Sorry. I shouldn't be making jokes like that.' She looked around to see if any guards had been listening. 'Need to ensure I come across as showing remorse,' she added.

'I don't think anyone's taking any notice of us,' Doreen said. 'Just don't make any jokes to the reporter when you meet with her on Saturday.'

June grimaced. 'Don't worry, I won't. I'm wondering if I should be calling the whole thing off. Leave here quietly without stirring up any issues before I go.'

'Stir away,' Doreen said. 'We need someone like you speaking up. You know that. Too many women have left quietly, and that's why there are so many victims behind bars, or whatever they're calling it. And who knows, it might be the thing that your daughter watches and comes to realise that there is another side to the story and one that she should be finding out more about.'

'Nicole?'

Doreen nodded. 'It sounds like something needs to wake her up. Perhaps it will be this.'

\* \* \*

Cole watched as Piper patted down the soil to protect the carrot seeds she'd planted. She'd spent the first hour helping one of the older members of the community garden transfer wooden stakes from the trailer he'd arrived with to the storage area and then used several of them to tie up seedlings that had been planted two weeks earlier. She'd done all of this without instruction.

'You're either a natural or you've had a good teacher. I know you said you learned quite a bit from your dad when we were here on Saturday,' Cole commented as they worked side by side, covering up the seeds.

'When he wasn't drinking beer, he loved to garden,' Piper said. 'He showed me lots. I probably should hate gardening because it's come from him, but I don't. I find it peaceful and relaxing. Sometimes, when he and Mum were fighting, I'd go out to the veggie patch and try and get away from it all. It helped remind me that he wasn't totally bad. If he had been, all of the veggies would have died, but they didn't. They grew enormous. I know it sounds stupid, but I used to convince myself that God was reminding me that even bad people must have some good in them.'

Was this really coming from an eleven-year-old? 'It doesn't sound stupid at all,' Cole said. 'From everything you've told me so far, it sounds like your dad's drinking affected how he acted.'

'Yep. There was one time when he said he wasn't going to drink ever again. It was when Katie needed stitches because he hit her by mistake.'

'By mistake?'

Piper nodded. 'I think he meant to hit Mum but he was too drunk, and his hand hit Katie's lip and split it open.'

'That's awful, no matter who he was meaning to hit,' Cole said, her stomach churning at the thought of the two little girls experiencing this.

'He was sorry that time,' Piper said. 'Anyway, Mum lied to the doctors about what happened, and the next day, Dad threw out all these cans and bottles and said he was quitting drinking. It lasted for a few months. He was so nice then. Like a great dad. I wasn't even scared of him then because I trusted him and knew that he wasn't going to yell at us or hit us.'

'But he started drinking again?'

'Yeah. He went on a fishing trip with some friends and came back drinking again and smoking. Not cigarettes, that drug stuff. Mum said that was good because that would make him more relaxed, but it didn't. He was horrible again.'

'It's an illness, you know?' Cole said, pushing down the soil. 'Alcoholism. I don't know enough about your dad and it's no excuse for what he did, but if he would accept help and get sober, it might bring back that dad that you liked.'

'Did your dad drink?'

Cole froze at the sudden change of topic. 'I don't think so,' she said, although both Lu and her gran would have a different answer. 'Not much anyway.'

As she said the words, she suddenly flashed back to her father. He was standing at the barbecue, turning sausages, while she and Lu ran to and fro under the sprinkler, wearing floppy bunny ears that their gran had found in a second-hand store and given to them. It was a hot day, and he was drinking beer while June cooked their dinner. Her mum had come out of the back door and called to the girls to say that dinner was nearly ready and to get their towels and dry off. Cole watched as her mother then turned and walked along the side of the house towards her father with a plate of bread in one hand and tomato sauce in the other.

'Don't you think you've had enough of those?' her mother said, loud enough that Cole could hear.

Her father hadn't answered, but in one movement, flipped a sausage with the tongs in one hand and threw the bottle at her mother with the other. It had shattered against the wall behind her, and she'd dropped everything she was holding and stopped frozen in her tracks.

'Daddy?' Lu had called out.

'It's alright, love,' Dad had called. 'I was throwing the bottle to your mum, but she dropped it. Be careful of the broken glass, okay? Mummy will clean it up once she gets some more bread. It seems she's dropped that lot.'

'You okay?' Piper broke into Cole's memories.

Cole looked at her. 'You made me remember something, that's all. Some things that were perhaps covered up because I was young at the time.'

Piper rolled her eyes. 'My mum always tried to cover up for my dad. I'm not sure how we were supposed to believe that a black eye and a broken wrist were accidents. Do you think my mum thought we were stupid?'

Cole was silenced by the comment, again thinking of her own situation. It wasn't a case of her mum thinking she was stupid. Maybe she *had* been stupid?

She drove away from the Gleesons' an hour later, having dropped Piper back to them. Katie was busy helping Anne with some cooking when she came in to say a quick hello.

'She's been a lot brighter since you took her out on Saturday,' Anne said. 'Whatever you're doing, if you're happy to keep doing it, I think we'll see her relax and come out of her shell a bit more.'

'She's a great kid,' Cole said. 'She's opening up a little. I'll have a chat with Mike about some of it, as I'd like to make sure her father's being assessed and getting some help. I'm still planning to visit her mother, too.'

'You think there's some hope for him?'

'Possibly. I'm only going off the little bit of information Piper's provided so far, but while our priority is to protect her and Katie, helping the family is also a high priority.'

Now, as Cole made her way toward home, her thoughts drifted back to her own family and the memory she'd had of her father throwing the bottle. She instructed her car to call Lu.

Her sister picked up almost before the phone had had a chance to ring.

'Are you returning one of my calls or texts, or have you lost your phone, and this is some random stranger calling me to tell me they have the phone?'

Cole couldn't help but laugh. 'Um, no. Why have you called today again?'

Lu tut-tutted down the phone. 'Twice if you bothered to check your messages. To say hi, nothing important. Now, to what do I owe this honour?'

'Strange question, but do you remember a barbecue when we were little? It was at home, and we were running through the sprinkler. We were wearing those bunny ears Gran gave us.'

'And those pink bathers you hated. Yes, I remember. How could I forget? I ended up in the ER getting stitches in my foot.'

Cole suddenly remembered that Lu had stood on a piece of the broken glass. 'That's right, from the beer bottle.'

'Dad blamed Mum for that,' Lu said, 'even though it was his beer bottle. Said she dropped it when he passed it to her and didn't clean it up properly.'

'Did you see him *pass* her the bottle?'

'No, I heard the smash. It was loud and gave me a fright. Mum dropped everything, the bread and sauce as well. I remember that because the sauce looked like blood, and then my blood got added to it.' She was silent for a moment. 'Why do you want to know about this?'

Cole took a deep breath. 'Because I had a weird flashback

about it today, that's all. I remembered what happened, and it kind of freaked me out.'

'Freaked you out? Why?'

'Because Dad didn't pass the bottle to Mum. He threw it at her, like he was throwing a baseball to home plate to get someone out. He was trying to hit her with it.'

'You're sure?'

'Yes. I remember it clearly. I can even picture the look of horror on Mum's face when it smashed on the wall behind her.'

'From what she's told me about Dad,' Lu said, 'most of the violence and threats happened when he was drinking, so he might have been drunk that day. Does this mean you're beginning to think that perhaps Mum was defending herself that night?'

'I'm not sure what I think. I wanted to check what your memory of that was. I was having a conversation with an eleven-year-old whose father gets drunk and violent when drinking. It's possible I've twisted that story into something it wasn't.'

'There's an easy way to find out,' Lu said. 'Ask Mum. Or I can, if you'd prefer.'

Cole was silent for a moment. 'I should go. Thanks, Lu, and have a good night if you're doing anything. Happy Valentine's.'

'You too, sis.'

\* \* \*

On Thursday morning, Tori arrived at the Hawthorn Community Wellness Centre a few minutes before ten. Alex was standing at the entrance. He smiled as she reached him.

'We're meeting Ethan Harris. He's one of the senior trauma counsellors, and possibly Mike Deans, the centre's CEO. This is a preliminary discussion to get a feel for how many people they think are likely to be involved. Scope the place out a bit to see what sort of footage we'll be able to get.'

Tori nodded. These meetings were generally the starting point for a story. 'I'm assuming we're checking out Ethan and any of the other counsellors to see how they'll come across on camera?'

'Definitely. I'm hoping they'll have a suitable female counsellor as well as a male.' He glanced at his watch. 'Showtime. We'd better go in.'

A short time later, they sat across the table from Ethan Harris, and Tori knew he'd come across well on camera. Perhaps too well. He was rather good-looking, and while she knew that the centre was hoping to attract awareness and bring in new clients, it was possible that Ethan's good looks might attract a less traumatised client than they were aiming for.

'We've spoken to some of our clients,' Ethan said as an assistant brought in coffee. He waited until he retreated from the room before continuing. 'We'll need a bit more time to get people confirmed, but there's definitely been some interest.' His lips turned up slightly at the edges. 'Although some of that interest was more about the *hot* reporter than helping others.'

Tori laughed as Alex flushed red, the irony not lost on her that she'd been thinking Ethan could cause similar issues if he was to be interviewed.

'It would be great if we could get a background on each person who is happy to be involved,' Alex said, shifting the direction of the conversation. 'That way, we can prepare some questions and run them past you before we do the filming. Ideally, we'd like to do some filming in their environments – not all of it here. Getting some candid footage of them at their homes and living their regular lives is always great to intersperse with the interview. Again, only those who are comfortable with that.'

Ethan nodded. 'We run trauma groups throughout the week here at the centre as well as one-on-ones with our team of counsellors. I'm sure you can get some footage from those sessions, too.'

'Perfect,' Alex said. 'We'd also like to interview you and Mike Deans to understand your role and the type of people you deal with. The challenges versus the rewards, that type of thing.'

Ethan nodded. 'Mike's an excellent spokesperson for the company. He's done a bit of media training, so he will probably come across better than I would.'

'What about any female counsellors?' Tori said. 'I assume you have some?'

Ethan's forehead creased with concern as he appeared to be thinking about the choices for this.

'They don't need media training,' Alex added. 'But do need to be confident to talk on camera.'

'I've been trying to convince Cole,' a tall, broad-shouldered man said, entering the room. He smiled at them, holding out his hand first to Tori, then to Alex. 'Mike Deans,' he said.

'Cole?' Tori asked, unable to hide the tremor in her voice. Surely it couldn't be? How many people went by Cole?

'Our other senior trauma counsellor,' Mike said. 'She's an incredible asset to the centre, and I think would add a lot of value to the segment.' He turned to Ethan. 'Would you agree?'

Tori watched with interest as Ethan appeared to be doing his best to remain calm. 'She's said no,' he said to Mike. 'She also asked us to keep her out of any discussions today.' The pointed look he gave Mike heightened Tori's senses even more.

'Cole's an unusual name,' she said before the topic was shut down.

'Not particularly,' Ethan said, 'but also not relevant as she's not willing to be involved, which we'll all need to respect. Now, would you like to tour the centre? We can show you the group training rooms and the outdoor space, which is unique and would probably film well.'

Tori followed the men as Ethan led them from one area to the next. She pulled out her phone and did a quick Google about the Wellness Centre as they walked and found the list of counsellors. Cole Langrell was at the top of the list. What were the chances? And how interesting it was that Cole had become a trauma counsellor. She'd love to be able to speak to her and find out more about her career choice and why she'd work with other trauma victims but not deal with her own mother. It was intriguing.

'Everything okay?' Alex asked as they moved to a beautiful outside courtyard area, and Ethan and Mike were out of hearing. 'You've gone very quiet.'

Tori kept her voice low. 'Remember the June Marlow story and how I told you one daughter refused to be involved?'

He nodded.

'She works here. The *Cole* Ethan mentioned who doesn't want to be involved. That's Cole Langrell, the eldest daughter.'

Alex's eyes widened. 'You're kidding?'

Tori smiled as Ethan approached them.

'As I said earlier, this space is special.'

'It is,' Tori agreed, observing the peaceful outdoor area, which boasted vibrant flower beds, shaded benches and a calming fountain.

'We conduct plenty of one-on-one sessions out here. People are often more relaxed outside and among some colour.'

'Can I ask you something?' Tori asked.

'Of course,' Ethan said, but Tori saw his eyes become guarded.

'Do you think there's any chance Cole Langrell would talk to us? I can see from your reaction that you've been given clear instructions to keep us away from her, but her story would be so powerful to include.'

'Cole's?' Mike joined them, confusion crossing his features. 'As in her story of working with trauma victims?'

Tori looked from Ethan to Mike. It was clear from Mike's face that he didn't know the details of Cole's past. She cleared her throat. 'Yes, we'd like to include a female counsellor as well as a male, so if you're able to get her to change her mind, that would be wonderful.'

'Poke your head in and say hello before you leave,' Mike suggested. 'Her office is the last one on the right before we get back to the reception area.'

'She won't appreciate that,' Ethan said, 'if she's even here. I'm sure she had meetings off-site all morning.'

'She's definitely here,' Mike said. 'She has a client one-on-one in about fifteen minutes. She doesn't have to be involved, but she can at least say hello. This story's going to bring a lot of attention to the centre, and I'd like to ensure she's across it, even if she's not directly involved. Some of her clients will want to know that she's supportive of their choice to be involved too.'

Tori could see Ethan wanting to object but he backed down. He did, however, slip his phone from his pocket, most likely to message Cole. Tori wasn't going to give him time.

'I need to use the bathroom, which I think was back down that way.' She pointed behind them. 'Wasn't it?'

Mike nodded.

'Great. Alex, I'll meet you in the foyer area after I've used the bathroom and said a quick hello to Cole.' She turned and hurried from the area before Ethan could stop her and before Cole could act on his text.

* * *

Cole was on heightened alert already, furious at having to be in the office, when her phone pinged with a text. She grabbed it, leaping to her feet the moment she read Ethan's message.

> Leave. She knows who you are.

She ripped open her office door, ready to take off down the hallway, but was stopped as her body collided with another person.

'God, sorry,' the other woman said.

Cole froze. It was Tori Blackwood. 'I can't speak to you.' The words were practically a whisper, and she honestly thought she might be sick.

'Hey,' Tori said, 'I'm sorry, I didn't mean to upset you. I wanted the opportunity to meet you. I met your sister yesterday, and she was lovely.'

Cole nodded before retreating into her office and sinking into her chair. Her legs were wobbly, and her heart raced. Even she could see this was an extreme response. All she needed to do was tell the journalist that she wasn't interested and she wanted to be left alone.

Tori entered her office and sat down in the chair across from her. 'Don't worry,' she assured Cole, 'nothing you say to me will be used for anything. We'd need your permission to film you or even quote you, and we're not the sort of show that goes against people's wishes.'

'And yet you're sitting here now,' Cole said. 'I'm sure Ethan would have made my wishes clear.'

Tori had the good grace to blush. 'He did. But the coincidence of you being here was too much for me. I had to meet you.'

Cole frowned. 'Coincidence? You didn't already know I worked here?'

'No,' Tori said. 'I was asked to tag along with Alex as this story is inter-related to the one we're doing on victims behind bars. I had no idea where you worked. I was planning to do my research and try and find you, but you've landed in my lap... so to speak.'

Cole couldn't help but smile. As much as she wanted Tori to disappear, she was personable. It was no surprise *Southern Insight* was so popular.

'A smile,' Tori said, 'does that mean I can stay a bit longer?'

'You can, but I'm not going to change my mind. I don't know what Lu told you, but I haven't spoken to my mum since she was arrested, and I have no intention of changing that.'

'Even if she gets out?'

Cole hesitated. She knew she was going to have to speak to her at some stage, but she didn't need to share that. 'No. She's a stranger to me now, and based on what she did, she was back then, too. She's not the woman I thought she was.'

Compassion filled Tori's eyes. 'It must have been hard for you. Then and now.'

Cole couldn't stop tears from filling her eyes. She wiped them roughly, annoyed at herself.

'I can't imagine what you've been through,' Tori continued. 'I'm an only child, and my parents are everything to me. I can't imagine losing them both like you did.'

Cole swallowed the lump in her throat. Most people only wanted to know why she refused to speak to her mother. 'I had my gran and Lu,' Cole said. 'I wasn't alone. But thank you. Not many people acknowledge that we lost both of our parents when it happened.'

'That you went on to do a job like this says a lot about you,'

Tori said. 'To help others when you'd experienced such trauma and loss.'

'I wanted to make a difference,' Cole said. 'Even if I could help one person, I thought it would somehow make what happened a little less awful. It doesn't really, but focusing on other people's hardships often helps put our problems in perspective. Life's hard and having a good support network makes a huge difference.'

A smile curled at the edge of Tori's lips. 'I know you don't want me to say this, and you'll probably throw me straight out, but that's exactly what we need viewers to hear. Honestly, it's the key to both the victims behind bars story and the trauma story we're here today about.'

Cole leaned back in her chair, realising she'd already said a lot more than she intended to but also recognising how clever the reporter was. 'You haven't mentioned my mum by name once,' she said.

'I assumed you wouldn't want to talk about her.'

'I don't... but have you met her yet?' Cole wasn't sure why this detail mattered to her.

Tori shook her head and stood. 'I'm still waiting for a clearance from the prison. I know I've ambushed you, and I appreciate that you didn't call security.' She took a card from her purse and placed it on Cole's desk. 'I don't expect to hear from you, but I would love to.'

Cole left the card where Tori had placed it.

'And, don't be concerned about the story we're doing here. You being involved would be great, but there's no pressure at all. Your involvement could be as simple as providing some information on the clients who choose to be part of the story. We'd then say, "One of the trauma counsellors was able to share with us that... et cetera." We're only trying to shine a spotlight on the amazing work you do here at the centre. We're not looking for a sensational story.'

Cole couldn't help but smile. 'So, if I said I was happy to go on camera meeting my mother for the first time in close to three decades and confronting her for killing my father, you wouldn't want the story?'

'Nope,' Tori said. 'Not interested in the least.' She tried to keep a serious face but ended up laughing. 'Okay, I'm assuming you'd never agree to that, so you can play the game your way, but yes, we'd probably pay big bucks for something like that.'

Cole shivered. Cashing in on the situation was the last thing she intended to do. 'I'll give it some thought,' she said, 'to help with some information for the trauma story. But nothing more. I will be asking that I'm not mentioned and that there's no connection from me to the victims behind bars story.'

'Perfect,' Tori said. 'And in return, I won't share any information with you about my visit to the prison when it happens so that you don't have to give that any emotional energy. Now, I'll leave you to recover from my ambush. And Cole, thanks for not throwing me out.'

Cole watched as Tori left her office, conscious of a mild feeling of disappointment washing over her. She should be pleased that Tori understood her position and wasn't going to talk to her about her mother, but a niggling part of her wanted to hear how the meeting with her mother went.

# 12

Tori woke on Friday morning, a mild sense of shock still hovering over her at the coincidence of meeting Cole the previous day. When Lu told her that her sister had refused to speak to their mother for all these years, she was expecting to meet someone cold and bitter. But Cole was neither of those. She was sad and vulnerable. What a shame for the family that this had happened. But it wasn't only the Marlows. There were hundreds of families around Australia, and no doubt the world, experiencing incredible distress and trauma.

She arrived at work a little late, allowing herself the luxury of stopping for a coffee and Danish at Future Blend, hoping to see Lu again. She wanted to tell her of the coincidence of meeting Cole.

'Not here,' Ali said, as she served Tori. 'Did you want me to pass on a message?'

Tori shook her head. 'No, I'll give her a call after I meet with her mother. I'm hoping that will be arranged for next week. I was wanting to share something unexpected with her if she happened to be here.' She picked up the coffee and bag with the

Danish Ali had prepared. 'Instead, I'll enjoy these. A birthday treat.'

'It's your birthday?'

Tori nodded. 'I'm not sure if I should be happy or be regretting how quickly I'm edging towards thirty.'

Ali laughed. 'Happy birthday, they're on the house.'

'No, I can't let you do that,' Tori said, pulling her phone out to pay.

'Yes, you can. If you like the coffee and food, tell your friends. That's payment in itself.'

Tori smiled, a little overwhelmed at her generosity. 'Thank you. That's made my day already. I'll tell my friends.' She hesitated. 'And, if you're open to it, we could do some filming here. We're often looking for venues for interviews. Putting people in familiar settings. It'd be great publicity for the café.'

Ali crossed her arms, considering the offer. 'How about when you interview Lu?' she said. 'That would make a lot of sense as she works on her art from here. And...' excitement suddenly filtered through her words '...maybe we could show some of her artwork off during the segment? She's got so much talent, but it's so hard to get recognised these days. I've suggested she do some art for the walls here, and we put her name and contact details beside them, but putting them on your show could open up all sorts of opportunities.'

'She's lucky,' Tori said. 'Here's me offering you the opportunity to drive business to the café, and you're on-gifting it to Lu. I don't know too many people who'd do that.'

Ali shrugged. 'She deserves it. She's...' She grinned. 'I don't even know how to describe her.'

'The look on your face described exactly how you feel about her. Like I said, she's lucky.' Tori held up her coffee and paper bag. 'And thank you again for these.'

Once she arrived at work, the day flew by. She'd had plenty of phone calls and texts, her mum being the first to call. She played along with it being nothing more than a birthday and not the day her father was also getting his test results. When they'd gone to end the call, she'd told her mother, good or bad, to leave the news until Sunday. As much as she wanted it to be good news, if it wasn't, she didn't want her birthday associated with bad news about her dad.

A cake had appeared for afternoon tea at *Southern Insight*, and a quick rendition of 'Happy Birthday' was sung. But with a show to be produced that evening, most of the team didn't have time to enjoy the pleasantries of a birthday.

A little after four, Penny had stopped by Tori's office. 'Just got a call from Winchester prison,' she said. 'You've got clearance to visit June Marlow tomorrow morning. I know it's Saturday, but I need you to do this.'

'No problem,' Tori said. 'I've been pushing for this to be brought forward, and it has been. I'll be there at whatever time they tell me. I won't have too big a night tonight.'

'Perfect,' Penny said, 'and more importantly, you will have a big night tonight.' She pouted. 'We've been planning this birthday for some time, me and the girls. No letting us down.'

* * *

As their main course plates were cleared, Tori soaked in the buzzing energy of Luna Noir, a contemporary Australian restaurant in Melbourne's inner-city suburb of Richmond. The industrial décor, with its exposed brick walls and steel beams, was softened by warm lighting and the gentle hum of conversation.

Tori shot Penny a look as three waitstaff appeared at the table, a cake with candles and sparklers lit. Her friend shrugged as the waitstaff started singing 'Happy Birthday', and she joined in, with both Jaime and Sam following her lead.

Tori shifted uncomfortably in her chair as her three close friends ensured the volume was loud enough to intrude on everyone's dining experience at Luna Noir. After twenty-three years of friendship, Jaime and Sam knew how much she hated this kind of attention, but they still insisted on doling it out every year.

Sam, Jaime and Tori had been inseparable throughout primary and secondary school. Jaime and Tori had grown up living next door to each other and had met Sam in their first year of school. Tori couldn't remember a year since then when they hadn't all celebrated each other's birthdays. She'd introduced Penny to the group on her twenty-fifth birthday when Penny, never wanting to be left out, insisted her friends would want to meet and include her, and it turned out she'd been right. Penny had clicked with the other two as if she'd been part of the friend group since day one.

When the singing stopped and the sparklers were extinguished, she blew out the candles and leaned back in her chair. 'I'm not sure whether to thank you or be mad at you,' she said, laughing. 'I don't think I'll ever enjoy that part of birthdays. Maybe we could stop once we hit thirty?'

'We should probably stop acknowledging birthdays altogether at that point,' Sam said. 'We'll be so old.'

'Hey,' Penny said, a quick reminder that she was five years older than the rest of them.

'Like I said.' Sam grinned. 'So old.'

Penny narrowed her eyes and threw a rolled-up napkin at Sam.

Jaime held up a beautifully wrapped gift, its silver paper enhanced with delicate gold and satin ribbons. 'It's from all of us,' she said, pushing the present into Tori's hands. Tori smiled and carefully undid the ribbons. 'It's too beautiful to rip open.' The friends watched on as she carefully removed the wrapping paper, unveiling a box. Without opening it, Tori was sure it would contain a voucher for her favourite day spa, and it did.

She grinned in delight. 'You know me so well. There's literally nothing I'd like more for my birthday than this. Thank you.'

'But how well do you know yourself?' Jaime asked, producing another beautifully gift-wrapped box and sliding it across the table to Tori.

Tori glanced at her friends. 'You shouldn't have done anything else, the spa voucher is extravagant enough.'

'This one doesn't have a monetary value,' Penny said, 'but like Jaime said, how well do you know yourself?'

Tori carefully removed the wrapping paper, a little worried as to what she was going to find with that cryptic question. She lowered her voice. 'This isn't a vibrator or something like that, is it?'

Sam laughed, quickly clasping her hand over her mouth.

'What?' Penny said. 'Where did you get that from?'

'I don't know. The whole *how well do you know yourself*?' She removed the rest of the paper, relief settling over her as she saw it was not anything she needed to hide but rather a Heritage Link branded box. 'Ancestry testing?'

'We thought it would be fun to all do the tests,' Sam said. 'Penny got some extra kits from your work for us.'

'A conversation I had with my mum now makes sense,' Tori said. She turned to Jaime. 'Apparently your mum's pretty upset at the prospect of you doing this. I had a phone call from Mum during the week.'

Jaime shrugged. 'I don't see what the big deal is, unless she's got something to hide. And if she does, then I want to know what that is anyway.'

'Are you going to tell her you're going ahead with it?'

Jaime shook her head. 'No, and don't say anything either to your mum. It's none of their business.'

Tori nodded, not sure if she agreed with this, but also knowing Jaime well enough to know that once she'd decided to do something it was virtually impossible to stop her.

'Our results aren't for the show, are they?' She looked to Penny for a response.

Penny shook her head. 'Not unless you find out something incredible that you want to share. I expect I'm related to the Hemsworth brothers so once that's confirmed I'll have the cameras rolling for my reunion with them.'

'I think mine will show I'm related to the British royal family,' Jaime said. 'I've always felt like I'd get along with Princess Kate.'

'She's not a royal by blood,' Tori pointed out.

Jaime shrugged. 'Doesn't mean she won't love having me in her life and inviting me to the palace. I'm happy to let her try on some of my clothes if she shares hers. I'd say we're about the same size. Definitely in tiaras.'

They all laughed.

'It would be amazing to find out you did have famous people in your bloodline, wouldn't it?' Sam said.

'Not so great if you find out you come from a long line of criminals,' Tori said. 'There was that story years ago, before the pandemic, about that guy, Eric someone, who found out he was related to a serial killer in California. The guy had murdered a bunch of people and raped at least fifty women.'

Sam's mouth dropped open. 'Maybe we shouldn't do it. I don't want to find out anything like that.'

Penny rolled her eyes. 'That was an extreme finding. You're

more likely to find out you've got some second or third cousins you didn't know about. Now, me, Sam and Jaime have already done our DNA tests and they're sitting waiting to be shipped back to Heritage Link. Drop yours into my office on Monday and I'll send them all off together.'

Tori nodded. She had to admit, she was curious. More so in Jaime's results than her own. She was intrigued to know if Mary Thomas was hiding something.

# 13

Cole had found it difficult to get thoughts of Tori Blackwood out of her head the previous day. Knowing that she would be visiting her mother any day now left her feeling restless. She'd spoken to Ethan briefly the day before and was beginning to wonder if he was right.

'The fact you're feeling uncomfortable about Tori visiting your mother suggests perhaps you want to be involved or at least know more than you currently do. It's not surprising that it's all coming into focus right now.'

'Focus?'

'The story at the Wellness Centre as well as the one about your mum. Something you've been able to keep at a distance for some time is creeping closer and closer. As much as you've wanted to consider her out of your life, I'm guessing that from time to time, there's been some curiosity around her, too.'

Cole would be lying to say this wasn't the case. She thought about her mother a lot. More than she'd ever admit to Lu or her gran.

'And,' Ethan had added, 'I imagine you've built up a lot of

anxiety around the thought of ever having to be in the same room as her again. If you do decide to talk to her, I think once you get that initial conversation over, you'll find the situation a little easier.'

Now, as Cole took the Mount Waverley exit off the Monash freeway, she wondered if he was right. She took a deep breath as she stopped at the traffic lights at Blackburn Road. *Mount Waverley*. What were the odds of Piper's parents living in this suburb? She'd also done her best to avoid it since moving away from it when she was ten. She'd never returned to the family home. She frowned as the lights turned green, and she continued towards Beechwood Drive, realising she didn't know what had happened to the house. She assumed it was sold, but what happened to the money? Perhaps her gran had used it to bring her and Lu up, or it might have gone to pay off the mortgage.

She glanced at the clock. It was a few minutes before ten when she'd arranged to visit Jacinta Dixson. She'd deliberately asked to meet her at a time when her husband wouldn't be home. She wanted to get a feel for the girl's mother without the influence of her abusive husband on the scene.

She pulled into the driveway of a tidy brick house. The lawn was freshly mown, and the garden was well kept. That made sense as Piper had learned her gardening skills from her father.

The door opened before she reached it, and a petite, blonde woman with a hesitant smile greeted her. 'Cole?'

Cole held out her hand, noticing the nervousness in Jacinta's eyes. There was a softness to her demeanour and a reticence Cole had seen in a number of domestic violence clients she'd worked with. 'You must be Jacinta.'

Jacinta shook her hand, her grip weak. 'Come in. Paul's not here.'

Cole followed her into the house and through to a family room. The house was tidy, but there was a stark emptiness to it, as if the life had been drained from within its walls.

Jacinta indicated to the couches. 'How are my girls?'

The emphasis on 'my' wasn't lost on Cole, but there was a wavering uncertainty in Jacinta's voice.

'As I'm sure social services have already told you, they've been placed with a lovely couple, but in all honesty, they're struggling,' Cole answered gently. 'It's not easy to be taken away from your home and your parents.'

Jacinta's face crumpled, and she looked away. 'I never wanted them taken away.'

Cole remained quiet, waiting to see what else Jacinta might offer up.

'Things got out of hand. Paul...' She stopped and wiped her eyes. 'Paul can be difficult to live with.'

'From what Piper's told me, he's more than difficult,' Cole said. 'Both you and the girls have been subjected to physical, verbal and emotional abuse.'

Jacinta lowered her eyes and slowly nodded. 'It's been hard on all of us. I'm not sure what to do.'

'You need help,' Cole said. 'So does your husband. But while you're living under the same roof with him, your girls will remain in care. They won't be returned to an abusive environment.'

'He... he's not that bad. The situation got out of hand.'

Cole's voice softened, a note of concern creeping in. 'But it's been out of hand before, Jacinta. This wasn't a one-off incident. What if he'd hurt one of the girls badly? Could you live with that?'

Jacinta's shoulders slumped, and she seemed to shrink into herself. 'No, of course not. I can't leave... I don't know how.'

'Because you're scared or because you love your husband?'

The confusion that crossed Jacinta's face made Cole realise it was possibly a combination of both. 'Your girls need to know you love them. Piper's hurt and angry that you've chosen your husband over her and Katie. As awful as the situation is for you, think about it from the perspective of the girls.'

'I love the girls more than anything,' Jacinta said.

'I'm sure you do, but letting them be taken into foster care and staying with Paul doesn't send that message to them.'

'I need to tell them. Try and explain that it's hard. I made a promise when I married Paul. I can't just turn my back on him.'

'Your husband made promises to you too, don't forget. Protecting you, cherishing you. His behaviour goes against all those promises. His behaviour doesn't show much love towards you.'

'It's when he drinks,' Jacinta said. 'When he doesn't drink he's lovely to me and to the girls. It's just that he's been drinking more than usual.'

'Does he want to stop drinking?'

'He says he does, but he hasn't. Since the girls have gone, he hasn't been violent though. If anything, he's sad. He's been crying a lot when he drinks.'

'He needs help,' Cole said. 'Help that social services can provide. I'm sure they've already shared information on this.'

Jacinta nodded.

'If he wants to see his girls again, he'll need to be sober and even then, there will be assessments to check if it's suitable for him to spend time around them. But he needs to want help. You both do.'

'I'll speak to him.'

Cole nodded. 'The girls would love to see you. I could speak with your case worker at social services and see if we can organise a supervised visit if you're up to it? Most likely, you would be visiting them at the house they're currently staying in, and it would be only you. The court isn't going to approve Paul visiting.'

Tears filled Jacinta's eyes. 'I'd love that.'

Cole's heart contracted at the sight of this broken woman. This wasn't a woman who didn't care about her children; this was a woman who had been so beaten down that she couldn't find the courage to fight for them. An image of her own mother flashed in her mind. She'd been in this situation, and she hadn't spoken up either. But when put in an extreme circumstance where she feared for her life and for that of her girls, she'd stood up to her husband and protected her family. Cole wasn't sure that Jacinta had that same strength. In fact, she was sure that she didn't. She was a woman who needed support and help around her to ensure that she and her girls didn't end up in the same position Cole's mother had.

Cole stood. 'Leave it with me. I'll get the wheels in motion with social services.'

Jacinta wiped her cheeks. 'If you see the girls, will you tell them I love them and that I'm sorry?' She took a deep breath and locked eyes with Cole. 'I need help.'

Cole swallowed and nodded. She knew how hard it had been for the woman in front of her to say those three words. She found she couldn't help herself and stepped forward and drew Jacinta into a hug. 'You can do this. You can be strong and show your girls that they can have a better life.' She squeezed her. 'They're counting on you, and you *can* do it. There will be plenty of help, but you'll need to step up too.'

Jacinta nodded as Cole released her from the hug. Cole had to blink away tears as she saw the woman do her best to stand up tall and convince herself she could. As Cole walked away from the front door towards her car, she hoped Jacinta was still standing tall, believing in herself, and that she wasn't a crumpled mess on the floor.

* * *

Tori felt like patting herself on the back the next morning when she woke up feeling refreshed and not hung over. She'd enjoyed a few glasses of champagne for her birthday but hadn't gone overboard like Jaime had. She was sure Jaime had made up for the drinks Tori had declined and would be paying for it today.

Instead of patting herself on the back, she'd spent ten minutes brushing Sunny before showering and making herself a coffee for the car. She'd made the appointment for ten and wanted to leave plenty of time as she knew the admissions process could be lengthy.

Her phone pinged with a text as she was leaving the house.

> I know you said good or bad to wait until tomorrow, but as the news is good, I wanted you to know today. Dad's all clear!

Tori had to blink back tears the relief was so huge.

> Wonderful news! Can't wait to see you both tomorrow to celebrate. Running off to a meeting. Love you. x

She smiled at the heart emoji that appeared instantly on her message.

At nine thirty, she turned her car into the visitor car park of Winchester prison. Nerves rattled in the pit of her stomach. She'd visited prisons before for work, but this was different. In many ways, she considered June Marlow to be an innocent woman, even though she was a convicted murderer. It was an unusual scenario. She entered the prison, waited while her paperwork was processed, and then followed the instructions to empty her pockets before passing through the X-ray scanner. She left her bag and sunglasses in a locker as directed before being escorted through a series of corridors to a door that led to an outside area. She swallowed, nerves still jangling as she geared herself up to meet this woman who'd been imprisoned for longer than Tori had been alive.

The facility was a lot nicer than Tori had imagined, but it had minimum security and was a fairly new establishment. The gardens were well maintained, with neatly cut lawns and flower beds overflowing with brilliantly coloured petunias and salvias. She was led out to an open area where several tables and chairs were positioned.

'She's over there,' the prison guard said, pointing to a table where two women sat. One was wearing the blue prison outfit Tori had already seen several women wearing, the other a tailored black suit not dissimilar to the one she wore.

She took a deep breath as she approached the table and hoped her smile looked kind and genuine.

Both women stood as she reached them, the suited one holding out her hand. 'You must be Victoria Blackwood,' she said. 'I'm June's lawyer, Mackenzie Sullivan. And I'll be sitting in the background today listening, so pretend I'm not here. This is about you and June.'

Tori shook her hand before holding it out to the other woman. She wondered if she'd made a mistake. Was she allowed to shake her hand? She'd been given a million instructions during the briefing process when she'd arrived at the prison, but she couldn't remember. Her mind had been racing so fast she wasn't sure if she'd absorbed anything she'd been told. She was relieved when June took it.

'It's nice to meet you, Victoria. I'm June, which you've probably already guessed.'

Tori smiled, nodding. 'Thank you for agreeing to meet with me. Please call me Tori.'

They sat down, and Tori began to speak.

'The purpose of today is to find out what you're comfortable talking to me about when we're filming. I have a list of questions to go through with you, not ones you need to answer today, but ones I'd like you to be aware of. I'm hoping to ask you when I have the camera crew with me.'

'Did you feel safe coming here on your own?' June asked. 'I'm surprised you didn't have someone from your station accompany you.'

'Should I be concerned for my safety?' Tori asked, a smile playing on her lips. The woman in front of her may be a convicted killer, but she also had a gentle warmth about her.

'Only if you drink the water,' June said. 'It's quite disgusting. Full of chlorine. They do offer bottled water if you would like a drink, though. Or tea or coffee.'

Tori laughed, relaxing. She unfolded the piece of paper she'd been allowed to bring in, which housed her questions. Within minutes of meeting June, she knew that the television audience would love her. If she didn't freeze up when the cameras arrived, she could already see people talking about her, like: 'Gosh, she could have been my mum or my grandma.' People would relate to this woman.

'The questions were sent to your office earlier in the week,' Tori said to Mackenzie. 'We removed what was the fifth question, as requested, and we can certainly remove or edit any others that June's not happy with. Also, there might be some specific messages you'd like to convey, June. We can add some questions in to ensure we capture those.'

'What was question five?' June asked.

'It was about Nicole,' Mackenzie answered. 'It asked how she'd coped with your imprisonment and what she was doing now. It also asked about your relationship with her.'

Tori noticed June's face pale as soon as Mackenzie mentioned Cole's name.

'We can't discuss my eldest daughter,' June said. 'She doesn't want anything to do with the interview or to be named or associated with me.' She gave a wry smile. 'That probably tells you exactly how she's coped and what our relationship is like, but that's off the record and not to be included in the program or questioning.'

Tori hesitated. Should she tell June she'd met Cole? Cole would probably prefer that she didn't, but she had a feeling June would love to know.

'Is there a problem?' June asked.

Tori shook her head. 'No. It's just that I met Cole on Thursday.'

June's eyes lit up. 'Really? She's willing to be involved?'

Tori felt bad having to let June down with her reply. 'No, sorry. We're doing a related story on trauma victims, and we happen to be filming at the Wellness Centre where Cole works. Her name was mentioned, and I put two and two together.' She blushed. 'I kind of barged my way into her office.'

June's hand flew to her mouth. 'She wouldn't have liked that. She's angry with me.'

'Maybe,' Tori said. 'She made it clear she wouldn't be involved in the story, but she did ask about you. Wanted to know if I'd met you yet, and I think if I had, she would have had more questions.'

'You'll need to respect her decision to not be involved,' Mackenzie said. 'If you don't, we may choose to revoke June's involvement.'

'Of course,' Tori said. She turned her focus back to June. 'We want to tell the story you want to tell. From everything I've read, you should have been given a medal, not handcuffed. You're a survivor of every woman's worst nightmare, and you ensured the safety of your children. The injustice of how events played out is a part of the story, of course, but one thing that hasn't changed, which we want to help fight, is women's confidence to speak up. To turn to the available help centres and know that they'll be protected and assisted. There are a lot more crisis and women's shelters now than there were when you were going through this, but even knowing that, not all women will come forward.'

'Admitting what you're going through is humiliating,' June said. 'It's absolutely degrading to be treated that way by a person who you thought loved you, but admitting that to your family and friends takes a lot of courage. Courage that I didn't have. I've read a lot about domestic violence since I was sentenced. Trying to get a better understanding of why I allowed it to go on for as long as I did, and I can now see that abusive men often pick a certain type of woman. Are you in a relationship, Tori?' June asked.

Tori found herself blushing.

'You don't have to answer that. I hope that if you are, he or she is a decent person.'

'No, I'm not currently in a relationship,' Tori admitted. 'My last boyfriend moved overseas, and long distance didn't work for us. But he was a lovely guy. I'm lucky to have been around nice men and not put in a situation like you were.'

'Lucky,' June said softly. 'That's a problem, isn't it? To think that being treated with respect and not abused is being *lucky* rather than it being mandatory.'

'Shall we go through the list of questions?' Mackenzie glanced at her watch.

Understanding that June was probably paying by the hour for her lawyer to be in attendance, Tori moved through the rest of the questions quickly.

'I'm not sure how my mother will go on camera,' June said. 'She might be a bit nervous.'

'That's okay,' Tori said. 'We'll have a bit of a chat and try to make it feel like the cameras aren't even there. I usually suggest to older people that we do the interview in a place they consider safe, such as their home or that of a friend. It usually helps them relax, and the conversation then comes across as quite natural.'

'My daughter, Luella, goes by Lu, and she'd be good, I think.'

Tori smiled. 'I had coffee with Lu on Wednesday. She's lovely, and yes, she'll be good on camera.'

June's eyes lit up. 'You met Lu? Why didn't you say? She's such an amazing artist.' June thought for a moment. 'She's also a *struggling* artist. I wonder if we could showcase her art in some way. Might save her from too much more dog walking.'

'Leave it with me,' Tori said, thinking back to Ali's suggestion that she interview Lu at Future Blend. 'She was doing some pieces for one of the local cafés when I met with her, and what I saw was exceptional. She's also got some amazing art on her Instagram account.'

June smiled. 'So, I've heard. One of the challenges I'm going to face returning to the real world is getting my head around social media. The internet and email were the big advancements the year I ended up here. I'm aware of how technology has progressed, but I certainly haven't been part of it. Lu's explained Instagram and other platforms to me. Facebook and TokTok.'

Tori didn't correct her. There wasn't a need. She didn't imagine June would be a big TikTok user when she got out. 'What I love about Lu's art that I've seen is that it's quite symbolic,' Tori said. 'Showing hope evolving from adversity. We'll make sure we include it and hopefully give her career a bit of a boost.'

'Thank you. There's so much to make up for both of my girls. This would be a good place to start for Lu.'

'Do you think,' Tori asked, 'that you owe them something?'

June nodded. 'Definitely. My actions changed their childhoods.'

'Your husband's actions could have seen you dead instead of him. Lu and Cole too.'

'Quite possibly.' June sighed. 'I guess the whole point of this story is to show women like me that there are much better options. If I'd had the courage to speak up, I wouldn't be here, Alan might be alive, and the girls wouldn't have grown up with my mother.'

'I'd be proud if you were my mother,' Tori said. 'For you to stand up for me like that. I wouldn't be expecting any form of apology or for you to make anything up to me. And from what I saw of Lu, I don't think she expects that either. She just wants you home.'

'Thank you,' June said, taking her glasses off and wiping her eyes. 'You're kind, which is why I love watching your show. I watch it as often as I can.' She blushed. 'You've kept me company for many years. Provided a much-needed distraction at times. Focusing on your stories helps put my problems in perspective. That there are people coping with much worse situations.'

'I should get you to speak to my mother,' Tori said. 'She's concerned that I'm reporting too much depressing news and should be providing light-hearted and uplifting entertainment.'

June shook her head. 'That's not you. Doesn't she realise

you're fighting for social justice? You're creating conversations and causing change. Don't ever stop doing that, Tori. It's people like you who help make the world a different place.'

A lump rose in Tori's throat. June had summarised exactly why she did what she did in a couple of sentences. 'When you're out, perhaps I'll get you and Mum together. You can share what you said to me and help her understand.'

June laughed. 'I have a feeling I won't be on top of people's invite lists when I'm out. It will be strange. I can hardly imagine having the option to go out for dinner or walk to the park. But I'm not expecting anyone who knows what I did to want to come within ten feet of me. They'll be expecting me to kill them.'

While June's words were delivered with a smile, Tori saw the real worry in her eyes was that she expected people to fear her.

'I don't know if you'd be open to this, and it's something that I'm only thinking of, but I'd be interested in talking to you about another story. About following your journey once you are released and seeing how you fit back into society. I'm sure the prison offers programs to help you integrate back in, but the station could also offer some of our contacts to help with the adjustment.' Tori was thinking of the Wellness Centre. They were dealing with trauma all the time. She wasn't sure if it got much worse than what June had experienced. 'No need to answer that one now, but it's something to keep in mind. I don't know much about transitioning from prison.'

June gave a wry smile. 'This will be a first for me, too. I'm expecting it won't be easy.'

The guard nearest to them had signalled a few minutes earlier that the time was up.

Tori stood, wishing she could spend more time with June. The audience was going to love her; that much she knew.

She said her goodbyes, the nerves she'd experienced as she'd arrived at the prison now replaced with a sadness she couldn't explain. As she drove along the Western freeway back towards Melbourne and St Kilda, she found herself wiping away tears. Tears for every minute June had missed out on. Tears for society convicting a woman who'd been dealing with trauma, and tears that not only had she lost her husband and her freedom that night, but that she'd lost her eldest daughter too.

## 14

Cole drove away from the Dixsons' house feeling hopeful. She could see that as beaten down as Jacinta was, she loved and missed her girls. A visit to them to convey this would make a huge difference for all of them.

She let out a breath as she took a right-hand turn off Beechwood Drive. Her mind was whirling as she turned into a random street. She slowed, realising that it looked familiar. Most of the houses were new, and she'd avoided Mount Waverley for years. She looked from house to house as she continued along the road, stopping as she reached one of the original houses. Every other block seemed to have a new house or dual townhouses on some. But this house didn't look like it had been touched since it was first built in the seventies.

She glanced at her car's GPS at the address and froze. Legions Crescent. Of course, she recognised the house she'd passed; it had belonged to the Wilsons, family friends who had been there when she'd grown up. She forced herself to continue along the road, slowing as she passed another three houses and stopping at her childhood home. Her heart raced.

This was also the original house, while the neighbours on either side were now brand-new homes. She recalled her grandmother saying that a lot of the houses in the area had been pulled down, and she hadn't appreciated how different it would look. But their house was exactly as she remembered, except for the large liquid amber tree that had been a feature in the front garden. That was gone. The garden wasn't anything flashy, just maintained to a bare minimum. It was neat and tidy other than a stack of flattened boxes piled high in the driveway.

She closed her eyes as a wave of memories and emotions overcame her. She could hear Lu's laughter as she rode her scooter up and down the driveway, calling out to Cole each time she passed her. Cole saw her dad on the lawn, a hammer in one hand, a beer in the other. He was building a cage for the guinea pigs he'd promised to get them for Christmas. Both Lu and Cole had been so excited at the thought of having pets of their own to look after. She flinched as more of the memory returned. Her father had gone inside for something, but she never found out what it was because there'd been a huge crash, like piles of glasses smashing all at once. Raised voices had caused her to rush to the door.

'Don't come in, Nic,' her mother had called, her voice unusually high-pitched. 'I've dropped a tray of glasses, and there's broken glass. I don't want you to get cut.'

Her father had appeared at that stage, the hammer and beer bottle still in his hands. He'd grinned at Cole and winked. 'Klutzy mum. Always dropping things. Now, let's keep building this cage. She's insisting she'll clean it up, as she's the one who caused the mess.'

Cole had laughed and followed her dad back outside.

She opened her eyes now, a tear rolling down her cheek as

she recalled her mother's bandaged hand and her father making light of it during dinner.

'First, you drop the tray of glasses, and then you cut yourself cleaning them up. We're going to have to change your name to Klutz, aren't we, girls?'

A car pulled up behind her, interrupting her thoughts, and Cole quickly wiped her face. A young couple with a child of about seven got out. The woman saw her staring and waved. Cole was about to drive on when the woman left her family and came over to the car. She smiled. 'You look a bit lost. Can I help you?'

'Do you live here?' Cole asked, nodding towards the house.

'We do,' the woman said, frowning. 'Any reason you wanted to know that?'

'I used to live here, that's all. When I was a kid. It's the first time I've seen it since I was about ten.'

The woman's eyes lit up. 'That's amazing. Come in for a tour if you like. You can tell us how much it's changed and anything you can remember about the house. We only moved in over the weekend and haven't caught up with any of the neighbours yet to get the low down. I love hearing the history of houses. What the people were like before us. What good energy they had and all that.'

Cole's stomach churned. She wondered if the woman had finished unpacking as she'd probably want to repack her boxes and flee the moment she found out there'd been a murder in the living room. Cole certainly wasn't going to be the one to tell her. 'Um, no thanks, I'd better get going. Sorry, I kind of ended up here by accident and need to be somewhere.'

'You know where we live. Drop in anytime.'

Cole forced a smile. 'Thanks.' She started the car and slowly moved on down the road. She shuddered as she considered going into the house. Just sitting outside, it had brought back memories. She hated to imagine what details she'd remember if she went inside. What if it brought back the memories of everything that had happened?

She thought back to Jacinta and her own realisation that Jacinta was unlikely to have the capacity to defend herself or her girls if she'd been put in the position her mother claimed to have been put in. *Claimed to be in.* When she'd had dinner at Gran's, Lu had asked her: *Would you ever disbelieve a woman who said she'd been abused without speaking to her or hearing her story?*

Of course she wouldn't. So why did she continue to dismiss her mother's claims? Lu certainly had an opinion on that. *While she's in prison, you have all the power. You can choose to accept a call from her or visit her. She has no choice, and all she wants to do is talk to you. Ask you to hear her side of the story. But no, you're exerting power, which I get, because you feel the need to protect yourself, but it's totally unfair to Mum. I can't imagine you ever agreeing with one of your clients that this is the right way to handle things.*

Cole let out a deep breath. Maybe turning around and going inside the house and remembering everything that happened was exactly what she needed to do.

She hesitated for a split second and then, deciding she wasn't ready to do that, turned onto the main road, making her way back to the Monash Freeway.

\* \* \*

June remained seated as Tori was led back into the prison to be taken through the administration and processing area again. She turned to Mackenzie. 'She's lovely, isn't she? Seems to genuinely care.'

Mackenzie nodded. 'Very impressive, and yes, I agree. That wasn't pretending to get a story. The questions she asked that weren't on the list were heartfelt and empathetic. No wonder she comes across so well on the screen. Now, I didn't want to speak about this until after she's left, but I got some news late yesterday about your release.'

June's heart thumped in her chest. 'And?'

'And, a parole hearing is scheduled for March 1st.'

'But that's less than two weeks away.'

'It is. Assuming the parole board grants parole, your release date could be a matter of days or weeks following it. The fact they've moved you here already suggests it's more likely to be a shorter time frame. I'm guessing most of the processing is already happening in the background.'

June swallowed. As much as she was looking forward to getting out of prison, the reality of it happening was overwhelming. 'I'd better let Mum know.'

Mackenzie squeezed her arm. 'I think what Tori said about surrounding yourself with some support systems will be key when you get out. I'm not saying you need to do it as part of their story, but it certainly will help with the transition. You've spent more of your adult years in prison than out of it. The world's changed a lot in that time.'

June smiled. 'But people haven't. Tori Blackwood is living proof of that. Hopefully, I'll find some other people who are as empathetic as she is. And you're right that the world's changed too. From everything I've read and seen it's a much more sympathetic place towards women and victims of violence than it was before. Even though I haven't had a chance to experience it myself, I believe social media and people sharing their experiences can be thanked partly for that. And, of course, I've got Mum and Lu. I'll take it slowly when I'm out.' She shivered. 'I can't believe that's about to happen.' She grasped Mackenzie's hand. 'Thank you. This wouldn't be happening without you.'

'Of course it would,' Mackenzie said. 'It's the system finally doing the right thing.'

\* \* \*

Lu couldn't believe how nervous she felt at the thought of showing Ali the first completed piece of work for the café. While her initial stages were to sketch the picture, she wasn't sure if Ali understood that what she was doing in the café was a sketch. She would then transition it to canvas before adding base layers with colour and building up touches to add texture and depth to the drawing. She'd worked until the early hours of the morning on this piece, as she often did when she got carried away with something.

She'd then slept for ten hours, completely spent from the focus she'd applied. The total immersion was why she loved what she did. It was why she was happy to live on minimal funds in a basic apartment and walk dogs for a living. To give her the flexibility and space to lose herself was magic. She often wondered if other artists felt the same way. She assumed they did, or why else would they do it?

She'd wrapped the canvas carefully in bubble wrap and had it in the boot of her car, ready to show Ali after dinner. She was picking her up and driving to the Dandenongs, Melbourne's nearby mountain range, for a picnic. She'd learned that Ali wasn't your restaurant type, which, considering she ran a café, was ironic but suited Lu. She didn't have the funds for an expensive dinner, but could put together a delicious picnic. She had the picnic hamper and blanket Cole had given her the previous Christmas, which was lovely and looked impressive. She'd thrown some cushions into the back of the car, which she'd use to set a lovely scene. Other than the café, Ali's house, and a burger at the beach, this would be the first proper date they'd been on, and Lu wanted it to be special.

She pulled up outside Future Blend to find Ali standing out the front waiting.

Lu grinned as Ali opened the passenger door and slid in beside her. She had to use every fibre in her body not to lean across and kiss her.

'Where are we off to?' Ali asked, returning her smile.

'My favourite stargazing place in the Dandenongs. It's a bit of a drive. I hope you don't mind?'

'Good tunes and good conversation, and I'm all set,' Ali said. 'And Lu—' Lu turned to look at Ali, her heart skipping a beat. 'Thank you. I can't remember the last time someone did something nice for me.'

Lu smiled. 'Says the gorgeous woman who has been so kind to me for months. But that's not why I'm doing this, to be clear.'

'Oh?'

Lu couldn't help herself. She leaned across and kissed Ali lightly on the lips. 'I'm doing this because I can't think of anything I'd rather be doing. Now, let's get out of here, or we're going to get distracted, and all my plans will go out the window.'

Ali raised an eyebrow. 'Would that be so bad?'

Lu let out a long breath. 'No, it would be amazing. But I want to get to know you. Take it nice and slow.'

Ali smiled. 'That I can do.'

It took them close to an hour to get to the spot Lu had pictured as perfect for their picnic. It was a clear night, and the sun was setting as they pulled into the empty car park adjacent to the lookout. The smell of eucalyptus trees hit them as they opened the car doors, and Lu inhaled deeply.

'How good does that smell? And to think we're not that far from the city. I love it here,' she added.

'It's gorgeous,' Ali said, looking out to the city and ocean in one direction and across to the Yarra Valley in the other.

'Let's get set up.' Lu took her picnic blanket and cushions from the car and walked down to a spot that she decided was far enough away from the car park but gave the best view of the city, and no trees would block the stars once they came out. Within a matter of minutes, she had the blanket and pillows expertly arranged and a little tray table set up that housed a charcuterie board, two champagne flutes and a bottle of Lu's favourite sparkling wine.

Ali shook her head as she looked at the set-up. 'Okay, you win. This beats anything I've served up at the café.'

Lu laughed. 'Definitely not a competition but come and sit down.'

Ali took Lu's outstretched hand and the two women sat down on the blanket. 'I'm so nervous right now. My legs feel like jelly.'

'You're nervous?' Lu laughed. 'I find that hard to believe.'

'Why's that?'

'I don't know. You're a business owner. You've got your shit together. You don't walk dogs and rely on kind café owners to feed you each day.'

'I should be flattered,' Ali said, 'that you think that I've got my shit together. You know that my grandma left me the café, don't you? She died a few years back. Before that, I'd been drifting from one job to another. No purpose, no real interest. She gave me something to focus on. I'm not like you, Lu. I don't have this great passion for art or any skill. My grandma gave me a foot up, but otherwise, I'm nothing.'

Lu stared at the woman in front of her. The vulnerability was so clear on her face. She moved closer and took her hands in hers. 'Please never say that you're nothing again. You are amazing. What I see is someone who's so kind, confident and caring.

Look at how you questioned the reporter from *Southern Insight* to make sure she wasn't upsetting me. Your customers love you. You've turned that café into a haven for other artists. Don't you see that?'

Ali shook her head. 'Until now, no, it's never crossed my mind that I'm doing anything other than providing coffee and conversation.'

'Oh hon.' Lu pulled Ali to her, her heart beating so fast she imagined Ali would ask if she was having a heart attack. But she didn't, and she quickly realised Ali's heart was beating as quickly as her own. She had hoped the night would end with this, but the timing was too perfect. She stroked Ali's cheek and then lifted her lips to meet hers.

Sometime later, Ali lay against Lu, the two women watching as the sun set and the stars rose in the sky. They each had a glass of sparkling wine in hand, but Lu had hardly touched hers. This was one of those moments when she didn't need food or drink or anything else. As she had this thought, her phone pinged with a text. She groaned. 'Don't worry, I have no intention of checking that.' She stroked Ali's hair. 'This is too perfect to interrupt.'

'It is,' Ali murmured as Lu's phone pinged again and then again.

'You'd better check it,' Ali said as Lu pulled the phone from her pocket to silence it.

She glanced at the screen and froze.

'What?' Ali sat up and turned to face Lu.

She held up the phone so Ali could read the message. Ali's eyes filled with confusion. 'But that's what you've been hoping for, isn't it?'

Lu nodded.

'So, it's good news.'

Lu nodded again. 'I can't believe it, that's all.' And she couldn't.

I think I might be ready to talk to Mum.

Cole's text wasn't something she ever expected to receive.

Ali smiled. 'Text her back, and then let's turn off our phones and shut the real world out.'

Lu sent her sister a quick reply.

Love you and am so glad you're thinking like that. Will ring you tomorrow. On a hot date. x

## 15

Cole had been doing her best to relax, if you could call it that, with a glass of wine when she felt the urge to text Lu. The visit to Jacinta that morning and then stopping outside their childhood home had turned her into a ball of anxiety. Lu's words kept playing over in her head. *You're exerting power, which I get, because you feel the need to protect yourself, but it's totally unfair on Mum.*

She'd dropped her head into her hands when she admitted to herself that Lu was quite likely right. The memories and flashbacks were telling a different story to how she'd previously remembered her childhood. Why had she taken her father's side in all of this? Even when both Lu and her gran had begged her to talk to her mother, she'd refused.

She'd done enough counselling to have a good idea of why; she wasn't sure that she could take more hurt than had already been inflicted upon her. At age ten, she thought she had the best family. Sure, some of her friends had nicer houses and went on exciting holidays where they stayed in a hotel rather than a tent, but they often ended up being looked after by babysitters or being put into holiday clubs. She and Lu spent all their time with their parents. They laughed and played games together. She didn't want to believe she'd imagined all of that.

If she believed her mum, then everything she'd thought about her dad and her family wouldn't be true. It was some fantasy. But then, that's where it all came unstuck. Both Lu and her gran confirmed that they'd had a lot of fun as kids and that they went on the holidays Cole remembered. But they'd also tried for years to make her realise that while her happy memories were true, her mother had done an excellent job at hiding the abuse from them.

Her phone pinged as she contemplated another glass of wine. She picked it up and read her sister's message.

> Love you and am so glad you're thinking like
> that. Will ring you tomorrow. On a hot date. x

Cole smiled. She wasn't sure if Lu had seen anyone since the surgeon who hadn't been the right fit. That didn't surprise her. Lu needed a free spirit. Another artist would be ideal. The one thing Cole recognised in her sister was incredible talent, and yet she hadn't had success with it yet. She sent her back a brief message.

> Enjoy! Chat tomorrow. x

She sighed, her thoughts drifting to Ethan and the wedding. It would be strange going as his date, or would it? She liked Ethan and, if she was being honest, found him attractive. But they were good friends and colleagues, and she'd hate to jeopardise that, and if they were to become more than friends, she could almost guarantee that's what would happen. She wasn't any good at relationships. That was one thing she felt justified in blaming her mother for. They'd had no good role models as kids.

Gran didn't date when they'd moved in to live with her. And it wasn't just her. The fact that Lu's love life was a mess wasn't any surprise either.

Cole had analysed her situation previously and concluded that with a murderer for a mother, she couldn't take the risk of getting close to anyone. What if the impulse to kill was genetic? She hadn't experienced a desire to kill anyone yet, but it didn't mean it wouldn't happen. It was why she lived alone, too. Lu had suggested she get a pet, but what if she killed it? She wasn't willing to take that risk.

'I'm going mad,' Cole said out loud. At least if she had a pet, it would justify having a conversation with herself. Why would she kill anything? She liked dogs and loved cats. In fact, she'd always wanted one, but this strange belief she might kill it had always stopped her. She sipped her wine. If she was willing to speak to her mother, then maybe she should also consider getting a cat. Tomorrow, she'd go to the shelter and see if she still felt that way.

* * *

Tori, having no Saturday night plans, was sitting in her pyjamas typing up notes from her meeting with June when her phone rang, the 'Don't Stop Believin'' ringtone signalling it was her mother. She reached across from Sunny, who was asleep on the desk next to her, and picked up her phone.

'Hi, Mum. Everything okay?'

'Of course. I was ringing to check that you're still coming for dinner tomorrow? That you hadn't got a better offer.'

Tori laughed. 'Is that your not-so-subtle way of asking if I'm seeing someone?'

'Maybe, but I also wanted to check that it still suited you.'

'Can't wait,' Tori said. 'It's such great news about Dad. You must be so relieved.'

'We are,' her mother said, but her tone lacked the enthusiasm and excitement Tori was expecting.

'He's definitely okay? You sound a bit, I don't know, less happy than you should be.'

'I'm over the moon about your dad. But yes, I'm a little concerned. Mary dropped in again today. She was acting very strangely.'

'Strange, how?'

'She said she spoke to Jaime about the DNA testing today and Jaime's told her she's going ahead with it even though she knows Mary doesn't want her to. Did you speak to her last night?'

'I did, but she's pretty set on doing it. I thought she wasn't going to tell Mary from what she said last night.'

'She also mentioned that you, Sam and Penny are doing them too.'

'Yes, it was part of my birthday present. The girls thought it might be a bit of fun.'

'It could lead to all sorts of problems though,' Sylvie said.

'Really? Like what?' Tori's investigative journalist hackles rose.

Sylvie continued. 'I've heard stories of these tests ruining families, and I don't want that to be us.' She appeared to force a laugh. 'Some people prefer the new relatives they've found to the old.'

'I'm not expecting I'll find anyone new,' Tori said. 'But I'm also happy not to do it if it makes you uncomfortable.'

There was silence at the other end of the phone.

'Mum?'

'I'm thinking. I know it's probably an overreaction, but yes, I think I'd prefer that we leave it alone. Rhonda did a family tree a few years back, and that was from one of these DNA kits, so we have all the information anyway.' Rhonda was Sylvie's younger sister.

'Did that show up anything strange?'

'No, it showed us that some of our ancestors came from Scotland when we'd thought they'd all come from Ireland. Other than that, I think there was one cousin we hadn't been aware of. Nothing earth-shattering.'

'In theory, mine should show the same on one side and then whatever Dad's side has. Dad's not hiding something, is he?'

'Of course not. Why would you think that?'

'Because I'm an investigative journalist, and you asking me not to do something makes me question why. If people don't have anything to hide, they don't usually make such requests.'

Her mother sighed. 'It makes me uncomfortable. I can't put my finger on exactly why, but it does. But my call isn't about me. It's about Jaime and Mary. Do you think you could have a chat with Jaime and suggest that she doesn't do the DNA test? Mary is very upset.'

'I'll give her a call before I see you and Dad tomorrow,' Tori promised. 'Although...'

'Although what?'

'The whole point is for a story for *Southern Insight*. Not one that any of us will be part of. We're using some spare kits. But it's supposed to be an uplifting, feel-good story. You know, exactly like you were asking for the other day.'

Her mother gave a wry laugh. 'Be careful what you wish for. I can't explain exactly why I don't like the idea of this, love. I've always felt that our lives play out as they're meant to, and as soon as we start messing with situations that should be beyond our control, we invite all sorts of trouble into our lives.' She sighed again. 'I'm probably being dramatic, but after everything that's

gone on with your dad this past year, I don't need more unexpected stresses.'

'Don't worry about it,' Tori said. 'I haven't even done the
cheek swab yet. I'll leave it for now and only revisit it if you're
comfortable.'

'Thanks, love. As I said, we've all been dealt the hand we
have, and I would hate to see anything upset that. And yes, I'm
being ridiculous and overly sensitive, but seeing Mary today
made me worry about it all. Anyway, let's talk about it tomorrow
night. See you at six thirty?'

As Tori ended the call, an uncomfortable weight settled on
her shoulders. She could understand that being adopted, Jaime's
mother might be nervous about what the DNA results would
show, but her own mother? If her mother had achieved anything
by her call, it was piquing Tori's interest in what her DNA testing
might reveal.

* * *

Cole figured she was having a midlife crisis. It made sense. First
agreeing to speak to her mother and now driving to an animal
shelter. What was wrong with her? She thought that maybe she
should pull over and call her gran or perhaps Ethan. Someone
who might talk some sense into her. But as she had this thought,
her phone rang. It was Lu.

'You need to stop me,' were the first words that popped out of
Cole's mouth.

'What? What's going on? Are you okay?'

The concern in Lu's voice caused a hysterical laugh to escape
Cole's lips. 'I'm going mad. I'm on the way to the shelter to adopt
a cat.'

She was met by silence and then laughter. 'Are you joking?'

'No, but I think I need help. Ever since I decided I should talk to Mum, every other thought I've ever had seems to be rearing its ugly head and expecting me to act on it.'

'A cat?'

'Maybe. I don't know. I need something in my life, Lu. Suddenly, I feel more alone than I ever have.'

'Because you're considering letting Mum in, and you're scared she's going to let you down, so a fluffy friend will give you a backup?'

Cole gave a small laugh, shocked that her sister had nailed it. 'I thought I was the psychologist, not you.'

'Get the cat,' Lu said, 'but don't let it stop you from having that conversation. Cole, our lives could be so much better if you decide to let Mum back in. Gran told me this morning that her parole hearing is on March 1st. She could be out days later. It's literally a matter of weeks now. I'd love it if we could all welcome her home. I know how much you've hurt through all of this, but I know she's hurt as well. And the difference is she hasn't been able to distract herself with work and friends and everything else. She's been rotting away for years. It's better now that she's been moved and might even get released, but what she went through at Trendall was awful.'

'Okay,' Cole said. 'I've promised I'll speak to her, and I will. Now, what's going on with you? How was the *hot* date, and who is she?'

'She owns Future Blend. I'm doing some artwork for her. It's a win-win. She's providing exposure for me and multiple coffees and meals per day, and I've given her walls a fresh look.'

'Meals per day? Lu, are you okay? I can always help if you're having any issues meeting bills. I'd much rather you spend your time on your art than worrying about money.'

'Thank you, but I'm fine. It was a deal we struck up. I'm

getting by. The one thing my ex instilled in me was that I need to grow up. Walking dogs and scraping by doesn't cut it when you're in your thirties. While it didn't work out with her, that advice has stuck with me.' She sighed. 'I'm thinking I might need to go back and do some studying and get some skills that translate to a proper job.'

'You've got such a gift, Lu, you can't give up on it. And that ex of yours, she was a surgeon, for God's sake. All about money. She wasn't right for you, and you should ignore everything she said.'

'You only met her once at Gran's,' Lu pointed out. 'And you deduced all of that from one dinner?'

'That and what Gran told me about her. Anyway, tell me more about your date. What's her name?'

Fifteen minutes later, Cole found herself walking into the animal shelter with a smile on her face. Lu deserved some happiness, and it sounded like she might have found some with Ali.

She asked for directions to the cats and found herself standing in front of an older cat's cage, her fingers poking through the door with a fluffy tabby cat rubbing up against her and purring. Cole couldn't help but smile as she noticed his tabby markings stopped at his paws, which were all white.

'I see you've found a friend,' one of the shelter workers said as she walked into the area. 'That's Socks. He's seventeen and you can probably guess where he got his name. He's been here for a few years, so we consider him part of the furniture. And, considering how he's taken to you, shows you must be the ultimate cat person.'

'Ultimate?'

She grinned. 'Socks doesn't usually talk to our visitors. He keeps his affection for the staff at the shelter. As a result, he's been with us for a long time. I'd say you're the first person in the last year that he's shown any love towards. Sometimes, it makes me wonder if he was rejected so many times that he's not willing to put himself out there in case it happens again. But then I think I'm being ridiculous, and cat psychology is probably not my thing.'

Cole forced a laugh, her stomach churning as she recognised the shelter worker might be speaking about the cat but had also summed her up.

'Are you looking to adopt?'

'Maybe. To be honest, this is a bit of an impulsive visit, so it might be better to say I'm browsing today and will come back another day when I'm sure I want to adopt.'

'Fair enough. Most people prefer to adopt a younger cat or kitten.' She grinned. 'Speaking of which, come and meet Oski. If Oski doesn't win your heart over and have you taking him home, no cat or animal ever will. This guy is the most cuddly and affectionate fluffball you'll ever come across. He got separated from his litter and arrived two days ago. We've only put him out for adoption this morning. He'll be gone by the end of the day.'

Cole patted Socks on the head one last time and followed the woman through to the cage that housed Oski. She opened the cage, took a kitten out and handed him to Cole. He was a total mismatch of colours. 'He loves cuddles,' she said as the cat buried himself into Cole, purring and rubbing his head into her chin. 'If you're after a kitten that loves you to death, Oski's who you want. He's gorgeous. Everyone's going to want him, so if you're interested, I'd at least put down a deposit.'

And he was gorgeous. While it had felt like an impulsive and possibly quite reckless outing, Cole was glad she'd come in search of a new friend. Knowing Oski would be snatched up quickly made the decision easy for her. Who would have thought, single one day, taking home a new dependant the next?

As she drove home with the cat carrier sitting on the

passenger seat beside her, Cole knew she'd achieved one of the two items that she had considered might confirm that she was going mad. She still had to tackle the other. She wasn't sure if they were nervous butterflies or nausea churning in her gut at the thought of making that next step and visiting her mother, but she knew she needed some guidance on this. Lu wasn't the right person. She'd be so happy Cole was going to see June that she wouldn't think through anything more than how happy it would make her mother and gran. Cole needed to speak to someone who would think about the impact on her, too. Ethan's image popped into her head.

'What do you think?' Cole said, addressing the cat cage. 'Shall we invite Ethan over?'

She grinned as a meow gave her the answer she was hoping for.

# 16

Cole opened the door a crack, confirmed it was Ethan and pulled him inside before slamming the door shut.

She'd sent him a text the moment she'd arrived home from the animal shelter asking if he was free later in the day or perhaps for a takeaway dinner. He was and said he'd come over around five, and they could order in.

'Interesting greeting,' Ethan observed. 'Everything okay?' He held out a bottle of wine.

Cole laughed, realising how ridiculous that must have seemed. 'Thank you, and yes, sorry, everything's okay. I didn't want my new housemate to escape.'

'Housemate?'

Cole nodded. 'Come and meet him. It's one of the reasons I invited you over. I wanted some advice.' She led Ethan through to the lounge area. 'He's behind the TV. He's been there for about five hours.'

Ethan raised an eyebrow before walking slowly over to the television and looking behind it. He chuckled before looking up at Cole. 'I wasn't sure what I was looking for, but it definitely wasn't this.' He reached behind the unit and extracted a gorgeous tabby cat. 'I never picked you as a cat person. I love his white feet. What's his name?'

'Socks,' Cole said. 'I had this urge to give someone a home today and went to the shelter. There was this beautiful kitten that they tried to get me to take. Fluffy, cuddly and so loving, but he was going to find a home easily, so I chose Socks. Actually, he chose me. He's seventeen, and in the last year that he's been in the cat home, he's not shown interest in anyone except me. I had to bring him home.'

Ethan laughed, still cradling the cat in his arms. 'And since you brought him home, what's the verdict?'

Cole frowned. 'That I should have gone with my original instinct that I'm destined to live alone. He has no interest in me. I have no idea what I'm doing. I think he tricked me at the shelter so I'd help him escape, but now he's acting all macho and couldn't care less about me.'

'What made you think I'd be able to help?'

Cole shrugged. 'No idea, and if I'm truthful, he's not the real reason I asked you over. Honestly, I needed someone to talk to tonight.'

Ethan put the cat down, grabbed her hand and led her to the couch. 'Sit. I'll open the wine, and then we'll talk. I can almost guarantee that if you relax, Socks will decide he wants to relax with you, so that will sort him out, too.'

Cole nodded.

A few minutes later, Ethan returned with two classes of the pinot gris he'd brought with him and a smug look on his face. 'Told you,' he said as he indicated to Socks, who was curled up on Cole's lap, his head in the crook of her arm.

Cole smiled. 'I can't believe he did that. Almost as soon as I sat down, he ran over and planted himself here. I guess he has to do things on his own terms. It's lovely. Can you hear him purring?'

'I can. You need to realise that he's the boss now,' Ethan said. 'That's all you need to understand. Go with his routine, and you'll be best of friends, although...'

'Although what?'

'We've got the wedding in a couple of weeks. Will you still be able to come?'

'Of course,' Cole said. 'I'll ask Lu if she can house and cat sit, or I'll put him in a cattery or something. I'll work it out. Actually, Lu was part of the reason I wanted your advice. I did something a bit stupid last night.'

'Oh?'

'I told Lu I was ready to speak with our mum.'

Ethan's eyebrows shot up. 'That's a big step. What made you make that decision?'

'A lot has been happening lately that has probably been leading to it, but something Lu said to me the other day keeps playing over in my head. That I'm the one calling the shots and by refusing to visit I'm not giving her the chance to tell her side of the story. Also, I'm having more memories and flashbacks from when I was a kid that are making me realise that she pretended all was okay when it wasn't. Perhaps I did get it wrong, what happened that night, and even if I didn't, I should probably hear her out.'

Ethan nodded. 'Okay, so what's the "but"?'

'But,' Cole said, 'how do I even start? I last saw her when I was ten years old. I'm now thirty-eight. It screams awkward.'

'It does. Honestly, I think you should visit her as a first step.'

'She might be out in a few weeks. I'm thinking maybe I'll leave it until then. She's got a lot going on with the whole release process.'

'You could if you think continuing to put it off is the best thing.'

'You don't?'

'It sounds like you're ready, so putting it off means it will ruminate in your mind for weeks, possibly make you even more anxious, and it's highly likely you'll change your mind between now and then. I think regardless of the outcome of seeing her, it will help you move on either with her in your life or without, but at least you'll have moved past wondering if you should see her.'

Cole nodded, stroking Socks's head as she considered Ethan's words. 'You're wise.'

He smiled. 'You'd be telling me the same thing if our situations were reversed.' His eyes travelled down to where she continued to stroke Socks. 'He's one lucky cat.'

'I think I'm the lucky one,' Cole said. 'Finally, a man in my life who won't run a mile when he learns what a mess I am.'

Ethan reached across and took her hand. 'I'm also not running.'

* * *

Late on Sunday afternoon, as she neared her parents' home in Chadstone, Tori remembered she hadn't called Jaime as she'd promised her mum she would. She'd spent the day immersed in research relevant to the June Marlow case and had even found herself walking down to Future Blend mid-morning under the guise of getting a coffee but hoping Lu would be there. Unfortunately, neither Lu nor Ali were around, so she'd settled for a coffee and muffin instead.

She instructed her car's audio system to call Jaime and hoped her friend would be available to chat. She picked up almost instantly.

'Hey, birthday girl.'

Tori laughed. 'Hey, drunken friend. How was the head yesterday?'

Jaime groaned. 'It was a good reminder as to why I rarely drink, and certainly not that much. I assume you pulled up okay?'

'Yes, I had quite a bit of work to do this weekend, so I couldn't go too crazy on Friday night. You're not at your mum and dad's, are you?'

'No, I'm at home, why?'

'I'm heading to mine for a birthday dinner and thought if you were, I'd pop next door and say hi. But this is probably better as I don't want your mum to hear our conversation.'

'Okay. What's going on?'

'Mum called me last night. Said your mum was upset about the whole DNA thing. Mum wanted me to let you know, that's all. Ask if you'd reconsider finding out.'

She was greeted by silence.

'J?'

'Yeah, I'm here, and yes, Mum's made it clear she's upset about it all.' She sighed. 'I wasn't going to tell her I was doing it but she asked me outright again yesterday and I couldn't lie. I told her I'd think about it, which I will. Have you done your cheek swab yet?'

'No,' Tori said. 'Weirdly, my mum doesn't want me to do it either.'

'Really?'

'Yes, after asking me to speak to you, she went on and on about how these kinds of findings can upset a family, and you shouldn't mess with the universe. She was kinda worried about it. And she claimed it was on behalf of your mum but then went on to ask me not to look at my results.'

'Wow! That's suspicious.'

'I know. I said I wouldn't do the test but after we ended the call I went and did it ready to give to Penny tomorrow. Her reaction made me want to find out what she's hiding.'

Jaime gave a wry laugh. 'What do you think she's hiding, if she's hiding something?'

'I'm not sure I want to know,' Tori said. 'But I'm thinking it might be something to do with my dad. We have the family tree on her side, and it's all clear, but they've always been vague about Dad.'

'Are you worried he's not your dad?'

'No, it crossed my mind, but there's no way Mum would have cheated or anything like that. No, I honestly have no idea what I'll discover, assuming there is something.'

'Now I'm more intrigued about your family than mine.' A doorbell rang in the background. 'Hey, I've got to go. But let me know when you get your results. And, when you see your parents, tell them I said hi, and I'll give thought to Mum's request.'

As she ended the call, Tori turned her Mazda into the driveway of her parents' elegant two-storey Victorian-style house, with its intricate wrought-iron balcony and gabled roof, feeling a wave of nostalgia wash over her. Her childhood home was full of so many good memories.

The front door opened before she was halfway up the path, and her father appeared, his lean figure reminding her of how much weight he'd lost over the past year. Where his dark hair had previously had flecks of grey, his grey hair now had a few strands of dark.

'Hey, favourite daughter!' He opened his arms as she walked towards him, a wide smile on her face. 'Happy birthday. I know it was Friday, but I haven't got to say it in person yet.'

'Hi, Dad.' She walked into his arms and hugged him back. 'Speaking of favourites, I brought yours.' She held out the bottle of red as they pulled apart. 'I believe we're celebrating some good test results tonight.'

'You didn't need to do that. But thank you,' he said, taking the bottle of expensive wine from her. 'I'd better have tests more often if this is the outcome. Although I'm sure this is a birthday celebration, not a medical test celebration!'

Tori laughed as she followed him into the house.

'Mum's in the kitchen,' he said, 'and if you can't tell from those delicious smells wafting down the hallway, it's roast lamb tonight.'

'I was hoping it would be,' Tori said.

'Tori!' her mother exclaimed and rushed to hug her as she entered the kitchen. You would have thought it had been weeks since Tori had seen them. She couldn't help but notice her mother's pale face, and even her fashionable glasses didn't detract from the dark bags under her eyes.

She hugged her mother, conscious of the extra squeeze she was given, often a sign that something was up.

'Everything okay?' she asked as her mother released her.

'Of course. You're here, and we're having lamb for your birthday. What could be better?'

'This,' Dion said, holding up the bottle of wine. 'Our favourite. Will go perfectly with the roast.'

'Lovely,' Sylvie said. 'Pour some glasses, and I'll serve up. The lamb's resting, and everything else is almost ready.'

Tori placed her bag on one of the stools at the island bench and moved into the kitchen to help her mother plate up and carry bowls to the table. Instinctively, as they placed the last of the dishes on the table, she hugged her mother.

'What was that for?' Sylvie asked. 'Not that I'm objecting.'

'Just to say thanks. This looks amazing, and I wanted you to know how grateful I am.'

Tori took her seat at the round table and smiled at her parents, her smile slipping as she saw her mother's eyes fill with tears. 'Mum? What's wrong?'

Sylvie took her glasses off and wiped her eyes. 'Nothing. I'm a bit tired after everything this week and being appreciated like that has made me a little emotional. Don't worry, they're happy tears.'

Tori looked at her father, noting the concern on his face. He reached out and squeezed his wife's hand.

'You've looked after me too well and exhausted yourself,' he said. 'After dinner, you're to go and put your feet up and let Tori and me clean up, and then you're not to come near the kitchen for the next week. Do you hear me? It's my turn to make the cups of tea and the meals.'

Sylvie wiped her eyes again, and Tori's heart squeezed at the love her parents shared. Married for nearly forty years, and they looked out for each other every day. She knew her father wasn't just saying words. He would actually insist he did everything for the next week. And it wasn't as if he didn't do a lot already. He cooked two to three times a week and did his fair share of the housework. Both of her parents still worked, and both contributed to the running of the house.

'Let's eat,' Dion said, handing Tori a bowl of roast potatoes. 'Your favourite, I believe.'

Tori smiled as she accepted the bowl and spooned some onto her plate. She glanced at her mother, concerned by her unusually emotional response. It wasn't like her, but neither had the phone call been the night before. She hoped the two weren't related.

'What are you working on?' her father asked once their plates had been filled and they'd started to eat.

'A couple of stories,' Tori said. 'One's about victims of domestic violence, and then there's another that looks at how trauma affects people. They complement each other to a degree. And then, earlier today, I had an email and information from Penny on another story – this one's about human trafficking – which led me down a rabbit hole of research this afternoon, that provided some interesting and frightening information around domestic servitude.'

Her father frowned. 'Domestic servitude? What's that?'

'It's a type of modern-day slavery,' Tori said. 'It's usually related to women and children, but basically, they're forced into domestic work in an exploitative way. They're abused physically and emotionally and threatened.'

'How is that different to domestic violence?' Sylvie asked.

'It's got similarities, but with domestic servitude, the victims are often isolated, forced to remain in the household. It's often women being brought in from overseas, too. They've been made all sorts of promises of a better life and then get here and discover they're at the hands of an abuser. Their isolation makes it impossible for them to speak up.'

'Sounds awful,' Dion said. 'Doesn't it get you down working on those kinds of stories?'

Tori shook her head, finishing a mouthful of lamb before she spoke. 'Exactly the opposite.' She thought of June's words as she said that she was fighting for social justice, giving people a voice. 'It empowers me to tell their story and hopefully make people aware of what's going on. Make people look for signs of unusual activity and report it. Imagine if you had a neighbour who you never saw or who never left the house. You'd probably be so busy with your own life you wouldn't even notice, which is why people need to pay attention. Check in on each other. It's the same for the domestic violence story I'm researching. Did you know there are women in prison who hurt or killed their attackers and are now being punished for defending themselves? It's awful.'

She noticed her parents had both lapsed into silence. 'Sorry, this isn't a cheerful topic. We should be celebrating Dad's results, not focusing on my stories.'

'Not at all,' Dion said, 'I think it's hard to hear that kind of stuff. Now, let's have a toast to being cancer-free and...' He stopped talking as Sylvie pushed back from the table, tears streaming down her face, and hurried from the room.

'Mum!' Tori got to her feet and was about to chase after her when her father laid his hand over hers.

'No, I'll go. I think she's overtired and a bit emotional. Help yourself to some more food, and I'll be back in in a minute.'

Tori watched as her father left the room, wondering what was going on. She took a sip from her glass, nausea swirling in the pit of her stomach. She wasn't sure she'd ever seen her mother react like she had tonight.

\* \* \*

'Sorry, love,' her mother said a few minutes later, coming back into the room. Her eyes were red-rimmed, her face still pale, but she'd plastered on a smile for Tori's benefit.

'No, I'm sorry,' Tori said. 'I should never have gone into all that detail. I get a bit carried away sometimes.'

'You're passionate about what you do, which is why we're so proud of you,' Sylvie said. 'But it's something else that's been worrying me, and I can't seem to get past it. It's what I spoke to you about last night.'

'The DNA tests?'

Sylvie nodded.

'You'll be pleased to know that I spoke to Jaime before I got here, and she's reconsidering whether she goes through with it. And, I won't access my results if it's going to upset you.' Tori examined her mother's face as she waited for a response. In all honesty, she wished she could see the DNA results right now to find out what the fuss was all about.

'I don't think that's necessary,' her father said. 'Your mother and I have discussed it, and we're happy for you to go through the process if it's something that interests you.'

Tori looked from her father to her mother, whose eyes were closed.

'Mum? You seemed worried that I might find something out that you didn't want me to find out.'

Sylvie re-opened her eyes and looked straight at Tori. 'It's not that I'm worried about what you *might* find out. It's what you *will* find out.'

Tori looked at her father. 'We already have information on Mum's side through Rhonda. Is there something or someone on your side of the family you want to keep secret?' She gave a little laugh, thinking of Jaime's comment about whether Dion was her father. 'Don't tell me you're not my dad, and I'm going to find out Mum was having an affair.'

Dion glanced at Sylvie, who gave a little nod.

He ran a hand through his grey hair, the way he did when he was stressed or unsure. 'No, your mother has never had an affair, and neither have I. But there is something we haven't told you.'

* * *

Lu hummed as she drove towards Malvern and her gran's house. She'd been tempted to invite Ali along after the amazing time they'd had together over the past twenty-four hours but decided not to rush any faster than they were already moving.

Their starlight date in the Dandenongs had continued when they'd arrived back at Ali's, and Lu had only gone back to her apartment to shower and change an hour before she needed to be at Gran's for dinner.

A text appeared on the Jeep's Apple Car Play, and Lu's stomach flipped.

> You're amazing. Last night and today were soooo special, and to top it off, the artwork is incredible. I'm so glad you're in my life. x

Lu smiled as she thought of Ali's reaction when she'd unwrapped the artwork and shown it to her. Blown away was an understatement. Ali had been so overwhelmed that tears had run down her cheeks, alarming Lu at first that she hated it, but it was quickly made clear that Ali's reaction was brought on by the emotionally charged piece of art. Lu hoped it evoked the same response in others. She'd taken the idea from her original discussion with Ali, who'd mentioned a rainbow after a storm. Her final piece depicted a dramatic post-storm scene where a vibrant rainbow emerged from dark clouds. The dark sky was interspersed with light breaking through the storm while the ground below showed signs of the storm's impact: puddles reflecting the sky, bent trees and scattered leaves. Amongst the chaos and destruction a single flower bloomed. A subtle sign of hope. A new beginning. In the foreground of the picture was a young girl looking up at the rainbow.

'She's so innocent,' Ali said. 'You can tell she believes there are brighter days ahead.' She'd looked straight at Lu when she'd said this. 'And there are, Lu; I know there are.'

Now, as she thought back to the night before, Lu realised she still hadn't spoken to Cole today. Her euphoria thinking about Ali was quickly replaced with disappointment. She'd left a message for Cole that morning and sent her two texts since, but no response. She wondered if her sister was drunk when she'd sent the text and now was regretting it or back-flipping. Back-flipping was the most likely scenario.

She sighed. She wasn't sure how much more of this she could take. Why couldn't Cole see how easily they could be a family once again?

She pulled up outside her gran's house, looking forward to telling her about Ali but also hoping she'd have a solution for how to deal with Cole.

## 17

Tori looked from one parent to the other, her stomach twisting into sickening knots. Her father's face had drained of colour, matching that of his wife. Whatever was going on was beginning to scare her. 'What do you mean there's something that you haven't told me?'

Dion continued to run his hand through his hair.

'Your father and I,' Sylvie started, 'were desperate to have children. We always imagined a large family with five or six kids. It was our dream. But when we tried to have a family, we struggled.'

'Struggled?'

She nodded. 'I had three miscarriages before we were lucky enough to be blessed with you and two more when you were still quite young.'

'Five miscarriages. That's awful. I'm so sorry.' Tori wasn't sure what to say. The pain in her mother's face showed that this was still as raw for her as the day they happened. 'It's a miracle I'm here then.'

'You're definitely our miracle,' Dion said, 'but there's more to it. We were incredibly lucky to be blessed with you, as your mother said, but it wasn't through our own genes that we did it.'

Tori waited. Were they going to say they'd used a donor and done IVF? Or something along those lines?

'Tori,' her mother said. 'There's no easy way to tell you this, but we adopted you, when you were only a few hours old.'

Tori stared at her parents, trying to comprehend what they'd told her. 'What?'

'There was a woman we were made aware of who was unable to raise her baby. She wanted the baby to go to a good, loving home. She agreed that we could have you within a few hours of the birth. And that's what happened. We brought you home and never saw or heard from her again. It was the most amazing gift we could ever have received. Not a day goes past when I don't think of her and the sacrifice she made that led to our happiness.'

Tori leaned back in her chair and drained the rest of the wine in her glass. How did she respond to that? 'I don't know what to say.'

They fell silent while Tori tried to comprehend what she'd been told. *She was adopted. These were not her parents.*

'And the only reason you're telling me now is because you were scared I'd find out from the DNA test?'

'We felt that if you were going to hear it, you should hear it from us,' Dion said. 'It's why your mother hasn't been able to sleep.'

'Who is she? My biological mother? You met her, so you must know.'

'One of the conditions of the adoption was that we are not allowed to reveal her identity. Your DNA test might tell you more, but we can't.'

'Did she know who you were?'

The guilty look exchanged between her parents was impossible to miss.

'She knew of us,' Dion said. 'She'd asked for a lot of information about us. She wasn't going to give you up to anyone. But she also made it clear that she didn't want you to know that you were adopted and certainly didn't want anyone tracking her down.'

Anger surged through her. 'I'm twenty-eight years old. You didn't think I had a right to know before now?'

'Of course, you did,' her father said, 'and we discussed telling you many times, but we also had to respect the wishes of your biological mother. As your mother said, it was a condition of the adoption.'

'And we weren't sure it would achieve anything,' Sylvie added. 'As far as we're concerned, you're our daughter, and you always have been. You've been with us since you were a few hours old. While we might not be your biological parents, in every other sense, we have been your parents.'

'The DNA test could tell me who my birth parents are.'

Sadness clouded Sylvie's eyes, and Tori knew why she hadn't told her. Her mother had had multiple miscarriages and had been desperate for a child. She didn't want to lose this one too. There was part of her that wanted to reassure her mother, to tell her that she was her mum and always would be, and this wouldn't change anything, but another side of her was angry that this had been kept from her.

Toni stood, her mind reeling. *She was adopted. These were not her parents. The two people she loved most in the world were not related to her at all. She had no biological family.* Tears filled her eyes.

'Tori,' her dad said. 'Don't rush off. We want to talk to you. Try and explain as best we can.'

'No, I need to process this. I'll come back and talk when I'm ready. This is a lot to digest. Now I can see why Mum didn't want me to do the DNA test.'

'I didn't want you finding out like that,' Sylvie said. 'I didn't want you finding out at all, if I'm honest.'

The thought of Jaime's mother crept into Tori's mind, and she understood how upset she'd been at the prospect of Jaime finding out information she didn't want her to know. Right at this second, she knew exactly how Jaime's mother felt. She wasn't sure if she ever wanted to know who her biological parents were, but if she did, she wanted it to be when she decided to initiate that process, not because of a birthday present.

She moved towards her parents, hugging each of them. 'I'll be in touch in a few days,' she said. 'Give me some time to process this, and then I'll drop over. I've probably got a lot of questions. I just don't know what they are right now.'

'We love you,' her father said. 'Always have and always will. And you're our daughter one hundred per cent as far as we're concerned.'

Tori pulled away, tempted to say *no, I'm not* but stopped herself. She could see the devastated looks on her parents' faces, and she didn't intend to hurt them more than they were already hurting.

'Tori, I'm sorry,' her mother said as she climbed into her car. 'I wish I was your biological mum. I'd give anything to be her.'

Tori couldn't stand the pain she saw etched in every line on her mother's face. This woman had loved her with a passion that had made her feel loved and secure for her entire life. She knew no different. She got back out of the car and put her arms around her. 'I love you. That's never going to change. I just need to understand how I feel about all of this. I'm sorry if that's going to hurt you, but it's something I'm going to have to work out.'

Her mother opened her mouth, but her father shut her

down. 'Sylvie, let Tori process this. We can talk another day about the details of her birth. That's not for tonight.'

As she drove along Dandenong Road on the return trip to St Kilda, Tori had to pull the Mazda over. Her tears had started a few minutes into the journey and were now flooding down her cheeks, and she was finding it difficult to see. She wiped at her eyes roughly with the sleeve of her jacket. She wasn't sure why she was so upset. Sure, it was a shock, but her parents had been the most loving parents she could ever have asked for. She'd probably been better off being adopted. Still, it would have been better to have known this from a younger age. That her parents had lied to her and only told her because they thought she was going to find out via the DNA test was the most upsetting part.

Her phone pinged with a text. She was going to ignore it, assuming it was her mother checking on her, but she saw Penny's name on the screen. Anger instantly welled in her. If it wasn't for Penny, she wouldn't be in this situation. Even though she thought it was unfair. Penny hadn't given her up for adoption, and Penny hadn't raised her and lied to her for her entire life.

> Emergency meeting at the studio in an hour.
> Breaking story. Human trafficking. Need to
> resource it. Confirm attendance. P.

She sent back a quick text confirming she'd be attending and pulled the car back out into Dandenong Road.

* * *

Tori pulled into the car park of Channel Six studios a little after nine. She would be early for the official meeting, but seeing the number of cars already parked, she knew the office would be buzzing.

She hurried to the front entrance, punched in her security code and waited for the doors to open. She did the same once inside the lifts and made her way up to level three. The lift opened, and nervous excitement buzzed through her as she heard loud, urgency-filled discussion wafting from the main meeting room.

She crossed the open-plan area to the meeting room and stepped inside. Five of the team were already present. Two of the camera crew, a sound guy, one of the scriptwriters and Penny.

'What's going on?' she asked, breaking into their discussion.

Penny gave her a strange look. 'The people-trafficking story got bumped up the list,' she said. 'I'll explain the situation in full once everyone's here, but the quick summary is we've been given a tip-off that the police will be raiding a home in Footscray early tomorrow morning. They've already surrounded the area, ensuring no one leaves, but it's believed that the house has at least four women and six children being held against their will.'

'How do they know this?'

'A woman was going door to door in the neighbourhood, fundraising for a charity. She told police that she met the man who lived there who was not only rude to her but tried to physically keep her away from the property. She was a bit shaken, and the woman from the next-door house brought her inside to calm her down. When she explained what had happened, the neighbour mentioned that a strange man lived next door. She thought she'd seen a woman there, maybe more than one, and even a child, but they didn't come out of the home, so they might have been visiting. Anyway, she thought it was unusual and started asking around as she continued her fundraising and knocked on doors. She heard enough unsettling information and speculation that she reported it to the police. They've been watching the property and believe there are several women and children being held there.'

'We're going to want you on the scene to interview anyone you can. Neighbours, police, counsellors. I'm not expecting you'll get much from any of the official parties, but the neighbours generally like to share their thoughts. We'll try to get footage of the rescue and, hopefully, the arrest, too. Then, we'll see what information will be released. It's unlikely there'll be any other news on the scene. We'll lead with it on the morning show as breaking news with live updates and then want it ready for a more comprehensive story tomorrow night for *Southern Insight*. Sound okay?'

Tori nodded, her adrenaline pumping. Breaking and same-day stories and deadlines weren't the norm at *Southern Insight*. It was a current affairs program that often led to weeks of research, interviewing and filming before a story was aired. A story like this one was more like working for nightly news. It was exciting. 'I'll get onto the background information.'

Penny nodded, her eyes scrutinising Tori's. She took her by the elbow, led her from the room to her office and shut the door.

'What?' Tori asked.

'You tell me? Are you okay?'

Tori took a step backward.

'Tori, your face is a mess. You've been crying. What's going on?'

Tears filled Tori's eyes again. The distraction of the last half an hour had taken her mind from her own problems.

'Hon?'

'Sorry, had a bit of a shock tonight.'

Penny didn't speak, waiting for Tori to continue.

She gave a little laugh. 'Actually, it's your fault.'

Penny frowned. 'My fault?'

'Your DNA tests scared the hell out of my parents. Made them realise they needed to come clean before the test exposed their secret? Turns out I'm adopted.'

Penny's mouth dropped open. 'What? Oh my God. I'm so sorry. It was supposed to be a bit of fun.'

'It's okay; it's not your fault. It's their fault for keeping it secret all this time.'

'Why did they?'

Tori wiped her eyes. 'Honestly, it's probably too much to process or get into right now. They had their reasons, and I'll talk to them more about them once the dust settles. When you rang, I was on my way home, probably going to open a bottle of vodka and drown my sorrows. But this is a much better distraction, so let's get on with making a story.'

Penny nodded. 'If you need anything or aren't up to this, tell me, won't you? I'm sorry, I really am. If I'd had any idea...'

'I know, and again, it's not your fault. I'll be fine for the story, but I will ask you to do me one favour.'

'Anything. Name it.'

'I'm still going to give you my DNA swab. I'm not sure I'll access the results, but I want to have the option to if I ever decide I'm ready.'

'Okay, then what's the favour?'

'When the results arrive, please don't access mine. I'm not sure if I ever will, but if I choose to, I want it to be when I'm ready, not before.'

Penny nodded. 'The results will come directly to you. I won't see them.'

'Okay, good. Now, I'm going to get to work. Call me when you're ready to brief the team.'

# 18

As the cool, early morning air whipped across her face, Lu turned to her gran as they stood outside Cole's apartment block. 'She's going to kill us.'

'Why? We come bearing warm croissants and all her favourite pastries. It's a nice thing to do for her.'

Lu rolled her eyes. 'On a Monday morning! How often have we turned up unannounced with breakfast? She's not stupid, Gran.'

'You asked for my help last night, and hopefully, she'll see the gesture for what it is. We love her, and we want her to act on meeting her mum while she's thinking it's the right thing to do. If she listens to her and believes her, it will make all our lives a lot easier when June's released. It's something I've been praying for, for years. You probably don't remember, but I even took her to the prison a few times when she was little, thinking she'd come in and talk to her, and that was all it would take.'

'I do remember,' Lu said. 'She refused to and stayed in the car each time.'

Elena nodded. 'So, hopefully, this will be an actual, proper visit... if we can get her there.' She lifted a finger and rang the intercom for Cole's apartment. It was six thirty in the morning. They were taking no risk that Cole had already left for work.

Cole's voice came through the speaker within seconds of them ringing. 'I thought you took the key,' she said. 'I'll buzz you back up. But, be careful with the door. Socks is sitting on this side of it.'

She hung up, and the door to the apartment building opened.

Lu looked at Elena. 'That was unexpected. Who do you think she gave the key to? And who's Socks? Maybe we should come back?'

Elena shook her head. 'No, this is perfect. If she's got a male friend there, she'll be so flustered we'll be able to get her to agree to anything.'

Lu smiled, loving her grandmother's manipulative side.

They took the lift to the third floor and made their way along the corridor to Cole's door. Lu had to admit she was a bit nervous but also curious. Cole hadn't mentioned anyone she'd have given a key to. If nothing else, this should be interesting.

She knocked on the door, and it opened. Cole's wide smile was instantly wiped off her face as she saw Lu and her gran. With a large fluffy cat under one arm, she poked her head out and looked towards the lift before facing them. 'What are you doing here?'

'Breakfast,' Elena said, holding up the basket of baked goods and pushing past Cole into the apartment.

Lu shrugged and grinned, mouthing 'sorry' as she followed Elena.

'This isn't a good time,' Cole said, putting the cat down and following them. 'I'm about to leave for work.'

'At six thirty in the morning,' Elena asked, 'when you live a few minutes from the office? Put the coffee on and come and join us. There's plenty of food here if you're expecting any other visitors.'

As she said that, a key turned in the door of Cole's apartment, and a male voice called out, 'Coffee's here. And I've got wedding news, too.'

Lu wasn't sure whether to laugh or feel sorry for her sister as Cole's cheeks turned bright red.

'Oh,' Elena said, 'sorry, Cole, we didn't realise you'd invited a friend over for breakfast.'

Lu had to turn away at this. The innocence in Elena's comment when she knew that this male visitor had probably been here all night was too much.

Cole let out a breath. 'Ethan, come and meet my sister and gran, who've dropped in to surprise me.'

The footsteps that had been clearly audible walking down the hallway stopped. The poor guy.

'Do you want us to go?' Lu asked. She put herself in Cole's shoes and knew how uncomfortable she'd be right now if they'd walked in on her and Ali.

'Yes,' Cole said, not needing to give any thought to her answer. But she threw her hands up and started to laugh. 'No, whatever, it's fine. Let me introduce you. Ethan's heard plenty about the two of you, so he'll probably be interested in putting faces to names.'

Lu shot her gran a look as a tall, dark-haired man with brilliant blue eyes and flawless skin entered the kitchen. She might not be into men herself, but she could certainly appreciate how lovely this one looked.

He grinned, his dimples adding a touch of charm as he sheepishly held out a coffee to Cole. 'I would have got four if I'd known you were joining us.' He put his on the bench and held out a hand to Elena. 'Cole's told me a lot about you, Mrs Langrell. It's lovely to meet you.'

Elena shook his hand. 'Elena's fine.' It wasn't hard to see that he'd impressed her.

He then turned to Lu. 'And you must be the brilliant artist Cole's spoken so highly of.' Lu shook his outreached hand. If he'd been shocked they were here, he'd certainly made a good recovery.

'Ethan and I work together,' Cole said. 'And we're good friends, so he knows a lot about what's been going on with Mum and *Southern Insight*. In fact, the two of you can thank him for me agreeing to speak with Mum. It's his words of wisdom that helped me see that I should speak with her.'

'And I dropped by to talk to Cole about one of our clients,' Ethan said. 'We often use Monday mornings for that. And, of course, the wedding I mentioned. There's been a slight change of plans.'

Cole laughed. 'As much as I appreciate you trying to cover our tracks, neither Gran nor Lu is stupid.' She slipped an arm around Ethan's waist. 'It's new, but yes, we've moved into something more than friends.'

Ethan's dimples deepened as his cheeks flushed red.

'I, for one, am delighted by this news,' Elena said. She opened the basket. 'Pastries to celebrate?'

Ethan's eyes widened. 'You're my sort of gran. Yes, please.' He helped himself to a croissant while Cole took some plates from the cupboard.

'And who's this?' Lu asked, scooping the cat up, which was rubbing around her ankles.

'That's Socks,' Cole said. 'He lives here now.'

'I know you said you were going to the shelter, but I didn't really think you'd get a cat. And certainly not an old cat!'

Cole nodded. 'He needed a bit of love, and I hope I can give him that.' She laughed. 'They told me I was the first person he'd shown any affection to in over a year. Looking at him now, I think perhaps I was set up.'

Lu stared at her as the cat nestled against her. 'Are you okay? This is not normal, ordered Cole behaviour.'

The intensity of the question made Cole laugh. 'Probably not. Now, I'll make you both some coffee in a minute, but why are you here?'

'Honestly?' Elena said.

Cole nodded.

'You said you'd speak to your mum, and we want you to lock in a time. After saying you'd speak to her, you ignored Lu's call and messages yesterday, and we're expecting you'll backtrack and decide you're not going to do this.'

'And you thought pastries would do the trick?' Cole's voice had an incredulous tinge to it.

'No, but if you do backtrack and refuse to see her, I'll comfort-eat my way through them,' Elena said. She tapped her rather rounded stomach. 'Eating my feelings is a tried-and-true method. You should realise that by now.'

As she continued to stroke Socks, Lu couldn't help but notice Ethan squeeze Cole's hand.

Cole closed her eyes momentarily before opening them and looking from Lu to her gran. 'I'll see her. How do I arrange a visit?'

Tears filled Elena's eyes. 'Really?'

Cole nodded. 'It's long overdue, and I'm only realising that now.' She let go of Ethan's hand and wiped at her own eyes. 'Talking to Ethan made me realise that I might have missed out on a lot by excluding her from my life.'

Lu shot Ethan a grateful look. 'Would Saturday work best, or would you like to go mid-week? They allow visits on some week-days, definitely on a Wednesday.'

'Saturday,' Cole said. 'I have a busy week, and I can't let my Wednesday group down by not being there.'

'They'd understand,' Ethan said.

'They would, but I'll be more relaxed on Saturday.' She gave a wry laugh. 'In reality, I'll be so anxious and highly strung that it won't be funny, but at least I won't be worrying about work as well.'

'Let me drive you,' Ethan said. 'I'll wait in the car while you have your visit. I don't think you should drive yourself.'

Lu could have hugged him. She'd planned to offer the same to Cole but doubted her sister would agree to her taking her. But to Ethan, she nodded. 'Thank you.'

'If you change your mind...' Elena began.

Cole reached out and squeezed her arm. 'I won't. I promise.'

* * *

A few hours after leaving Cole's, Lu and Ali stood back and looked at the artwork that Ali had now hung on the main feature wall of the café. Ali slipped an arm around Lu's waist. 'That's amazing. I feel like I've taken advantage of you. To get something like that for the price of a few coffees and some food. It's got to be worth thousands.'

Lu laughed. 'Only if someone's willing to pay thousands, and as they haven't ever suggested they were before, I doubt this one will be any different.'

'Well, if someone does offer thousands for it, I'm happy for you to sell it to them.'

'No way,' Lu said, turning to face Ali. 'A deal's a deal. You've paid for it, and I still owe you another four. If you're happy to put my name up on the wall, that would be great, of course. Who knows, someone might approach me to do a commission for them.'

Ali leaned forward and kissed Lu lightly on the lips before moving away. 'I'd better not start that, or no one's going to get any food or coffee today. Now, you said Tori was coming to talk to you again.'

Lu nodded. She'd received a text from Tori saying she'd dropped in hoping to see Lu the previous day and would try again this morning. She glanced at the clock on the café wall. It was already ten. The early morning visit to Cole and then dropping her gran home again had eaten up some of the day already. She was usually at her most creative early morning, and by this time of day, it often felt like the window of opportunity was closing. 'She'll probably be here any minute. I might get set up if you don't mind, and at least I'll start giving thought to my next piece.'

'Coffee?'

Lu shook her head. 'No, I'll wait for Tori. But thanks.'

Lu could only imagine how surprised Tori would be when she found out Cole would be visiting their mother on Saturday. Who knows, with Cole adopting cats, starting a relationship and agreeing to visit their mother, she might also agree to be part of *Southern Insight*'s story. Lu had a feeling that that would be pushing it.

She opened her sketchbook and started thinking through her next piece. She already had an idea from something Ali had said on their date up at the Dandenongs as they'd watched a butterfly flit around a sunflower. *Imagine transforming from a caterpillar to something so beautiful. It's like the ultimate take on freedom and pushing past challenging circumstances. I'll not only get through this, but I'll also come out the other side, which is magnificent.*

'Lu,' Ali called, interrupting her thoughts.

She glanced up to find Ali pointing to the television. She was in the process of pointing the remote control at it to turn up the volume. Lu stood, seeing Tori on the screen.

'Is that live?'

Ali nodded. 'Yes, they're saying it's breaking news, so she's probably not going to make your meeting this morning. They said they'd been camped out at the property before daylight.'

Lu sat down on one of the stools by the counter, her eyes fixed on the screen. 'How awful,' she said as she listened to Tori explain the details of what they knew so far.

*'We believe there could be as many as six women and nine teenage girls being kept prisoner on the premises...'*

God, and Lu thought she'd had a rough childhood.

Ali had come around beside her. 'You okay? You've gone pale.'

Lu nodded. 'I can't imagine being put in a situation like that. Those poor women. They'll be ruined for life.'

'Maybe. Or, hopefully, they'll see their release as a second chance. A chance to heal and rebuild. Like you did.'

Lu looked at Ali, seeing the concern in her girlfriend's eyes.

'You talk about Cole a lot,' Ali added, 'as if she's the only one who went through this terrible trauma. You did, too, Lu. Look at how amazing you are. Do you consider yourself ruined for life?'

Ali was right. As awful as losing her dad and her mum's imprisonment had been, never had she considered herself ruined. She considered herself lucky that she'd been able to visit her mum and that she'd be able to welcome her home soon.

'Tori looks awful,' Lu said. 'I think she's crying. I'm not surprised. That must be confronting.'

They stood in silence, watching as the footage showed a man being walked towards a police car, his hands cuffed. The women and children were being led to ambulances that were waiting, being carefully covered by blankets to hide their identities.

'You never know what's going on in other people's lives, do you,' Ali said. 'How quick people are to judge and to think they've got problems. Then you see something like this, and it puts how lucky we are into perspective.'

Lu could only nod in agreement.

* * *

Tori let herself into the house a little after two, feeling absolutely wiped. Sunny came racing up the passageway and threw himself on her feet, meowing. She scooped him up and planted kisses on his head. 'I'm so sorry, Sun. Let's get you brushed and get you something to eat.'

She should feel guilty that she hadn't given him a thought overnight. Luckily, she'd fed him before going to dinner at her parents', and he always had a bowl of biscuits he could access, but he wasn't used to her being out all night and half the day. Guilt, however, was the last thing she felt right now. She was exhausted.

The news from the previous night and then seeing the terrified women being extracted from the house this morning had been overwhelming. She'd found herself crying mid-report at the sheer horror of the situation the women had been through. She'd assumed they would have cut to other footage or one of the other reporters, but Penny had said no. They'd kept the camera on her. Her reaction was so raw and emotional that ratings had gone through the roof. 'You'll have had half of the country in tears watching your reaction,' Penny said. 'The story will get a lot more media attention moving forward because of that. People are invested, and that's thanks to you, Tori.'

Tori watched Sunny gobble down the tuna she gave him. She couldn't help but smile. You'd think he hadn't been fed for a month.

She kicked her shoes off and, phone in hand, headed toward her bedroom. Right now, all she wanted to do was sleep. She wasn't expected back in the studio until the next day, for which she was grateful.

A text message arrived as she put her phone on the bedside table to charge and lay down. Her mother.

Worried about you. Love you. x

She closed her eyes. She should have texted her mum and reassured her, but right now, she needed some space. She didn't want anything to do with anyone. An image of Cole Langrell flittered into her mind. She imagined this was how Cole felt when it came to her mother. Just wanting to be left alone.

She sat up and grabbed her phone. She'd completely forgotten that she'd arranged to see Lu that morning. She sent her a quick text apologising.

Lu's response came back a minute later.

Saw the live show, so knew you were busy. And we thought we had problems! Those poor women. Hope you're okay. I'll be at the café the next few mornings. x

Tori gave the message a thumb up and lay back down as Sunny jumped up on the bed and pushed his head against her. She reached down and stroked him, glad of his company, and closed her eyes. She couldn't imagine being able to get to sleep as images of the women's distraught faces filled her mind. How did you ever recover from something like that? She guessed people did, and the segment they were doing on trauma victims certainly helped show that. She sighed, thinking of what her mother had said about news stories being depressing and that she would prefer lighter stories. Right now, Tori had to agree with her.

\* \* \*

Cole waited until mid-afternoon to speak to Ethan about the visit from her gran and Lu in the morning. He'd headed home before they'd left the apartment to get changed and ready for the workday.

She'd, of course, had to listen to Gran and Lu drool over him, which she had to admit had been rather nice.

'He's lovely,' Gran had said. 'Exactly the sort of man I've always pictured you with. Strong, caring.'

'Gorgeous too,' Lu had added.

Now, as she walked down to his office, she hoped he hadn't been scared off by how full on her life currently was. He looked up from his computer as she knocked on his door, his smile widening as she walked in.

'I'm sorry...'

He held up his hand. 'Stop. There's nothing in the past...' he glanced at his watch '...twenty or so hours that you could possibly need to apologise for.' He stood and walked around his desk and took her in his arms. 'This has been the best twenty hours of my life... so far.'

Cole blushed. 'I was worried that my stuff's a bit full on, that's all.'

'Which I was aware of before spending the night with you. The way you conduct yourself is what I love about you. You carefully consider what you're going to do. You ask for help and guidance, and you use them to make your decisions. Yes, you've had a difficult time, and who knows what's going to happen next? It's nothing that scares me. I want to be with you through this.'

A lump formed in Cole's throat. She could see how genuine he was and how much he cared about her. She hoped she wasn't going to let him down.

He kissed her and then pulled away. 'We'd better be a little bit careful at work. I'll let Mike know that we're seeing each other. Are you okay with me doing that? Full disclosure and all that.'

She nodded and smiled. 'Are you sure you're happy to take me on Saturday? It could be a lot of waiting around.'

'That's okay. I'm reading a great book, so I'll enjoy some forced reading time, and if you're up for it, we can get some lunch or something afterwards. And if you're not, we'll come home and curl up with Socks.'

Cole frowned. 'I hope he's okay. I felt bad leaving him on his own this morning.'

'He'll be fine. I can almost guarantee he's fast asleep. Probably in the middle of the kitchen table or anywhere else you've told him he's not allowed to go.'

Cole laughed. 'I don't mind what he does. He's proven to be well-behaved so far. I'd better get back to work.' She turned to leave his office and stopped. 'I forgot to ask. When you came back with the coffee this morning, you mentioned a change of plan for the wedding.'

'Nothing to worry about,' Ethan said.

Cole frowned as he averted his gaze from hers. 'You're not a good liar. Which is a good thing, I guess. What's going on?'

Ethan sighed. 'The wedding's off. Mum's upset about it, as am I. I was looking forward to introducing you to everyone.'

'That's terrible. What happened?'

'The groom got cold feet. To be fair, that's not quite accurate. He decided committing to one person might be too much to handle. My sister discovered he's been cheating on her.'

'That's awful, but probably better to find out now than in a few months.'

Ethan smiled. 'You and Dad will get along well. That was what he said. The only difference is he went around and flattened Jonno, too. Mum's worried he might press charges.'

Cole couldn't help but smile.

'It's not funny,' Ethan said, even though he was smiling too.

'I know. I'm just glad to see that there's some dysfunction in your family, too. While it's not at the level of the Marlows, I'm sure you can help bridge the gap with some encouragement.'

Ethan laughed and pulled her to him again. 'We can still go to Sydney if you like. Although, with everything going on with your mum, it might be better to play it by ear. And I can think of plenty we can do to pass the time.' She melted against him as he kissed her.

'Sounds perfect.'

# 19

Cole found it hard to hide her delight when, on Wednesday afternoon, Piper threw her arms around her when she came to collect her from the Gleesons' for another after-school gardening session.

'Wow, that's quite a welcome,' she said, laughing as she hugged Piper back. 'Not that I'm complaining.' She looked over Piper's shoulder to Anne Gleeson, who stood smiling as she watched on. Anne gave her a thumbs up in response to Cole's questioning look.

Cole knew that Jacinta had visited the girls after school the previous day, and from this reaction, she assumed it had gone well.

'Mum visited,' Piper said as she pulled away, confirming Cole's thoughts. 'She told us that she was sorry and that she should never have let us be taken into foster care.' She flushed and turned to Anne. 'Sorry, it's really nice here with you and Zane.'

Anne smiled. 'No need to say sorry. We love having you here, but we'd also love it if your mum was able to have you home again. Don't forget, she did explain it wouldn't happen immediately. While your dad's in the house you can't return.'

Cole was pleased to hear that that information had been conveyed. She didn't want Jacinta giving the girls false hope that they'd be home soon.

Piper turned to Cole. 'She said you'd spoken to Dad, and he was going to get help.'

Cole smiled. 'I spoke with your dad yesterday morning, and yes, he's checked into a facility that will help him.'

Paul Dixson had phoned the Wellness Centre, wanting to speak to Cole. She'd taken the call, half expecting him to lash out at her for visiting Jacinta but had been relieved when he said he wanted help. She'd arranged for the case worker from social services to visit him at home and make the arrangements needed to get him a place at Serenity Springs Rehabilitation Centre in Brunswick. He'd been admitted later that afternoon.

'Do you think he'll get better at the treatment place?' Piper asked.

Cole wanted to reassure Piper he would, but she knew better than to give her false hope. 'I hope so,' she said. 'It's up to him to put in the hard work. I don't know if your mum told you, but it could be quite a long process before he gets out and before he'd be able to live with you again.' *If he was ever allowed to.* Not that she added that.

Piper nodded. 'She did. But she said that Katie and I might be able to go back and live with her.'

Cole smiled. 'Yes, which will be good for all of you. Your mum's going to need support and help, too, though. She's had a hard time with what your dad's put you all through. So, we're looking at getting her into some programs at the Wellness Centre to help build her strength up again.' Building Jacinta's mental strength was going to be crucial for having the girls return to her, and one of the programs run by the centre would help her with that. It would help rebuild her self-worth and give her coping strategies for moving forward.

'Now,' Cole said. 'Are you up for some weeding and watering? And, if it's okay with Anne, I thought we might grab a burger for dinner afterwards. If you'd like?'

Piper turned straight to Anne. 'Can I?'

Anne nodded. 'Definitely, and Cole, thank you.'

Cole knew that Anne was thanking her for more than the offer of a burger. She hoped that Jacinta would be able to step up for their girls, but unfortunately, without a crystal ball, only time would tell.

\* \* \*

Work had proven a good distraction for Tori on Tuesday and Wednesday. In addition to putting together a follow-up piece on the women who'd been released from the Footscray house, she'd been doing more research on the trauma story and found both stories helped to put her own situation in perspective. She'd grown up in a loving environment with two people who'd do anything for her. She'd never gone without and never suffered any ill treatment. When she looked through the files of some of the clients of the Wellness Centre who'd volunteered to be involved, her stomach churned at their experiences.

How did you recover from finding your father hanging from a rope in the garage at age thirteen like one of the women had? Tori guessed you didn't, which is why Lisa, now in her forties, continued to have therapy sessions at the centre. As much as the story saddened her, she was looking forward to finding out more about how it had shaped Lisa's life. Without even delving into

Cole Langrell's life, she could see how badly she'd been affected by her father's death.

Now, as she was nearing the end of an early morning walk along the St Kilda foreshore, she wondered if Lu was likely to be at Future Blend this early. She had said in her text that she'd be there the next few mornings but didn't specify what time. She decided to try her luck.

It was close to seven thirty when Tori pushed open the door of the café to be greeted by a smile from Ali, who, with a quick nod of her head in the direction of Lu, answered Tori's question before she asked it.

Tori smiled and walked over to where Lu was totally engrossed in a drawing at what Tori suspected might be her favourite table, tucked away in the corner. She hesitated, wondering if she should come back later and not disturb her.

'Lu!'

Tori couldn't help but laugh as Ali made the decision for her, the sound of her name being yelled jolting Lu back to the present.

Her cheeks reddened as she smiled at Tori. 'Let me guess, you've been standing there for half an hour?'

Tori grinned. 'No, just got here. I was debating whether to interrupt you or not. You looked so focused.' She couldn't help but notice Lu slide a piece of paper over her drawing, not wanting to share it.

'Coffee?' Ali asked, coming over to the table.

'Sure,' Tori said. 'And whatever Lu would like. If you've got time for a quick chat that is?'

'Yes, of course. And I think I'll have tea. I'm getting fat with all these lattes and meals. I think my figure prefers me to be a starving artist.'

Ali laughed. 'Not starving for long. Once people start to see your work, it will change.' She turned to Tori. 'Did you see that one?' She pointed at the lone picture that now held pride of place on the main wall of the café.

Tori walked over to the artwork. The detail was exquisite. She couldn't take her eyes off the young girl in the foreground, looking up at a rainbow that had broken through the dark clouds. Lu had captured a look of hope and belief on the girl's face that sent shivers down Tori's spine. This had to be Lu weathering the storm that was her life. She wondered if she'd drawn this a few months earlier before there was any talk of her mother's release, whether they'd be looking at a dark sky. This picture depicted hope, which might not have been on the table a few months back.

'You're incredibly talented,' Tori said, returning to Lu's table and sitting across from her.

Lu smiled. 'Thanks. Now, how are you after Monday?'

Tori frowned. How did Lu know about her situation?

'The women in the house?' Lu prompted. 'You looked so upset doing the story, which is no surprise. I can only imagine how much some of these stories must affect you.'

A minor sense of relief came over Tori. Of course, Lu wouldn't know about her personal problems. 'Yes, they do from time to time. It's hard not to be affected when people are going through such awful situations.'

'You look pale and tired,' Lu said. 'I expect you can't stop seeing the women and imagining how he mistreated them.' She shuddered as she spoke the words.

Tori closed her eyes momentarily and took a deep breath.

'Sorry,' Lu said. 'I didn't mean to bring it all up for you.'

Tori opened her eyes and shook her head. 'No, it's not that. I've had a tough few days on the personal front as well as the work front. It's...' She stopped. She was supposed to be talking to Lu about her story and her life, not her own.

'It's what?' Lu asked as Ali delivered the coffee and Lu's tea. She retreated to the counter quickly, possibly sensing the serious turn their talk had taken.

Tori smiled. 'It's nothing. Now, I came to talk to you about the visit I had with your mum, who's amazing, and to lock in an interview time with you and your gran if you're happy to speak to her about some dates. It will make sense if we do the interviews on the same day. I had a word with Ali last week, and she said we could do the interviews here, which would be perfect.'

Lu sipped her tea. 'Whatever's going on, if there's anything I can do to help, let me know.'

A lump rose in Tori's throat at the sincerity of Lu's words. She could tell she meant every one of them. 'It's not a big deal,' she finally said. 'When you think of what you've been through and the women from the Footscray house.' She took a deep breath. 'I found out on Sunday that I'm adopted. I'm still trying to put my head around it, that's all.'

Lu's eyes widened. 'That's all! Are you kidding? That's huge. No wonder you look, no offence, but... kind of terrible.'

Tori couldn't help but laugh at Lu's honesty. 'I feel kind of terrible. I'm unsure what to do next. Should I track down my biological family, for example? Do I even want to know who they are? I'm not sure about any of it.'

'I guess there's no rush to make any decisions,' Lu said. 'You've gone years without knowing anything about them. Waiting until you're sure of how you feel isn't going to change anything.'

Tori considered Lu's words, realising how insightful she was. She was right. There was no urgency to do anything other than let it settle on her.

'How're your parents going with you finding out about this? If they didn't tell you for all these years, I imagine it's not easy on them.'

Tori felt a rush of guilt when she thought of the brief text message she'd sent her mother to say she was alive and would be in touch when she was ready to talk. 'I haven't spoken to them since they told me on Sunday.' She sighed. 'I'll drop in after work today or tomorrow to let them know that we're good. Now, speaking of mothers, yours is the real reason I wanted to catch up with you. And I should apologise. Unloading my personal problems isn't something I usually do. I'm normally much more professional than this, I promise. So, your mum, she's an amazing lady.'

'There's no need to apologise,' Lu said, 'but as for Mum, yes, she is. And...' she smiled '...you'll never guess who's visiting her on Saturday.'

Tori shook her head, not knowing where this might be going.

'Cole,' Lu said, laughing as Tori's mouth dropped open.

'No way?'

Lu nodded. 'She's got a new man in her life. You might have met him with the story you're doing at the Wellness Centre. Ethan?'

'I did meet him,' Tori said, remembering the good-looking trauma counsellor she'd met. 'That's great news on both fronts. Although is she meeting your mum with any agenda in mind? She's not going there to yell at her, is she?'

'No. She's started having some flashbacks and remembering some of Dad's violent and aggressive behaviour.'

'That's fantastic,' Tori said and then backpedalled quickly. 'Not that it happened, of course, but that she's realising that your mum is a victim. I wonder if she'll be willing to be involved in the story.'

'Probably best to see how the visit goes first,' Lu said. 'I'll chat to her afterwards if you like though, and let you know.'

'That would be great, and in the interim, if you can check with your gran what day suits her for an interview, I'd appreciate it. I've left her a couple of messages, but I haven't received a response.'

Lu laughed. 'She hardly uses her mobile phone, so if you're calling that number, you probably won't get a response. Best to try her landline. But as far as interviews, we can probably work around you. I don't think either of us are even a tenth of how busy you are. Just give us a few days and times to choose from.'

'Sounds good,' Tori said, sipping her latte. 'Now.' She nodded towards Lu's sketchbook. 'We need to plan a way to get you some exposure.'

Twenty minutes later, Tori left Lu and walked at a brisk pace back to her apartment. She was still in her activewear and needed to get ready for work. She wondered if she could give Cole Langrell a call but dismissed the thought as quickly as she had it. The last thing she wanted to do was put Cole off a visit that was so many years overdue.

Cole had tossed and turned the previous night, grateful for Ethan's strong arms around her, even though she knew she was keeping him from sleep. At one stage, when she was thinking through what she was going to say to her mother, she wondered if she was unable to sleep, too. From everything her gran had said when she'd called Cole late that afternoon to check she was still going, she assumed her mother was also having a sleepless night.

Now, as they drove into the visitors' car park at Winchester prison, Ethan reached over and squeezed Cole's knee. 'You okay?'

Cole's response was internal. No was the answer. Her stomach was churning, and she was glad that she hadn't eaten anything that morning, or she assumed she'd be seeing it again.

'It's completely understandable if you're not,' Ethan continued. 'I imagine your mum's probably a nervous wreck as well. This is something she's dreamed of for the past twenty-eight years.'

Cole nodded. He was right, of course. She turned to Ethan as he pulled to a stop. 'Thank you.'

He switched the car off and turned to her. 'For what? I haven't done anything other than drive you here.'

'Yes, you have. You've been my sounding board and helped me decide to do this. And knowing you'll be here after this visit means a lot. I have no idea how I'm going to feel.'

Ethan squeezed her hand. 'There's no right or wrong way to feel. You know that, don't you?'

Cole nodded. 'I say it to our clients almost every day. It's much easier to preach this stuff than live it.' She took a deep breath and opened the car door. 'Here goes.'

\* \* \*

June sat on her bed, her leg tapping nervously. She'd been awake all night, trying to work out the best approach to talking to Nicole. She still wasn't sure what she was going to say or how her daughter was going to receive her. What if she started yelling at her like Doreen's son did? Should she sit there and take it? She guessed she wouldn't have much choice. If that's what Nicole needed to do for her own healing, then there would be at least one positive outcome.

But that wasn't all that was worrying her. One of the guards had given her news before breakfast that she had another visitor requesting to visit her the next day. Her best friend – her best friend, who she'd asked to keep a secret that could destroy everything she held dear.

She stood and started pacing for the millionth time.

'Would you sit down?' Doreen said, walking into June's room. 'We can hear your feet scuffling on the floor from miles away.' She smiled so that June knew she was kidding. 'Should I ask how you're holding up? I can see the answer, but it feels rude not to ask.'

June forced a smile, her thoughts moving back to Nicole and not the other visitor. 'As much as I'm looking forward to this, I'm kind of wishing it was already over with. Or at least the first few minutes so that I know how she's going to react.'

'Unfortunately, if I'm speaking from personal experience, I don't have a good story to share. But hopefully, your daughter will be more mature than my son and be ready to have a proper conversation.'

June nodded. She hoped so, too. But now, she was faced with another concern. What if Nicole did forgive her, and they were able to move on, and then her secret was revealed? She closed her eyes. She couldn't bear the thought of possibly having Nicole back in her life and having her ripped away again. She opened her eyes again, mustering as much strength as she could. For almost three decades, she'd lived one day at a time, putting one foot in front of the other. Today was no different. She needed to see her daughter and worry about the other situation if it became relevant.

## 20

Cole's stomach churned as she went through the admissions process. It was hard to believe her sister and gran did this on a regular basis, and she imagined the procedure at the maximum security had been even more gruelling. When her details had been approved and her bag stored in one of the lockers, a guard motioned to her to follow her. She walked down a long corridor until they reached a secured door that led outside. She followed the guard out to an inviting garden area. There were tables with chairs scattered around, mostly occupied by people. The women in their blue prison uniforms all looked so normal. She wasn't sure what she'd expected: shaved heads and neck tattoos, perhaps. They ranged in age, too, from much younger than herself to women who looked like they should be in nursing homes, not prisons.

'She's over there,' the guard said, pointing to a woman sitting on her own at the table farthest from them.

Cole hesitated as she locked gazes with her mother. Her eyes instantly filled with tears. No matter what her mother had endured in the years she'd been inside, her eyes still held the same warmth and love she remembered as a child. Today, they had an added layer of fear. Cole stopped, realising she'd seen that look in her mother's eyes before. She closed her eyes momentarily, trying to move past the memory, but she couldn't. She must have only been seven or eight and remembered her mother waking her in the middle of the night, saying they needed to go next door. She couldn't remember exactly what reason her mother had given, but she did remember that look in her eyes. She opened her eyes again and continued walking. Why did she only remember this now and not earlier?

June was wiping her eyes as Cole reached her. They stared at each other for a moment before June spoke. 'You've no idea how long I've dreamed of this moment. I've missed you, Nic, sorry, Cole. I've missed you so much.'

Cole continued to stare at her mother. Her memory of her mother was of a woman who would have been a similar age to Cole now. In her thirties, young and attractive. She was still attractive, but she was an old woman compared to Cole's last recollection of her.

'Would you like to sit down?' June asked, indicating to the chairs.

Cole sat, unsure of what to say. Finally, she managed to speak. 'This is strange.'

June nodded. 'For me, too. I'm sorry for everything you've been through. I do have some idea of how hard this has been on you. If I could turn back time, I'd do everything differently, and we wouldn't be sitting here today as strangers.'

Cole nodded. 'I've been starting to remember some things about Dad.'

'About that night?'

Cole shook her head. 'No, but other incidents. The time he threw a beer bottle at you, which ended up cutting Lu's foot. And just now, I remembered you waking us in the middle of the night and taking us next door. There are other memories, too, but they're currently the clearest ones.'

'Your father was a troubled man,' June said. 'He loved you and Lu. You were the most important thing to him in the world. Never believe otherwise when it comes to that. He also never hurt you.'

Cole's fingers moved up to her forehead. 'What about this scar? I can't remember where I got it.'

'You tripped on the rocks leading to the front door.'

'So, nothing to do with Dad?'

June looked away.

'Really?'

June let out a breath. 'Indirectly related to your dad. You and Lu were playing outside and he was angry with me. He threw a vase and it missed and hit the wall behind me. You heard the smash and were running in to see if everything was okay when you tripped and fell. Your dad was at your side within seconds and had you to the emergency department of the hospital within about ten minutes. They glued it but it didn't need stiches. You falling was an accident. Your dad didn't hurt you.'

'Why did he hurt you then?'

'I wish I knew the answer to that,' June said. 'It's a question I've asked myself again and again. All I can say is that it's what he grew up with. His father was an abusive alcoholic, and that behaviour can repeat itself, particularly in men. What was different was that Alan's father beat all the family, including your dad. When he drank, your dad was violent and verbally abusive, but only ever to me. It's like he had to have an outlet for it, and they often say people take out their problems on the person they love most. I hope that was the case anyway. I need to have something to take away from this that wasn't truly terrible.'

Cole thought of the various clients she'd worked with over the years who'd dealt with this kind of abuse. Many had said similarly that it was the underlying love their spouse had for them that kept them in the relationship for longer than it should. 'Did I see what happened that night?'

June considered the question. 'You have no memory of it?'

Cole shook her head.

June remained silent for a moment before taking a deep breath. 'Yes, you did see what happened, and the fact that you were in the room at the time was my biggest regret. I'd put you and Lu to bed an hour or so earlier, but you'd either not been asleep yet, or maybe you'd heard your dad raise his voice. He'd had too much to drink and was extremely angry. He'd been verbally abusive to begin with, but then had left the room, and I hoped he'd finished. But then he returned with the block of kitchen knives.' June closed her eyes. 'Told me to pick one.'

Cole's hand flew to her mouth as a visual image of the knife block flashed across her mind. 'I remember those knives.'

'Then when I didn't, he took out his own choice of knife and threatened me with it. It was the first time he'd ever gone that far, but he had a look in his eyes that frightened me more than any other time. I truly believed he was about to stab me. It was at this point that you appeared in the doorway of the kitchen.' June shuddered at the memory. 'You looked terrified: a reflection of how I felt.'

Another memory flashed in front of Cole's eyes. Her father had turned to look at her but then had looked back at her mother.

'He saw me,' Cole said, 'but I don't remember anything after that.' How could she have blocked this out for so long and done her best to convince Lu and their gran that their mother was a liar? That their father had been a great man?

June nodded. 'He looked at you, which is possibly what saved me. He turned towards you, and that's when I pushed him away and grabbed another knife from the block. And... well, we know the rest.'

The two women sat in silence.

'I'm sorry if that's brought up memories for you,' June finally said. 'Part of me has always been relieved that you had blocked it out, but another part wanted you to remember so you knew it was self-defence. I'm not sure what he was capable of that night, but I think it could have easily been me who was killed. I'd like to think he wouldn't have hurt you or Lu, but that night, I wasn't convinced that he wouldn't.'

'Gran said you tried to save him, even after you stabbed him?'

'I never meant to kill him,' June said. 'I just didn't want him hurting us. He was on the floor with blood pouring out of his stomach. I grabbed clothes and an old sheet and, with your help, we tried to stop the bleeding. You were almost hysterical at this stage. I remember thinking that I'd ruined your life. That you'd never recover from this and that I should never have allowed us to be in that situation. That I should have got out much earlier.'

'I don't remember that,' Cole said. 'I have this image of blood washing down the plughole in the shower, but I always assumed I imagined that.'

'Mum, as in your gran, came over straightaway. I called her after I called the police. I imagine she got you cleaned up – the blood was real. We were both covered in his blood from trying to stop the bleeding. They took me away as soon as they arrived. Asked a few questions, but I told them straight up that I'd killed him, so I guess they didn't have any reason not to arrest me. I am sorry. You've no idea what torture it's been reliving that night again and again and wishing I'd done everything differently.'

Cole nodded, the lump in her throat so large she couldn't speak.

Tears continued to run down June's cheeks. 'Lu said to me that both of you remembered your dad as a generous and loving man, and that's why you found it so hard to believe me. I want you to know that you aren't wrong in that memory. When he was sober, he was a fantastic dad. He loved the two of you so much, which was probably the only thing that stopped him from opening a bottle of beer as soon as he woke up. He used to take you on outings and read to you and make up a lot of games.' She gave a brief smile. 'Do you remember Pussycats Rush?'

Cole nodded. It was a game her father had made up. She and Lu were the cats, and he would stand between them and their target blindfolded. When he would call out "Pussycats, rush", they'd run as fast as they could to try and get past him.

'You played that for hours, always ending up in a heap on the ground laughing.' June wiped her cheeks. 'I think this is part of why I didn't leave. I knew he was a great dad. But he was a terrible drunk.'

'We had a lot of good times, didn't we?' Cole felt that she had to check that she hadn't been looking at her childhood through an idyllic lens.

June nodded. 'We did. Outings and family holidays, as well as having fun at home. For me, there was always the black cloud, wondering if the day would merge into the night and continue to be fun or whether I could expect a beating. And often, on the days after there had been an incident with your dad, he'd be extra lovely towards you girls. I wasn't sure if it was because he felt guilty or because he thought he'd rub my nose in it that he loved the two of you but perhaps didn't love me.'

'I don't know why I convinced myself that you attacked him unprovoked,' Cole said.

'You were ten,' June said. 'The memory you have sounds like what was shown on the news at the time and what ended up in the court reports. If you blacked out the actual events of the night, then it would be easy enough for the false reports to create an image in your mind.'

'I wonder if I'll ever remember everything?'

June sighed. 'In all honesty, I hope you don't. It was an awful scene. He didn't die immediately, so he was suffering, and there was more blood than you can imagine. Then the emergency services...' She shuddered. 'It's something I do my best not to relive, and I'd suggest the same for you.'

\* \* \*

The two women lapsed into their own thoughts before Cole broke the silence. 'I'm sorry.'

Tears filled June's eyes.

'I should have been more open to believing your version of the story. One of the many therapists I've seen over the years told me that I needed to acknowledge that I was holding on to the anger I felt towards you for abandoning Lu and me and that had clouded all my thought processes. It's only more recently that I've begun to realise the truth in that.'

June closed her eyes, the resentment and anger she'd done her best to keep suppressed for years rising within her. When she'd first been imprisoned and Cole had refused to visit, she'd felt hurt, but also understood that her daughter had experienced a traumatic event, and it would take time. But when years passed and still no contact, anger had mixed with that hurt and had grown.

She opened her eyes, trying her best to control her voice. '*Abandon?* I didn't *abandon you*, I was protecting you. Both of you.

Who knows what he would have done that night if I hadn't taken charge? I saved all of us and I lost my freedom and my chance of a normal life in the process.' June did her best to keep her anger from showing. 'Do you really not understand what I did for you and Lu?'

'You left us without parents,' Cole said, her voice rising a notch. June watched as her daughter took a deep breath, visibly trying to calm herself. 'Yes, I get that you gave up a lot. Lu, Gran and many of the counsellors I've dealt with have tried to convince me of that for years. What they can't convince me of is that it needed to happen. If you'd spoken up earlier, you wouldn't have put any of us in that situation. Why didn't you?'

June stared at her daughter, the resentment she'd felt only moments earlier fizzling out at her words. She was right. Their lives could be very different if she'd made different choices and decisions.

'I wasn't a strong person, back then. The way Alan spoke to me, I honestly thought I deserved the treatment he gave me and because he could be so lovely I didn't think anyone would believe me. And I didn't want to take your dad away from you and Lu. In hindsight I know he was a terrible husband and man, but he loved the two of you and he made sure you knew it. I was a different person, Cole. That's what it comes down to. I was weak.' She locked eyes with her daughter. 'And I'm sorry.'

The two women lapsed back into silence, each digesting the other's hurt and words.

'You're a different person now,' Cole said. 'You're stronger.'

June nodded. 'As you can imagine. I've learned a lot from what I've been through. I have so many regrets, but all I can do is live each day as it comes and hope for a better life.' She smiled. 'Having you here today, even if what we have to say is difficult, is one of those better days for sure.'

Cole nodded, a lone tear running down her cheek. 'I could have been visiting you for the last twenty-eight years.'

'And as much as I wish you had been, it could be argued that it's probably better that you didn't. The last place was quite confronting compared to this.' June nodded towards her surroundings. 'Winchester is like a holiday camp in comparison.'

'Was it that bad?'

'Yes. But the one thing I learned from maximum security was to only look ahead, never look back. I'd say that to you, too. Don't look back to that night or anything relevant to my prison stay. Let's look ahead now and hopefully have a chance to get to know each other again. If you're open to it.'

Cole nodded slowly. 'I think I am.'

\* \* \*

June reached across and squeezed her hand. 'Tell me something about your current life. Both Lu and Mum have kept me up to date to an extent, but I'm sure there's a lot about you that they don't even know.'

Cole smiled. 'I'm not sure where to even start. If I'm not looking back, then I guess it's the current situation. I have a great job working at a Wellness Centre in Hawthorn, which is also near where I live. And then there's Ethan...' She blushed as she said his name. It was all still so new, but now that both Lu and her gran knew, her mother might as well, too.

'What's he like?'

'Lovely and gorgeous,' Cole said. 'We've got him to thank for me being here. He made me think about what I had to gain from talking to you rather than what I had to lose. He's waiting out in the car for me.'

'Please tell him thank you from me,' June said. 'And that I hope I get to meet him once I get out.'

'Lu said you have a parole hearing on March 1st,' Cole said. 'That's next week. How are you feeling about that?'

'Nervous,' June admitted. 'Nervous that it might not happen and nervous that I might get out too. I'm not sure how adjusting to the real world is going to go. They've started sessions here trying to get me ready in case it does happen. But I don't think anything will prepare me, to be honest. I'm grateful I have somewhere to go. I've known women who got out of Trendall and had no one. They were relying on shelters.'

The conversation continued, and Cole couldn't believe it when a guard told them there were only five minutes left.

When the five minutes were up, Cole stood and stared at her mother. They'd chatted for close to two hours, and she had to admit, she'd loved the time they'd spent together. 'You're the same,' she said as they were about to say their goodbyes. 'I wasn't sure what to expect, but it feels the same to be around you.' And it did. The feeling of comfort and security her mother had always emitted was still there.

'The strength and independence you had as a ten-year-old is still there too,' June said, 'but seeing you as a woman is quite a shock.' She self-consciously touched her hair. 'No doubt it's a shock to see me looking so old. I know it is for me anytime I look in the mirror. Now, you'd better not keep Ethan waiting any longer, and again, thank him from me.'

Cole nodded. She desperately wanted to hug her mother but wasn't sure if she should. Would it seem strange that she'd gone from hating her for years to needing that comfort from her?

Her mother appeared to sense her dilemma and opened her arms.

Cole walked into them and found herself wiping her face

seconds later as tears cascaded down her cheeks. June wrapped her arms around her and held her tight, exactly as she'd done when Cole was a little girl. Any time she'd hurt herself or something had gone wrong, she'd known she could count on her mother to be there for her. Her tears increased as she again questioned why she hadn't been there for her mother.

'You're here now,' her mother said, seeming to understand what the tears represented. 'And I couldn't be happier.'

'Marlow,' one of the guards interrupted them. 'Time's up.'

Cole squeezed her mother one last time, and they broke apart. She smiled. 'I'll arrange another time to come back and see you.'

June wiped her eyes. 'I'd love that.'

June couldn't suppress her tears after Cole's visit. She lay on her bed, a mixture of gratitude and terror swirling through her. She and Cole had had the opportunity to voice their underlying anger and resentments and they'd forgiven each other. There was a chance for a relationship to move forward. A chance to have her family back.

But her visitor tomorrow also had the power to destroy all of that.

Why would she be coming back now? There was no scenario June could imagine where the visit wasn't going to bring with it bad news and possibly destroy her family relationships.

She thought of her dead husband as she wiped her tears. What had she done to deserve this punishment? While on paper, she might be a convicted murderer, she'd always tried to be a good person and look where it had landed her. The one thing she did know was if her secret was revealed – and her relationships with her mother and daughters were destroyed – then she'd wasted the last twenty-eight years trying to survive. Without her family, there'd be nothing to live for.

\* \* \*

Lu found herself walking miles on Saturday. Her clients, William and Kate, two large Bernese mountain dogs, were happy with the extra attention. She found it difficult to call these two by name. They had big floppy ears and tongues that hung out of their mouths as they panted through the walk. They should have been called something like Daisy and Pete, not named after the royals. Still, that was the least of her worries. Her mind was distracted by thoughts of her mother and Cole.

She glanced at her watch as she passed Future Blend for the third time in the past two hours. It was almost two already. The visit would have been over a couple of hours ago.

'Hey, speedy,' Ali called to her from the café window. 'Those dogs probably need a drink, even if you don't.'

Lu stopped, realising Ali was right. She was thirsty, too, and other than a banana, she hadn't eaten anything all day.

She tied the dogs to a pole outside the café and met Ali, who was already coming out of the door with two bowls of water. She passed one to Lu.

'Are you being paid for this long with these two? I thought it was usually for an hour.'

Lu smiled. 'It is normally. I'm distracted and have nothing better to do. Kate needs to lose some weight, so it'll probably help.'

'Thinking about your mum?'

Lu nodded. 'It'd be so amazing if Cole hasn't backed out and even forgiven her. I think I'm probably dreaming on both accounts, but I'd give anything for that to happen.'

'I think you're about to find out,' Ali said, indicating behind Lu.

She turned to see Cole and Ethan walking hand in hand towards them. Nervous energy rippled through Lu. This was a good sign, wasn't it? That they'd come to see her? But then again, why would she bring Ethan unless that was for moral support because it hadn't gone well?

'Relax,' Ali said in a low voice. 'Whatever's happened has happened. You can't control this one, hon.'

She was right, of course, but telling someone to relax was never received well, and it wasn't on this occasion either. Lu was tempted to snap back at Ali but instead took a deep breath, concentrating on the fact she'd called her 'hon' instead. None of this was Ali's fault.

She smiled as they arrived at the café. Regardless of the outcome of the morning, she was happy to see Cole with such a nice guy. But before she could stop herself, she blurted out, 'Did you go?' She bit her lip. She had planned to let Cole do the talking when she was ready, so it was not a great start.

'Hello, Lu,' Cole said, sarcasm dripping from her greeting as she laughed. 'And how are you this fine day?'

Ethan poked Cole in the side. 'Don't torture her.'

Cole dropped his hand, stepped towards Lu and gave her a hug. 'Thank you.'

'What for?'

'For pressuring me for years to go and visit. I know it ended up being a few decades overdue, but I'm so happy I went today. We had a long talk, and I was reminded of what a great mum we have.'

Lu pulled back from Cole to look her in the eye. 'You forgave her?'

Cole nodded.

'Have you told Gran?'

'Not yet, I wanted to tell you first. I'll give her a call later.'

Lu shook her head. 'No, she'll be sick with worry.' She slipped her phone from her pocket. 'I'll call her now.'

'Just tell her it went well, and I'll phone her for a proper catch-up later today.'

'This calls for a celebration,' Ali said as Lu walked away from the group to make her call.

When Lu returned, Cole and Ethan were seated at the outdoor table closest to the two dogs.

'Ali's bringing us coffee and cake to celebrate,' Cole said as Lu slipped into a seat beside her.

'Gran started crying,' Lu said, wiping her own eyes as she relayed the information. 'Said it was the happiest day of her life, and she can't believe she's alive to see it.'

She saw Ethan squeeze Cole's hand and instantly loved Cole's boyfriend for it. Lu was sure he knew Cole well enough to know that the comment she'd made might upset Cole. That she'd caused so much unhappiness for both Lu and their gran. But Lu wasn't going to apologise either, as this is how it was.

'So, what now?' Ali asked, delivering a tray of food to the table and sitting next to Lu. 'Coffees will be here in a minute.'

'What now is a big celebration when Mum's released,' Cole said. 'Just us, as I'm sure it's going to be overwhelming enough when she does get out. But I was thinking we should try and remember all her favourite foods from before she was arrested and make sure there's a huge spread.'

'Great idea,' Lu said. 'Gran should remember a lot of that. I can't remember too much about food, except that she always drank a lot of tea. She had that friend with the funny teapot. Remember, she lived next door. What was her name?'

Cole frowned. 'I can't remember, but I should remember. Her husband was nice too. They called Mum "Ju". I remember that cause I thought that it was weird that Mum had another name. I guess we heard Gran and Dad call her June, but Ju was different. Like she was another person, not our mum.' Cole smiled. 'I was little, I guess. We spent heaps of time with them. Didn't the guy help Dad renovate that back part of the house? We ended up having it as a playroom.'

'That's right,' Lu said. 'And she made those yummy brownies. I remember that.'

'And the raspberry sponge cake,' Cole said. 'Mum used to say we liked the neighbour's cakes better than hers, and Dad said the only way we could test it was for Mum to make more cakes, so we had something to compare to. I remember them laughing, because Mum clearly knew he loved her cakes and wanted more.'

They lapsed into silence at the memory.

Eventually, Lu spoke. 'Imagine how different life would have been if Dad had been like that all the time? I wonder where we would all have ended up.'

'And the neighbour, Mum's friend. I wonder what ever happened to her,' Cole said. 'Has she ever mentioned her?'

Lu shook her head. 'No, although I do recall Gran mentioning a friend who had abandoned Mum when it all happened and how she would never be able to forgive her. I wonder if that was her?'

## 21

Following a second sleepless night, June's heart thudded as she watched her visitor walk along the path to the outside area. It was hard to believe it was the same woman who'd been her best friend for years. A woman she'd cut off within months of her arrest, their final conversation where June had thanked her for agreeing to keep her secret but had made it clear that she was never to contact her again.

Now, almost three decades later, tears filled her eyes as Vee approached her. Had June made the right decision to end their friendship all those years ago? She wondered if the situation had been reversed, whether she would have been willing to keep the secret that Vee had.

She wiped her eyes and stood as her former friend got closer. She imagined Vee was taking in how much June had aged over that time, in the same way she was. The last time she'd seen Vee, she had been in her early thirties, with jet-black hair and smooth skin. Now, presumably in her early sixties, her hair had turned a soft silver and was cut into a neat bob. Her brow was creased with lines, and her blue eyes, which had always been filled with joy, were swimming behind her fashionable glasses with a combination of tears and concern.

June opened her arms and pulled Vee to her. She felt the other woman melt into her, and they stood in silence until the guard called a gentle reminder. June pulled away and squeezed Vee's hand before indicating to the chairs.

'It's so good to see you,' she finally said, and even though she was worried about what the visit might bring, it was true. It was good to see her friend.

Vee's smile was tentative. 'I wasn't sure if you would agree to see me or not. You've got no idea how many times I've wanted to reach out. We wanted to let you know we were thinking of you. I know why you cut off all communication, and there's part of me that's always been grateful we've had so many years without having to face this, but there's part of me that's missed you so much. How are you, Ju?'

June closed her eyes momentarily. *Ju,* she hadn't been called that since before the night her life had changed. It was a reminder of a lifetime ago. She re-opened her eyes and smiled. 'Right now, I'm good. Very good. This prison is like a holiday camp compared to the maximum-security one, and I've got a parole hearing on Friday, so it's possible I'll even be leaving here soon.'

'That's wonderful news. That you're getting out, I mean, not that maximum security was so awful. The girls and your mum must be thrilled. How is Elena?'

'She's good. Always the trouper. I don't know how I can ever make it up to her. Having to raise the girls in the way she did.'

'You'd have done the same for anyone else,' Vee said. 'You know you would have. I'm sure she wouldn't have wanted it any other way.'

June nodded slowly. 'Yes, I'd like to think that I would have.'

'And the girls?'

'Lu's ecstatic. She's been wonderful since it happened. Coming in with Mum when she was little and then visiting on her own, once she was old enough to drive and make independent decisions. As much as I've missed out on, I still feel like I know her, which is amazing.'

'And Nicole?'

'She goes by Cole now,' June said, smiling. Having met her grown daughter the day before, she saw that the name fit her. It would still take some time to get used to, but at least she hadn't got rid of Nicole altogether. 'She changed her name when it happened, and took on Mum's surname too. And, you probably won't believe this, but yesterday was the first time since the night Alan died that I've seen her.'

Vee's mouth dropped open. 'What? Why?'

'She blamed me for destroying the family. For leaving them without parents.'

Vee frowned. 'That doesn't make any sense. Nothing that happened that night was your fault. You were put in an impossible situation.'

'It was impossible, yes. But Cole doesn't remember the night. Doesn't remember Alan going crazy or anything else. It's not uncommon to block out traumatic experiences, so up until recently, what she believed was what she read in police reports and the trial notes.'

'That's so unfair. Alan was a monster. I'm so sorry that I never saw what was going on. That you never felt comfortable to tell me.'

June sighed. 'Me too. In hindsight, I wish I'd done so much differently. I needed him out of our lives, but having covered up everything prior to that night so that we appeared like a happy family, I couldn't see any way out. Mum didn't even know what he was like until after I was arrested.'

'But the girls lived in the same house. Surely they were aware?'

'No, he was clever, and that's why Cole didn't believe the story of self-defence. He held it together in front of the girls and would leave it until they were out of the house or asleep.' June shuddered. 'He'd keep me up all night, tormenting me, threatening me and leaving bruises where no one would see them.' She cleared her throat as she forced the next admission out. 'He had even started raping me when he'd had a few drinks in him.'

Vee's eyes filled with tears again, and June's heart ached for her friend. She could only imagine how she would feel if their situations were reversed, and she was discovering that her friend needed help all those years ago and that she was oblivious to her situation. 'I remember one morning after he'd left me sore and terrified, coming into the kitchen to find him cooking pancakes for the girls, laughing and joking with them and then insisting we all go to the zoo for the day. I wanted to curl up in the foetal position and instead spent the day putting on a brave face for the girls and having to pretend we were a happy family. I look back now and can't believe that I went along with it. That I didn't ask for help. I must have been so weak.'

'You're the strongest person I know,' Vee said.

'You believe that, even with what I asked you to do?'

Vee nodded.

'I'm dreading asking this question, but as you've honoured my request not to visit or communicate for the entirety of the sentence up until today, why are you here?'

A cloud passed over Vee's face, causing June's heart to beat faster.

'You're not here with bad news, are you?'

Vee met her eyes, understanding June's concern. 'No, nothing like that.' She took a deep breath. 'As you know, you asked me to keep a secret when you were sentenced. A big secret.'

June nodded. 'I've thought about it every day since.'

'Yes. Unfortunately, we're not going to be able to keep that secret much longer.'

June closed her eyes. Vee had spoken the words she'd been up all night dreading. She could only imagine how Cole and the rest of the family would react. A cold, clammy sensation spread across her skin as she opened her eyes and struggled to find her voice.

'What? Why?'

Vee took a deep breath and began to explain.

'Should I be worried about you?' Doreen asked as June continued to stare at the television screen.

'What? Sorry?' She turned her attention to Doreen.

'Ever since your visitor was here, you've sat in front of the television staring at it, a blank look on your face. You didn't even notice that I turned it off after *Southern Insight*.'

June had noticed. She hadn't had the energy to comment.

'That anchor you like wasn't hosting tonight. The other one was back from maternity leave.'

June nodded.

'I guess you'll see her when she comes back to do your interview,' Doreen said.

June sat up taller. 'The interview. I'd forgotten about that.' She stood. 'I need to speak to my lawyer.'

'June, what's going on? You're acting strangely. What did your visitor say to you today? Was she family?'

June shook her head slowly. 'No, although years ago we were as close as family. I can't go into the details of what she said – all I can tell you is that I'm not doing the interview. Being on television and bringing any attention to myself is the last thing I need right now.'

## 22

Tori responded to an email from the Wellness Centre confirming the filming schedule for later in the week and pressed send, sighing as her inbox refreshed and six new emails arrived. As much as she loved her job, the administration side was, at times, overwhelming. She glanced through them, noting one was an approval for filming at Winchester prison. That was good. She wanted to speak with June again before confirming the date for the interview but had been waiting for the approval first.

She glanced at the other emails, hesitating when she saw one was from Heritage Link. The subject line read: *Your Heritage Link DNA results are in!*

She hesitated before opening the email. It provided a link to her account where her results were now sitting. She closed it again and squeezed her eyes shut. It had only been a little over a week since she learned she was adopted. Did she want to learn any more than that now?

'Knock, knock.'

She opened her eyes to find Penny standing in the doorway of her office. Anger welled up inside her. While the results and

Tori's past weren't Penny's fault, an irrational part of her wanted to blame someone and Penny was an obvious target.

'You okay?'

She nodded.

Penny moved into the office and sat in the chair across from Tori. 'You sure? You don't look it.'

'There's a lot going on.'

Penny nodded. 'Okay, well, to add to that, I came in firstly to let you know that my Heritage Link results arrived this morning, so if you don't want to know what your results are, delete the email when it arrives.'

'Did you look at yours?'

'Of course.' She grinned. 'Not related to the Hemsworths, though, so that's a good thing, I guess. Leaves the door wide open for something romantic to happen, but it turns out I'm part Italian!' Her eyes sparkled. 'I always wondered about those pasta cravings. And get this, I also have a bit of Irish and Scottish in me. Apparently, some of my ancestors lived in the Highlands. There are plenty of DNA matches too, but second cousin was the closest match. I had a quick look and the second cousin had put quite a lot of information in to their profile so I'll check that out later. The only drawback in finding relatives is that they need to have done the DNA testing through Heritage Link and shared their profiles.'

'But you didn't find any unwelcome news, like being adopted or having a different father than you thought or anything like that?'

Penny managed a wry smile. 'I'm not sure that the report would come right out and say that, but no, sorry. I kind of wish I had to make it up to you.'

Tori sighed. 'It's not your fault. It's unfortunate, that's all. My results arrived, but I'm not sure if I'm going to look at them or not. Have you spoken to Jaime or Sam?'

'No, I've messaged them and suggested we catch up for drinks soon if you're keen. That way, those who want to look at their results can share what they've found out. Think about it; we don't need to know your results, and it's a good excuse to have a drink together, not that we normally need an excuse.'

'I wonder if Jaime's going to look at hers,' Tori said.

'My guess is yes,' Penny said. 'And possibly keep them to herself.'

'I've got to admit I'm intrigued about what she might find out,' Tori said.

'Imagine if you lot let me film you for the story,' Penny said. 'We've probably got more drama unfolding around our personal quest than we're going to find in any of the others we're interviewing.'

'No thanks,' Tori said. 'I'll stick to being the interviewer, not the interviewee.'

'Speaking of interviewees,' Penny said, 'I'm sorry to say I'm also the bearer of bad news. June Marlow's lawyer contacted me this morning. They're declining the interview.'

Tori sat up straighter. 'What? Why?' All thoughts of the Heritage Link results were forgotten.

'They're concerned it will affect her chances of parole.'

'But it was confirmed that as long as we stick to the interview questions and Correctional Services sign off on the final copy before we go to air, it wouldn't.'

'I reminded the lawyer of that, but she said it wasn't negotiable. That we'd need to find someone else to tell their self-defence story.'

Tori's heart sank. 'But we're almost ready to film. There's been a heap of work put into this story already. The interviews with the mother and one of the daughters are scheduled for this week. I'm even hoping to get the other daughter to agree to be involved.'

'Salvage what you can, meanwhile we'll see if we can find ourselves another "June",' Penny said. She stood. 'Let me know about drinks when you can.'

Tori watched as Penny left her office, disappointment settling in her gut. June Marlow had been perfect for the interview. She was so relatable and so easy to feel sympathy for. Yes, she'd killed her husband, but regardless of what the law states, many viewers would feel he deserved it. No doubt there were other women in the same situation as June out there. It was going to be finding one that would be difficult.

She picked up the phone, all thoughts of her DNA results forgotten, and called Lu.

\* \* \*

Tori pushed open the door of the bustling Espy Hotel where Lu had suggested they meet. The place was lively, with patrons chatting animatedly and the clinking of glasses filling the air. She spotted Lu at a table near the back, looking pensive as she sipped her beer.

Sliding into the seat opposite her, Tori gave Lu a concerned look. 'Thanks for meeting me,' she said, her voice tinged with worry. 'I'm hoping we can do something to change your mum's mind. I'm just not sure what.'

Lu sighed. 'Her lawyer's still sticking to Mum's story that she's worried it will affect her parole, but when I spoke to her on the phone after you rang me, there was something in her voice... a hesitation. I think there's more to it than the parole concerns, but her lawyer wasn't sharing that information. I'll see what I can find out on Wednesday when I visit Mum.'

Tori nodded. 'Hopefully, you can convince her that it won't impact her parole. We can assure her that everything will be approved by Correctional Services before it airs, as well as by her and her lawyer. I tried to set up a meeting with her, but she refused.'

'Mum's not great with confrontation.' Lu gave a wry laugh. 'Which got her into this mess in the first place.' She shook her head. 'I shouldn't be joking about it, but you're right; you need to speak to her. Why don't you come with me on Wednesday? Maybe hearing it directly from you, with me there, will help ease her worries.'

'I doubt she'll agree to me visiting.'

'Leave it with me, I'll convince her to approve you.'

'You'd do that?'

Lu nodded. 'Absolutely. I want to tell her story as much as you do.'

Tori felt a weight lift off her shoulders, grateful for Lu's support. She stood. 'Let me get some drinks. Another beer?'

Lu glanced at her half-full glass and shrugged. 'Sure, why not.'

Tori realised an hour later that the discussion had mainly turned to her and how she was coping with the knowledge of being adopted.

'My mum's upset,' Tori told Lu. 'I dropped in and saw them over the weekend to let them know that they're still my world and all that, and I need some time to work out what I want to do if anything.' She narrowed her eyes and looked at Lu. 'What would you do?'

Lu considered the question. 'If I found out I was adopted. I'm not sure. I think the fantasy of finding some amazingly wonderful family is exactly that: a fantasy. I can't believe anyone who is in a great place in their life is going to give up a baby, so we can assume whatever the circumstances were, they weren't great for your mum. Your birth mum,' she corrected. 'Also, she hasn't come trying to find you either. She might not be alive, or she might have good reasons for why she doesn't want you to know who she is.'

'You're thinking along the same lines as me,' Tori said.

'But,' Lu added, 'I also know what I'm like, and even though I'd like to think I would respect her right to privacy if I had information on who she was, I'd probably still look at it.' She shrugged. 'Sorry, I realise I'm no help at all.'

Tori laughed. 'No, I think you're a lot of help, and you're probably confirming what I was thinking. I did an ancestry test a little while ago through Heritage Link, before I knew I was adopted. It was a birthday present. Supposed to be a bit of fun. But now there's the real possibility I could find out information about where I came from. I'm not sure I'll be able to not look at it.'

'Definitely not,' Lu said. 'Not knowing will eat away at you. Let's assume the DNA results tell you, or at least give you clues as to who your biological parents are. There's nothing to say you need to act on it. Although, I have to say, exploring family history's great. I did one a few years ago and loved finding out information about my grandparents and great-grandparents and where we originated from in the UK and Europe.'

'Did you reach out to any of the people?'

Lu shook her head. 'No, I was more interested in learning about my background. It'd be a bit weird suddenly getting in touch with distant relatives. Also, with Heritage Link, you only get their details if they happen to have done the DNA testing and set up a profile. I did have one third cousin message me through it but I was a bit vague in my responses. What was I going to tell her? That my mum killed my dad?' She grinned. 'I'm not sure they'd be rushing to invite me to Christmas lunch.'

Tori laughed. She loved Lu's outlook on life. This woman had been through a horrific trauma as a child but saw things with such clarity. June Marlow was lucky to have a daughter who was so easy-going and realistic in her outlook.

She glanced at her watch and sighed. 'I should get going. I've got a tonne of work to do tonight in preparation for the filming at the Wellness Centre. I was hoping to bump into Cole and see if I could get her involved in your mum's story now that she's visited, but if there's no story, that's a bit pointless.'

Lu stood. 'Hopefully, we can change Mum's mind on Wednesday and cross the Cole bridge afterwards.'

## 23

Cole wasn't sure whether to be happy or annoyed as the focus of her Wednesday group shifted away from the discussion around support systems and coping strategies to the interviews that *Southern Insight* was conducting.

'They asked if they could film me at home,' Lisa said. 'And now I feel like I need to get a cleaner in and possibly renovate the whole house first.'

Roberto's booming laugh had the group smiling. 'I think the program is about trauma,' he'd pointed out, 'it's not a home renovation show.'

'For those of you who've agreed to take part,' Cole said, 'how are you feeling about your stories being shared in this way?'

'I wasn't going to do it,' Shane said, 'but then I changed my mind. I'm not sure if telling my story will help anyone, but hopefully it does. I'm not the only one who hasn't been able to save my family, but I live with that every day. Coming here is helping.' He glanced at Roberto and smiled. 'Even putting up with you and your outbursts is strangely enjoyable.'

Roberto threw his arms in the air. 'I am here to help in whatever way I can.' The group laughed. It was nice to have a light-hearted mood for a change, although Cole didn't miss the look Roberto threw in Tom's direction. 'Are you going to talk about your trauma with the reporters?' he then asked Tom.

Tom's cheeks reddened. 'What, so other people can dismiss the extent of my trauma too?'

'I do not dismiss it,' Roberto said. 'I have come to realise that not everything is what it seems. That we don't always remember how events happened or want to remember what happened.'

Cole swallowed. Roberto was looking at her now. Did he know something about her situation?

'Do you agree, Capo?'

Cole nodded. 'Sometimes trauma is too much to cope with, so we don't. Our brains can block the memories or twist them into something they might not have been.'

Roberto continued to stare at her, and Cole shifted uncomfortably in her seat. How had he found out?

'I'm a good detective,' he said, his eyes trained on her face. 'Your own story might help others here.'

Bile rose in Cole's throat. She forced a little laugh, trying to shrug off the discomfort she was feeling. 'Let's move on,' she said. 'Ethan's asked those of you involved in the TV show to drop into his office before you leave today so you can discuss *Southern Insight*'s schedule further, but for now, I want to focus on your support networks and who, outside of here, makes up your team.'

Cole was still feeling rattled when the session wrapped up, and Lisa and Shane made their way to Ethan's office while the others said their goodbyes.

Roberto waited until everyone had left before standing and addressing Cole. 'You are so good at what you do, yet you do not share your story. Why is that?'

Cole's cheeks flushed. 'Firstly, there are professional boundaries as to what would be appropriate to share with the group, but also, I have no interest in sharing my personal life with the group. And how do you know my story?'

Roberto tapped the side of his nose. 'It was not hard to find out about your mother. The detective in me was curious. I am sorry for what you've been through.'

Cole nodded. She wasn't going to discuss her situation with Roberto.

'If I can do anything to help.'

'You can. Please don't talk about my situation to anyone or bring it up in our sessions again. It's been difficult and stressful.'

Roberto nodded. 'Your mother is also to appear on *Southern Insight*?'

Cole stared at him. None of that was public information, so how did he know? Her phone pinged with a text, giving her an excuse not to respond. She slipped the phone from her pocket.

> Mum's called off the TV interview. Going to visit later today to see if we can talk her around. Her story's too important not to share.

'Bad news?'

Cole looked up to see genuine concern in Roberto's eyes.

She shook her head. 'In answer to your question, no, my mother will not be telling her story. She's called off her interview.'

Roberto sighed. '*Che peccato*. Such a pity. I imagine she could help many women in similar circumstances to speak up and ask for help.'

Cole had to admit that she'd been relieved to read Lu's text, and she didn't want her mother's story to be made public. But, listening to Roberto now, she thought of women like Jacinta and what her mother's story could do to help them. She wondered why her mother had changed her mind. She'd find out from Lu later. For now, she needed Roberto to give her some space.

'I thought you were supposed to be finding out about Tom, not me,' Cole said.

'Ah, yes, and I have my feelers out. There is more to his story, but interestingly, several of the case files have restricted access, and my contacts haven't been able to give me too much information. Yet.' He smiled and tapped the side of his nose again. 'But don't worry, I will find out.'

Tori stepped out of her Mazda, glancing at the looming structure of the prison under the grey Wednesday morning sky. Lu climbed out from her Jeep and waved. She looked tense but determined, and Tori felt a surge of hope that this visit might persuade June to move forward with the story.

'She really agreed to see me?'

Lu nodded. 'It took a lot of persuading but eventually she agreed that she needed to tell you no in person.'

After navigating through the necessary security checks, they were led to the visiting area. June was already seated at a weathered picnic table, her expression hard to ascertain as they approached.

'I only agreed to this meeting, to not appear rude,' June said before either Lu or Tori had the chance to say hello. 'I won't be involved with the program and I'm sorry for the late notice with this. I'm sure you'll find someone else who you can feature.'

Tori looked to Lu, conscious that June couldn't meet her eye. She did her best to keep her tone calm and professional. 'I appreciate your concerns, but June, I promise we're here to help. If you were to change your mind, we can ensure that everything will be approved by Correctional Services before anything goes public. It won't impact your parole. Your story is too important not to tell. You could help countless women.'

June's expression turned stony. 'You don't understand. Of course I want to help others, and that is why I said yes to begin with. And it's not only about my parole. There are other factors.'

Lu frowned. 'What other factors?'

June's eyes darted around the room. 'I'm not going into that. I've been told it could affect my parole, and that's enough to turn me off the idea. The hearing's on Friday and confirming that I'm not going to participate removes it from being an issue, when they consider my release.'

'Who told you that?' Lu asked. 'I spoke to your lawyer, and she said no one has advised her of that, but she was following your wishes to pull out of the story.'

June shook her head. 'She shouldn't be telling you anything. And no, it wasn't Mackenzie. I haven't told her or anyone the full story. There are things you don't know, and I don't want them becoming public information because of a news story that doesn't benefit me in any way.'

Tori and Lu exchanged puzzled glances. 'What do you mean?' Lu asked gently. 'If there's something else going on, we need to understand. We want to help you.'

June averted her gaze, unable to look at either of them. 'There's information that will come to light in the coming weeks. When it does, you'll understand why I'm reluctant to share anything now. Just know, it's for the best.'

The conversation continued in this odd, unsettling manner, with June alternating between coherent arguments and cryptic warnings. Despite her controlled anger, there was an underlying fear that neither Tori nor Lu could quite grasp.

The visit ended on a strained note, with June standing abruptly and signalling to the guard that Lu and Tori needed to be escorted out.

Lu hugged her mother. 'Sorry, I didn't mean to upset you.'

'Oh, Lu,' June said, her pale face clouding with concern. 'It's not you. As I've said, there's something else going on, and I haven't worked out how best to deal with it. Once I do, I promise you'll have all the answers you need, and to be honest, you will probably wish you didn't have them.'

Tori followed behind Lu as the warden led them back to the main administration building to collect their belongings and go through the sign-out process.

Outside the prison, Lu let out a deep sigh, her shoulders sagging. 'I'm so sorry. I didn't expect her to act like that. I knew she was worried, but this, this is unexpected.'

Tori shook her head, trying to process the strange interaction. 'It's okay. I can see she's dealing with more than we thought.'

Lu nodded, looking troubled. 'I don't understand what she means by things coming to light and it all being for the best. I hope she's not going to end up back in prison after all.'

'Maybe it's the stress of everything?' Tori suggested. 'Being in here for so long, the pressure of parole and being released, and now the idea of going public with her story. For someone who's had little interaction with the outside world for close to three decades, it's a lot to handle.'

Lu sighed again. 'You're right. But she's made it clear that there's more. Something big by the sounds of it.'

Tori placed a reassuring hand on Lu's shoulder. 'We'll get to the bottom of it. One step at a time.'

Lu gave an appreciative smile. 'Thanks. I'm worried about her. More than ever now. I'm not sure any of us can take any more than we've already been through.'

Tori had to admit, she was worried, too. She hoped that whatever June was talking about wasn't going to affect her release or bring more stress to Lu and the family.

'Let me talk to Gran,' Lu said. 'If anyone can talk sense into Mum, it's her.'

Tori nodded. She was sure that today's visit to June was the last she would see of the Marlow family, but she could only hope she was wrong. This was a story she felt passionate about. One that needed to be told.

## 24

June was a bundle of nervous energy when she woke from a fitful sleep on Friday morning. The parole hearing would take place at ten o'clock, and Mackenzie promised to visit June as soon as she received formal notification of the outcome. June wasn't required to attend, and from everything her lawyer had advised her, it sounded like it would be a straightforward decision.

'There's nothing complicated about your situation,' Mackenzie had explained when they'd met earlier in the week. 'I'm guessing they'll have a decision quickly, most likely in your favour, and then they'll work out any conditions that might be imposed. You're not a threat to society, so I'm not expecting that to be much more than being assigned a parole officer and possibly counselling or a rehabilitation program. They might put restrictions on travel, but I'm not sure if they'll go to that extent.'

June wasn't sure there'd be any condition that would faze her as long as she could go home. *Home*. Her childhood home. She certainly wouldn't be returning to the Mount Waverley house. It would have been sold years ago, but it wasn't something she even wanted to see again.

'How are you holding up?' Doreen asked over a cup of coffee in the breakfast area.

'Nervous,' June admitted. 'I've been waiting for this day for so long.'

'And you've got a lot to look forward to now,' Doreen said. 'With Nicole also on the outside waiting for you. That must be a huge relief.'

June nodded. She hadn't admitted to Doreen that if her secret was revealed her whole world might come tumbling down. She was doing her best not to think about that and concentrate on one thing at a time.

Time appeared to stand still for most of the day, and June could only assume that when three o'clock came around, and she still hadn't heard anything from Mackenzie, the hearing hadn't gone well. It was taking too long.

'Marlow, visitor.'

June looked up from the garden bed, where she was crouched over, pulling weeds. The guard stood waiting for her.

'My lawyer?'

He nodded. 'Your mother and possibly your daughter are with her.'

'Did they look happy?'

The guard frowned. 'They're visiting a prison. No one looks happy. Now, come on.' He pointed to a nearby tap. 'Wash your hands, and then let's get moving. This is outside of official visiting hours, and the prison has made an exception.'

June hurried to wash her hands and followed him back into the building and to one of the visitor rooms.

Tears filled her eyes as she took one look at her mother and Lu's faces. Their cheeks were wet with tears but also flushed with happiness.

'Release was approved,' Mackenzie said before June had the chance to ask.

Her mother flung her arms around her and hugged her tight. She didn't need to say anything. The hug said it all.

Lu was next, and to her surprise, Cole had slipped into the room and offered her arms. June closed her eyes as her eldest daughter hugged her.

'I've missed a lot,' Cole said, 'but I wasn't going to miss this.'

'So,' Mackenzie said once they were all seated. 'It was straightforward as we expected. No objections or complications. There's some processing to be done, and you're set for release on the fourteenth.'

June's mouth dropped open. 'That's less than two weeks away?'

Mackenzie nodded. 'The conditions of the parole are good. Fortnightly meetings with a parole officer, a rehabilitation program, and, if you're open to it, a training program to help you get back into employment. That won't start for two weeks after your release to give you the chance to settle back into the outside world. Parole officer meetings will start immediately, the first being within a week of your release. This will all be gone through with you prior to the fourteenth in more detail.'

'I don't know what to say,' June said. 'I feel like I'm dreaming.' She smiled at Cole. 'Having you here is what also makes this feel like a dream. I can't believe it.'

Cole smiled. 'Believe it. I'll take the day off so I can come and collect you with Lu and Gran.'

Lu reached across and squeezed her hand. 'Yes, Mum, believe it. You're coming home, and nothing's going to ruin that.'

June closed her eyes, willing with every bit of her that Lu was right. That everything would go smoothly. Surely, after everything she'd been through, she deserved a chance at happiness.

\* \* \*

Lu found herself knocking on the door at Future Blend, a bottle of champagne in hand. She could see Ali behind the counter and knocked again.

Ali hurried over to open the door, her face breaking into a wide smile when she saw what Lu was holding. 'I can only imagine that means she's being released?'

Lu nodded, so overwhelmed she wasn't sure if she could even speak.

Ali took her in her arms. 'This is the best news ever. I'm so happy for you, hon. I can't wait to meet your mum. I'm guessing you get a lot of your strength from her. I love that you've pushed Cole to reconnect with her and that you've stayed strong by her side for all these years. You're an inspiration.'

Lu blushed at Ali's enthusiastic praise. She wasn't sure she was as deserving as Ali was making out, but it was nice to know she had her back. She held out the bottle of champagne. 'All I know right now is that I want to celebrate, and there was only one person I wanted to do that with.'

\* \* \*

Tori was glad the week was over. Being Saturday morning, she'd enjoyed lying in bed later than usual. Sunny had curled up with her initially and purred as he slept in the crook of her arm. But he'd eventually remembered it was way past his breakfast time and demanded Tori get up and feed him.

Now, mid-morning, she sat at the kitchen table, her laptop open in front of her and a cup of tea growing cold beside it. Sunny was stretched out on a chair next to her, snoring softly.

Her heart raced as she stared at the email notification from

Heritage Link. Lu's words had played over in her mind since their drink earlier in the week when she'd confided in her. *Not knowing will eat away at you. Let's assume the DNA results tell you, or at least give you clues as to who your biological parents are. There's nothing to say you need to act on it.*

Lu was right. She didn't need to do anything more than hopefully gather some information about where she came from. Like Lu said, it could be interesting to find out some of her history.

With a deep breath, she clicked on the email. The words swam before her eyes for a moment before they settled into clarity. *Your Heritage Link DNA results are in!*

She clicked on the link, her mind buzzing with anticipation and dread. She clicked through various screens to explain how to interpret her results and what they could mean, stopping when she reached the key information.

She frowned as she read through the initial findings. Was this some kind of joke? There's no way this could be correct. Absolutely no way. She refreshed the screen, seeing the same information. No, it couldn't be right. This was saying she shared 2800cM – centimorgans – with a close family member.

She'd already realised in reading through how to translate the results that the level of centimorgans was relevant to a full sibling. But she didn't have a sibling. She leaned back in her chair, realising that, of course, it was possible that she did. It hadn't crossed her mind that her biological parents had more children than her. She'd assumed that she was an unwanted pregnancy to a couple that were unlikely to be together. But a full sibling suggested this wasn't the case.

Sunny stretched, opening one eye, and looked at her. She reached across and stroked his head, feeling some comfort from its softness, before clicking on the link that showed her DNA match. Her mouth dropped open. She knew this person.

She clicked on the profile and saw a second sibling, parents and grandparents listed. If this was her biological family, there would have been a lot of them.

'This can't be right, Sunny. It can't be.' Her pulse throbbed in her temples, and the room tilted slightly.

As Sunny moved himself onto her lap, she scanned the results further, and the implications deepened. Siblings. She'd always dreamed of a sibling when she was growing up, and it turned out she had them. She hadn't known. She also had grandparents, possibly aunts and uncles too, although they weren't listed. Her thoughts raced, trying to piece together the puzzle. She had always thought of herself as an only child, but now, family were out there, connected by blood.

The one thing she needed was answers. Her parents had implied they knew nothing of her biological parentage. What else had they lied about?

She lifted Sunny from her lap and stood abruptly, the chair scraping against the floor, and paced the room. The cat wriggled in her grip and meowed.

She kissed him on the head and put him down on the couch. 'Sorry, Sun, I've had a bit of a shock.' That was an understatement.

After a few moments of frantic pacing back and forth, with Sunny watching her as if he were watching a game of tennis, she stopped and took a deep breath. Her parents had always been there for her. It didn't take a genius to understand why they'd kept this from her.

She picked up her phone and called her mother. Her fingers felt numb, and the ringing seemed to stretch on forever before her mother's familiar voice answered.

'Hi, darling. What's up?'

'I need to talk to you and Dad. It's important. Can I come over now?'

'Of course. Is everything okay?' She could hear the guarded concern in her mother's voice. No doubt she'd been expecting this call. Why hadn't she told Tori rather than letting her find out like this?

Tori swallowed hard, fighting back the wave of emotions threatening to overwhelm her. 'I'll explain when I get there.'

\* \* \*

Cole poured the tea into the two cups her grandmother had taken from the cupboard and placed them on the kitchen bench while Elena put the pastries she'd brought with her on a plate.

'I'm getting fat,' Elena said, patting her soft belly. She gave a little laugh. 'I've always used your mother's situation as my justification for eating my feelings. When she gets home, I won't be able to continue to do that. I'll either need to start exercising or, better still, have some self-control.'

Cole laughed. 'I'm guessing Mum might want to indulge in some treats when she gets home, so either choose the exercise option or delay doing anything for a few weeks.'

Elena nodded and Cole found herself studying her gran's face. 'Are you okay? You don't seem as excited as I thought you would be.'

Elena picked up a Danish and took a bite. She chewed it slowly, appearing deep in thought. 'As excited as your mother was about her release, I thought she seemed quite distracted yesterday. Like there was something else going on.'

'I imagine it's overwhelming,' Cole said. 'I wouldn't read too much into it.'

Elena opened her mouth, about to say something, but closed

it again. She sighed. 'Hopefully you're right. I'm not sure I can take too much more if there is something else.'

'Let's assume she's a little unsettled at the prospect of getting out,' Cole said. 'Now I want to make it up to her. Don't worry. I know that I'll never make up for what I did, but I can at least start trying to make a difference. Throwing a welcome-home party is a starting point. Something small: you, me and Lu, and Ethan and Ali, if you think Mum can handle meeting a couple of new faces?'

Elena nodded. 'I think that number will be fine. But I'll check with your mum first. She might prefer it just be you, me and Lu, and we can invite the others over on another day. Coming home will be a big deal.'

'I want to make some of her favourite food, too,' Cole said. 'I remember she loved tea, but I don't recall her drinking alcohol.'

'She didn't,' Elena said. 'She told me later that it was because of your dad. She didn't want you girls to grow up thinking drinking was normal, so she didn't drink at all. We should get some champagne, regardless. Even if she had been a drinker, she wouldn't have touched a drop for all these years, so I'm sure it's not something that she'll care about either way.'

The reference to alcohol made Cole think of Paul Dixson. She imagined he wasn't having too much fun now. She hoped that he stuck the rehab out.

'I'm proud of you,' Elena said. 'That you've taken the steps to allow your mum back in your life. I know it wasn't easy.'

'You shouldn't be proud of me,' Cole said. 'If anything, I'm more surprised that Mum's willing to forgive me.'

'Oh, Cole, she's more than aware that if she'd spoken up earlier the situation today would be very different and there'd be nothing to forgive. But, as she proved that night, she'd do anything for you and Lu. I can't imagine there's anything either of you could ever do that she wouldn't support you in, or in her case, protect you from. If you take nothing more from this, know that she was always your biggest supporter and protector, and I'm guessing she'll step straight back into that role if you'll let her.'

Tears welled in Cole's eyes as the truth of her grandmother's words settled over her.

\* \* \*

For Tori, the drive to her parents' house passed in a blur. She barely remembered navigating the familiar streets, her mind a whirlwind of thoughts and emotions. When she arrived, her parents were waiting in the living room, concern etched on their faces.

'What's going on?' her father asked as she sat down opposite them, clutching her hands in her lap. Their faces were as pale and strained as she imagined hers looked.

'I opened my DNA results today.'

Her mother let out a soft moan.

'We thought you'd decided not to find out who your biological family were?' her father said.

'Really? That's your response?'

Her parents exchanged a glance.

'No, of course not,' her mother said. 'As you can imagine, we were hoping you would choose not to find out, and we could forget all about it.'

'Forget that I have a whole family that I've been kept away from for my entire life? These aren't strangers either. They're people I've met. Neither of you thought I might be able to be a sister to my siblings? Have them to lean on and vice versa? Why didn't you tell me?' Tori's voice broke. 'Why keep this a secret?'

Her mother sighed; her eyes filled with tears. 'It wasn't our place to tell you, that's why. Your biological mother was never going to raise you and never planned to tell the rest of the family that you existed. Surely now you've learned who they are, you can understand why?'

'But we had a right to know. Me and my siblings. My extended family, too. Do you believe my mother told no one?'

'I know that's the case,' her mother said. 'She gave us the greatest gift anyone could ever give someone, and in repayment, we agreed to her terms. We moved away from the area and had a fresh start, which meant no one knew she had another baby, and no one knew you weren't biologically ours.'

'We promised never to make contact with her or any of the family again,' Dion added.

Tori lapsed into silence. If she removed herself from the situation and put her reporter's hat on, she could see what a brilliant plan they'd hatched. If it wasn't for the DNA test, there was no reason anyone would have ever known the truth.

'You'll need to speak to her, love,' her father said. 'She's the only one who can truly convey the state she was in when she made the decision to give you up.'

'Give yourself a day or two to process all of this,' her mother added. 'It's a lot. Once you're feeling up to it, you can consider reaching out to her. I'd be happy to come with you if you want to meet with her in person.'

Tori wasn't sure whether she'd want her mother there or not. In fact, right at this moment, she didn't know what to think at all.

## 25

Tori walked along the path, the late-afternoon sun casting long shadows on the ground. The air was warm, and the scent of freshly cut grass filled her senses... but she barely noticed. Her mind was consumed with thoughts of the woman she was about to meet with, the woman who had given her life and handed her over to another woman only hours later.

She'd been told where she'd find her mother and spotted her at one of the picnic tables that ran alongside a large, flowering garden bed.

Her biological mother looked up as Tori approached, her face a mix of apprehension and hope. She gestured to the seat across from her. Tori hesitated for a moment before sitting down, her eyes never leaving the other woman's face.

'I realise this is a huge shock.'

Tori didn't respond, allowing the silence to stretch between them, thick and heavy. Eventually, she took a deep breath, her hands clenched on the table.

'Why didn't you tell me when you first met me?' Tori's voice was barely above a whisper, but the intensity was unmistakable.

'I didn't know. I only found out a few weeks ago. The irony is I've been watching you on *Southern Insight* for many years and always felt a connection with you. It never occurred to me that you were my biological daughter.'

They sat in silence for a few moments.

'Can I ask you something?'

'Of course.'

'Did you name me? Surely that would have been a dead giveaway?'

She shook her head. 'No, I deliberately didn't, and I asked your mum and dad not to share what they named you with me. And their surname is Cox, not Blackwood, so there's no reason I would have ever thought it possible.'

'Cox wasn't a good television name,' Tori admitted. 'I was asked to change it.'

'I need you to understand that giving you up was the hardest thing I've ever had to do.'

'Even harder than murdering your husband.'

Silence settled between the two women as June digested Tori's angry words.

Eventually, June nodded. 'Yes, even harder than that.'

Tori ran a hand through her hair. 'Sorry, that was uncalled for. I'm struggling with everything right now.'

June looked down at her hands, her fingers twisting nervously. 'I thought it was for the best. After what happened...'

Tori's heart pounded. 'When we first spoke, you told me that your husband, my father, had taken to raping you. Was I the biproduct of that?'

June couldn't meet her eyes. 'I'm sorry, Tori; I am. It's one of the many reasons I didn't want you to find out. If Alan hadn't died that night, I would have taken off with you and Nicole and

Lu. It was what I'd been planning for the previous two weeks before the night of his death.'

'Did he find out?'

June nodded. 'I thought I'd been so meticulous in my planning and had everything worked out to the finest detail. I didn't count on him wanting to take us all to New Zealand to see his parents. He came looking for the passports and discovered mine and the girls' missing. I tried to play it down at first, but he made me show him where they were, and they were in an envelope with the birth certificates and a doctor's letter confirming my pregnancy.'

'That was the night he found out you were pregnant?'

'Yes, and he wasn't happy about it. Accused me of having an affair, which of course I hadn't, and the argument escalated.'

'And you killed him.'

June nodded.

Tori sat for a moment, processing this. 'If you hadn't been pregnant, do you think the argument would have had the same outcome? That he'd still be dead?'

June bit her lip, the tension on her face intensifying. 'Are you asking if being pregnant with you was the reason I killed him and I'm in prison?'

'I guess.'

'I think finding the passports packed up as they were would have sent him over the edge anyway. He was an intelligent man and would have put two and two together. Suitcases were also packed and hidden, which wouldn't have taken much for him to find. So yes, it would have had the same outcome, and you are in no way responsible for anything that happened. He was angry and threatened me with a knife.'

Tori let this sink in before moving on to a different direction of questioning. 'Are you planning to tell Cole and Lu about me?'

'Yes.' June's eyes filled with tears. 'I'll be telling my mother tomorrow and then Cole and Lu. Unless you'd prefer I didn't?'

'They should know,' Tori said. 'They should have known when I was born.'

'Maybe,' June said. 'But I need you to know that it was never an easy decision. I desperately wanted to tell my mother, but I knew she'd either talk me out of giving you to Sylvie and Dion or refuse to let them raise you without her involvement. She was almost sixty and suddenly forced to raise two young girls. Adding a newborn to this load was too much to ask.'

'Surely that was her decision to make?'

'She'd agree with you there, but I don't. There was more to it than that. I had no idea in those early days what impact killing Alan was going to have on Cole and Lu. I was thinking the very worst – that I'd destroyed their lives. How could I do that to a third child? One who didn't ever need to know what had taken place?'

June wiped a tear from her cheek and continued. 'When I was about six months pregnant I refused visitors except for Sylvie and Dion so Mum wouldn't know I was pregnant. With Sylvie and Dion's financial help we engaged a lawyer to make plans for you. There were a lot of legal hoops to jump through to have consent for adoption approved, but we were able to make it happen. I thought you would have a better life without the stigma of what I'd done hanging over you. It was an awful thing to do to Mum and the girls, and I've felt guilty ever since the day I kissed your forehead and told you I loved you. However, I knew that Sylvie and Dion would give you a good life. One that I couldn't give you. I was just grateful that the courts agreed and allowed them to take you home shortly after you were born.'

Tori digested June's words. She was right. Of course June couldn't have given her a good life, and knowing her mother was in prison could have affected Tori in many ways. Look at how it had shaped both Cole and Lu.

'There is one thing that I've been wondering about,' June said, 'and that's you doing the story for *Southern Insight*. It seems like too big a coincidence that you'd turn up here to do a story on me. It's one thing that you did a DNA test that would have led to me eventually but having already met all of us before you found out. That seems a little too convenient. And that you met Cole at the Wellness Centre before you met me the first time.'

Tori stared at her. She was right, of course. 'I was asked to cover both of those stories by the show's chief executive,' Tori said. She shook her head even as she said it.

'What is it?' June asked.

'The chief exec – Gav – is a friend of my parents. Could he have known who you were when he insisted I do the story?' She frowned. 'The DNA test was a present. I guess he might have been involved in getting me to take that. I'd like to think he wasn't, though. Penny, one of the producers of the show, is a good friend. I'd hate to think she was part of it.'

'The chief executive being involved makes sense,' June said. 'Although, if he was a friend of your parents, I wonder what he thought he'd achieve?'

Tori thought of her interactions with Gav over the last six months or so. 'My dad has had a battle with cancer,' she said.

'Oh, I'm so sorry,' June said. 'Vee didn't tell me that when she visited.'

Tori gave a wry smile. 'I'm guessing she had other priorities to discuss. Anyway, he was given the all-clear a few weeks ago, but Gav was worried about him. I'll speak to him and find out, but it might have been to give me some kind of security or extra family if Dad hadn't made it.'

June nodded. 'Possibly.'

Tori lapsed into thought. It was also quite possible that Gav was looking to boost ratings. She hoped that wasn't the case, but it was something she'd need to find out. 'I don't know what to do,' she admitted, her voice trembling.

June reached out, her hand hovering uncertainly before resting on the table. 'Take your time. This is a lot to take in. But know that I love you, and I always have. I only wanted what was best for you. I've thought about you every day. Wondered what you were doing. Your birthday and Christmas were particularly hard. If you're open to it, I'd like to get to know you.'

Tori stared at the woman who had given her life. 'I need to think,' she said, her voice barely audible as she pushed back the chair and stood. She beckoned to the guard that the visit was over, and she needed to be escorted out.

June nodded, a mix of sorrow and hope in her eyes. 'I'll be here.'

\* \* \*

When Tori left the prison, she'd gone straight to Gav's house. She'd been so worked up when she got there that it had probably been a good thing he wasn't home. She wasn't sure what she would have done. She'd sat outside his house in her car for two hours before giving up and taking herself for a walk along the track that wound around St Kilda's foreshore. Her thoughts were still quite jumbled by the time she let herself into her apartment that evening, but she'd decided the best thing was to try and get a decent night's sleep and tackle it at the office the next day. There was so much to get her head around. June Marlow was her mother. Cole and Lu were her sisters, and her own parents had kept all of this from her. She wasn't sure where she needed to start to unpack all of this, but a conversation with Gav would certainly help her unleash some of her anger.

Now, on Monday morning, she took deep breaths as she made her way to Penny's office, willing herself to calm down. She'd done her best to remind herself that her parentage wasn't Penny's fault. However, she was in the mood to demand some answers.

'She's in a meeting, Tori,' Penny's officious assistant said as she approached Penny's office. 'Would you like me to make time for you to see her?'

Tori looked through the glass walls into Penny's office. Her friend was having an animated discussion with none other than CEO Gavin Barnett.

'No, now's a good time.'

Without waiting for a response, she pushed open the door, causing Penny and Gavin to turn to her.

'Everything okay?' Penny asked, her eyes flicking from Tori to the red-faced assistant who'd followed her into the room.

'No, it's not,' Tori said. 'And I need to speak to both of you, so now seems like a good time to do that.'

Penny looked to Gav, who nodded. Tori imagined he had a good idea of where this was going.

'Thanks,' Penny said, nodding at her assistant. 'Please close the door, if you don't mind.'

Tori bit her lip as she waited for the assistant to leave.

'Sit down,' Gav said, indicating an empty chair next to him.

Tori shook her head. 'No, I'm fine. I need to speak to you both about the June Marlow story.'

'Okay,' Gav said, wariness showing in his eyes. 'You've got our attention.'

Tori locked gazes with Penny. 'Did you know? When you gave

me the ancestry test for my birthday? Did you already know what I was going to find out?'

Confusion flickered across Penny's eyes. 'No. I've already told you that I had no idea you were adopted. Why? And what does this have to do with June Marlow?'

'Why don't you tell her?' Tori folded her arms and looked at Gav.

Gav ran a hand through his thinning hair. 'I'd been at your dad for months to tell you, and when he wouldn't, I guess I decided to take it into my own hands. I hadn't planned for you to find out through the ancestry test. I thought it would be enough to put you on both the June Marlow story and the one at Cole's work. I figured that surely, if you started being part of their world, Dion and Sylvie would feel obligated to tell you. Or that you might notice how much you look like Lu. The fact you did the ancestry test was a bonus and saved me telling you outright if they didn't.'

Penny looked from Gav to Tori. 'Can someone tell me what's going on here?'

'June Marlow is my biological mother,' Tori said.

Penny's mouth dropped open. 'What? No way.' The horror on her face brought a mild sense of relief to Tori that Penny wasn't involved in Gav's plan.

Penny turned to Gav. 'Gav?'

He threw his hands up in the air. 'Fine. I've been at Dion for years to tell Tori. Even before I started working here. His cancer scare was worrying me, and I pushed him to tell her. If he died, it would leave her with one parent and nothing else, when she has siblings and other family. She had a right to know.'

'Surely it wasn't your place to tell me any of this?' Tori said. 'Why didn't you tell Dad your plans and give him the option to tell me?'

'Because it would make an amazing news story,' Penny answered before Gav had the chance to speak. She shook her head. 'You know, I'd heard stories about you before you came to *Southern Insight*. That you were ruthless and would put a story and ratings before people. I'd hoped it wasn't true.'

Gav folded his arms across his chest. 'It was a win-win. Dion's been battling cancer, which might have left Tori with one grieving parent. That's a lonely place to be. June Marlow's story should be told. I've thought that since the day Dion told me everything, but I respected my friend's request to keep it to myself. Until now. This show needs a boost, and what better way to boost it than with a human-interest story that involves one of our most beloved reporters?'

'You're not seriously suggesting we out Tori as June Marlow's daughter on national television?' Penny stood. 'Gav, I know you're the boss of this place, but right now, I'm going to respect-fully ask you to leave my office.'

'But...'

Penny pointed at the door. 'Leave. I need to get my head around all of this. Tori's one of my staff members, and I don't care what your relationship is with her family; you've crossed a line. Human resources will be informed.'

Gav pushed his hand through his hair. 'I honestly felt you should know you had sisters and other people that are family.'

'Get out,' Penny said, pointing to the door again.

Gav hesitated, as if about to say something else, before thinking better of it.

Tori sank into the chair he'd vacated, and Penny dropped into the one across from her.

'I had no idea. I promise,' Penny said. 'I thought it was strange that he was making decisions on some stories and specif-ically asking you to be involved, but I was also conscious of the ratings needing a boost, so I assumed that's why he was suddenly being hands-on.' She shook her head. 'I can't believe I suggested the ancestry testing. That played right into his plan. I'm so sorry.'

Tori forced a smile. 'The one good thing that's come out of the last few minutes is seeing your reaction and knowing you had nothing to do with it.'

'June Marlow is your mother?' Penny continued shaking her head.

'She didn't know,' Tori said. 'She's only just found out too. My mum was her neighbour and best friend. But when she adopted me, she made a promise never to tell June who I was, or vice versa. But Gav obviously planned to tell one of us – no doubt with the cameras rolling – before the DNA test did that job for him.'

'What about the sisters and other family?'

'I've loved getting to know Lu, in particular. However, I haven't spoken to her or Cole since I found out that we're sisters. Or Elena, who is my grandmother too.' She let out a breath. 'It's overwhelming.'

'I'll bet.'

'But?'

Penny raised an eyebrow. 'But what?'

'We both know this would make an incredible story. Which is obviously part of the reason Gav pushed it to start with.'

'That's on you,' Penny said. 'Yes, it would, but there are plenty of other stories out there. I'd get your head around everything for now. Worry about stories later. And then there's your new family. You don't know how they'd feel about this side of it being told. All we wanted was to shine a light on the injustice of June's sentence.'

'What she gave up protecting her family is what keeps coming back to me,' Tori said. She sighed. 'And no, I don't want to be part of a story like this. I'm just finding it hard to remove myself completely when I know how powerful it is.' She stood. 'I need to speak to my parents. Let them know what Gav did. Dad's going to be gutted.'

* * *

June sat on a bench in the gardened meeting area of the minimum-security prison, the sweet scent of blooming flowers contrasting sharply with the tension she felt. Other prisoners were scattered around, meeting with family members under the watchful eyes of the guards.

She spotted Elena approaching, her mother's face a mix of apprehension and concern. June's heart ached to see the lines etched deep on her face. She hoped her mother wouldn't get up and walk out when she told her what she'd kept from her all these years.

'Juney,' Elena said softly, sitting down next to her and taking her hand in hers. 'Is everything alright? There's not a problem with your release, is there?'

June shook her head. 'No, Mum, nothing like that. Sorry if my call asking you to visit scared you.'

Her mother didn't respond, confirming what June had thought when she'd ended the call the previous day. The prison had been accommodating of June's extra visitors and allowed a phone call. She knew they were being more lenient on her due to her upcoming release and appreciated it.

June realised her mother would have been worried. In the years she'd been imprisoned, she'd never asked her to visit, suggesting there was any urgency. She swallowed hard, her eyes meeting her mother's. 'There's something I need to tell you. Something I should have told you a long time ago.'

Elena's eyes narrowed, a hint of fear creeping into her expression.

June could only imagine what she'd be thinking. That she'd done more than murdering her husband. Mind you, she wasn't sure it got much worse than that. She took a deep breath, her grip on her mother's hand tightening. 'Do you remember how I refused visitors when I was first put in prison?'

Elena nodded, confusion flickering in her eyes. 'Yes, you said you needed time to adjust, to come to terms with everything. You don't know what a relief it was when you agreed we could visit. It was months.'

June averted her eyes, unable to meet her mother's gaze. 'I wasn't trying to adjust. I was pregnant.'

Elena gasped. 'What?'

'I found out two weeks before Alan's death. The night he died I was trying to leave him. I didn't want anyone to know because I'd already made a plan.'

'Did… did he find out?'

June nodded. 'That night. I'd hidden the girls' and my passports with some other documents, including confirmation of the pregnancy. He found them and went ballistic.'

'And that's the night he died?'

'Yes. And I went to prison and didn't tell anyone until I knew I couldn't hide my bump any longer.'

'But during your sentencing, surely I would have noticed? That didn't happen for a few months after you were arrested.'

'I think I was about five months when that happened. I was small like I was with the other two girls and wore baggy clothes. There's no reason you would have noticed.'

'And you told no one?'

'No, actually I did tell one person, two in fact. Do you remember my friend, Vee?'

'Of course I do.' Elena's face darkened. 'Wasn't her full name Sylvie? She was the one who cut off all communication once you were imprisoned. Unforgivable.'

'I asked her to cut off all communication,' June said.

Surprise replaced the disgust in Elena's eyes. 'What? Why?'

'Because with the help of social services and a good lawyer, I gave the baby to her and her husband, Dion.'

Elena stared at June, her mouth hanging open.

'She and Dion had struggled for years trying to get pregnant, and I knew they'd give my baby the best life possible. I couldn't bear the thought of hearing anything about the baby and what I was missing out on. It was bad enough to miss out on Lu and Nicole's lives, so I thought it would be easier if she didn't contact me again. Then of course there was the baby too. She didn't have to know her mother was a murderer. She was the only one of my three children I could protect from that.' Tears filled June's eyes, and she wiped them away. 'It was the hardest decision I've ever had to make. To lose my baby and my best friend in the same moment.'

Elena was silent, taking in all that June had told her. Finally, she spoke. 'I would have raised the baby. She would have had a happy childhood and been with her sisters.'

Tears welled in June's eyes. 'I know you would have, but I didn't want to ask even more of you than I already was asking. You should have been enjoying retirement, not raising my girls. And like I said, it was protecting her too. Not knowing where she came from would allow her to have a normal life.'

Elena's voice trembled. 'So you have another daughter?'

June nodded. 'Yes, I have three daughters.'

'And Sylvie never contacted you again?'

'Not until recently. She told me who her daughter was and

that she'd done a DNA test and was likely to work out who I was. And she did. She visited me yesterday.'

'You met your daughter? My granddaughter?'

June nodded again. 'It was one of the hardest conversations of my life. This one is pretty hard too if I'm honest.'

'And so it bloody well should be,' Elena said, her voice low but the fury in her tone growing with each word. 'How could you do this to any of us?'

June wiped away more tears. 'I was trying to protect everyone. To give the baby a chance at a normal life and not to burden you with more than I already had.'

'Burden? You really think raising my granddaughter would have been a burden?'

'She was a newborn; it would have been exhausting. You already had Cole and Lu to deal with and all the counselling and nightmares they were dealing with after I was arrested. I thought it would be too much.'

'It might have been exactly what we needed,' Elena said, the fury in her voice dissipating a little. 'A distraction from the awfulness of everything else. A sister for the girls to love and protect. You didn't even give us a chance to be involved in that decision.'

June closed her eyes. Her mother was right. She should have involved her in the decision-making process. Except her mind had already been made up and nothing Elena said would have changed it. She opened her eyes. 'I'm sorry. I'm sorry for everything I put you through back then and for this now. I think we can both agree that from the moment I met Alan I haven't made the best decisions.'

Elena sighed. 'No, you haven't. But you've also been punished more than anyone ever should have been. There's not a lot of benefit in me getting angry with you, even though I think I have every right to be.'

'You do,' June agreed.

'And you've met your daughter,' Elena said. 'She must be in her late twenties by now.'

'She is. And, unbelievably, it's someone we already know. Tori Blackwood, the journalist.'

Elena's mouth dropped open. 'That's not possible, surely? Didn't you recognise her surname? We've been watching *Southern Insight* for years.'

'Blackwood isn't her real name. Sylvie and Dion's surname is Cox. It wasn't the best name for a television celebrity, so she changed it.'

'I don't know what to say.' Elena wrung her hands. 'Tori Blackwood is your daughter. What about Lu and Cole? Are you going to tell them?'

June sighed deeply. 'I have to, but I'm scared of how they'll react. I've put them through enough already. How do I tell them I have another daughter? Honestly, I don't know what to do. I feel like I've betrayed everyone. Tori, Lu, Nicole, you. I kept this secret for so long, and now it's all unravelling.'

'As secrets usually do,' Elena said. 'You need to be honest with them. They deserve to know the truth. And if Tori knows, then it's likely she'll reach out to them, so you need to do it before she does.'

June took a shaky breath, feeling the weight of her mother's words. 'You're right. Do you think you could ask them to arrange a visit as soon as possible?'

Elena sighed. 'I can, but I honestly don't know how they're going to react. Cole especially. She's finally ready to have a relationship with you and she's going to find out you've lied about something so significant. Don't be surprised if it's the last conversation you ever have with her.'

## 26

Cole arrived at her grandmother's house first, coming to a stop in the first of the two parking spaces on the wide driveway. The front garden was immaculate, with roses in bloom and salvias providing a stunning array of deep purples and reds, a testament to her grandmother's love of gardening. She stepped out of the car, clutching a bouquet of flowers she had picked up from the market.

As she walked up the path towards the older-style brick bungalow, a flood of memories enveloped her. For everything that had happened when she was little, this house always brought her a feeling of peace and comfort. Her grandmother had not only provided her and Lu a haven but also a loving home. As she reached the front door, now painted a cheerful blue, Lu's car pulled into the driveway next to hers.

She gave a little wave and waited as Lu stepped out, reaching across to the passenger seat for a large tote bag, which she slung over one shoulder.

'Hey, sis,' she called as she walked toward Cole. 'Nice flowers.'

'Thought as I've contributed nothing to Mum's room, I could at least thank Gran for all she's done.'

They reached the front door together, and Elena opened it before they had a chance to knock, her face lighting up with a warm smile.

'Hello, my darlings! Come in, come in.' She ushered them inside, taking the flowers Cole held out to her. 'These are lovely, thank you.'

'You deserve them,' Cole said. 'It's a little thank you for everything you're doing for Mum's return.'

Elena put a hand on her arm. 'You don't need to thank me, but I appreciate the sentiment. Now, come in.'

They followed her through to the back of the house, where the kitchen opened out onto a dining area and living room.

The moment they stepped into the house they were greeted by the comforting aroma of freshly baked bread.

Cole couldn't help but laugh as Lu threw her arms around Elena. 'You're the best gran ever.'

Elena tutted. 'I'd like to think you'd be doing that if you couldn't smell food, but I think we all know you well enough, Lulu.'

Lu laughed. 'You're still the best gran ever, but the food does help.' She took a bottle of Sauvignon Blanc from her tote bag and held it up. 'I'll pour the wine. Courtesy of Ali. She said to say hi.'

'It's going well then?' Cole asked.

Lu blushed as she reached for some wine glasses. 'Very well. She gets me in a way that no one has before. But it's early days, so we'll see.' She put the glasses on the kitchen counter and opened the bottle. 'I guess I can ask you the same thing. Ethan's so into you. It's written all over his face.'

It was Cole's turn to blush. 'Let's hope I don't mess it up. I've never been great with relationships.'

'That's not true at all,' Elena said, taking the bread from the oven. 'It's what you've told yourself to stop getting close to people in case they let you down like your father did.'

Lu raised an eyebrow at Cole as Elena looked up at them both.

'Did I say that out loud?'

'Sure did,' Cole said.

'Oh. Well, it probably needed to be said. You're both good, caring people who deserve to have lovely partners. And by the sounds of Ali and Ethan, you do. With them beside you, you'll be able to handle anything.'

Cole glanced at Lu and mouthed 'handle anything?' What was their gran about to drop on them?

'Now, come and sit down, and I'll serve the soup. It's nothing fancy tonight, just my minestrone.'

'*Just my minestrone,*' Lu parroted. 'As if it wasn't practically an award-winning soup.'

Elena laughed, and a few minutes later, they sat across from each other, large bowls of steaming soup and thick, crusty slices of bread in front of them.

Cole picked up her wine glass and held it in the air. 'We should toast Mum's release.'

She glanced at Lu, who'd picked up her glass and frowned. It was as if their gran hadn't heard her. She was staring at the soup, deep in thought.

'You okay, Gran?' Lu asked, putting down her wine, and Cole noticed how pale her grandmother's face was. Had it been that pale earlier?

'Yes, fine.'

'You look like a ghost all of a sudden,' Lu said. 'Is it something to do with Mum?'

'I'm fine,' Elena repeated and spread a napkin across her lap.

'Are you sure you're okay?' Cole asked. Lu was right. She didn't look well. 'It's understandable with Mum being released that you might be a bit worried.'

Elena hesitated.

'Gran?'

Elena took a deep breath. 'I found out something yesterday that I wanted to speak to you about. And yes, it does concern your mother, but no, I'm not worried about her release. That can't come quick enough.'

'What is it?' Lu asked.

Elena gripped the edges of the table. 'I'm not sure I've come to terms with this myself, and I'll warn you, what I'm about to say is a shock.' She looked at Cole. 'I hope we'll all be there for each other. You've come such a long way forgiving your mother, Cole, and I want you to understand her motives behind what I'm about to tell you before making any decisions about it... or running out of here.'

'You're scaring me,' Lu said.

Cole had to admit she was beginning to feel scared, too. 'She didn't kill anyone else, did she?'

'Jesus,' Lu said, her eyes shooting daggers at Cole. 'That's what you jump straight to?'

Cole threw her arms up in the air. 'What am I supposed to think?' She took a deep breath. 'Gran, why don't you tell us what's going on.'

Elena closed her eyes briefly, re-opened them and began to speak. 'Firstly, I want you to know that after giving this a lot of thought, I decided it was best for me to share this news with you, not your mother. I'm hoping you'll be less angry with me and by the time you're ready to speak to her you'll hopefully have cooled down and can let her explain her reasons behind why she did what she did.'

Cole looked to Lu, whose face was now as white as Gran's. She opened her mouth to speak and closed it again. She wasn't sure how much more she could take in relation to her mother and what other awful things she might have done.

Elena took a deep breath. 'Your mother was pregnant the night your father died.'

'What?' Cole said. This was the last thing she would have guessed.

'Why didn't you tell us?' Lu added.

'I'm telling you now,' Elena said, 'because I only just found out. June never told anyone. She'd only just had the pregnancy confirmed when your father died, so she wasn't showing and then concealed the pregnancy while in prison. You might not remember, but we didn't visit for a few months. She told me she couldn't face us because of what she'd done and needed to come to terms with it. It turns out that wasn't the only reason. It was a few weeks after the baby's birth that she allowed me to visit.'

'She had the baby?' Cole asked.

Elena nodded. 'She did, and she arranged a private adoption with a couple that had been close friends of hers to adopt and raise as their own.'

'The neighbours?' Cole said. She looked at Lu. 'The ones we were trying to remember the other day.'

'Yes, Sylvie and Dion Cox,' Elena said. 'They lived next door and were close to your mother.'

'The baby would be a full sibling,' Lu said, looking at Cole. 'That's crazy. We have a brother or sister out there.'

'One, who thankfully, grew up not knowing who their mother was.' Cole sighed. 'I guess I can see why she did that. It was for the baby, wasn't it? So he or she didn't have to live through what we have.'

Elena nodded. 'From what she's told me, yes. It broke her heart to give her up, but she had to for everyone's sake.'

'*She*. We have a sister,' Lu said.

'Why is she telling us now?' Cole said. She pushed a hand through her hair. 'I was trying to wrap my head around forgiving her for everything else, and now, suddenly, there are more lies to deal with. Thank God she said no to the television interview. Imagine this all becoming public information.'

'Is this why she said no?' Lu asked Elena.

Elena nodded. 'Yes, but not for the reason you're thinking. Of course, she wanted the story to remain private, but she also wanted the identity of your sibling to remain private.'

'She knows who she is?' Lu asked.

'Yes, the baby reached out to your mother,' Elena said. She gave a strangled laugh. 'Not so much a baby now. And, in a bizarre twist or touch of fate, depending on how you look at it, she happens to be Tori Blackwood.'

'What?' both Cole and Lu spoke in unison.

'No way,' Lu said. 'There's no way that could be true.'

'Apparently it is,' Elena said. She went on to relay what June had told her about the circumstances.

'I don't know how to feel,' Lu said when Elena had finished. 'Tori... our sister?'

Cole stood abruptly, her hands trembling as she pushed back the chair. 'You should feel *angry*; that is how you should feel! First at Mum for keeping another secret from us, and then at Tori. She turned up in our lives suddenly, pretending to care about Mum. What was she going to do, a big reveal on live television and embarrass all of us?' She shook her head. 'I can't believe this! I finally listen to you all and welcome Mum back into my life and this is what happens.'

The room blurred around her, Lu's voice fading into a distant hum as she struggled to process what had happened. Another sister. A manipulative, uncaring one at that. How could her mother keep such a secret? How many more lies had she told? 'I have to go,' Cole managed to murmur, her voice strained and shaky.

'Hold on,' Lu said. 'We need to discuss this. Work out what we do about Tori and about Mum. I agree that it's a bit too convenient that she got assigned to do a story on us, but how did she find out about Mum in the first place?'

'A DNA test,' Elena said. 'It linked her to a lot of information that had already been posted on some ancestry website.'

'By me,' Lu said, her face flushing red with anger. 'Remember I did the DNA test and some of the family tree a few years back. But Tori discussed this with me when we had a drink last week and acted as if she had only just found out she was adopted. I agree with Cole though. This is way too much of a coincidence.' She shook her head, disappointment written all over her face.

'I have to go,' Cole repeated. She shook her head, her chest suddenly restricting. Great, now she was having a heart attack. 'I'll call you tomorrow. I can't do this.' And she couldn't.

## 27

Cole was grateful that neither Lu nor her grandmother followed her out to the car. Once she reached it, she leaned against it, gasping for air.

She hadn't had this kind of reaction in years. For years after her father's murder, she'd been gripped by panic attacks on a regular basis. She'd only have to try to recall details from the night of his murder and end up dizzy and disconnected from reality with panic gripping her.

She took a breath, reminding herself that this was temporary. She needed to push through the feeling, and she'd be back to normal in no time. She pictured herself standing on top of Mount Kosciuszko. The view was stunning, and the warmth of the day seemed to wrap itself around her.

She pressed her forehead against the cool metal of the car, trying to keep her focus on her breathing and the mountain. It took a few minutes, but her heart rate slowed, and her vision returned to normal. She no longer felt dizzy and felt well enough to open the car door and flop into the driver's seat.

As quickly as relief settled over her that she was okay, anger built in her. How many years had she spent trying to stop the panic attacks when she was younger? There had been hours of therapy and so many techniques she'd been taught to use. There was so much delving into her past and trying to get to the root of why she reacted the way she did. Honestly, no psychologist needed a degree to be able to work that one out. But now, all these years later, letting her mother back into her life was causing more stress.

She was grateful to have at least backed out of the driveway when the door opened again, and Lu appeared. Her sister called to her, but she wasn't going to stop. With a quick wave of her hand, she pulled out into the street and drove away.

* * *

It was an hour and a half later, sitting on her couch, a strong vodka in one hand and stroking Socks with the other, that Cole allowed herself to look at her phone. There were two missed calls and numerous messages from Lu, one from her Gran and one from Ethan.

She put down her drink and opened Ethan's message.

Hey there, what time should I come by? My ESP senses tell me you need company.

Cole smiled. He was certainly tuned in to her, and she would love to see him. She quickly typed her reply.

Now is perfect, or sooner if you can! But, I've had a bit of a shock today so might not be the best company.

On my way. I'll bring wine. x

She glanced at the near-empty glass in front of her. It was the third drink she'd had since she arrived home. She sighed and, gently moving a sleeping Socks, stood. She'd at least make herself look presentable before he arrived.

Ethan arrived twenty minutes after their text exchange with two large pizza boxes in hand and a bottle of wine balancing on top.

Cole smiled. 'The ultimate comfort food – you must have known what you were heading into.'

'Just a hunch I had today that something might be going on. So, let's pour a drink, and you can fill me in.'

'I should warn you,' Cole said as they made their way through to the kitchen, 'I've already had three vodkas.'

Ethan raised an eyebrow and deposited the pizzas and wine on the kitchen counter before turning and pulling Cole to him. 'In that case, I'd better kiss you before you pass out.'

Cole melted into him, only pulling away when he did.

'As much as I want to scoop you up and take you straight to bed, it might be better to chat about your day first. Make sure you're not distracted and can enjoy yourself when I do scoop you up and take you to bed.'

'In that case, let's pour the wine, and I'll fill you in.'

Ethan filled the glasses while Cole got out plates for the pizza. They took the food into Cole's cosy living room and sat down. Socks stretched and repositioned himself on the couch, his eyes firmly closed.

'Socks looks like he's settled in.'

Cole nodded. 'I can't believe what good company he is. I think he knew I was upset and came and planted himself next to me.' She smiled. 'He's probably disgusted at how much I've drunk. I know I am.'

'I'm not sure cats are ones to judge,' Ethan said with a smile.

'But the whole time I've known you, I don't think you've ever had more than a couple of drinks. I'm assuming this is about your mum. They haven't changed their mind about her release, have they?'

'No, it's not that.' She took a sip of the wine. 'Gran dropped a bombshell on Lu and me tonight. When I think I've made big steps in reconnecting with her, we find out there's more that she's lied about.'

Ethan's eyebrows raised. 'What happened?'

'It turns out that when she was arrested, she was pregnant. We now know why for the first few months of her sentence she refused all visitors. Well, all visitors except the friends she gave the baby to.'

Ethan let out a low whistle. 'You're kidding?'

'Nope. But—' Cole took a gulp of her wine '—it gets crazier. Our biological sister is none other than Tori Blackwood.'

'No way?'

Cole nodded, tears filling her eyes. 'Yep.'

Ethan reached out and squeezed her hand. 'I'm not sure what to say. I'm assuming Tori knew who you all are, and this was going to be part of the story.' He shook his head. 'Unbelievable.'

Cole nodded again. 'There's no way this was some kind of coincidence. I'd say she orchestrated the whole thing. Probably planned to reveal the truth during her interview with Mum and then do the same to me and Lu if we'd agreed to be involved. Imagine the ratings for capturing that kind of emotion. Probably would have won her a Logie or some other award.'

As the bitterness of Cole's words reverberated in the air, Ethan continued to shake his head.

'No wonder you've had three vodkas. I probably would have drunk the bottle if I was you. Have you spoken with Tori since you found out?'

Cole shook her head. 'No, I only found out a couple of hours ago. I'm not sure I'll ever speak to her. Imagine a sister acting like that towards her family?'

'Perhaps she's angry,' Ethan suggested. 'That she was adopted out and didn't get to be part of your lives.'

'Mum could hardly have raised her in prison. Considering her high-flying career, I'd say she's probably been given a good life. I don't know when she learned about who her mother was, but we can probably assume it was only recently, and that's why she's telling the story now. If she'd learned the truth years ago, she would have been sniffing around a lot earlier. The timing of Mum's release is perfect, too. She can have some wonderful reunion with *her mother* when she gets out of prison.'

Ethan pushed the pizza box towards Cole, and even though the last thing she felt like was food, she slid a piece from the box. If nothing else, she needed to start soaking up the alcohol.

He sipped his wine, his eyes trained on Cole. 'You know, you're amazing. Dealing with all of this, you're still able to put other people's problems ahead of your own.'

Cole snorted. 'I don't think you can say that tonight. I'm wallowing in self-pity.'

Ethan laughed. 'Maybe, but overall, you've had a shitty time of it, and you're still putting one foot in front of the other. There are a lot of clients at the Wellness Centre who'd be going through a much rougher time than they currently are if you weren't there supporting them. I think a lot of people would curl up in the foetal position if they were dealt the hand you've been dealt.'

'It's highly possible I still might,' Cole said. She shook her head. 'From everything Lu told me, Tori was so empathetic towards Mum's situation and never let on that there was a connection, or that she had an ulterior motive. She acted so surprised to see me at the Wellness Centre. But of course, she must have known I worked there and set that up. You often hear about how unscrupulous the media are. I never thought it would be relevant to us.'

'It suggests she's not interested in getting to know any of you,' Ethan said. 'You're hardly going to do that, but then turn around and say, "Surprise, I'm your sister. Let's get to know each other."'

Sadness settled over Cole as his words sank in. As angry as she was with her mother and Tori, there was part of her that, in different circumstances, would have been curious about her sister and wanted to have spent time with her.

'How's Lu doing with the news?' Ethan asked. 'And your gran?'

Heat flooded Cole's cheeks. 'I kind of ran out of Gran's before I was able to check on either of them. I had a bit of a panic attack. I used to have them a lot after Mum was arrested, but this was the first one in years. I felt like I couldn't breathe. I think it was too much. I've spent most of my working career focusing outward on other people and their issues. Turning it back and focusing on me and my dysfunctional family is more than it appears I can handle. I should probably give Lu a call.'

'Do it now if you like,' Ethan said, helping himself to another slice of pizza. 'She's probably worried about you if you ran out like that.'

Cole got up and walked over to the kitchen bench where she'd left her phone. She'd silenced it after she'd sent Ethan the text earlier.

'You're right, she's worried,' Cole said, noting the additional missed calls and text messages.

She pressed on Lu's number and put the phone to her ear.

'Are you okay?' The worry in Lu's voice was clear. 'I'm outside your apartment with Ali. I was about to press the buzzer.'

'I'll buzz you in,' Cole said, walking over to the intercom

button. 'And Lu, I'm sorry. I should have called you earlier.' She ended the call and turned to Ethan. 'Do you mind if Lu and Ali join us?'

'Of course not. Hopefully, they're hungry,' Ethan said, nodding toward the barely touched pizzas.

Cole opened the door to Lu and Ali, who looked equally anxious.

Lu stepped straight towards Cole and hugged her. 'You scared me,' she said when they pulled apart.

'Sorry,' Cole said. 'It was all too overwhelming.'

'Mm, something smells good in here,' Ali said.

'Pizza,' Ethan called out. 'And wine if you're interested.'

'Or vodka,' Cole added. 'I'm going through it all tonight.'

Ethan stood as the women entered the lounge room. He walked straight over to Lu and hugged her. 'Sounds like a rough day.' He turned to Ali. 'Wine?'

Both Lu and Ali accepted glasses of wine and plates for pizza.

'Do you think she definitely knew who we were?' Lu asked once they'd all settled onto Cole's couches. 'She seemed genuinely lovely. Like she cared and wanted to share Mum's story. I find it hard to believe someone so nice was so calculating.'

'It's just too big a coincidence,' Cole said. 'I'd like to believe our new sister is someone we'd want to welcome into the family with open arms, but I can't believe it's the case.'

'I hate to say it,' Ali said, 'but I agree with Cole. It's too far-fetched. And she's a reporter. I'd say they're probably happy to go to any length to get a story.'

'It's so disappointing,' Lu said. 'It would have been a silver lining to find out we had a sister we wanted to get to know. She looks a bit like me too.'

'A lot like you now that we've made the connection,' Cole said.

'Perhaps you need to speak to her,' Ethan said. 'We're assuming she's an awful person, but she might be as innocent in all of this as you both are.'

'It is possible,' Ali added, although the look on her face belied her words.

'I think I'll visit Mum,' Lu said. 'I want to hear the details from her first before I speak to Tori again.' She turned to Cole. 'Any chance you'd come with me?'

Cole didn't respond immediately. Not because of her mother or Tori, but because of the look on Lu's face. She was beginning to realise how much Lu had carried over the years in relation to her mother. She hadn't given her the support she should have, and it must have been hard for her.

'Don't worry,' Lu said when she still hadn't responded. 'I'm not expecting you to.'

Cole bit the inside of her lip. Everything inside her was telling her to run, but she felt like she owed Lu. 'It looks like you've got one sister who's going to let you down. I'm not going to be the other one.'

'You'll come?'

The incredulous look on Lu's face caused guilt to stab in Cole's gut. She'd been so wrapped up in self-preservation over the years she hadn't looked out for Lu. It was time she stepped up.

She nodded.

\* \* \*

June's leg bounced up and down as she waited for Lu and Cole to arrive. She'd spoken to her mother briefly the previous day to learn that she'd told Lu and Cole the news about Tori and that they were both in shock. She wasn't sure what type of reception she was going to receive. They had every right to be angry. If her mother had hidden a pregnancy, she knew she'd be shocked and upset. Mind you, her mother had no reason to, as she wasn't in prison for murder.

'Marlow. Visitors.' The warden nodded in the direction of the door. The outdoor area was closed for visiting due to the stormy weather that was circling the facility, so a more formal indoor area was used. It was still private, with the meeting areas spaced apart, but June still wished they could be outside, which felt less institutionalised.

Tears filled her eyes when the girls arrived. This was her third visit with Cole in all these years, and it was for this reason. As they neared her, she saw how pale Lu was versus how angry Cole looked.

'It's okay, Mum,' Lu said as she reached her and opened her arms to hug her mother. June's tears spilled down her cheeks, with the relief she felt from those three words. She couldn't lose Lu, too.

They pulled apart before they were asked to by the guard, and June turned to Cole. She certainly wasn't expecting a hug but still wasn't sure what Cole was likely to serve up. The fact she'd come was hopefully a good sign, although it was quite likely she was there to tell her exactly what she thought of her.

When Cole didn't react, June sat down and faced her daughters. 'I'm sorry,' she said. 'I know that doesn't mean much, but I honestly thought I was doing the right thing all those years ago.'

'And do you now?' Cole asked. 'Now that we know the truth?'

June nodded. 'I wouldn't have changed anything that I did in relation to Tori. Sylvie was my closest friend and someone I knew I could trust implicitly to give Tori a good life.'

'Why didn't you tell Gran? I get that me and Lu were too young, but not even your own mum?'

June thought about her answer. 'I couldn't. Mum had lost her husband, my dad, only three years earlier. She'd been talking about taking early retirement and travelling and suddenly she's being asked to raise you two girls. She took it in her stride as if it was the most normal thing to be asked to do, but it wasn't. I was worried that she'd struggle with you two and a newborn would have taken that struggle to a whole other level. I knew she'd then be feeling guilty that her attention was on the baby and not the two of you who were processing the trauma of losing both of your parents.'

'So, you were looking out for Gran?' Lu said.

'And myself,' June admitted 'If Mum had known, Tori would have been brought up in conversation over the years, and I don't think I could have handled that. I thought of her every day and often wondered what she was doing, but I needed to be able to compartmentalise that. Put it away when it hurt too much and not have the risk of Mum suddenly bringing her up.'

'You lost so much that night, didn't you?' Lu said.

June's eyes flooded with tears again at the understanding she could hear in Lu's tone. She wasn't sure if anyone ever understood how much she'd lost.

'I lost everything,' she admitted. 'Alan, you girls, the baby, Mum, my freedom. Some days, I look back and wonder how I even lasted this long here. Not that I would ever have put you girls through that, as well as everything else.'

'Didn't you think that as we got older, we should have known we had a sibling?' Cole asked.

'I couldn't tell you,' June said. 'Sylvie and I made a promise to each other that we'd never tell Tori or any of you. I wanted the baby to have the opportunity to grow up without the stigma of having a murderer for a mother. I'm sorry I couldn't offer that to the two of you as well.'

'We're upset that you lied about this,' Cole said, 'but I think I can speak for both Lu and me when I say that we do understand why you did that. Whether we would have done it differently in the situation, we'll never know. But we're probably more upset with Tori at this stage. She clearly manipulated the situation for a news story. That's the awful part in all of this.'

June frowned. 'I'm not sure what you mean. Tori didn't do anything wrong.'

'She found out her DNA match through Heritage Link and then evidently set up this whole *Victims Behind Bars* story so she could ambush us all during interviews with the news that you had a baby, and it happened to be her. It would have made compelling television.'

June was silent for a moment. 'I think you should speak to her. She's visited me, and I had the same question for her. I told her that it's not believable that this was some kind of coincidence.'

'What did she say?' Lu asked.

'She said she'd been instructed by the show's chief executive to do the story on me and assist her colleague on the story at the Wellness Centre where you work, Cole. The chief executive is a friend of Tori's dad, and she was going to check with him about what was going on. But she was so shocked by everything when she visited me, I don't think she knew what to think. I think the friend of her dad must have wanted her to know the truth. But the one thing I can say is that I believed her. I think she's as innocent in all of this as you both are.'

'We need to speak to her,' Lu said. 'Find out for sure. There's no point guessing and not listening to her side of the story.'

Cole's cheeks turned red at Lu's words, and June felt heartened that she'd made the connection that guessing and not listening to her side of the story was how Cole had treated her mother.

'What?' Lu said, looking from her mother to Cole. 'Don't you think we should do that? It'd be nice if she turned out not to be some awful leech.'

Cole laughed, and June smiled, relieved that Cole's anger had disappeared.

'It would be nice,' Cole said. 'And yes, we should hear her side of the story before we jump to too many conclusions.'

Lu's eyes widened. 'Sorry, I wasn't having a go at you. And you'll come with me to speak to her?'

'Yes. Something Gran said the other night about me protecting myself, so I don't get hurt resonated, that's all. I'm always telling my clients that they need to try and unpack some of that hurt so that they can open themselves up to having love in their life and friendships that they might otherwise not have. I'm trying to take my own advice.'

'Good,' Lu said. 'About bloody time.'

# 28

All thoughts of Tori and Lu were erased from Cole's mind when she received a call from Anne Gleeson. Piper and her sister were scheduled to spend some time with their mother at their home with Anne accompanying them, but Anne was feeling unwell, so unless Cole or another social worker could stand in, the visit would need to be postponed. Cole could imagine how upset the girls and Jacinta would be if that happened and agreed to take them. Anne gave her the details of their case worker at Child Services, and Cole gave her a quick call to check that she could take Anne's place.

Two hours later, after ticking all the legal boxes, Cole found herself driving towards Mount Waverley with Piper and Katie in the back seat.

'I can't believe we're finally getting to go home,' Katie said. 'Do you think Mum will have made a cake?'

Cole glanced in the rear-vision mirror to see Piper debating her answer.

'Maybe,' Piper said. 'But she's probably missed us heaps and might not have had a chance to do that. She might be a bit upset about what's happened, so if there's no cake, don't mention it, okay? We can always get something later.'

Cole felt unusually emotional hearing an eleven-year-old doing her best to protect both her sister and her mother. 'I checked with Anne, and she's happy for us to stop for pizza on the way home. So, as Piper said, if your mum hasn't had a chance to prepare anything, we can fill up later.'

Katie smiled, hugging herself with her arms. 'I can't wait to see Mum.'

Cole's nerves were on edge when she pulled into the Dixson's driveway. She prayed that this went well for all of them. The girls needed reassurance of their mother's love, and she hoped they would get it.

When the front door flew open, and Jacinta came running out, her arms stretched wide as the girls climbed out of the car, she knew no one was going to be disappointed. She embraced the girls, tears flowing freely down her cheeks.

'I'm so sorry,' she said, again and again. 'I love you both so much, and I'm so sorry.'

'Why don't we go inside?' Cole suggested when it appeared Jacinta wasn't going to let the girls go.

She let go and gave a small laugh. 'Sorry, it's so good to see my girls. Of course, come in. I've got something to show you.'

A delicious smell hit them as they walked into the house, causing Katie to squeal. 'I knew you'd make a cake. And that's your chocolate one, isn't it?'

'It sure is, Katie-pie. And it's got chocolate buttons on it, your favourite.'

Piper met Cole's eyes, and Cole saw the relief in them. Like Cole, Piper had been hoping Katie wouldn't be disappointed. She had to stop herself from pulling the little girl to her and hugging her. She had such a generous heart. Cole knew she could learn a lot from her and already had, particularly when it came to forgiveness.

They entered the kitchen, and Katie squealed again when she saw how the table had been set up. It was like a party, with balloons tied to two of the chairs, streamers and some delicious-looking biscuits and chocolates on the table.

'I wanted today to be special,' Jacinta said. 'You girls have been so brave, and I wanted to tell you how proud I am of you both. And,' she said, her eyes gleaming with a mixture of tears and excitement, 'I have a surprise for you. Do you want to have cake and treats first, or the surprise?'

'Surprise,' both girls said at once, and Cole laughed, realising it was the thought that had popped into her head, too.

'It's in your room,' Jacinta said.

Piper grabbed Katie's hand, and the two girls rushed from the room in the direction of what Cole assumed was their shared bedroom.

'You're doing an amazing job,' Cole said when the girls were out of earshot. 'This is what they needed today. To know how much you've missed them and love them. I'm feeling quite emotional myself seeing the effort you've gone to.'

Shrieks of delight erupted from the bedroom before Jacinta had a chance to respond.

'Cole!' Piper called. 'Come and look.'

Jacinta nodded, and Cole hurried down to the bedroom the girls shared. She laughed as she entered the room and saw Katie hugging a Cavoodle. The brown, teddy-bear-looking dog was licking Katie's face, its tail wagging madly.

The delight on Piper's face was quickly replaced with concern. 'But Dad said we could never have a dog. He'll be mad.'

Jacinta wrapped an arm around Piper's shoulders. 'I told Dad when I visited him that I'd be getting you a dog. He wasn't mad.

He knows he won't be coming home to us for a long time and agreed that a dog would be good for all of us.'

'How long's a long time?' Katie asked.

Jacinta pulled Katie into their hug. 'I'm not sure. Once he's well enough we'll start with a visit to him and go from there. We can't have him home again until we know for sure that we'll all be safe.'

Cole was pleased that Jacinta wasn't sugar-coating the process and promising the girls that he'd get better and come home to them.

'In the meantime, once you girls are back home with me, we'll look after each other and of course the dog can help too.'

Piper smiled and laughed. 'This dog is incredibly cute, but he's not going to be able to look after us, Mum! He's not exactly a guard dog.'

'Does he have a name?' Katie asked.

'Teddy,' Jacinta said. 'He's not a puppy, which is good because he's trained, but he won't get much bigger than he is now.'

'That's perfect,' Piper said. 'Not like Bruiser.'

Katie giggled as the dog licked her again. 'I love him.'

'Good,' Jacinta said, 'because so do I. Now, let's go and eat. Bring Teddy if you like. I've got some special treats for him, too, which he can have while we try the cake.'

Two hours after they'd arrived, the girls said their goodbyes to their mum, Jacinta assuring them that she'd look after Teddy until they were back in the house full-time and could look after him. Cole checked they were securely fastened in the back seat before she spoke with Jacinta out of their hearing.

Jacinta's emotions were clearly written all over her face. They'd had a wonderful afternoon, but having to say goodbye wasn't easy.

'They can come back next weekend for another visit,' Cole

said. 'And I know the assessments are underway to try and get them back to you full-time. That could happen within a matter of weeks.'

Jacinta nodded. 'I know, and as much as I want them here now, I also know that I need to do a lot of work on myself. The sessions I've had at the centre have already helped. I feel stronger, like I can maybe get through this.'

'Not maybe,' Cole said. 'Definitely.'

The girls' enthusiasm to wave to their mum as they drove away didn't go unnoticed by Cole. Not at any point during the afternoon had Piper or Katie asked their mother why she'd allowed them to end up in foster care or allowed their father to abuse any of them. Those questions would no doubt come later, but it was plain to see that today they just wanted their mother. They wanted her love and the warmth of being with her.

Why had she herself been so quick to reject that as a kid? It made no sense. She knew how desperately Lu had wanted their mother after she'd gone to prison. She'd cried herself to sleep every night for months. But Cole hadn't. She'd felt nothing other than the need to distance herself from it all. She sighed. It was her coping strategy, she guessed. Block it out, walk away. Avoid, avoid, avoid.

'That was nice,' Piper said as they drove back towards Camberwell and the Gleesons'. They'd all eaten so much cake that Cole wasn't sure they'd fit any pizza in, but the girls had assured her they would try.

'I can't believe Daddy didn't get mad about Mum getting us a dog,' Katie said. 'He must love us after all.'

'He loves us,' Piper said. 'He's sick and needs help. Once the doctors fix him, he'll be able to be with us again.'

'What if he hurts us?'

'He won't,' Piper said. 'They won't let him back with us until they're sure he's better. Zane told me that. But if we were ever worried, we'd call Cole, wouldn't we, Cole?'

'Definitely,' Cole said, again amazed at the maturity Piper was showing and again realising how badly she'd failed Lu on this front when they were kids. 'I'll be visiting you and checking in regularly, as will your case worker. There are a lot of people looking out for you now, and our main aim is to get your family back together. It can take time, but if everyone works towards it, it's likely to happen.'

Cole's emotions were all over the place by the time she dropped the girls back to Anne and Zane later that night. Piper was like a different child from the one she'd met only a few weeks earlier.

'What will happen when we go back home?' Piper had asked after polishing off her second slice of pizza. 'It's a long way to come back to the garden.'

'Not on a weekend,' Cole said. 'I can come and get you if your mum can't bring you over. In just a few weeks, you've become invaluable at the community garden. We'd all miss you if you couldn't help.'

The relief on Piper's face confirmed for Cole that while she was excited and happy at the thought of going home, she still needed the security of Cole being there for her. It made Cole realise again the ways she hadn't been there for her own sister, and she vowed she would make a difference now. As she had this thought a sick feeling spread through the pit of Cole's stomach. She glanced at her watch. She was supposed to be meeting Lu and Tori in St Kilda in ten minutes. Once again, she was letting her sister down.

She stood, apologising to the girls. 'I need to send a quick text. I'll be a few minutes.'

\* \* \*

Tori pushed a stray hair from her eyes and gratefully accepted the glass of wine Dion set down in front of her. She'd been surprised to get the text message from Lu on Friday night asking if she and Cole could meet her. She'd assumed they would suspect this had all been a set-up and never speak to her again. She had, of course, planned to get in touch with them to explain but was still putting all the pieces together herself. The fact that Cole was also coming was the biggest surprise. If anything, she'd worried Cole's forgiveness of her mother might have been taken back off the table once she'd learned of Tori's existence.

'You don't think you should have let them know I was going to be here?' her father asked, sitting down next to her. 'They might feel like they've been ambushed.'

Tori shook her head. 'I think it's the only way Cole will believe me. And to be fair, I wouldn't blame her if she still didn't. I'll have to get Gav involved if she doesn't, to convince her once and for all. I still can't believe he did this.'

Dion sipped his beer, shaking his head. 'If he wasn't working at the show and had done it genuinely because he was worried about you not having family if I had died, then I'd possibly believe it was for our best interests. Mind you, as I said to him when he came over to apologise the other night, he could have waited until Mum and I were both dead before that was even relevant. But he's got this big job at a network where ratings need a boost and clearly thought "look at the story I can hand the station". Let's say it's the last thing he'll ever have to do with our family.'

'I'm sorry, Dad,' Tori said. 'You've known him for so long.'

Dion shrugged. 'You don't always know a person, Tori, remember that. Alan Marlow was a good friend of mine, too, and

I had no idea what was happening behind closed doors. I feel I've let June down on two counts now.'

Tori squeezed his arm. 'No, you haven't. And you've been an amazing dad to me. I couldn't have asked for a better childhood than the one you and Mum gave me.' She removed her arm. 'Here's Lu and her girlfriend,' she whispered under her breath.

They both stood as Lu and Ali reached the table.

'This is my dad, Dion,' Tori said before anyone had a chance to talk. 'I wanted you to meet him and hear from him. This is Lu and Ali,' she said to her dad.

Ali shook Dion's hand before turning to Lu. 'I'll get us some drinks,' she said and disappeared in the direction of the bar.

'Cole's not coming,' Lu said as she sat down across from Dion and Tori. 'She's had a work emergency and only sent me a message a few minutes ago. She said to say she was sorry.'

'I didn't expect she'd come,' Tori said. 'After everything that's happened, I thought she'd run a mile.'

Lu smiled. 'Normally I'd agree with you, but her text was uncharacteristically lengthy in her apology. She suggested we reschedule but as we were almost here, I figured it'd be better not to delay this. It's such a bizarre situation. Cole had an elaborate plan to ambush you so that we could get some answers.'

Tori nudged her dad in reference to the ambush. It sounded like they all had similar plans.

'Ali and I talked her out of it,' Lu continued, 'which is why you got the message from me asking to meet. One good thing out of all of this is that she said she wanted to hear your side of the story. That she recognises she should have done this with Mum years ago and won't make the mistake again of making up her mind without giving someone the opportunity to explain.'

Tori was surprised by this revelation. 'That's incredible,' she said. 'Good for her. Now, Dad's going to tell you everything. Since he was there when I was a baby, I thought it would give you a better picture of everything that happened, if it came from him. I hope you're okay with that?'

Lu nodded.

\* \* \*

Ten minutes later, Lu reached across the table and took Tori's hand. 'Hey, sis.'

A lump formed in Tori's throat. She squeezed Lu's hand, surprised at the relief the simple gesture brought her.

'I take it you believe me now that I didn't set this up. That Gav, who Dad's been telling you about, is responsible for how it all played out at work? Penny, the show's producer, is planning to be in touch with both you and Cole to explain this too.'

Lu nodded. 'Honestly, I didn't want to believe you were behind this when I first heard about the supposed coincidence. And now I'm relieved, because I liked you when we first met. Something clicked, and that tells me that my senses aren't that far off after all.'

'I've been so worried as to what you, Cole and June must be thinking of me. But before realising you'd think it was a set-up, I thought you might hate me anyway.'

Lu frowned. 'Hate you? Why would I hate you?'

'I don't know. Growing up without the knowledge you and Cole had about the family? Being sent to private school and given opportunities I know you both didn't get?'

'None of that's your fault. If anything, I'm just sad that we didn't know we had another sister until now. It might have helped Cole deal with everything. She's a protective person, and I can't imagine her turning her back on Mum in the same way that she did if you'd lived with us.'

'Did she say that?'

Lu shook her head. 'No, she flipped out when she found out who you were. But, like I said, she was planning to be here, and I'm sure she'll believe what you and Dion have told us. I'll call her later tonight.'

'How are you holding up, Lu?' Dion asked. 'I've heard a lot from Tori about how Cole's struggled but not a lot about you. This can't be easy, any of it.'

'She's amazing,' Ali said before Lu had a chance to answer. 'She's the backbone of the family, but doesn't realise it.'

Lu blushed. 'I'm not sure about that, but the one thing I've always wanted was a bigger family. A happy family that spent time together. I know we did when I was little, but I was only six when Mum was put away, so my memories are a bit blurred. I'd like to make a lot of new memories, hopefully, ones that Tori, you – Dion – and Sylvie are part of, too. I do remember spending time with you and Sylvie when I was little,' she added. 'We loved coming to your house. I bet Mum would love to have you back in her life.'

'I don't think you'll be able to keep Sylvie away,' Dion said with a smile.

'What's going to happen to the story?' Ali asked. 'This would add an incredibly powerful element to it.'

'It would,' Tori said. 'But I've already told my producer I won't be touching it. It's too personal. I want to move on. Hopefully, we'll get to know all of you and see where that takes us. What I'm hoping is that there won't be any other life-changing secrets pop up along the way.'

It was close to two hours later that they decided to call it a night. Tori was grateful that not only had her dad joined them, but also that he'd shared numerous stories about Lu and Cole when they were kids living next door. They were happy stories, and she could see how much they meant to Lu to hear them.

Tori hugged Lu as they all said their goodbyes outside the pub. 'Thank you for listening and for believing me. The good thing that's come out of all of this is us. I can't wait to get to know you more and hopefully Cole too.'

Lu hugged her back. 'Ditto. Mum's being released on Friday, so as you can imagine, there's a lot to organise, and it's going to be a big week. I'm sure she'll want to see you once she's out.'

'Sylvie's hoping she'll see all of us,' Dion said. 'As soon as June's up to it, we'd love to have you all over or meet somewhere. Whatever she's comfortable with. We're assuming it's going to be quite an adjustment for her.'

'For us all,' Tori added.

* * *

Cole ended the call with Lu and took Ethan's hand. They were sitting on her couch, Socks on Ethan's lap, purring in amongst his snores.

'I only heard your side of that conversation,' Ethan said, 'but I take it Tori is as innocent as you and Lu in all of this.'

Cole smiled. 'She is, which is a huge relief. The show's producer set the whole thing up. He's a friend of Tori's dad, and he decided to play God.'

'What does that mean for you and Tori?'

'I'll give her a call,' Cole said. 'Apologise for jumping to conclusions, and I guess take it from there. How weird to have another sister.' She laughed. 'I wonder if Lu minds now being the middle child.'

Ethan squeezed her hand. 'From what I've seen so far of Lu, I'd say she's happy that your family is coming together in ways that no one ever expected. First, your mum is being released, and now this. It's incredible.'

'It is,' Cole agreed. She turned to face him. 'Thank you. You've been amazing through all of this. I'm not sure many guys would have wanted to get involved with all this drama unfolding.'

Ethan carefully picked up Socks and moved him off his lap. He turned back to Cole and pulled her to him. 'Watching you handle this, on top of seeing how you interact with clients at the centre and generally carry yourself, is why I want to be here. Look what you've done for Piper and her sister, too. You go above and beyond.'

'Except for my own family,' Cole said. 'I'm not sure how I get past what I did to Mum.'

'It was an exceptional circumstance,' Ethan said. 'You witnessed something horrific and were expected to process it and deal with it as a ten-year-old. The way you handled it was completely understandable. And now, you get a chance to move past that night and welcome your mum back into your life.'

'Tomorrow,' Cole said. 'It's hard to believe that it's happening.' She sank into Ethan's embrace, grateful to have him with her. She hoped she had, as he said, moved past that night. Regardless, she knew she was looking forward to welcoming her mum home the next day, something she wouldn't have believed possible even a few weeks ago.

## 29

Doreen squeezed June tight. 'I never want to see you again, you hear me?'

June squeezed Doreen back before pulling away. 'Thank you, that means a lot. But, when you do get out, feel free to look me up.'

Doreen shook her head. 'No. I think once we leave this place, we never want to be reminded of it again. As much as I've loved getting to know you, June Marlow, after today, I never want to hear your name again.'

June wiped her eyes as the other woman's eyes filled with tears. In the short time she'd been at Winchester, she and Doreen had become close. She hoped the woman's son would start being kinder to her.

She picked up a box from the shelf in the cell and handed it to Doreen. 'At least enjoy these. It's my tea, some chocolates and some soap.'

Doreen took the box and pointed to the door where one of the prison guards was waiting for June. 'Go on, out with you. And no coming back, remember.'

June impulsively pulled Doreen into a hug before walking out of the cell and following the prison guard. She was led to a private area where she could change out of her prison uniform. Lu had brought a complete set of clothes for her mother: smart pants, a stylish top and comfortable shoes. As June went through the bag, she discovered new underwear and socks. Lu had said leaving all her prison clothes behind would be symbolic of a new beginning. Nerves rattled through her as she had this thought. She was only moments away from being free.

She slipped on the fresh clothes, and the sensation of the soft fabric against her skin was both exhilarating and emotional. This was the first significant moment in her transition from imprisonment to freedom. She stuffed the prison clothes into the bag provided and left them on a chair in the room before following the guard to the next stage of the processing.

When they reached the administration area, paperwork was placed in front of her to read and sign. In comparison to the lengthy process of admitting her to Trendall twenty-eight years earlier, the process, while surreal, was quick. She was handed a bag of personal items. She glanced inside, the sight of her wedding ring causing a spike of pain to reverberate through her. She would need to get rid of that as soon as possible. The fewer reminders of her past life, the better.

'Good luck, Marlow,' Wendy, the prison guard, said as she led her to the doors that divided the administration area from the public waiting room. 'I'll reiterate Doreen's words and remind you; we don't want to see you back here. Ever.'

June managed a smile. Wendy, like many of the guards at Winchester, showed a kind and compassionate side. Something she hadn't seen much of at Trendall. 'Don't worry, you won't be seeing me again.'

Wendy keyed in the access code, and the doors opened.

*The doors to freedom,* June thought as she stepped into the adjoining room. Her mum, Lu and Cole stood huddled together, waiting. Elena started wiping her eyes the moment June made eye contact with her.

June hurried over to the group and pulled them all to her, tears freely flowing down her cheeks now.

'Let's go,' Cole said as soon as they pulled apart. 'You've spent too many years imprisoned already. Let's not waste another minute.'

June put an arm around her mother and followed Cole outside. She stopped momentarily.

'You alright, love?' her mother asked.

June nodded. 'Just savouring this moment. I'll never take my freedom for granted again. That's one thing this whole awful experience has taught me.'

\* \* \*

Cole pulled her Honda into her mother's driveway, trying to put herself in her mother's shoes. It was obvious from the few comments she'd made on the way back from the prison that overwhelmed was one emotion she was feeling.

'The traffic's so busy,' June had said as they made their way across the Bolte Bridge, 'and the city's so built up. It's at least twice the size it was! What's that big Ferris wheel thing?'

'The Melbourne Star,' Lu had said. 'It's closed. I think Covid might have put an end to it. The CBD was like a ghost town during the pandemic.'

'This is at least familiar,' June said as she stepped out of the front passenger seat and onto her mother's driveway. 'The garden looks lovely,' she added as she looked around.

Cole had to hand it to her gran. She'd made the place so

welcoming for June's return. She hoped it all went as smoothly as possible.

'Come in and see the house,' Elena said. She gave a mild chuckle. 'You'll probably be more horrified at the lack of what's been done rather than the amazing changes and renovations. Other than the odd lick of paint here and there, it's probably not much different to the last time you were here.'

'Except Mum's new room,' Lu said. 'That's different and lovely.'

'I'll make tea and coffee,' Cole said, 'while you show Mum around. It's all Gran and Lu's doing. I can't take any credit for what they've done.'

Ten minutes later, they joined Cole in the kitchen. The table was laden with pastries and cakes, and the aroma of coffee filled the air.

June wiped her eyes, the emotion all too clear on her face.

Cole smiled. 'They did an amazing job, didn't they?'

June nodded, her eyes widening as she took in the selection of cakes and pastries. 'As have you by the looks of it. You can't imagine when I last ate something as delicious as those cakes look.'

'Lu's girlfriend, Ali, is to thank for these,' Cole said. 'Other than being a barista today, I've not added much to any of this.'

June squeezed her arm. 'You're here. That means more to me than anything. The fact I have you, Lu and Mum, and I'm not going to be told visiting time's over. I did wonder if Tori might come today too but understand it might be too early for everyone for that to happen.'

'If you're up for it,' Elena said, 'I've invited Tori, Sylvie and Dion for afternoon drinks on Sunday. I thought we could sit out the back and have a relaxed catch-up. I'm hoping the girls will bring Ali and Ethan with them too. Dilute it a bit. I spoke to Sylvie last night and told her I'd confirm once you were home.'

'How do you girls feel about that?' June asked.

'Fine by me,' Lu said. 'Tori and I get along well already.' She turned to Cole. 'What about you?'

'We can leave it if you're not ready,' June said. 'This is a lot to ask of any of us, and there's certainly no rush.'

'Invite them over,' Cole said. 'Now, tea or coffee?' she asked her mother.

'Coffee would be lovely,' June said. 'The prison coffee was terrible.'

Cole smiled and poured her mother a cup from the plunger. Nerves rattled her stomach as she thought of the catch-up with Tori. Ideally, she wanted to meet with Tori on her own. She wondered if Tori would have time tomorrow.

As a text pinged on her phone, Tori slowed her run to a walk and slipped her phone from her pocket. She stopped, surprised to see the message was from Cole. Cole, who'd ignored her previous phone call and two text messages.

> Hey Tori, any chance you're around tomorrow?
> I'd like the opportunity to meet you one-on-one
> if possible. Sorry for the delay in responding.
> Cole.

Before Tori had a chance to consider her response, her phone pinged again. This time, it was her mum.

Hi love. Drinks are confirmed at Elena's Sunday afternoon at 3. Do you want to come to us first and go together? x

Well, that explained the text from Cole wanting to catch up before the group gathering.

She quickly sent a message to her mother saying she'd pick her parents up on the way the next day, and then she sent Cole a message.

Would love to. How about X-Café in Richmond? It's licensed so gives us the option of a coffee or a drink. 4pm?

Perfect. See you there.

Tori slipped the phone back into her pocket with mixed feelings. She hoped Cole had reached out because she believed that Tori had been set up by Gav, but having seen how Cole had operated to date, she wasn't confident.

## 30

Cole hugged her mother, who'd insisted on accompanying her out to her car.

'The fact I can walk outside of my own free will and do this will take some getting used to,' June said as they pulled apart. 'And thank you. For being here today and for the effort you're making. I know you're still struggling with everything.'

Cole blushed. 'I'm not struggling. I'm glad you're home, and I'm glad you're back in my life.'

'I know that. But I can see that you're still torn over losing your dad. I get that, you know. Even if it was all those years ago, it's hard to come to terms with, and my getting out will bring up lots of repressed feelings and possibly memories. We need to work through it all and check in on each other. Make sure we're all okay.' She pulled her in for another hug. 'Drive carefully, okay, and we'll see you on Sunday. I'm looking forward to meeting Ethan too. Although, honestly, I'm a bit nervous.'

'Why?'

'I'm not sure how people are going to view me. I'm a convicted murderer, don't forget.'

'That's not going to faze Ethan,' Cole said. 'Nothing much does, and don't forget, he's a trauma counsellor. He's heard plenty of horrifying stories. He's not someone who's going to judge anyone. And regardless, he knows it was self-defence. He doesn't think of you as a murderer.'

Cole waved as she drove away from her gran's house, the image of her mother standing in the driveway taking her back to when she was eight or nine. She remembered her mum running out to wave her off as she set out for a sleep-over at her friend Ruby's. Ruby lived across the street and about five houses along, and Cole had insisted she was old enough to walk there herself. It hadn't stopped her from dropping her bag and running back to give her mum a cuddle. She'd then taken herself off to the sleepover. A lone tear ran down Cole's cheek as she thought back to this and how much she and Lu had then missed out on. Not having their mum there when they had friends for sleepovers, when they went on first dates, and when they had their high school formal and valedictory dinners. They'd all missed out on so much.

She wiped her cheeks. She needed to look on the positive side. They now had a chance to gain a lot. They wanted to spend time with their mother, include her in life's big and small moments, and, most bizarrely, get to know their sister.

* * *

On Saturday afternoon, Tori paid the Uber driver and stepped onto the footpath outside X-Café, one of Richmond's newer establishments. She'd suggested it, feeling that it was good neutral ground. If Cole was going to be angry or cause issues, she didn't want her doing it at one of Tori's favourite St Kilda haunts.

She'd also chosen not to drive, thinking she might need a couple of drinks after this meeting.

As she pushed open the café door, the quiet of the Saturday afternoon enveloped her. The rustic café was often buzzing with customers, but she guessed they'd picked a time between the busy lunchtime crowd and those arriving later for a boozy night out. Tori's eyes quickly found Cole already seated at a table near the window. Cole stood up nervously as Tori approached, her anxiety palpable even from a distance. Tori's heart ached with a sudden rush of empathy. This was her sister, her own blood, and the enormity of their shared connection struck her as she made her way across the room.

She stopped as she reached the table and offered a wobbly smile. 'This is a bit weird, and even weirder that I think we have the same nose.'

Cole let out a nervous laugh, clapping a hand over her mouth. 'Sorry. And yes, you're right, it's weird; your nose looks very familiar. So does the shape of your eyes. Your whole profile could be Lu actually. God, now I'm rambling. I don't know why I'm so nervous. If I'm honest, I don't know what to think. I didn't want to do this tomorrow with everyone else around. I thought it would be better if we met today.' She motioned for Tori to sit down, and both women sat across from each other.

'How are you doing with all of this?' Tori asked. 'I imagine it's been a lot to come to terms with. Forgiving your mum and then her being released. I've been thrown a curveball that I'm adopted and have another family, and I have to deal with that. That's been a big enough struggle, but I haven't had years of pain to deal with like you have.'

Cole's eyes filled with tears.

'Sorry, I wasn't trying to upset you. I know that if I was standing in your shoes, I'd be struggling, that's all. And I'd like to be someone who comes into your life to make it better, not harder. I know Lu believed me that I only found out we're family after I'd been assigned to the stories, and I'd already met you.'

Cole nodded. 'I do, too. Lu filled me in with the catch-up she had with you and your dad. He must be angry with his friend.'

Tori blew out a long breath. 'That's an understatement.' She grinned. 'Almost gave me another story of what drove him to murdering his best friend.' Her smile slipped. 'God, sorry. That was so insensitive. I wasn't thinking.'

Cole smiled. 'Don't worry, you'd be surprised at how often murder comes up in conversation. Speaking of that, I could *murder* a real drink right now. You?'

Tori laughed. 'Assuming this is now a "let's get to know each other" catch-up, then yes. I had thought you might be here to run me out of town.'

'No, and in fact, what I'm going to say to you will probably make your head spin. Let's get some drinks first, though.'

\* \* \*

'She what?' Lu pulled the phone away from her ear and put it on speaker, so Ali could hear the conversation.

'We had a drink yesterday afternoon,' Tori said, 'and Cole told me that she wanted to do the story. She's realising more and more that your mum's story needs to be told and the enormous loss that she suffered by being put away for so long needs to be shared. From what I gather, Cole's feeling guilty about abandoning June for so long and not being there to support you.'

'How do you feel about doing it?' Lu asked. 'Does she want to include the story about you too?'

'She does, and if the story wasn't about me, I'd be doing

everything possible to convince you all to tell it. It's an incredible story of sacrifice and love.'

'But?'

'But now it *is* about me, and I need to give it more thought. June pulled out of the interview a couple of weeks ago, so she might not want to do it anyway.'

'That was because she was worried we'd find out about you,' Lu said. 'That was the only reason. It had nothing to do with her parole or whatever she made up at the time. We do know about you, so that's no longer a reason.'

'I think Cole's going to bring it up this afternoon at the drinks at your gran's,' Tori said. 'I wanted to give you a heads-up.'

'But you had a good catch-up with Cole? Tell me she believes you were set up.'

'Definitely,' Tori said. She gave a little laugh. 'And we polished off a nice bottle of wine, so I'd say it was a good catch-up. Now, I'll see you this afternoon at your gran's.'

'Your gran's too,' Lu said.

Tori fell silent for a moment. 'That's hard to get my head around. Even though you're all technically family, I definitely feel like an outsider.'

'That's understandable,' Lu said. 'We need to get to know each other and spend time together. There's no rush, and I guess there's no guarantee we will ever feel like we're truly family. But hopefully, we will.'

## 31

June's nerves were at an all-time high. To think that for the first time ever, she was about to see her three daughters together. She wondered if they appreciated how big this moment was.

'Ready, love?'

Her mum came into the living area of June's room. She was dressed in smart pants and a lovely turquoise top.

'You look beautiful.'

Elena blushed. 'Thank you. It seems like a rather significant moment, don't you think? Not only are you home, but the strength of our family will all be together at once, too.'

'The strength?'

'The women,' Elena said. 'All five of us. I'm hoping Sylvie or Dion will take a photo for us. This photo would have been taken when Tori was born if life had been kinder.'

It was impossible to ignore the bitter edge to her words.

Elena forced a smile. 'Sorry. It's going to take some time for me to come to terms with missing out on so much of her life. I keep reminding myself that life could have turned out differently, and we may never have known about Tori's existence.'

June blinked back tears. Her mother had done so much for her, and it killed her to see the hurt in her eyes and hear it in her tone as she talked about Tori. Sorry wasn't enough, but she wasn't sure what she could say to make things right.

Elena sighed, reading her thoughts. 'I know you're sorry, love, just give me time. I'm looking forward to getting to know Tori, as I'm sure you are.'

June nodded. 'I am. And Cole, as well. While I had ten years with Cole, I don't know her as an adult. I feel like I'm starting again.'

'I, for one, am glad that you're starting again. There was a long time there that I thought this day would never come. Seeing you back in the house. Getting on with your life. I know it's early days, but you're still young, June. Plenty of years to get back out there. Work if you choose, travel and have some fun.'

June smiled. 'I think work will be essential. I can't expect you to pay my way.'

Elena frowned. 'But there's the money from the house, don't forget. I used some of it for the girls like you instructed, but the rest was invested, and for close to three decades. You won't be short of money.'

'Really? I'd assumed it had all been used for the girls. I hope you used it for you too?'

The doorbell rang before Elena had the chance to answer. 'I'll let them in,' she said. 'You finish getting ready and meet us out the back. And June, don't be nervous, be happy. Everyone's here today because they love you and are so glad you're part of our lives again.'

\* \* \*

Cole's grip on Ethan's hand tightened as she waited for her gran to open the door. 'I'm nervous,' she said. 'It seems so weird bringing us together, and it probably shouldn't. Mum and Sylvie are great friends, and Lu and I both like what we've seen of Tori so far. I've no idea why I feel like this.'

'Because it's all brand new, and you've spent a lot of years protecting yourself from getting hurt,' Ethan said. 'Just try and enjoy this. It's the start of a new chapter that includes both your mum and your younger sister.'

'You're the first to arrive,' Elena said, hugging Cole and hugging Ethan, whom she'd only met once before. 'I feel we have a lot to thank you for,' she said as a way of explaining her emotional reaction to him. 'And we're grateful. Now,' she said, turning to Cole. 'Your mum's understandably nervous about today, so we need to be gentle with her, okay? I think we should try to keep all talk about the future and not go back in time if possible. We don't want anyone reliving events of the past if they don't have to.'

Cole nodded. 'Ethan said to me it's a new chapter, and I agree with him.'

'Me too,' June said, joining them, a tentative smile on her face. She held out her hand to Ethan. 'You must be the wonderful man I've been hearing so much about.'

Ethan's dimples deepened as he took June's hand. 'I'm going to be leaving here with an overinflated ego if everyone keeps talking like this... not that that's a bad thing, of course,' he said, and they laughed. 'It's lovely to meet you, Mrs Marlow.'

'June. I haven't been called the other in years and would prefer not to be now.' As the words left her lips, June considered her surname. Would she change it back to Langrell, like Cole had? She wondered how Lu would feel about that, as she'd kept the Marlow name. She pushed the thought away. Not something she had to resolve right away. 'Now, having only had one drink in more than twenty-eight years, which was to celebrate my homecoming, I'm in need of another for some Dutch courage. I'm nervous about seeing Tori, Sylvie and Dion with you all. I'm responsible for all of this, and that makes me uncomfortable.'

'I had a drink with Tori yesterday,' Cole said. 'It's the first time I've spent any real time with her, and she's lovely. She wants to get to know us but is also finding the whole thing overwhelming. At least you and Sylvie and Dion are good friends. It's not like these people are complete strangers turning up.'

June nodded. 'That's true.' Her eyes shone with tears. 'It was wonderful seeing Sylvie when she visited. If life had been different, we would have spent the last three decades growing old together.'

'Older, thank you!' Sylvie's voice travelled down the passageway, and she, Dion and Tori were ushered in by Elena with Lu and Ali close on their heels.

'And we can spend the rest of our lives growing old together,' Dion added.

June laughed and embraced her friends, leaving her final hug for Tori.

Cole watched as Tori hesitated at first and then walked into June's embrace and stayed there for longer than any of them probably thought she would. She couldn't imagine how Tori was feeling.

'Okay,' Elena said, 'let's all go out into the back garden. We've got a lot of catching up to do, a lot of celebrating and a lot of eating.'

'Your gran wasn't exaggerating about there being a lot of eating to do,' Ali said a few hours later when they'd all eaten and drunk far too much.

It had been a lovely afternoon, all relaxing in Elena's beautiful back garden.

'I'd love to get some photos,' Elena announced at one stage, and Ethan offered to be the photographer.

'I've got something I want to say,' Cole said when the photos were complete and everyone was sitting together, with a drink in hand, relaxed. 'It's not to spoil the afternoon, and I did talk to Tori about this yesterday, but I really think we should tell Mum's story to the world.' She looked at her mother. 'What you went through was horrendous and possibly avoidable. I know you cancelled the story, but that was because of the Tori situation. I think adding that would be so powerful. The personal sacrifice you made to protect all of us, both when Dad was alive and after his death, is incredible. You shouldn't have had to do that, and there might be other women out there your story can help.'

Cole's thoughts went to Jacinta Dixson. She was getting help, but her situation could have ended up differently and still might. She continued. 'To provide them with information on what to do and who to turn to. I don't know if Tori, Sylvie and Dion would be willing to be involved, but sharing how heartbreaking the decision would have been to leave your friend in prison and walk away with her baby because she asked you to is mind-blowing.'

'It's an incredible story,' Lu agreed. 'But we'd also understand if you wanted to forget everything and move on. Wouldn't we, Cole?'

'Of course. I wanted to put it out there as, previously, I was against this and against being involved, but now I think it shouldn't be swept under the rug. Anyway, I won't say more as it's Mum's decision and then Tori's if she still wants to do it and wants to be involved.'

\* \* \*

Tori was surprised when, one by one, June, Elena, Lu, and even her own parents agreed with Cole. She'd been the only one to not contribute to the discussion that erupted after Cole broached the subject.

'You don't have to make a decision now,' June assured her. 'This is a one-off for us, but you're already in the public eye, so I imagine it has far bigger consequences for you. And another option, of course, would be to do the story, not mentioning who my baby was.'

'You want to do this?'

June nodded. 'No one should end up in prison for self-defence. If telling my story helps one other woman not go through what I did, it would be worth it.'

'What about you?' Tori asked Sylvie. 'You and Dad would be in the limelight if you do agree to this. It won't just be *Southern Insight*. This is the type of story that the newspapers and plenty of the magazines will want to pick up.'

'If June wants to tell the story, then I'm happy to support her,' her mother said. 'Your father and I wish we could have supported June better all those years ago. If we'd known what was going on, we might have prevented everything from happening.'

Tori wondered if her mother realised that this would have included not being the ones to raise her. As much as she couldn't imagine not growing up with Sylvie and Dion as her parents, growing up with siblings and her biological mother was something that might have been as wonderful. It appeared now she'd get to enjoy the best of both worlds.

But it also made her realise that no one should be put in the position June was, or to end up in your late twenties finding out your life wasn't at all what you'd been led to believe. If she could help another family avoid this, then she was willing to be involved.

## 32

'I found out the truth about Tom,' Roberto said to Cole as he entered the Wednesday trauma group room before the rest of the participants arrived.

'How?' Cole said. 'Did you speak to him?'

Roberto shook his head. 'No, I pulled some strings with my colleagues on the force. They managed to access some of the restricted files I mentioned. Your big boss, Mike, was right about how I would feel when I learned the truth. It changes everything I thought about him.'

Twenty minutes later, the focus of the group moved away from more talk of the *Southern Insight* interviews, which were already underway with Lisa and Shane, to the whip-around Cole liked to do. It gave each person an opportunity to talk about something that might be concerning them or that they were having a hard time dealing with. She was surprised to see Roberto wipe his eyes as it was his turn.

'Joss said something a few weeks back,' Roberto said, 'that I was getting angry at others to avoid dealing with my own grief and situation.' He met Joss's eyes. 'And she was right. I come here, and I have a lot to say about all of you, what you're going through, and what I think you should do, but it is all to avoid facing my own demons.' He took a deep breath. 'My beautiful Maria is dead, and I was unable to prevent it. In fact, I am responsible for her death. We argued that night, and Maria said she was going to see her sister. But she was upset, and she shouldn't have been driving. I didn't stop her, and she had an accident.'

The group fell silent.

'She was hit by a drunk driver,' Roberto said. 'Killed instantly.' He closed his eyes. 'And while you can say it is the drunk's fault, my Maria was only on the road because we argued. She had no plans to visit her sister until I made her angry.'

Cole imagined everyone else was holding their breath like she was. The pain in Roberto's words was heartbreaking. She'd heard his story many times during their one-to-one sessions, but there was an added rawness to his pain as he shared it with the group. 'Do you think Maria would blame you?' she asked gently.

Roberto kept his eyes closed and, after some time, shook his head. 'But she was too nice. That is the only reason why. She would say it was all part of God's plan, and it was her time to go. But I cannot believe that or forgive myself.'

'You have to learn to live with it,' Tom said. 'There's nothing more you can do. We can all tell you it wasn't your fault, and to be fair, it probably wasn't. There are usually two people involved in an argument. Am I right?'

Roberto nodded.

'And you're Italian,' Lisa added, 'and fiery. I bet you argued lots and made up lots.'

Roberto blushed but nodded again.

'So, you have to live with it,' Tom said again. 'You remember all the good times the two of you had and try to live your life how Maria would have wanted you to.'

'Is that how you live your life?' Roberto asked him, opening his eyes. 'You have learned to live with your situation?'

'It's a bit different,' Shane said. 'No offence, mate,' he added, looking at Tom, 'but we can't compare your dog to Roberto's situation.'

'I disagree,' Roberto said, looking at Tom. 'Have you learned to live with what happened to you?'

Tom stared at Roberto. They could all see that the question was genuine and far removed from Roberto's usual goading of Tom. Tom swallowed, his Adam's apple visible. 'No,' he said finally. He gave a wry laugh. 'I can't even talk about my situation, so how do I learn to live with it?'

'Hold on,' Joss said. 'I'm confused. We all know about your situation. That your dog died, and you saw it happen. That it was, of course, traumatic.'

Tom let out a breath and closed his eyes. 'It wasn't only my dog who was killed. It was also my older brother.'

Cole's stomach clenched as the pain in Tom's voice silenced the room.

'I was nine at the time it happened. It was a home invasion. David was fourteen and was looking after me while our parents went out for dinner. The invaders smashed a window to get in. David and I'd made popcorn and watched a movie. As soon as the brick came through the window, our dog, Shilo, went crazy, but she was shut in the backyard and the window they smashed was at the front. David pushed me into a cupboard where we kept coats and shoes by the front door. I saw everything through a crack.' He shuddered and opened his eyes.

'They wanted money, and he didn't have any, so they pushed

him down and started to kick him. Then one of them grabbed the poker we used for the open fireplace and started hitting him with that.' Tears ran down Tom's face as he recounted the event. 'I remember hearing Shilo's barks change to a weird cry and then she went quiet. I found out later that one of them had hit her with my cricket bat they'd found in the yard. So, I've never been quite truthful when I said I saw her get killed. While all this happened, I did nothing. I watched as they beat David to death. I knew he was dead and I stayed in that cupboard until my parents came home from their dinner. They found him dead on the floor, and Shilo dead in the backyard and I did nothing. I did nothing to stop them.'

At this stage, Tom started to sob. He put his hands over his face but shook uncontrollably as the sobs racked his body. Cole had seen it many times before, that moment when everything that was pushed deep inside was unlocked. It was overwhelming to go through and overwhelming to witness.

Roberto stood and moved over to Tom and placed a hand on his back. 'If you'd come out of that cupboard, you would be dead too, Thomas. Your family would have lost both of their sons that night. You did not have a chance against those men. In my line of work, I have seen many bad outcomes, and that is what would have happened that night.'

'But...'

'No buts,' Roberto said. 'You did what you needed to do. If you were dead, the invaders would not have been found. You would not have been able to describe them, and justice would not have been served.'

Tom wiped his eyes and stared at Roberto. 'How do you know that justice was served?'

'I do not,' Roberto said, doing his best to cover his tracks. 'But I am assuming and hoping that was the outcome. That while you have not wanted to talk about that night with us or anyone else, you did speak up at the time.' He put his hands on each of Tom's shoulders. 'You are a good man, Tom. I know that you spoke up.'

Tom nodded. 'I did, and the police found the men. One was killed in prison, and the other two are still there.'

'Justice was dealt,' Roberto murmured.

* * *

Cole found herself staring out of her office window an hour after the Wednesday group had finished. She'd asked Tom to stay back and spent more time with him after the session to check he was okay and to line up some additional one-on-one counselling starting the next day. She'd also been grateful to see Roberto waiting outside the meeting room when Tom was ready to leave.

He'd clapped Tom on the back. 'Now, Thomas, my friend, tonight I plan to introduce you to the joys of fine grappa, and then we shall dine at Trattoria da Luca, a hidden gem in the heart of the city. There will be no arguments. This is my treat. You've had a big day, and you should not be alone.'

He was a good man, Roberto. A very good man. Cole imagined that his wife had adored him and would be devastated to see the impact their argument and her death had on his life.

She couldn't help but compare Tom's experience with her own. The difference was he did know what had happened that night, but had chosen to change the narrative because it was too hard to face. Whereas she'd chosen to believe the narrative she'd wanted to, because she'd blocked out what had happened. A tear rolled down her cheek as she considered how different life would have been if she'd been able to speak up that night. To stand up for her mother instead of telling the social workers and police how wonderful her father had been and inadvertently helping convict her.

As much as she loved that she was rebuilding her relationship with her mother, and did believe her mother's story, she knew it was going to take a long time to come to terms with her own part in what happened.

## 33

It was less than a week since June had been released from prison, and Future Blend had been transformed into a film set for *Southern Insight*'s interviews with June Marlow's family.

As she'd previously suggested, Tori confirmed with Ali that they could use the café to shoot the interviews and booked it for Thursday afternoon. Ali agreed to close at 2 p.m. to give them the rest of the day for the filming.

Now, with the café lit and ready for the interviews, Tori couldn't help but smile when she saw what had been set up.

'Nothing to do with me,' Lu said as soon as she walked in.

Tori couldn't miss the smile Lu shot Ali. 'It looks incredible,' she said, and it did.

Two chairs had been brought in for the interview, and a makeshift set was established with one of the café walls as a backdrop. Plants flanked both sides of the set, but the feature was Lu's artwork. It was positioned in the centre of the wall with the two chairs slightly offset so that the full artwork would be shown. It was a new picture; the one Tori had seen Lu working on the first day she'd met her. It wasn't a grey pencil drawing now though. This was a full-colour artwork, showing a woman in torn clothing standing looking through a barred window at a garden where flowers were blooming under a vibrant blue sky. The hope on the woman's face was heartbreaking. A young girl stood in the garden beyond the bars, reaching out towards the woman. If anything told June and Lu's story, it was this picture.

'Has your mum seen that picture yet? It's powerful but possibly quite confronting for her.'

'She'll love it,' Elena said. 'This sums up Lu's experience for me. I'm sure she'll see that too.'

Tori nodded. It did. She planned to interview Lu, Elena, her parents and Cole this afternoon if time permitted. They'd leave June's interview and her own interview for Friday when they had more time booked in.

'You look great,' she said as Lu sat down on the chair across from her. 'Try to treat it like a chat between us if you can and forget about the cameras and lights.' She laughed. 'Easier said than done, I know.'

By four thirty, Tori was surprised at how effortlessly the interviews were going. Lu and Elena were naturals on camera, and Tori knew the audience would love them. They became emotional at times and the tears flowed freely, making them even more relatable. Her own parents were less natural and more nervous, but that was totally normal. She planned to use a lot of the interview footage as voice-over and overlay it with visuals so the nerves would be less obvious.

They took a break after Sylvie and Dion's interview with Ali preparing tea and coffee for everyone. She'd been amazing with an incredible spread of food, which Tori knew her crew were loving.

'Thanks again for letting us use the café,' she said to Ali. She nodded towards the wall. 'Love what you did with the artwork.'

'And I love that you asked Lu about it during her interview. Will that stay in the final cut?'

'Definitely. I've made sure the crew have filmed the other piece of Lu's art and the bit about the café. In fact, we've taken some footage outside of the café, which we'll show before the first interview, so people know where we filmed it and where the artwork is. Hopefully, you'll see an increase in customers.'

'Regardless, the fee you've paid to use the café is very generous.'

'Just the usual location fee,' Tori said and smiled as Cole joined them. 'Ready?'

Cole nodded. 'I think so. We're sticking to the questions you sent me?'

'That's the plan,' Tori said. 'Although sometimes the answers you give lead to other questions being asked. Are you okay with that? Like I said earlier, I'll show you all the footage for approval before we go to air with anything. There will be no surprises.'

\* \* \*

As the audio guy hooked up a microphone to her shirt, Cole found Tori's words: *there will be no surprises* repeating in her mind interspersed with Roberto's words from the day before: *justice was dealt*. She tried her best to relax and be ready to answer the questions Tori had prepared for their interview.

Her heart was racing, and she felt like she would break into a sweat at any moment. Since Tom had shared his story, Cole had found herself reliving more moments from her childhood. She wasn't sure why Tom remembering his trauma had triggered memories of her own, but she was. She was putting pieces together of a father who she'd learned was a terrible man. But she was also guilty of having seen some of the abuse and choosing to believe her father's stories that nothing was wrong. Why had she been so eager to believe him rather than see that her mother needed help?

She answered some general questions Tori had asked about who she was and where she worked before the *real* questions started.

'You were there that night,' Tori said, her voice gentle. 'When your father died. You were only ten, but you tried to help your mother stop the bleeding and save his life.'

Cole nodded. 'I did, but I don't remember any of it.' As she said the words, she had a flashback of the family room. She was in a cupboard looking through the crack at her father, who was yelling at her mother. She shook herself. This wasn't her memory. This was Tom's. For a start, there was no cupboard in their family room. It was all getting mixed up.

'It must have been a dreadful shock for you,' Tori continued, 'to learn in the days following that your father was dead, and your mum had been arrested.'

'It was awful,' Cole admitted. 'I don't remember the actual night he died, but I do remember feeling like my life was over, and in some ways, I guess the life I'd known up until then was.' She closed her eyes as she shook her head. She re-opened them and kept her focus on Tori. 'The hardest thing was not remembering. I was taken off to a bunch of psychologists who asked me a million questions. As an adult, when I look back on this, I realise that a lot of this was police questioning, hoping to get more information to confirm what my mum had told them was true. Of course, I didn't know she'd said it was self-defence until later. I told them what I could remember, which wasn't a lot.'

'Do you regret that now?' Tori asked.

Cole nodded. 'Absolutely. I played a part in sentencing my

own mother because I couldn't remember what happened. At the time, I didn't see my father as someone who'd been abusive.'

'But you do now?'

'I've had flashbacks more recently of events that I now realise were when he was physically abusing or threatening my mum. But he did a great job of being the best dad in the world, too, so he was able to hide that side of himself from me and Lu.'

Cole was hit by her father's raised voice. Her heart beat faster as she heard him clearly yelling at her mother.

'*You slut. Tell me who he was. We both know this baby's not mine.*'

She glanced over at her mother, who was watching the interview. Her face was pale as Cole answered each question. That memory *was* from that night. How was it she hadn't been able to remember that before?

She closed her eyes as more memories washed over her.

'*I'll cut that baby out of you right now,*' *her father was yelling at her mother.*

*Nicole was hiding out of sight around the side of the family room door. She was trembling at the anger spewing from her father. He wouldn't really hurt her mother, would he?*

*She peeked around the door to see him with a large knife in his hand, holding her mother by the hair.*

'*I'll kill you if that's what it's going to take, you disobedient bitch.*'

*It was on the tip of Nicole's tongue to scream, but at that moment, her mother saw her in the doorway and locked eyes with her. She didn't need to speak. Her eyes were filled with terror, and Nicole, in that instant, knew she had to help her.*

'Cole?'

Cole was brought back to the present, realising she hadn't heard Tori's question.

'I asked how you coped when your mother was officially sentenced. If you remember, of course.'

'I refused to listen to anything good anyone had to say about my mum,' Cole said. 'I blamed her for killing my dad, and I was angry. In fact, I still am angry. For different reasons now though. It was only recently that I believed she was an abused woman and that I'd been awful to her. She was the victim in all of this.'

Cole looked across to her mother, who was wiping her eyes on her sleeve at this admission. Cole froze. That action of wiping her eyes like that. She'd done that that night. She'd put a blanket over her husband and turned to Cole, wiping her eyes as she did.

*'Oh, Nicole, we need to stick to the story, okay?'*

*Nicole was shivering. She was covered in her father's blood, and he was dead. Her dad was dead. They'd been unable to stop the bleeding and he'd bled to death.*

*'If the police ask you, you say you came in the room when you heard me screaming and that I asked you to help me stop the bleeding, which is why you're covered in his blood. Okay?'*

*Nicole nodded.*

*'And that's all you say. Nothing else.'* Her mother had tears rolling down her face as she made Nicole promise over and over that she'd stick to this story. She wiped her eyes on her sleeve.

Cole locked eyes with her mother. Oh my God, she was going to be sick.

'Cole?'

She heard Lu's voice through a thickness that had enveloped her. She stood, wobbly on her feet. She had to get out of there.

'Cole,' Tori said, taking her by the arm. 'What's going on?'

'I remember,' she said, her eyes locked with her mother's.

June shook her head. Her eyes pleaded with Cole. 'Don't say anything, Cole. Let's end the interview and go and talk.'

'Hold on,' Tori said, looking from June to Cole. 'Are you saying you remember your dad's death?'

Cole nodded.

'You remember seeing him being stabbed?'

She nodded again.

'Is it difficult to have your mum here while you relive that?' Tori's voice was gentle, but Cole realised Tori had no idea why she was reacting the way she was.

'Very difficult,' she croaked.

'I think we should stop this,' June said. 'Cole doesn't need to relive this now. Especially not while you're filming. The world already knows I killed Alan. We don't need another rendition of it.'

'No,' Cole said. 'I remember. I remember *everything*.' She shook her head, tears rolling down her cheeks. 'How could you? You lied. It's all a lie.'

\* \* \*

Lu watched from the sidelines as Cole's memories flooded back, and a cryptic conversation took place between her mother and sister. She could see Tori motioning for the camera crew to continue filming. She wasn't sure why, as none of this made any sense to her. But she guessed they could edit it out later.

'How could I not?' her mother answered Cole's question.

Cole was white as a sheet and looked like she'd be sick at any moment. She sank back into the chair and put her head between her legs.

Lu looked at her gran, who was frozen while watching the scene play out.

'We need to stop,' June said again. 'Cole's clearly not feeling well. Let's stop the cameras and get her some water. She seems quite delirious and is rambling now. Let's let her gather her thoughts and start again later or tomorrow.'

If anyone was rambling, Lu thought it was their mother, not Cole. She wanted this shut down. That was obvious.

Cole looked up at Lu. 'I'm sorry.'

'What for?' Lu was even more confused.

'For everything. I...'

'No.' June raised her voice, cutting Cole off. 'Like I said, this needs to stop. Let's take a break.' She turned to Tori. 'Stop filming and get your crew out of here. Now! I mean it.'

Tori nodded. 'Cut,' she called. 'And guys, please leave the room. I'll call you back when we're ready to continue.'

Lu watched the film crew leave the room, surprised Tori had agreed so readily. However, her mother's authoritative tone had everyone on edge. The room was charged with emotion.

'Cole,' June said. 'I want you to stop. You've muddled up your memories and should speak to someone. A psych or someone, to get them in order. Blurting out thoughts now isn't a good idea.'

Lu looked to her gran, whose face was pale and her lip trembling and then to her mother, Cole and Tori, all of whom looked like they might be sick at any moment.

'Oh God,' she said, suddenly realising where this was heading.

'I killed him,' Cole said. 'It wasn't Mum. It was me.'

Silence filled the room, and June dropped her head into her hands.

'He was going to kill Mum. He was threatening to cut the baby out of her.' She looked at Tori. 'He was going to kill *you*. I couldn't let him do that. It was like something took over, and I had no control. I went to the kitchen and took a large knife from the drawer. Then I went into the lounge room and screamed to stop him from hurting Mum. I had the knife behind my back, and when he saw me, he rushed over to me, trying to convince me that they were playing a game.' She wiped her eyes. 'I didn't hesitate. I slammed the knife into him as hard as I could.'

Lu turned to their mother. 'Is this true?'

June shook her head. 'No, of course not. Cole's remembering it all wrong. She screamed. That bit's true, and that was my chance to grab the knife and stab Alan with it. It only took one stab. Luckily, or unluckily, depending on how you view it, I hit the aortic artery, and he bled out within a few minutes. We did our best to stop the bleeding, but we had no chance.'

Cole closed her eyes, and Lu could almost see her reliving every second of what had happened. Cole was shaking her head. 'That's not true, Mum, you and I both know that.'

June walked over to Cole and took her hands in hers. 'You were ten, and you've blocked this out for nearly three decades. You're remembering it in parts. But I swear to you, you did not stab your father. I killed him, not you.'

Cole continued to shake her head until June shook her, and her eyes flew open. 'Cole, I spent twenty-eight years in prison for a crime *I* committed. Let's not turn it into something it wasn't. We've all got the chance to move on now and live our lives. There's no point reliving it all, especially when you're remembering a different version of events. A version that didn't happen.'

Lu watched as Cole locked gazes with her mother, tears pouring down her cheeks. It was at that moment she understood how huge her mother's sacrifice was.

# 34

Ethan's arms stayed tight around Cole as her tears flowed. He'd been standing in the background at the café during the interviews, wanting to make sure it all went well when the shock of Cole's realisation had become apparent.

He'd quickly realised with June's forceful words, asking Cole to stop, that this was something that needed to be a private conversation, not one in front of the rest of the family and a film crew. He'd walked onto the makeshift set, taken Cole's hand and pulled her to him.

'I'm taking Cole home,' he'd said, realising that no one, not even Cole, was going to object. They all looked shell-shocked at her admission. And while June had done her best to contradict Cole, it was obvious that no one believed her.

Tori and Lu had nodded, and Ethan had led Cole out to his car and driven her home.

Now, they lay on her bed with his arms firmly around her. Neither of them had spoken, and he would be lying if he didn't admit that he was worried. Cole had killed her father. She might only have been ten at the time, but she'd taken a human life. It was going to be difficult for her to not only come to terms with that but also come to terms with the sacrifice her mother had made. Ethan's respect for June had gone through the roof when he'd grasped during the interview what she'd covered up. The authority with which she'd demanded Tori stop was frightening and impressive all in one.

Ethan's heart ached for the pain he knew Cole was suffering.

'Thank you.'

They were the first words Cole had said since leaving the café two hours earlier.

'There's nothing to thank me for,' Ethan said, stroking her hair.

Cole shifted on the bed and turned to face him. Her tear-stained face was a mess, her eyes red and puffy. He wiped the tears from her cheeks.

'You're still here for a start,' Cole said. 'You're dating a murderer, and you didn't run away.'

Ethan smiled. 'You were ten, and you saved your mother's life. That doesn't make you a murderer. It makes you a hero. And that's exactly how your mother saw you, which is why she protected you.'

'But I was ten,' Cole said. 'I wouldn't have gone to prison like she did.'

'No, but it probably would have messed you up,' Ethan said. 'Look at some of the people in the trauma groups we deal with who witnessed traumatic events and how it's impacted them. To have lived with the knowledge you killed your dad would have affected you massively. I doubt you would have turned out so level-headed and be doing the job you're doing. We'll never know where it would have led you, but you could have ended up with substance abuse issues and all sorts of problems trying to hide from the knowledge of what happened.'

'I still could,' Cole said.

Ethan laughed. 'Not with me around, you won't. Once you get over the shock, you'll also see that what you did was protect your mother. Imagine if he'd killed her that night. That would have instantly killed Tori, and he might have then killed you and Lu, too. He could hardly talk his way out of stabbing someone to death.'

'I think I'm more devastated at how I treated Mum,' Cole said. She shivered. 'Imagine being sentenced to life imprisonment and the only person who refuses to visit you is the person you've given up your life to protect. It's awful.'

'No,' Ethan said, 'It's love. You were a kid, and your mum knew that. I imagine she was relieved that you've gone all these years without knowing what happened. Not blaming yourself and not messing you up. She would have done anything for her kids. She's proven that with Tori too. Her actions were utterly selfless when it came to giving her up. Imagine the torture of kissing your baby goodbye and making a condition that you never hear anything about her, and you lose your best friend at the same time.' He shook his head. 'Your mum is the most amazing woman I've ever had the honour to meet. Of course, you need to speak to her about what happened, but I think you also need to respect what she's going to ask of you.'

'To let everyone believe she's a murderer?'

Ethan nodded. 'She gave up a lot for you, and if you're ever going to thank her, this will be your chance to do that.'

\* \* \*

June sipped the peppermint tea her mother had made for them and let out a long sigh. 'That didn't go quite to plan.'

'No, it didn't,' Elena agreed. They sat in silence for some time before Elena spoke again. 'I don't understand why you did it.'

'Did what? Killed my husband?'

Elena raised her eyebrows. 'I think we can drop that charade after Cole's revelation. And yes, I'm happy to go along with it when anyone else is around. I agree with you that now, after serving all that time, there's not much point in trying to clear your name and dragging Cole through the wringer. But, back then, she was ten. She would have been seen as protecting you rather than you murdering your husband. No jail time would have been served.' She shook her head. 'I don't understand.'

'Really?' June asked. 'What if it had been me as a ten-year-old killing Dad to protect you? Would you have wanted me to live with the knowledge of what I'd done and probably ruin my life, or would you have done anything possible to protect me?'

Elena nodded her head slowly. 'I'm beginning to understand.'

'The fact that Cole blocked it out from the start made it so much easier,' June said. 'I prayed that she wouldn't remember and go to the police and confess. I would have told them she was being ridiculous and wanted me out of prison, so I doubt it would have had any impact, but at least she wasn't living with the guilt.'

'She will be now,' Elena said. 'My guess is that the guilt will be over her turning her back on you, more so than killing Alan. She's a complex character, our Cole. This isn't going to be easy.'

'Thank goodness for Ethan,' June said. 'I think he'll help her see that moving forward is all we can do now. I'll talk to her in the coming days. Make sure she knows that what she did that night was the most courageous act anyone could ever do.' Tears filled her eyes. 'And it was. She loved Alan so much. It's a shame his violence started this horrible chain of events. If he'd survived,

I'd like to think I would have left, and life would have been different.'

'Do you think it's why Lu likes girls?' Elena said.

June gave a startled laugh. 'I wasn't expecting that change in direction. And no, I'm sure she was hard-wired to like girls. She believes me about the abuse, but doesn't remember it happening at the time, so I don't think it was a case of Alan putting her off men forever.'

'Ali obviously cares about her,' Elena said. 'Did you see that studio she'd set up today? It all focused on Lu's artwork, which itself is quite astonishing. She's wasted walking dogs.'

'That's one of the many things I will agree with you on,' June said. 'As much as I know Cole's suffered through all of this, I think Lu's the one who's been affected the most. She's been there for me every step of the way, but I worry that's been at the expense of her own happiness and her career. It's like she's kept her life on hold. I hope that's not the case, but I have a feeling she hasn't been able to move forward with me in prison and Cole not accepting the situation.'

'I'd say that's an accurate summing up,' Elena said.

June wiped a tear from the corner of her eye. 'Poor Lu, she didn't deserve any of this. She's such a loving, beautiful person.'

'None of us deserved any of *this*,' Elena said. 'Juney, you have to remember that any time you have a thought like that. Yes, I agree that it's affected Lu, but look at what you'd put up with and what you did to protect Cole and her sisters.' She shook her head. 'You've carried this all alone. Giving up Tori, protecting Cole, loving those girls so much that you would do anything for them. Lu knows that, and I can guarantee she won't be looking at how the situation affected her. She'll be looking at the fact that she had a mother who would kill for her children and, if she had to, probably die for them, too. What you've sacrificed is beyond comprehension, and all I want you to know is that I couldn't be prouder to call you my daughter. I'm sure your dad's looking down at you now with tears running down his cheeks, as he appreciates this incredible person we created.'

The lump in June's throat was so large she couldn't do anything but nod and wipe her tears. Her mother's words, while beautiful and true, weren't describing her. They were perfectly describing Elena herself. She wished she'd been able to embrace her mother's strength a lot earlier and walk away from Alan and not put any of them through what she had. While she might not have killed him, she wasn't sure she'd ever be able to forgive herself for staying in a marriage she should have left years earlier.

## 35

Cole realised as her mother looked around the café she'd chosen for their catch-up that, other than the interviews at Future Blend, this was probably her first outing.

'This place is so modern,' June said, pointing to the sleek, minimalist light fixtures hanging from the ceiling and the industrial brick feature on the back wall of the café. 'Cafés were more, I don't know, rustic or something when I was going out. Future Blend is more like what I remember cafés being like.' She laughed. 'Ali might want to think about renaming the café to Vintage Blend or something more appropriate.'

Cole wasn't sure how to start the conversation she wanted to have but waited until their coffee and the mud cake they'd ordered to share arrived.

Her mother jumped in before she had a chance. 'I know we need to have this conversation, but surely you realise why I did what I did?'

Cole nodded. 'I do. And I'm not sure whether I should be apologising or thanking you or both.'

'Neither,' June said. 'Cole, he was about to kill me. Which

meant Tori would have died too. And as much as he loved you girls, I don't know what he would have done then. It's quite possible none of us would be here today to even wonder about that.'

'But why didn't you tell the truth?' Cole asked. 'I was ten. I've worked in the system long enough to know I wouldn't have been held responsible. There would have been a lot of counselling and support, but that was probably the extent of it.'

June took a deep breath. 'I think right now I'm a much stronger person than I was back then. Don't forget I didn't admit to anyone, not even your gran or Sylvie, my closest friend, what had been going on with the abuse. I guess I didn't trust that we'd get the help we needed. And I felt guilty. How could I let you take the blame for a situation I should never have allowed you to be in? The only person at fault was me, and I hadn't asked for help. I hadn't removed us all from that situation.'

'Do you believe that?' Cole asked. 'That you were the person at fault?'

June nodded.

'What about Dad? Surely, he's to blame for everything?'

'Ultimately, yes, but I should still have protected you and Lu. And I didn't. I was weak. I was ashamed, and I was embarrassed. Traits I'll probably never forgive myself for, but I will never repeat. So, as far as asking for forgiveness, that's my job, not yours. Yes, I went to prison for all those years, but look at how it impacted you, Lu and Gran. You've all dealt with your own versions of prison over that time, and regardless of who's to blame, it's something we need to all move on from.'

'I want the truth to be told,' Cole said. 'It could help a lot of women if we tell your story.'

June shook her head. 'I agree that telling a story about being able to ask for help and not putting up with abuse could be powerful, but I won't agree with you saying you were responsible for Alan's death. And all these years later, no one's going to believe you anyway. What purpose would it serve at this point? There'd probably be a full investigation, and who knows what would come out the other end of that, other than a lot of stress and heartache. We can't do that to Gran or Lu.'

Cole nodded her head slowly. Her mother was right. It wouldn't serve any purpose other than to clear her conscience.

'It's time we put your gran and Lu first,' June said. 'They bore the brunt of what happened, and if you want to do anything right now to make this right, you'll help me in ensuring they don't deal with more stress over it.'

'I can do that,' Cole said, 'and I should.' She shook her head. 'And I'll find a good therapist. This is going to take some unpacking.'

'I think you've already found an unofficial one,' June said, her eyes twinkling. 'And if I was you, I wouldn't let him go.'

## 36

Three weeks after the interviews were finalised, the entire family, including Sylvie, Dion, Ethan and Ali, settled down in Elena's living room to watch a draft version of the *Victims Behind Bars* story.

Cole's phone pinged with a text and she smiled as she glanced at the screen. 'Piper,' she said when Ethan raised an eyebrow in question. 'Letting me know that she and Katie are officially back home again.'

'What about the dad?' Lu asked.

'Still in rehab,' Cole said. 'It's going to be a long journey to get him back to them, if that ever happens. Small steps. They'll get to visit him once he's finished the program and social services approve a visit, but whether he ends up back in the family home will be a question of time and whether Jacinta wants him back. She's a lot stronger now and with the support she's getting will continue to get stronger still.'

'Support I should have asked for,' June said.

'Support that this story will encourage a lot of other women to seek,' Cole said, offering her mother a sympathetic smile.

'And we can still make changes if absolutely essential,' Tori said, 'but at this stage, the station is hoping we'll sign it off and they can air it next Sunday night. That will give them over a week for plenty of promos and build-up. Sunday's the highest ratings night of the week so it should get a very good audience. And,' she turned to Lu, 'I have some news not related to the story to share.'

'Related to me?'

Tori nodded. 'More specifically to your artwork. One of the post-production guys also happens to be married to an art enthusiast who's set up several galleries through regional areas in Victoria and New South Wales,' Ali said. 'Apparently she's interested in talking to you to find out if you'd be interested in doing a roadshow to each gallery.'

Lu's eyes widened. 'Really?'

Tori nodded. 'It will give you heaps of exposure in the smaller towns and hopefully lead to some bigger events in the cities. If you're interested, I'll set up a meeting between the two of you.'

'Of course she's interested,' Ali said, flinging an arm around Lu's shoulder. 'I told you you're amazingly talented.'

'She is,' Cole added. 'Lu, you have to do it.'

'Of course she does,' June said.

Lu laughed as Elena and Ethan nodded in agreement. 'Thank you,' she said to Tori, 'and to you,' she said, turning to Ali. 'You've made this happen for me, firstly getting me to create the art and then promoting it so well.'

Ali shook her head. 'It was always going to happen, Lu, it was just a matter of timing. And now, with your mum home and everything falling into place, it's the right time.'

Lu smiled. 'It is. Now don't keep us in suspense,' she said to Tori. 'I want to see how we all look.'

Tori glanced at June. 'Ready?'

June nodded. 'As ready as I'm ever going to be.'

'Don't forget when it's aired the anchor will introduce it, and then it will play. So, it won't start straight in the story as it's going to now.' She took a deep breath and pressed play.

Twenty minutes later, there wasn't a dry eye in the room.

'That was incredible,' Dion said.

'It's been done so well,' Lu added. 'I can't imagine anyone will believe Mum should have gone to prison after seeing that.'

'I'm surprised you got Gavin Barnett to agree to allow you to say he set this up,' Ethan said. 'I thought he'd want to run and hide.'

Tori gave a wry laugh. 'Gav's working on a new show called *The Moment of Truth*. Basically, reporters uncover and reveal hidden scandals, capturing the shocked reactions of those exposed as their stories go live on air. *Victims Behind Bars* is fantastic advertising for the show.'

'For Channel Six?' Lu asked.

'No, he got fired from *Southern Insight*, and I'd be surprised if he ever works for the Six network again. No, it's for Channel Eight. Something to compete with *Sixty Minutes* and our show.'

'And you're going to be okay with this?' June asked Tori. 'I imagine you're going to be flooded with interview requests after it airs.'

'That's something I wanted to talk to you about,' Tori said. 'You're free to do any interviews you like, whereas my contract is exclusive to Six, so I won't be talking to anyone else.'

'Mackenzie has advised me not to speak with anyone without her present,' June said. 'She's suggested I engage a publicist for after it airs. She thinks if we're approached, then some of the publications with large female readerships are worth talking to, but otherwise, to say no. We want to make a difference, but we don't want this to drag on forever. We're all victims of our pasts, and now, we need to move forward and never settle for less than we deserve.'

Elena nodded. 'It's time to get back to living.'

Cole raised her glass. 'That's definitely toast-worthy. Let's get back to living.'

## MORE FROM LOUISE GUY

Another brilliant, emotional book from Louise Guy, *A Mother's Betrayal*, is available to order now here:

https://mybook.to/AMothersBetrayalBackAd

# ACKNOWLEDGEMENTS

It's always an exciting, yet scary process to publish a book. How will it be received? Will the characters and elements that are so special to me resonate with you? There is, of course, only one way to find out, and I truly hope you enjoy *To Save my Daughters* as much as I loved bringing June, Cole, Lu and Tori's story to life.

The publication of a book, plus its subsequent life cycle, is carried out by a large team – a team that I would like to extend a massive thank you to...

Firstly, to my editor, Isobel Akenhead. Your insightful comments consistently elevate my stories to a new level. A huge thank you to you and the team at Boldwood Books for your support in bringing this book to publication and for the care it will receive during its release and promotion.

To the wonderful reviewers, bloggers, Facebook groups and everyone else who spreads the word about books to read – your enthusiasm is invaluable.

To the librarians and booksellers, your dedication to connecting readers with stories never goes unnoticed – thank you.

A special thanks to my early readers and those who offered to proof the final version, with appreciation to Judy and Maggie for your invaluable feedback.

To Diane, Rosa and Ruby, thank you so much for checking Roberto's Italian phrases for me – discovering one in an early draft was actually French showed me the importance of an authenticity check (and not relying on Google translate!).

To the authors and friends in my writing community, thank for your continued support, sharing of information and ideas, and friendship.

And, most importantly, to you, the readers – thank you for buying and borrowing my books, for leaving reviews, and for telling your friends. Please continue!

# ABOUT THE AUTHOR

**Louise Guy** is the bestselling author of eight novels, blending family and friendship themes with unique twists and intrigue. Her characters captivate readers, drawing them deeply into their compelling stories and struggles. She lives in Australia.

Sign up to Louise Guy's mailing list for news, competitions and update on future books.

Follow Louise on social media:

facebook.com/louiseguyauthor

bookbub.com/authors/louise-guy

## ALSO BY LOUISE GUY

My Sister's Baby

A Family's Trust

A Mother's Betrayal

To Save My Daughters

BECOME A MEMBER OF

# THE SHELF CARE CLUB

The home of Boldwood's
book club reads.

Find uplifting reads,
sunny escapes, cosy romances,
family dramas and more!

Sign up to the newsletter
https://bit.ly/theshelfcareclub

# Boldwood

Boldwood Books is an award-winning fiction publishing company seeking out the best stories from around the world.

## Find out more at www.boldwoodbooks.com

Join our reader community for brilliant books, competitions and offers!

Follow us
@BoldwoodBooks
@TheBoldBookClub

Sign up to our weekly
deals newsletter

https://bit.ly/BoldwoodBNewsletter